Unauthored Letters

by

Tara C. Allred

ISBN: 061586337X
ISBN 13: 9780615863375
Library of Congress Control Number: 2013914423
Patella Publishing, American Fork, UT

to
Jeff

WINTER 1984

PROLOGUE

Milton Haight looked out over the fog-covered Pacific from Robert Brownell's expansive estate. Across the peninsula, up the rolling hills of the elite Southern California town of Palos Verdes, and along the private lane, the midmorning fog swirled, beckoned, and moaned, as if Robert Brownell's ghost was trapped within.

Perhaps he was there, begging Milton not to reveal his last will and testament. But it was too late. The recently deceased could not change their wishes.

Yet if he could . . . If so, Milton would not be there to ring the Brownells' doorbell. Rather, his boss, Issac Warner, would be there.

But Warner was not.

Instead the housekeeper escorted Milton inside, where he became lost among the high ceilings, the ornate marble, the Persian rugs, and the array of museum-quality sculptures and paintings. In silence, he followed the housekeeper toward the study while he contemplated his situation. Then the French doors glided open. Milton stepped inside, and a sudden heaviness seeped into his mind.

Across the expansive room, two pairs of eyes stared at him. One set was dim and gray, and belonged to the stern, protective face of Robert's close friend, Rick Downley. The other eyes sparkled green, brimmed with tears, and belonged to Robert's fifteen-year-old daughter, Becca. Both sat in chairs that faced a distinguished desk.

Milton drew in a breath, then cleared his throat. "Hello." His small voice faded as it crossed the room.

Rick reached for Becca's hand, and his voice boomed through the silence, "Where's Warner?"

Milton inhaled again and stepped forward, passing the extensive masterpieces of elegant antiques, artifacts, and furniture, while the coldness settled around him.

"Where's Warner?" Rick demanded.

Milton paused and looked at Rick. "He . . . he couldn't make it."

Rick remained seated. "Why?"

Milton sighed and wished he could speak the truth, yet he could not be that bold. Instead, Milton reflected back to precisely 9:32 that morning, when Warner had thrust the documents into Milton's briefcase and pushed Milton out the door, alone, to face the grieving group.

Since this was a prized account, Milton had questioned such odd behavior.

For many years, Warner had managed all the legal documents centered on Brownell's wealth. The seasoned attorney took pride in this association, and although the Brownell family was private and disconnected from the community, Warner could claim to be one of the few people who actually knew Robert Brownell.

Of course, no one really knew the recluse well, except perhaps Rick Downley.

For this precise reason, Milton struggled to find his voice as he now faced Mr. Downley. Against his sudden dry throat, he managed to say, "Warner had a conflict, so he asked me to go over some details with you."

Milton stood still while Downley's eyes scanned the top of Milton's thinning blond hair all the way down to Milton's lightly-scuffed leather shoes.

Surely, Rick Downley saw through the lie and sensed the truth—that to avoid facing him, Warner had delegated this unpleasant duty to the newest member of his practice.

So Milton stood there, regretting that he had not succumbed to his early-morning desire to wear his prized Armani suit. Instead, he felt completely unprepared and too inexperienced to know how to manage the erupting tension.

Since Downley refused to offer him a seat, Milton took the only spot available, the sleek office chair stationed behind the large executive desk. Such placement gave Milton hope for a sense of authority. Yet as he settled across from Rick's stone-focused face, the dense cloud in Milton's brain thickened.

Rather than entertain Downley's powerful stare, Milton reached for his briefcase and shuffled through the bag.

The file was right where Warner had placed it, clearly labeled, and easy to find. However, Milton searched aimlessly in hopes of clearing the haze trapped within his mind. At last he raised his eyes, only to see Rick's face roiled in anger. "What did Warner tell you?" Milton asked cautiously.

"What he didn't tell me is that he was sending *you*."

"Yes, well . . . he's concerned that before Robert passed away . . . he may not have told you all the details of the will. Everything might not be as you'd hoped."

Rick glanced at Becca. Fear covered her face. Like a father, like the guardian that the will specified him to be, Downley took her hand. "Don't worry," he said softly. "I'm here to take care of this."

The concern lifted from her face. "Do I need to be here?" She put the question to Downley yet watched Milton.

Rick shook his head. "Not if you don't want to be."

"I don't."

She stood, as did Rick. "Since Warner isn't here," he said, "we can discuss all this later."

Becca nodded and then hugged him. "Thank you."

A smile crept across Rick's face. Then his lips grazed her ear. "Why don't you go lie down," he said quietly. "You look tired, and I know you didn't sleep well last night."

Something in the exchange disturbed Milton. As quick as the inappropriate thought came, Milton dismissed such scandalous speculation; certainly the family was odd, but Downley was at least twenty years her senior.

Once Becca exited the room, Rick's soft demeanor also fled. Instead, he stared directly into Milton's eyes. "You know Warner should be here."

"Yes."

"And you know that I was there when Rob and Warner drafted that will."

"I know that Warner understands your concern—"

"No," Rick cut him off. "You know if there's been a change—then there's been a mistake."

Milton heaved out a sigh. "Warner and I wish there were. As I was saying, Warner tried to find a loophole. He's looked. And his only counsel for you is to walk away from this. You don't have to fulfill Robert's wishes."

"Let me see the will."

Without protest, Milton handed over the file. On the top lay the previous will, signed in 1980, that everyone had come to accept, value, and regard; hidden underneath lay the one-page handwritten will with the firm's summer intern shamefully listed as the witness. Until Robert had died, no one had known of the modification.

Now Milton watched while Rick's neck muscles tightened and his gray eyes narrowed as he read. Then silent fury followed.

"This is a mistake." He tossed the file back at Milton. "You know that."

"I wish it were."

"So what happens to Becca?"

"Since the final will doesn't mention those items, we refer to the 1980 document. However, Warner wants you to know that you don't have to be the executor over the estate, and you don't have to be her guardian either. You don't have to fulfill any of Robert's requests."

Rick glared at Milton. "What happens to Rebecca?"

Milton gazed down at the papers, then carefully scooted the documents into an orderly stack. He picked up his Warner & Berk ballpoint pen and clicked it twice before glancing back at Rick. "If you chose not to care for her . . . because she has no living relative, she'd go into the care of Child Protective Services."

"No," Rick stated firmly. "She has me, and that's enough." He strode over to the window and stared out over the fog-covered peninsula.

Meanwhile, Milton glanced back at the documents. Although the 1980 will requested that Rick Downley be the executor over the estate and Becca's legal guardian, the handwritten modification had altered Rick's inheritance. Robert had left his friend with nothing.

With Rick aware of these changes, Milton's task was complete. Milton tucked the file back into his briefcase and prepared himself to leave. "Warner will be in touch."

"Wait."

Milton sunk back into his seat slowly. "Yes?"

Rick turned around and, in a controlled voice, said, "Stay. I want to show you something." He moved swiftly past the antique books, the gallery of fine art, and the custom furniture, until he stopped at an enclosed curio cabinet in the far corner of the room.

"Do you see that?" Rick pointed at a small terracotta statue of a woman holding a young child. "Four hundred AD from Teotihuacan, Mexico. Do you know what 'Teotihuacan' means?"

Milton shook his head.

"'The City of the Gods,' or 'Where Men Become Gods.' Rob purchased this at an auction in Zihuatanejo. He bought it for Mia while they were staying in La Vida Que Cubra, on the day he learned she was expecting. A symbol of his love." Rick studied the statue. "But then she died when Becca was only two." He glanced back at the young attorney. "Did you know that?"

Again, Milton shook his head.

"Mia died when Becca was two," he repeated. "And Rob needed a friend—so he turned to me. He relied on me. It was me who gave him the strength to cope . . . and in exchange for all I offered him, he promised me a chunk of his inheritance. We discussed this, just like we discussed all our business affairs. He mentioned stocks, bonds, gold, specific property. All this in exchange for the friendship I offered him.

"I gave him a great deal. Our lives intertwined in business, in travels, in personal affairs, in the caring for his daughter. He needed me, and I was there. I was always there, like a brother."

Milton nodded, searching for a way to wrap up the conversation. Yet Rick was absorbed in his thoughts. "I did everything I could for Rob. I tried to save him. I did. But it became clear he was past any point of help. He was miserable, extremely depressed. It wasn't a question of *if* he was going to take his life, but rather *when*. That's why our discussion of Becca carried such weight. When he asked me to care for her when he was gone, I understood. I knew what would be required of me. I accepted that duty. Of course it's a huge responsibility . . . but I love that girl."

Bothered by Rick's tone, Milton placed his hand on his briefcase and glanced at the door.

"Let me see the document again," Rick said.

Milton bit down on his lip. Against his wishes, he carefully opened his case and retrieved the will. After he handed it over, he painfully watched Rick rescan the words that minimized his past and demolished his future.

Once the verification was done, Rick dropped the document onto the desk. "You'll pay, Brownell."

Then he strode back to the curio cabinet, and with one jerk of his wrist he flung the cabinet door open and grabbed the Teotihuacan statue. For long, heavy seconds, he stared at the figure. Slowly, his fingers glided over its ceramic hair, nose, lips, and breasts. In time, his eyes lifted, and he scanned the entire room, taking in the array of world wonders, only to realize that none of these riches would be his.

When his eyes turned back to the statue, he touched it one more time. Then his face twisted into a grin. He drew his arm back and launched the statue across the study. A deafening crash filled the room as chunks of plaster scattered across the floor. "Enjoy hell, Rob."

Milton flinched and Rick smirked.

"Does hell bother you, Mr. Haight?" Without waiting for a reply, Rick returned to the cabinet, swung the door shut, and snapped the latch back into its place.

A knock sounded from the study's entrance.

"Yes," Rick said coolly.

Becca's head appeared in the doorway. "Is everything all right?" Her voice sounded shaky.

Rick studied her, smiled, and nodded. Then his index finger beckoned her back into the room. "You didn't lie down, did you?"

She kept her eyes on Milton.

"Come," Rick ordered.

She obeyed, and after approaching him, he locked her into a hug. For a few uncomfortable seconds, Milton watched as Rick held her tight. Finally a sob slipped from her lips.

Rick grabbed her shoulders and held her at a distance. "Your father took care of you." He grinned. "And"—he wiped a tear from her cheek—"it's official. He's made me your guardian."

Becca glanced at Milton, then back at Rick, and smiled. "Thank you," she said to both of them. She returned Rick's hug and said softly, "This is good."

"Yes. It's very good," Rick said.

LATE AUTUMN 1989

On a magnificent sunny day almost six years later, Milton Haight's Mercedes ascended up the Brownells' drive. This time Rick Downley had requested Milton specifically, and while this surprised Milton, it was not unusual. His responsibilities had grown, especially since Warner's wife had been diagnosed with terminal cancer. Now as Warner became less involved with the firm, Milton's opportunities increased, greatly helping him wade through his law school debt.

After parking at the top of the Brownells' drive, Milton looked out again over the peninsula that jetted out into the Pacific. Any person could see why Robert Brownell had chosen this location.

Before ringing the doorbell, Milton ran his hands through his hair and straightened his tie. Then, seconds later, a beautiful woman in her twenties greeted him.

"Hello. I'm Milton Haight. I'm here to see Richard Downley."

"Yes, come in." She motioned him to enter the lobby, and then softly added, "I remember you."

The charming smile made Milton grin, yet he had no recollection of the beauty.

"You're the attorney." She shifted her focus to a wrapped blue blanket tucked against her left arm.

"You're . . . Becca?" His voice revealed the shock.

She glanced at the ground. "Yes."

"Yes, Becca Brownell," he stammered. Truly she had grown into a lovely woman.

"It's Becca Downley."

"Oh . . . I . . . I didn't know."

"We were married on my eighteenth birthday."

"Oh . . .um . . .well, congratulations."

Her eyes shot back at him. "You're here to make the divorce legal."

"Oh . . . uh." His stammering increased. "Rick said it was to go over some paperwork."

"I divorced him this week, on Monday, after I had my baby." She twisted the bundle toward Milton.

"Oh." Suddenly, he remembered the mental fog from years past. "Congratulations," he repeated. Yet he saw no infant in the bundle. So he stepped closer, only to still see nothing; and for the slightest moment he considered touching the fabric and pulling down a corner, in hopes of revealing the odd couple's offspring.

Instead Becca stepped away, her hands tightening around the bundle. "My baby was born the night before last."

Milton looked again at the blanket. No swaddled infant appeared to lay there. He peered closer, causing Becca to twist the bundle from his view. Helplessly he asked, "Boy or girl?"

"I named him Robert, after his grandfather."

"Milt," a booming voice echoed down the hall.

Milton cringed. Until then, only his law school nemesis had referred to him as Milt. Slowly, he turned to see Rick striding forward then circling around until Rick blocked the exit from Milton's view.

"Sweetness," Rick said to Becca and grinned, "Milt's here to provide you with your request." A deep scowl transformed her beauty into the appearance of an immature yet submissive child. "So I ask you to be a dear and leave us men alone. Do you understand me?"

"Of course. I need to feed Robert." She tightened her grip around the blanket, spun around, and marched through an open door.

While he watched her leave, Rick exhaled a defeated moan. "That girl." Then he turned back to Milton. "Thank you for coming, especially on such short notice. Can I get you something to drink?"

"No, I'm fine."

"Good." Rick laughed. "Otherwise I'd have to call Becca back to retrieve it."

Milton glanced around. "Is your help not here?"

"We get along fine without them these days . . . Well, we did until . . ."

"Yes." Milton hesitated. "Congratulations on the baby."

Rick shot Milton a concerned look. "She's crazy. You see that, right?" Before Milton could answer, Rick turned and motioned down the hall. "Come. Let's talk in the study."

They entered the study, and other than sunlight beaming through window, Milton noted how little had changed. Quickly, he glanced toward the spot on the wall, but no trace of that hole remained.

"Here, sit." Rick motioned at the seat opposite the grand desk while he settled into the master's chair. "So, do you know why you're here?"

"No."

"It's actually Becca who requested you here."

"Well, she mentioned the . . . the . . ." He struggled for words.

"The arrangement," Rick stated.

"I'm not a divorce attorney," Milton blurted out. "We deal with finances and estates."

Rick smirked at him. "That girl—she certainly likes to make my life easy." The two men stared at each other, and for a moment, neither said anything. Then Rick ventured forward. "Glad she explained the circumstances. So yes, due to her condition, we're both requesting that you help us with some legalities here."

"I can't."

"I'm sure you have your resources."

"I can provide you with a referral."

For a long moment, Rick looked at Milton.

Then he arose, stepped around the desk, and touched the back of the small leather chair. A sigh expelled from his lips before he leaned down and spoke into the young attorney's ear. "Milt, we both know that when someone wants something, he finds a way. Which means, I know, that you know, that you can find a way. Becca's done here. She wants out of her comfortable life, so she requested this divorce. She wants a new life, and I expect you to help me give her that."

Milton tensed. "I can't."

"Milt. I need your help." The hand lifted and suddenly Rick was sitting in the chair next to him. "I promised her father I'd care for her, but she's crazy. You saw that. You can't deny that. She told you she had a baby two nights ago, and believe me, that's absurd, especially since I haven't touched her in years."

"I don't need to hear this."

"No, listen. Things were once good between us, really good. But lives change. You know how it is—she changes, I change, other people come into our lives. It's all part of our changing."

"Other people?" Immediately Milton regretted his words.

The question brought Rick's face back to the coldness from years before. "What do you want?" he asked.

"What do I want?"

"Name your price," Rick said.

"What do you mean?"

"Everyone has a price. What's yours?"

"I don't understand."

For a moment, Rick examined Milton; then he stood up and turned his back on Milton. "I was afraid of this, so I made the terms clear." He approached his briefcase and played with the lock until the latch's pop echoed through the room. Then he returned, the arm again around Milton's back while he thrust a form into Milton's grasp. "You sign here." He pointed at the form's designated spot. "And I'll sign here. We could make this verbal, but since you're an attorney, I figured you'd appreciate this legality."

Milton began scanning the document, but within seconds Rick distracted him. "Do you understand that with us in agreement, you get adequate pay?" He extended a thickly bound wad of cash with an attached slip noting the amount. Milton's eyes strayed from the document to glance at the slip. Quickly, his eyes got stuck reading zeros.

"Milton Haight." Rick spoke as if chiding a small child. "Nullify this marriage. Do everything in your power to break this. And once this marriage is annulled, I need you to remember this marriage never existed. Do you understand?"

Milton kept his eyes on the cash while Rick pushed it closer. When the money brick grazed past Milton's index finger, the rest of his fingers hungered for it.

Suddenly Rick dropped the cash directly into Milton's lap. With no forethought, Milton picked it up and clearly read the slip. Yes, there indeed were five lovely looped zeros with one incredibly important numeral one to start the valuable sequence.

"This is the first installment." Rick pointed at the cash. "Just the beginning. All I ask in return is a clean slate for both Becca and me. Give us each the freedom to move on. Don't tie us down with the legalities of divorce, the long paperwork, the battle over the estate, the minute details."

"What details?" To be responsible, Milton let his eyes wander over the document while his fingers stroked the cash. The offer was incredibly desirable.

"Don't worry." Rick sat again next to his guest. "I won't need visitation rights to see her *baby*." Such mockery caused Milton to stir. He paused to examine Rick, which turned Rick's tone stern. "You know she's crazy, Milt. Just within the seconds you saw her, you understood that. The woman needs help, and I need to move on. Consider this your opportunity to serve two people, to give each a chance at a new start, a beginning we both need." He pointed at the cash still held tightly in Milton's hands. "It's yours, if you annul the marriage."

"And what about the estate?"

"She doesn't want it; she doesn't want any of it."

Milton raised his eyebrows.

"Ask her yourself. All she wants is that pretend baby. Then she's extremely happy in her new life, delusional as it may be."

Now the pieces fell into place. "So you get it all." Milton slid the contract to the center of the desk then set the cash directly on top of the contract. But his eyes could not leave the little slip's line of zeros.

"Of course not." Rick patted Milton's shoulder. "I promised Rob I'd care for her. He could break promises, but I can't. She's in no shape to manage finances, but I can. I've already spoken to the owner of a reputable private facility. The arrangements are all made. The funds will be used to provide her with optimum clinical care. She needs help, and I've arranged for her to receive the best. You don't need to worry about how the funds are addressed. At the moment, she wants none of them, which is why I must still manage her inheritance. I must do what best suits her needs. Do you understand that?" Rick picked up the cash and set it closer to Milton. "I will get her the help she needs."

With its new proximity, the cash held an even greater weight. 1-0-0-0-0-0. From the slip of paper, the long numbers stretched out in front of him. 1-0-0-0-0-0. Milton thought about all the freedoms he could enjoy if he provided this simple service. Just for ending a marriage, making it no longer exist, and giving both partners exactly what they wished for. What harm was there in granting those wishes?

He drew in a breath and tried to push the lingering concern from his mind. "She'll be taken care of?"

"Absolutely." Rick clicked the ballpoint pen into place and handed it to Milton. "What kind of person do you think I am?"

Milton nodded. He would accept that answer.

"Use this installment to eliminate the traces of the marriage. Prove to me that it never existed, and the next installment is yours. Got it?"

Milton looked at the cash and grinned. The request really was quite simple—surely something he could find a way to address.

Since all parties gained and no one lost, this made absolute sense. Milton looked at Rick and nodded.

Rick squeezed Milton's shoulder. "Excellent." He pointed at the document and Milton scribbled his signature across a form that no one else would ever see. Then Milton Haight tucked the cash into his briefcase.

A simple gift for a simple favor.

EARLY AUTUMN 1995

CHAPTER ONE

The morning breeze floated through the apartment's open window and swayed past the bare walls, the sparse plants, and the personal library of textbooks and psychological journals. Dr. John Sanders inhaled the air while his long body stretched out on the old brown sofa. He reviewed casually Dr. Norman Vincent Peale's *The Power of Positive Thinking*, until a sudden knock at the door surprised him.

When he opened the door, he found Lisa Henley there holding a cardboard box and a bag of groceries. She flashed him one of her perfect smiles with her blue eyes sparkling at him. "I'm here to make you breakfast." On tiptoes, she pecked his cheek.

"Really?" John reached for the bag of groceries. "Allow me to help you."

Quickly she placed the box on the dining room table and then handed John a newspaper from the bag. "You haven't read the latest articles, have you?"

"No. Not yet."

Her eyes lit up. "Dr. Gravers's and Mayor Downley's conduct is being questioned by the appropriate sources."

"Excellent." He sat at the table and unfolded the paper, only to be distracted by her fingers that grazed past his hands to flip through the pages. Such proximity caused him to smile. Yesterday evening had been their first kiss, and John hoped that she, too, was interested in more than just offering her professional assistance.

"Here's my article." Lisa pointed at the story with photos of Clearcreek Mental Care Center and its corrupt president, Dr. Steven Gravers. She pulled out a chair, sat next to John, and then leaned in close. "And none of this would have happened had you not been there."

Her statement humbled John, and tenderly, he reached for her hand.

She interlocked her fingers with his. "Because of you, your patient got the help she needed. And because of you, Dr. Gravers no longer can accept bribes from Richard Downley to keep her there. You stopped both of them from ruining her life."

She beamed at John until he drew her into their second kiss. It was slow and soft at first, but as the seconds passed, the intensity grew. Finally Lisa slid away.

"I saw Landersen yesterday." Her eyes teased him. "He's back from his family vacation."

Her shift left John in a daze. Yet he paused to focus on his former supervisor. It was Gary Landersen, after much of John's prodding, who had uncovered the final pieces of Clearcreek's corruption. "Where did he go?"

"He says his trip led him to Arizona."

"Arizona." John's heart rate increased for a different reason.

"Yes." She smiled, waiting, playing with the information.

"Did he . . . ?"

"Yes. He saw your patient."

"He did?" John grinned back.

When Dr. Gravers knew that his secrets were about to be exposed, he began covering his tracks. He had quickly relocated this prized patient to a separate facility outside of California. But Dr. Landersen had found her. "What did Gary say? How is she?"

"Good. Very good." Her perfect smile grew wider. "In fact . . . he asked me to deliver this." She picked up the cardboard box.

John reached for it. "Thank you, Landersen."

But she retained the box, and in a teasing voice whispered, "You should know . . ." She moved closer. "This is from her. She asked Gary to deliver it to you."

"It is?"

She kissed his cheek, and then her lips glided toward his ear. "I'll start breakfast while you open it."

He grinned as she handed him the box. Then, after she walked away, his eager fingers fumbled with the tape.

Hours after Lisa left, John reopened the package and reread the letter.

Dear Dr. Sanders,

When I was sent to this new hospital, I knew it was because of you. You remembered me and were still helping me. It gave me courage to keep trying. Thank you.

It's been a good place for me. Dr. Steel is a good doctor. He talks to me like you used to. You would like him. He plans to retire soon. I'm glad he was here to help me.

I told him I wanted to share with you a few of the things he told me. He suggested I write you this letter.

Dr. Steel and I read my father's journal. Years ago, I read parts of it, but I never wanted to finish it. If I reached the end, he would be gone. But if I left some parts unread, it was my way of keeping him alive. Now, Dr. Steel has helped me move forward. I asked him if we could copy a few of the entries that I thought you would find interesting. Dr. Steel thought that would be okay.

The letter stopped. Six photocopied pages of her father's journal followed.

September 21, 1963
    The beast. He comes
    It used to be seldom

In the dark corners of my life
But now he comes more frequently
Seeping into my mind
Turning me into a man I do not know
Yet this is who I've become

February 26, 1965
  Mia does not know
  She says she loves me
  So she must not see
  The beast keeps me hid
  Long journeys to strange lands
  She will not discover me there
  But the silence
  I miss her face
  I want to return
  To see her
  Touch her
  But I cannot stay long
  She cannot know who I am

August 5, 1967
  A little Mia
  Or a tiny me
  Let it not be like me
  I would destroy the young lad
  I need help
  Someone to release me from the beast
  So I can stop hiding from Mia
  And what is to come
  But until then Mia must not know
  It would destroy her
  As it has destroyed me
  And my child to be

It must not learn
That a beast lives in my soul

September 4, 1970
    Mia is gone
    Never shall I touch her face
    The beast visits frequently now
    Calling me away from my home
    I miss my dear Becca
    If I stay I could hold her again
    She has Mia's face
    Her cheek, her nose and chin
    How I miss my love
    I should stay
    Mia would want me here
    But my Becca cannot discover
    She is young still
    Doesn't know who I am
    I must keep this secret forever

August 6, 1983
    The beast frightened me today
    Always seeping into my mind
    The public fears me
    They stare . . . hiss
    Today a lady spit at my feet
    They now see the beast
    Beast
    Everyone sees the beast
    I cannot hide him
    So I hide
    In the dark rooms of my locked closet
    I send away my help

I cannot feast
Sleep tires me
Nights with the beast are more fearful than the days
He has almost consumed my soul

January 4, 1984
Rick has seen the beast
He says he understands
If I don't return
He says he will care for Becca
All arrangements are made
I can leave
Where the winds take me
I do not need to return
Everything is in order
The Beast is waiting
He smiles at me
He is happy
And so I go
Everlasting
We shall be one

On a separate sheet of paper, Rebecca's letter continued.

Dr. Steel pointed out these passages. There are a few other entries where father mentions his sickness. I never knew.

I've learned that despite my father's failures, I can rise above my own weaknesses. Dr. Steel helped me see that, and many other things.

Yesterday, I visited a halfway house. Dr. Steel asked if I could make this my family. I said I would try. This is my new goal.

I'm doing well. Thank you for everything, Dr. Sanders.

        Love,
        Rebecca Ann Brownell

John grinned. She had succeeded.

Although she still did not know all the forces which had kept her at Clearcreek, she had overcome her personal demons, and John rejoiced over this news.

However, there also was a faint sadness, an odd feeling that John could not place. Perhaps it came due to the finality—her goodbye amid all the events and memories.

Suddenly, the front door burst open. "Greetings, neighbor," Randy Case hollered as he stepped into the apartment.

"Hey." John folded up the letter while his friend proceeded to the kitchen. He heard the fridge door open. "Help yourself," he mocked.

Moments later, Randy reappeared with a soda, then picked up the TV remote and plopped his lanky body down on the other side of the sofa. His Saturday attire typically included a baseball cap, used to contain his tousled sandy curls, but today the cap was absent. "What's that?" He pointed at the box.

"Nothing." John set the letter in the box. "Just something from a friend."

Randy's bushy eyebrows scrunched upward. "You have other friends than me? Who's it from?"

"You don't know the person."

"I've known you for how long? Since our first day of college. So let's see . . ." He began counting the fingers on his hands. When he reached the end he counted another two digits. "That's twelve years."

"Yep."

"That's a long time, buddy."

"It is."

"I know most of your friends, and the few I don't know, I've heard of. So who's it from?"

John drew in a breath. In truth, Randy knew more than he should—like the precise details on why John was removed from Clearcreek. "It's from my patient."

"Your patient." He glanced at the box resting on John's lap. "You mean *the* patient?"

"Yes."

"The *one*."

"Yes." John shifted the box until it perched on the armrest next to him. "It's from her."

"So . . ." Randy kept looking at it. "What is it?"

"It's a blanket."

"A what?" Randy sat up. He placed the soda and remote carefully onto the coffee table, glanced at John, and then leaped for the box. "What do you know?" He set the box on the table and unveiled the blue fleece. "A blanket—a cute little baby's blanket."

"Wow." A grin crept over John's face. "You're a quick one."

"So . . ." Randy sank back into the couch while clutching the blanket in his hand. "What does a smart clinical psychologist such as yourself infer when a former patient sends you an old baby blanket?"

John reached for the remote. "Nothing."

But his friend cuddled up against the blanket, stuck his thumb in his mouth, and then pulled it out to add, "No, Doc, what does it mean?"

"She's making a statement."

"A statement?"

"Yes. She's doing well."

Randy lowered the blanket to his lap and stroked it. "So was it worth it?"

"Worth what?"

"Giving up your career?"

"I haven't given up my career. Clearcreek was a corrupt place."

"Okay. So no regrets?"

"None."

Randy leaned back, lifted his legs onto the coffee table, and crossed his feet. "Good. Cause you were a bit OCD with the whole thing. For a while, you really got obsessed about everything. But you did piece all this together. So does that make you sort of like a genius or something, Johnny Boy?" He tossed the blanket back into the box. "Maybe for your next job, you should apply with the FBI."

John laughed. "I don't think so."

"But seriously look at your skill, Detective Sanders—figuring out the scoop on your patient and that politician. My dad wanted that Downley guy to win the Senate race, but not since I've educated him. Nope. Now we've determined he's the type that belongs in the sewers."

Too many long days had been spent dwelling on this man; and lately, just speaking his name sparked John with intense anger. "He did benefit at her expense, but have you seen today's paper?"

"No." Randy's eyes scanned the room. "Are you in it again?"

"It's on the table."

Randy stood and retrieved the *Times*. When he returned to the couch, John could see Downley's picture beneath the headline, Scandal Creates Campaign Danger for Santa Barbara's Mayor.

"Wow. Richard Downley on the front page." Randy whistled. "Can you believe it?"

As Randy read, John glanced at the blanket still sticking out of the box. It was a day for rejoicing, yet the photo of Mayor Richard Downley, with his politician smile, haunted John.

From all he had gleaned about Downley, this man would retaliate.

The question now was when.

CHAPTER TWO

Retaliation began Monday.
That evening, unaware, John sat on his couch skimming through an employment list of psychiatric services provided by Dr. Landersen. In red, John crossed off places he had tried or those he had no interest pursuing. Then he drew circles around the desirable ones. This prized list served as a strong prediction that a new job was soon ahead.

Until a sudden knock caused John to jump.

He was further startled to see Lisa on the porch, crying. Her tailored jacket was unbuttoned, her silk blouse untucked, and several strands of hair fell against her face.

"Come in." He ushered her into the living room, and she sank into the couch but said nothing. Instead she rubbed her swollen eyes.

John moved his employment list to the coffee table, sat next to her, and watched her blue eyes glisten with tears.

Finally she said, "It's not good." She glanced around the room and shook her head. "I'm sorry. I want you to know I'll be up all night writing an opposing article for this. But first . . . I needed to tell you. Before you read it."

John lowered his head. "It's about her, isn't it?"

She slid her hand into his, but her face turned away from him. "Rebecca. Rebecca Brownell." The fragile words were out. "The details are there," she said. "And they're not pretty."

"So you've seen the article?"

"Bill wrote it. I've been talking to him, trying to get him not to run it. But it's part of the business. It's news."

He let out a heavy sigh. "What does the article say?"

"As I expected, Downley used political charm. He portrayed her as a deranged beast and himself as an innocent, virtuous saint."

John's body sagged into the couch. "Did we have other choices? Could we have exposed Clearcreek in another way?"

"At this point, the press is free to throw around her name." Lisa used a tissue to dab at her eyes. "He said she endangered his welfare and that he was the victim of her frenzied mind. He claims he suffered and that his hardest choice was leaving her in a place that could ultimately offer her the best care."

"What about Clearcreek's arrangement to keep her there?"

"He denies that." She tucked a loose piece of hair behind her ear. "Instead, he says he sent generous donations to Clearcreek out of love and respect for his ex-wife."

"He's a liar."

"And he's had no continued contact with her because he had to move on, so he blames Gravers. He claims Gravers misinterpreted his generosity. He says that had Rebecca been released, he would have likely ceased those donations and used the money to support her in other helpful ways. His charity to Clearcreek was entirely for her benefit."

John slammed his fist against the armrest. "He can't come off looking innocent."

Her face tensed up, and tears seemed close again. "It's worse, John."

"You can do something, can't you?" As if to ward off the growing pain, John rubbed his forehead.

"Gravers is fighting back too."

John paused. He looked at Lisa, and his shoulders relaxed. "Good. If Mayor Downley plans to make Gravers take full responsibility, Dr. Gravers had better speak up."

"No, John." She tightened her fingers around his hand, drew in a long breath, and then spoke the words slowly. "He's fighting against *you*."

"Against me?"

"That's why I'm writing this counter-article." She released his hand, rubbed her temples, and stood up. "I'll be working on it all night."

Suddenly John's throat felt tight. "What's he saying?"

Her eyes clouded with tears. "It's not good."

"What's he saying?"

She folded her arms and stared at the ceiling.

"Lisa. What is Gravers saying?"

"That you were . . ."

John's voice stayed soft, yet strong. "Tell me."

She took in a long breath and held it. Then, after an extended, tense exhale, she said, "That you were controlling Rebecca."

"What?"

"That you used your skills as a therapist to manipulate her for your own passions."

Her words shocked John.

"His staff," her voice continued, "has verified that you were meeting with her in secret, after hours."

John's head dropped into his hands. "He's twisting facts."

"He says once he discovered your unethical conduct, he immediately dismissed you. As a result, you were furious." Lisa stepped toward the corner. "You distorted the truth to seek revenge against him."

John stood up, rubbed his forehead, and paced the room. "He can't do this to me."

"John?" Her eyes searched his face. "Did something happen?"

"No!" He wanted to punch a wall, a door, or preferably Gravers's face. "I've given everyone the truth." His fingers pressed into his forehead. "But now you're questioning me."

"No." A tense quiet followed, until Lisa wiped her eyes, and said, "I'm here to help you . . . and I believe you." She approached him, slid her hands down his arms, and pulled him forward. "I believe you. Just—before I write this, I needed to ask."

Reluctantly, he gave into her hug.

"This'll ruin my career." John's head pounded. "Dr. Gravers knows that. It's why he's doing this."

"I know. He's trying to turn the media's focus onto you."

"I'm going to be judged and questioned. My integrity will be under fire. I'll never get a job."

Her hands tightened against his back. "John. The facts are there. Downley and Gravers will fight. But ultimately, they'll lose."

He shut his eyes, hoping to block out the approaching terror. When he opened them again, he said, "You don't know that."

"Court action is underway. Gravers's preliminary hearing starts next month. Mayor Downley's will be slightly slower. But there's rumor he may be removed from the Senate race, so your career isn't the only one at stake."

John gave her a heartless smile. "It better not be. Especially since I'm innocent . . . but I'm the one who'll be ruined. Look at their revolting crimes, and now they're attacking me—and her—but . . ." John clenched his teeth. He could only shake his head.

"But"—Lisa attempted to finish his sentence—"we have facts. Dr. Gravers and Mayor Downley are guilty, which means in time you'll be seen for the person you truly are."

"Let's hope." John looked past the curtains' small opening and out into the darkness. Mayor Downley had obtained his position of power through manipulation, whereas John had labored for years to obtain his right to serve.

Yet tomorrow, John's sound reputation would be attacked.

CHAPTER THREE

The week exploded with strange phone calls, evil looks, and speculative reports. Unknown sources published John Sanders's picture, and slander clung to his name. Thanks to the press, the public viewed him as a disgrace.

As a result, an epidemic of black **X**'s slashed across Dr. Landersen's list of psychiatric services. The list that had once held small circles of employment hope now grew dark with despair.

After two days of this media madness, John shut himself off from the world. He avoided all newspapers, television, and radio. Of course he was not everywhere in the local news, but a simple hunt brought disturbing results. Rather than face the slander, John silently withdrew.

Then, during the following week, a ration of good news arrived. Since Dr. Landersen shouldered a small portion of blame for Clearcreek's demise, he appeared eager to correct some unfortunate consequences—one being John's job status. Therefore, on Wednesday morning, Dr. Landersen made numerous phone calls on Sanders's behalf. By midafternoon, John had a contact name, which led to an immediate interview and a strong promise for work.

Although it was not an ideal position, John understood currently it was his only hope. By Friday, he was employed again, and this news washed away some of the preceding week's dirt. In triumph, John turned his focus to celebrating.

That evening, at ten minutes to seven, he heard his apartment door open, followed by a familiar, strong voice: "Greetings, newsworthy neighbor."

"Hey, Randy." John turned from the kitchen to see his friend examining two paper bags that had been left on the table.

"What you got here, Johnny Boy?" Randy pulled out the white Chinese takeout box and opened the lid. "Oh, perfect! Kung Pao Chicken—you must have been expecting me." He selected a chicken piece and tossed it into his mouth.

John grabbed the box and shoved Randy away. "It's for Lisa."

"Lisa, huh?" He pulled out a chair and sat. "Well, the two of you won't mind if I join you." Then he reached for the other bag.

"Don't touch." John scowled, then returned to the kitchen to gather plates. When he came back, Randy had wooden chopsticks in hand and was chasing a clump of rice around the table. "Want to play chopsticks hockey?"

"Where's Lily tonight?"

Randy cocked his head to the side, batted his eyelashes, and raised his voice an octave higher to mimic his girlfriend. "Randy's insensitive." He shrugged his shoulders and returned to his normal voice. "Me, insensitive. Who knew?"

"I've got a great idea. Why don't you go make up with her?"

"What?"

"Right now."

"You want to get rid of me?"

"Lisa will be here in ten minutes."

"Okay. Fine. Situation comprehended." Randy stood up, drew in a strong breath, then sat back down. "But first, tell me—am I insensitive?"

John pulled the last containers from the bags. "Probably not."

"Here's the situation. I'm at school, got ninth-grade biology on the brain. The bell rings, last period ends." Randy opened a lid and dumped more clumps of rice onto the table. "I've got students who want to talk, ask me questions. But Lil shows up. That's fine, but she needs me pronto. Emergency status. She's upset." With the chopsticks, Randy separated out each grain of rice. "She didn't make it into the nursing program. It's been her lifelong dream, you know?" He held a small clump of rice between his chopsticks, which he popped into his mouth. "So I stop life for her, spend two hours consoling her. Two hours!" He raised the sticks up to John's face. "I brought her back to my place and tried to calm her down. By five o'clock we were grounded again. No more urgent crying. So I start making plans for Friday night cuddling. Whoa, did that suggestion make her mad. She said I was insensitive, that she needed real sympathy. Like what I gave her wasn't *real*?" His chopsticks mashed against the small pieces of rice. "So she asks to use my telephone and calls a friend. For over an hour and a half she's been talking. That's ninety minutes. Five thousand four hundred seconds. Five million four hundred thousand milliseconds. In other words—a very, very long time. What I want to know is how someone can even talk that long!" For a moment, Randy paused; then he actively used his chopsticks to rebuild a mound of rice.

"That's too bad for Lily." John wiped the table and swept Randy's rice out of reach.

In response, Randy began whirling a chopstick around his finger. "Just like that, I'm called insensitive. Apparently this friend who can give real sympathy is in cosmetology school. Before I know it, Lil remembers that her real lifelong dream was to make other people fancy. They're talking about hair, nails, pedigrees—"

"Pedigrees?" John grinned. "You sure it wasn't pedicures?"

"I don't know. When she started talking about waxing, I was done. So I told her I had to call you, and do you know what she said?" He slammed the chopstick down. "She told me I could walk over here. That you and I live in the same complex, so why did I need the phone line? Hello! Why did I need the phone line? Whose phone is it anyway?"

John grabbed the abandoned chopsticks. "Sounds like a tough evening ahead."

"Not really." He pulled open another container. "Chinese is my favorite."

John took hold of the box. "Not tonight."

Randy laughed. "I'm kidding, Johnny Boy. What do you think, I'm blind? You've got some fine dining plans this evening. And kid, I'm proud of you. I'd like to think that everything you know, you learned from Master Rando."

"I wanted to do something special for Lisa."

"Special." Randy's eyebrows moved up and down. "Say no more. I'm out of here." He stood up, took one step toward the door, and then turned around. "However, lest you forget, I'm forever to be praised for bringing you two together."

"Oh, yes, Great One. If you remind me, I'll kneel next time you enter." John pointed at the door and grinned. "See you later."

Randy stepped toward his exit only to turn around. "Actually, I'd like to see you kneel right now."

"Randy, go."

A big smirk crossed his face. "No, better yet, what I really want is for your girlfriend to teach my girlfriend how to write articles about me being the Hero-Man."

John paused. "You read Lisa's article, huh?"

"Well, usually I'm aware of current events right about the time they've expired. But these past weeks, the teacher's lounge keeps buzzing about your name. You, John. I'm just a little high school biology teacher, and here's my good buddy appearing almost daily in the news."

"Believe me," John scoffed. "It's no honor."

"Well . . . just so you know, I've stuck up for you. Had a few spats with some know-it-all teachers, but I stand by you, buddy."

"Did you read the other articles?"

"About you? I skimmed a few. Some left me a bit nauseated."

"Yeah." John looked down at one of his shirt's buttons. A thread had begun to unravel.

"If I were you," Randy said, "I'd hang Lisa's article around my apartment. No. Better yet, I'd wallpaper my walls with those words." His voice jumped an octave. "John Sanders—he's my hero. He should be everyone's hero. He's so dreamy." Randy waved his hands in an exaggerated feminine fashion. "He saves all women in distress, even the mentally unstable. There's not one ounce of corruption in his noble soul. No Big Bad Wolf of mental hospitals should ever say such nasty, untrue things about our community hero, my hero: Dr. John Harold Sanders, Esquire."

John released a short laugh. "Let's hope no one else interpreted the article like that."

"Hey." Randy's eyes turned sober. "It was a very good article. The truth."

"Thanks."

"How is"—Randy struggled for the words—"all that?"

"Things are quieting down. Yesterday only three women attacked me with handbags."

Randy shot him a grin.

"It's tough," John said. "At Clearcreek, I tried to do what I thought was right. I tried to help the patients. It's ironic that in my struggles to be good, the community feels a need to create evil motives for all my actions."

"It's that Gravers guy." Randy leaned his weight against the door. "He's out to get you."

"But now the media's in on it."

"So do you have people trying to get interviews with you? Wanting your picture?"

"Yeah."

"That's cool."

"No. It's not."

For a moment, the room was silent. Then Randy asked, "So what've your parents said?"

"When the news reached San Jose, my dad called."

"Your mom's a wreck, huh?"

"Actually, Dad says she's been modifying her vocabulary to properly express her attitude toward Steven Gravers."

Randy chuckled. "Way to go, Cindy Sanders."

"Yep, Mom decided he's the devil, but she adores Lisa and has her article cut out and stuck to the fridge."

"Definitely sounds like your mom."

"Dad bets she'd try and get the local paper to run Lisa's article, except she'd hate to tip off the neighbors, on the chance they may have missed it."

"I'm glad Cin and Hal are supportive."

"Yeah. They keep saying that they're here for me. That I can move back to San Jose, and get away from all this."

"Would you?"

"Sure." John's voice lacked enthusiasm.

"Really?"

"Lisa's here . . . and I've seen her daily for the past two weeks."

"Oh yeah?" Randy's face held a proud smile.

"But if I couldn't find work, as a last resort, I've considered it."

"No luck, huh?"

"Actually—that's the reason for this." John pointed at the Chinese food. "I finally have a job and wanted to celebrate the news with Lisa."

"Glad to see a poor man knows how to celebrate." Randy smirked. "Congratulations. I'm happy for you."

"Honestly. It's with the county clinic and it's not a sought-after position. But it's temporary, just until the firing squad's done."

A sudden knock made Randy turn. He shot John a smile, then approached the door, opened it, and drawled, "Well hello, Lisa."

"Hi, Randy." She stepped inside. "How's Lily?"

"Hopefully off the phone." Randy gave her a tense smile. "I guess I better get back to her." He leaned toward Lisa's ear. "You've got some fine dining ahead. Wish I were him. Enjoy." He walked through the door frame, then turned back and hollered, "Bye, Johnny Boy."

As soon as he left, Lisa said, "Randy's odd."

John pulled her into a hug. "How are you?"

"Overwhelmed." She looked up at him and studied his face. "Have you been listening to the news?"

"I try to avoid it lately."

"Well, you've missed the six o'clock, but you'd better catch the ten."

He released the embrace. "If it's about me, I want to miss it."

"It's not."

"Then that's good news." He wanted to kiss her, but she had already moved away. "Should we eat?" he asked. "The food may be getting cold."

She paused, then stepped toward the table. "Sure."

In a systematized order, John opened up containers and placed them around her plate. Lisa watched him while her fingers tapped against the chair. With each tap, the intensity grew. Finally he stepped back and looked at her. "What?"

"John, I'm going to burst. Aren't you the slightest bit curious what the big headline is?"

In truth, he was not. Over the last couple weeks, before his own name had been slandered, he had saturated himself with updates. From then on, he had received a rapid tutorial on how callous and subjective some reports could be. But out of respect for Lisa's career and passion, he politely answered, "Of course I am. Is it Downley or Gravers?"

"Downley's disappeared."

"What?"

"They think he's dead."

The food was forgotten. "Are you sure?"

"Yesterday he took his sailboat out, even though there were warnings about a coastal storm. He was last spotted going straight into fifty-mile-per-hour winds. This morning, they found his cap-sized boat about twenty miles from shore."

He starred at her. "What else?"

"He was alone." She sat down, and John followed her lead. From across the table, he watched her and waited. Finally she continued, "They're not sure, but there's speculation it was suicide."

"Really?" His voice was quiet.

"The scandal's been hurting him. The Democrats are furious enough to disavow him. He's losing ground with his hometown. And across the state, people are starting to despise him for manipulating Rebecca and stealing her funds."

"What about the innocent picture that he painted of himself?"

"Well, judging from the response, his attempts weren't good enough. Seems a fair amount of people can't separate the fact that, until this broke, no one knew about his ex-wife. Not even his current wife. It just doesn't look good for him."

"At least some of the public has some common sense."

"He's a fraud." Lisa said. "And people are now seeing that."

For a moment, they sat quietly, looking at each other. Then John calmly said, "But suicide?"

"If he was after fame, the disgrace may have been too much. If he can't rise above this scandal, his political career is over. Plus there's been talk that Gravers will turn against him."

John rubbed his forehead, looked at the food, and curtly said, "We'd better eat."

Lisa nodded. The two dished up and then ate in silence. John seldom looked up. When the meal came to a close, Lisa reached across the table and touched his arm. "You okay?"

He shook his head. "Gravers won't turn against Downley, especially if Downley's dead. Gravers will keep his focus on me. He wants me to carry his shame."

"I don't know. If Downley's dead and it's a suicide—none of that looks good for Gravers."

John sighed. "I hope. It all seems unfair, especially if Downley ends his life to avoid consequences and Gravers gets a better sentence from the results."

"Do you know what I think?" She arose from the table and approached him. "You're bruised." She placed her hands on his shoulders and began to massage them. "But the game's not over yet. So you can't jump to conclusions. Gravers will be punished. Be patient, and justice will pull through."

John closed his eyes and gave into the soothing touch. "And in the meantime . . ." As her fingernails glided across his neckline, his lips parted into a pleasant smile. ". . . I should focus on other things?"

"Maybe for right now, that's a good idea."

"Perhaps I should look at other aspects of my future." He touched her soft hand. "Right?"

"I think so."

"Landersen's already moved on with life. Rebecca's getting on with hers. It might be time for me to enjoy some things too."

Lisa grinned while she pulled him up and steered him toward the old couch. With his hands around her waist, she wrapped her arms around his neck. "Tell me, John Sanders, what do you enjoy?"

For a long minute, he kissed her. "I have you in my life." He continued with another drawn-out kiss, and then whispered, "And I have a new job."

She pulled back. "You do?" Her eyes searched his face. "John, that's wonderful! When? Where? Why didn't you tell me?"

"It'll be perfect." He smiled, feeling no desire to share more. Instead, he pulled her into a stronger kiss and focused on keeping her close. She responded, accepting his touch, until a series of beeps erupted from her purse.

The noise caused her to pull back, and John let out a perturbed sigh. "Does that thing always have to go off? Or just lately, when you're with me?"

"I'm sorry, John." She released herself from his embrace.

"Why are you even bothering to check it?" he asked. "You know who it is. And you know what he wants."

She retrieved her beeper, then picked up John's telephone and made the call. "Hi, Bill. It's me." Her eyes pleaded apologies to John, but her ears, mouth, and mind began shifting elsewhere. "I can't," she said into the phone. "I'm in San Bernardino." Then she turned so her back faced John. "It'll be over an hour . . . Yeah . . . I'm taking that into consideration . . . I know it's a good opportunity . . . Of course I respect you, and you've been patient . . . I'll have an answer for you soon." She paused. Then her voice changed in intensity. "Really?" She laughed into the phone. "You're serious? You'd give me that story?" Silence, and then her words filled with confidence. "Okay. If it's a reliable source—then we'd better grab it. I'll be there as soon as I can. Thanks, Bill—you're brilliant." Her body shifted; and John caught sight of the beaming smile, which he was excluded from.

"I know," she whispered into the phone. "I can't keep you waiting. I'll make a decision soon." She giggled. "Yes, you've made it very clear what I should do." She smiled, listened, and then whispered again, "Thanks for the encouragement, Bill—and for this opportunity. See you soon."

She placed the phone back in its cradle. For a moment, her fingers tapped against the phone book.

"You're leaving," he said.

Slowly she turned to face him, yet her eyes avoided his. "I have to go." She folded her arms against her chest. "There's more on Downley, and it's big."

"Of course." Everything with Downley was big.

"Bill thought I should know."

John tried to hide his disappointment. "And he offered you another chance to be a part of it."

"His wife found a suicide note." She moved anxiously toward the kitchen table. "It said he wanted to be out at sea when he killed himself . . . and his gun's missing."

John shook his head.

"The money's gone, too," she said as she reached for her handbag.

"The money?"

She turned to face him. "In the note, he apologized for their financial situation. So his wife called their broker, only to discover that many of their assets were gone."

"You sure?"

"I need to go. We need these details—and right now Bill's working on an interview with Anne Downley."

"His widow?"

"Yes." Lisa eagerly scanned the room. "Do I have everything?"

"Are you sure this is a good time to talk with her?"

"It's my job, John."

"How much money is gone?"

"I don't know, but Bill says it's my story if I hurry."

"That's not all Bill said." Her eyes returned to the phone, and a slight smile crossed her lips.

"What does he want?"

As her smile vanished, she twirled a ring around her middle finger. "Just work issues."

John tried to be kind but bold. "What else, Lisa?"

"He's been pushing this on me for a while. He needs me to make a decision."

"About what?"

"They want me there in LA." Her fingers stopped moving. "It's a promotion, a great chance."

John glanced at the ceiling and then down at her. "One you'd be crazy to pass up."

"When Clearcreek and Gravers were making headlines, it made sense to be here. But with most of those details covered, things are slowing down. But now, with Downley's death, plus this new issue about the finances, we've got news for a good month." Her voice became strong. "I need to be close. These stories are front-page material. And I have an opportunity to be a part of it."

John walked past her. He reached for the doorknob and gave her an encouraging glance. "I don't want to slow you down."

"They like my work." She searched his face. "They've made a spot for me in LA."

"I know."

She walked over and touched his arm. "I'm sorry."

"Why didn't you tell me sooner?"

"I don't know." She touched his chest. "Maybe I was afraid."

"Congratulations." He hoped he sounded sincere. Then he twisted the doorknob open. "You'd better get going."

She walked toward the door, but then turned back. "It's not that far away. There's the weekends, and—" She gave him an apologetic look.

"I know."

She took a step away from the door and closer to him. "I want this promotion, John."

"I know you do."

Her eyes searched for his acceptance. "Then I'll call you later, okay?"

"Okay."

She smiled, and with one quick kiss, she was gone.

When John shut the door, his apartment felt empty. He returned to the table, picked up the leftover food, and discovered the fortune cookies still in the bag. He tore open one of the packages, broke the cookie, and pulled out the slip.

Business matters around you will bloom.

John's fingers curled around the cookie pieces. He tightened his hand into a fist and then slowly released his grip over the white bag. Piece by piece, the crumbs fell.

Of course she wanted this. This was her dream, and the opportunities had come. If he truly cared about her, he needed to support this.

Otherwise she would let him go.

CHAPTER FOUR

Over a week later, on an extremely quiet evening, John sat on his couch and rested his feet against the coffee table. Erich Fromm's *The Art of Loving* lay in his hands. He skimmed page 17, contemplating the theory of mature love, when the phone rang. It was Lisa.

Her zealous voice made his heart race. He dropped his book and sat up straight. "How are you?" he asked.

"Great. I love this place. You should see the view from my office. Picture this—I'm on the eighteenth floor and it looks out over the street. I can see everything. The lights, the traffic, the diversity." Her pause was brief. "It's amazing. I'm living a life that belongs in a dream."

"How are the deadlines?"

"Exhausting." She laughed.

"How's your apartment?"

"Cute. Smaller. Rent is unreal. But it's worth it."

He had offered to help her move, but she had denied him the chance. "So it's a good place?"

"It's a great place—you should come see me."

John smiled. "I want to."

"Okay, then come."

"I'll be there this weekend."

"Oh, John. Not this weekend—it's not a good time. I'm working with some chief editors to consolidate the details on Downley. We're selling the concise report to Newsweek." She paused, clearly waiting for him to be impressed.

But it was too much. He allowed his voice to reveal the dejection. "Oh."

"Have you followed the story?"

"Some." He looked out the window to see gray clouds approaching. "When I get time. Especially if I know it's your article."

"It's fascinating. His wife, Anne—sweet lady. Conservative, not a person I'd place alongside Downley's liberal views. But people who knew them said she never sparked wars. She supported him and stayed neutral. I suspect it was required."

"How's she taken the death?"

"Pretty well." She paused. "I guess."

"What happened to the money?"

"Apparently there's some left. Less than all of us expected. But there's some. In fact, if Rebecca wants it, now's the time. You should contact her. She certainly has a right to it."

"No. I'm not getting involved."

"It'd be a fight, no question about that." She released a low whistle. "Anne was clueless about Rebecca. No idea . . . until everything turned public. Now she says she's not giving handouts. What's hers is hers. So there's already been talk of this turning into quite a war."

"But its Rebecca's inheritance?"

"Well, there may be some confusion around what's left. What's considered Rebecca's compared to what Anne brought to the marriage?"

John thought of Rebecca facing such an ordeal and his neck muscles tightened. "She'd need a good lawyer."

"She would. So let her know the options. Then find a good lawyer."

"Lisa." John clenched his teeth. Such a suggestion was dangerous. "I don't know where she is."

"You could find her."

"When she sent that package, she was in a hospital in Arizona. It's been over two months now, and she was leaving there. At this point I have no way to reach her."

"Landersen would. You know that. Have you talked to him recently?"

"Not since he helped me get my job."

"Your job? Oh, John." Lisa laughed. "I'm forgetting those things these days. How is it? I'm sorry, I've been so busy. I —"

"It's fine," he cut her off. "Work's fine." He had no desire to talk about his time with state-ordered clients who did not see a need—or have a desire—to change their self-destructive behavior.

"Is it good?" she pushed. "Your job? Are you happy?"

"It's okay."

"Are you happy?" she asked again.

He sighed, and then aimed to sound upbeat. "Clearcreek unsettled my plans. Now I'm readjusting and figuring out exactly what I want."

"Well . . . if I can help, let me know."

"Sure."

"Okay. Well, I'd better go. Please talk to Landersen. Find out where Rebecca is. At the very least, let's help her know she has these options."

To avoid her approaching goodbye, John quickly said, "Are you happy?"

"Of course." She laughed. "I'm living my dream."

An awkward pause followed.

"Are you there, John?"

"Yeah, I'm here."

"Well, I just looked at my watch. I need to go. Anyway, I wanted you to know that Rebecca deserves what's left. Find her. I'll talk to you soon."

When he heard the click, John released a heavy sigh. Slowly he arose to place the receiver back in the cradle. Then he saw their framed picture resting on the end table. In the photo he and Lisa both were full of smiles. They held the *LA Times* that bore the head-line "Mayor Downley and Clearcreek Mental Care Center face their doom." It had been taken during the final days of Downley's life, the end of Gravers's success, and possibly the beginning of the end of this joy John had envisioned for himself.

He picked up the picture frame and examined her smile. That day she had been extremely happy. They both had been happy. But now, their lives seemed vastly different.

Maybe it had always been that way.

He released a sigh, slid open the end table's drawer and carefully tucked the picture inside. Then he shut the drawer and walked away.

CHAPTER FIVE

A week later, John scanned Capello's Deli for Gary Landersen. Although the restaurant was small, it was clearly a favorite of the local lunch crowd.

From across a group of business professionals, John spotted Landersen waving his thick arm. Then, as soon as John slid into the booth, Landersen handed him a menu.

"How's the job?" Landersen's gaze traveled down the menu.

"Good," John said. "Thanks for the referral."

"It's the least I could do. You been here before? I hear the club sandwich is good." Earlier in the week, Landersen had selected the deli because it was one of the few venues his wife permitted during their joint diet.

John smiled. "The club sounds good."

In haste, Landersen flagged a server, but once the order was placed, he shifted his portly body further into the booth and smiled. "How are you, Sanders?"

"I'm hanging in there."

Landersen nodded. "It's been a tough transition for us all." Yet his face seemed more at ease then when John had last seen him. "I talked to Hunter the other day. He moved north and works at the state hospital in Napa. It sounds like he's doing well. Lumber's unemployed, struggling to get by. Did you know Hooper?"

"Of course."

Landersen nodded. "Well, he may write a book on the whole fiasco. If he does, he'll want to interview you. Are you okay with that?"

"Sure."

"Good." Landersen clasped his hands together and set them on the table. Then he looked John straight in the eyes. "If you do meet with Hooper, could you present me in a good light?" His tone softened. "I know I made some mistakes, but didn't we all?"

For brief seconds, John reviewed his year at Clearcreek. It had been a year which had deeply changed him. A time where his innocence had been stripped, and professionally he had been left alone to reevaluate the world around him. During that year, he and Landersen had held different views on Rebecca's progression. But now, none of those misunderstandings mattered. The truth was out and Rebecca was healing, which meant it was time for him to start healing too.

John maintained eye contact with Landersen and felt the residual strain of the last year leave him. "Yes." He smiled softly. "We all made mistakes, but we did the best we could with the information we had."

Landersen nodded. Then his tone shifted back to his normal jovial nature. "Occasionally I see Anita at our post office on the mountain."

"I do miss the mountain." John sighed.

"Well, come on up some time. We're only about fifteen minutes from Clearcreek. It'd make my wife happy. I think she blames me for sending all of the staff out into unemployment. She said that she never liked Gravers and that I should have seen through him clear from the beginning."

At that moment, the food arrived and Landersen attacked his sandwich. Apparently, hourly starvation was part of his diet plan.

"Mmm," he muttered between bites. "Told you—good sandwiches, huh?" Landersen smacked his lips and smiled at his meal.

Amid bites, John asked, "Who else do you hear from?"

"Dr. Blythe started her own practice." Landersen picked up the second half of his sandwich. "She's an amazing lady."

"She is."

"I call her the cayenne pepper of the human race. She's the penetrating type. You get too much of her and she'll bring you to tears. But overall, life's richer because of her zest." Then he added, "She was the best Clearcreek had." He mumbled between a large bite. "Certainly those publications and seminars set her up for the shift."

"She'll be excellent."

"She already is. I send most of my crisis patients straight to her for counseling." Again he bit into his sandwich, and then as an afterthought added, "Oh, you'll find this interesting." He ground through a few chews and said, "With this last referral, when I called to give her some background information, we got chatting. She asked about you, wanted to know where you'd ended up. She playfully cussed me out because I got you that job. She said she needed an assistant and had thought of you."

Suddenly John swallowed too large of a bite and gasped through some coughs. "Me?"

"I don't know if she was serious, but she mentioned it. Anyway, she's since hired some guy I've never heard of. I think he's new to the area."

Over the past weeks, John had struggled to convince himself that he appreciated his job, and that he was satisfied to have something to wake up for and a paycheck, small as it was, to place in his bank account. Now, Landersen's nonchalant remark blasted John's tactics for contentment.

Finally he said, "Thanks for the job."

"Don't mention it."

Quietly, he added, "Clearcreek really hurt my career."

Landersen stopped chewing and studied John's face. "Hey, the public can be quick to judge and slow to forgive, but they will forgive you. Do your best where you are and you'll be rewarded."

Although unsure of the accuracy of those words, John drew in a long breath and spurred himself forward. "Probably not the best time to bring this up, but Lisa insisted that I ask."

Landersen stopped hunting for crumbs and smiled. He grabbed a napkin, wiped his mouth, and asked, "How is that girl?"

"Good. Got a great promotion with the paper and now lives in LA."

"An amazing gal. The entire metal health community owes her a lot."

"Yeah." John's heart beat through the pain. "She's amazing."

"Beautiful and talented."

A sigh slipped from John's lips. Then he quickly pressed forward. "She thinks Rebecca should be entitled to her inheritance."

"Oh. Tragic about Downley, wasn't it? Some freak storm that cost him his life, especially after he was so confident about coming off clean."

John's neck muscles tightened at the name. "Yeah."

"So Rebecca needs to claim her money?" Landersen asked.

"Lisa thinks so. Personally, it seems like an extra stress for Rebecca."

"Would it have to be?"

John shrugged his shoulders. "I don't know. Lisa thinks Downley's widow would put up a good fight, which doesn't seem like a positive thing for Rebecca, does it?"

"I wonder how that girl's doing." Landersen rubbed a layer of chins. "It never dawned on me that she'd be in for an economic culture shock in addition to everything else. Here she was, spoonfed all her life, and then Clearcreek continued that feeding. Now she's supposed to rough it on her own. If she's told to put on some red vest and stock shelves with toilet paper, I wonder how she'll fare."

John placed his elbows on the table and rubbed his temples. "It doesn't get easy for some people, does it?"

"How much money?"

"Lisa speculates $1.5 million."

Landersen groaned. "That's sure money I'd like to have." He shook his head and grinned. "She needs the option."

"You think?"

"Well, I can call her present therapists and see what they say. But think about it. If you had access to $1.5 million and people don't tell you, how would you react?"

"Health is more important than money."

"Maybe she can have both."

John drew in a long breath. "Where is she?"

Landersen smiled. "This time I did something good for her. Arizona was always meant to be temporary, but I've done some pleading, and they've agreed to keep her there while she's still in the public eye. But she'll need to come back soon. In fact, now might be a good time. Hmm. Guess the best thing would be for me to talk to her directly." Dr. Landersen squinted, then rubbed his chin. "Unless you want to?"

John cleared his throat. "Could I?"

"Sure. Why not?"

"What about all this media?"

Landersen chuckled. "It's just a phone call. Besides, you're only statewide news. Arizona's got its own problems."

John grinned, and his heart raced.

"Hmm." Landersen looked off in the distance. "Now that I'm thinking about it, maybe the recommendation should come from you. You've already built that relationship, and she trusts you, which means you could give a good assessment—give her clear council. Yes, it should be you that talks to her; it'd be better that way."

CHAPTER SIX

A green highway sign announced the good news—only forty miles remained. Although his legs felt stiff, eagerness pushed John toward Tucson.

That Saturday, as early as four in the morning, he had lain awake contemplating what he would say to her.

It had been months since he had last seen Rebecca. In the beginning, he had wondered about her, sometimes often. But as time moved on, he had learned to control his thoughts. Yet routinely she had surfaced back, and now that he had an invitation to contact her, his mind raced with questions.

He wanted to know about her healing, her progress, her triumphs. Most importantly, he wanted to know if she valued her life.

Two hours later he determined a phone call would not suffice. He had to see her. He needed to witness her progress for himself then he could assess whether she should fight for her inheritance. So around 7:30 a.m., after leaving a message on Dr. Landersen's answering machine, John sped toward Interstate 10.

Now, six hours later, after John had passed vistas of tumbleweeds, cacti, and dry land, the town finally came into view.

John's heart rate increased. Perhaps this was extreme. Perhaps a phone call would have sufficed.

But he continued forward.

He reached her complex, then followed signs through the adobe building toward the office.

A strong woman in her mid-forties sat behind the desk. "You John Sanders?"

"Yes."

She peered at him while her tongue played with a graying piece of gum. "Want me to buzz her? Or do you want to go get her?"

"Did you speak to Dr. Gary Landersen?"

"Talked to somebody. You want me to buzz her down here?"

"No." John drew in a tight breath. "What room?"

"Twelve. Down on the left and up a flight of stairs."

He acknowledged his thanks, then headed down the hall and up the stairs. With each step, he contemplated the words he would say.

When he knocked on the apartment door, Rebecca responded quickly. And there she stood, with her green eyes alert, her smile bright, and her fingers tugging on a long, dark curl. "Hi, Dr. Sanders."

Seeing her outside of Clearcreek's walls made John feel displaced. Yet he gave her a deep smile. "How are you?"

"Good." She nodded. "Very good. You'd be pleased."

"That's great to hear."

"And I'm ready. I just need to get my bags."

John continued smiling, yet her comment confused him. "Your bags?"

"When I got the call, I thought it was fast. But I suppose I understand."

"Call? From who? Dr. Landersen?"

"No, Dr. Steel. He still sees me weekly like the other therapists. It seems we're constantly in sessions here."

"Oh," John said quietly, still feeling confused.

"But today Dr. Steel came to say goodbye," she continued. "He said that Dr. Landersen called him this morning and told him you were coming to get me and that you'd take me back. I wondered if that meant to Clearcreek, but then Dr. Steel said it was closed down, that you would explain, and that I was on California State care, so I needed to get back to California for treatment. But I didn't know any of that before today. I didn't know it was temporary here."

She wore a white cotton dress, thin sandals, and turquoise jewelry. Since her time at Clearcreek, her cheeks had filled out slightly, and her arms and face had tanned. Her words were strong, her eyes clear and focused.

"It's good to see you like this. You look great."

She grinned. "It's good to be like this." Then she pulled her suitcase forward. "Are we ready?"

"I'm taking you back?"

She looked puzzled. "Dr. Steel said you were."

"Do you have a phone in here?"

"No. You'll have to use the office. I'm confused. Aren't you here to take me back?"

"I came to discuss options with you. Unless Dr. Landersen did. But I was supposed to talk to you about them. Not him."

"I didn't talk to Dr. Landersen."

"What did Dr. Steel tell you?"

She dropped her suitcase to the ground. "What I said. He said if I had any questions about my treatments, or where I was going, or anything else, that you would answer them for me. I wasn't confused then, but I am now."

John lifted his index finger. "Give me a minute."

He headed back to the office and phoned Landersen.

"What were you thinking?" Landersen asked. "7:30 on a Saturday morning—that's just too early! It's wrong. Even though I heard the rings, I was still waking up. Then after you left, I recognized the benefits. Our time to keep her there has run out, and since you were heading down there, it just made sense. If you'd given me warning, we'd have provided you with a State vehicle, but you're there now. Anyway, record your expenses."

"You're okay about all of this?"

"It's good that Dr. Steel's so positive about her. She needs to come back here. This setup was always temporary, and Dr. Steel says that now would be a good time. I booked two rooms for you at the Desert Inn. It's about five miles from her place. Go get some food, have a good rest, and start back whenever you need to. When you're back in town, give me a call. I've got a place ready for her tomorrow night. From there I'll take over, do some testing, and finalize where she should be. Oh—what'd she say about the money?"

"I just got here."

"Okay. Well, Dr. Steel agrees—give her the choice. But after you tell her, tell me what you think."

That evening, Rebecca recommended a small restaurant famous for its blue-corn tamales. After the first order, John found it necessary to order more. The food was exceptional, the conversation priceless, and John wanted to remain sitting there in their little booth for as long as he could.

He felt like a former coach who had missed out on a star player's important game. Now he wanted her to recap every play, every event, every success, and Rebecca was eager to talk.

"When I left Clearcreek, I knew it was because you believed in me." Her eyes were active with life.

"I did," John grinned. "And I still do."

"That's what helped me. I could picture you encouraging me forward, and that gave me the courage to keep trying and not to give up."

"I'm glad you listened."

She grinned back at him. "At Clearcreek I tried to hide from my fears. There was so much I was afraid of: my past, the unknowns, things I couldn't control, future failures. But then suddenly I was leaving Clearcreek, and I knew . . ."

John watched her as she looked down at the table. There were still a few more bites of her meal, but the food had long since been forgotten. Now she appeared lost in thought.

After a few seconds, John prodded. "Knew what?"

She quietly chuckled, then looked up, and their eyes met. "Can I share something with you?" Her voice dropped to a whisper. "Something I haven't shared with anyone?"

John leaned in closer. "Please."

"Once I came here, during the first week, there was one morning that changed everything for me. I remember it so clearly. I looked myself in the mirror and I said out loud, 'This is it.' And I knew it was. This was my chance to choose what kind of life I wanted. And I knew I had to hold on to this chance."

"Good for you, Rebecca." A year ago she had fought against his goals for her. Now she embraced those goals with intensity and hope.

"So I want to do everything that I need to," she said. "I want to listen, I want to learn, and I want to do what I have to so I can heal. I'm choosing the life I want to live." Her eyes glistened, almost as if a light shined from within. "And I'm so happy right now."

"I am too," John said.

The meal became a celebratory dinner. Prior to this night, John could have never imagined this reward.

Tomorrow he would need to tell her about the other things—the true events that had triggered her freedom, and how she had originally been trapped.

But all that could wait.

Tomorrow would be about new beginnings; tonight was about an ending, and a happy one at that.

The following morning, after breakfast, the two loaded up Rebecca's luggage. When she slid into the passenger seat and buckled her seatbelt, John reflected on the irony that he would be the one delivering her back. The thought caused him to smile. Then he glanced at her. She was smiling too.

"You ready?" he asked.

She nodded, and they began their journey home.

But instead of being enthused and vocal as she had been last night, this morning Rebecca remained quiet as she watched the town fade into a sea of dry sand and cacti.

Then, thirty minutes into the drive, she softly said, "It's good to be alive, and it's even better to know that."

Again she gazed out the passenger window and let several seconds pass before adding, "Dr. Steel said that in order to heal I must learn to love myself. I must believe in myself, and remain confident that I can have a positive life."

John nodded. "He sounds like a good man."

"Yes. It's been a very good few months."

"He was definitely the person you needed."

"He told me to think about the positive things in my life."

"And do you?"

"Mostly. Sometimes it's a challenge, especially when I feel empty, like I have nothing."

"How often do you feel that way?"

"Not as much as before. Life is good. I know that. I feel happy to be alive, and when I think about that goodness, I feel hopeful. I get excited about the person I want to be."

John shot her a glance. "At Clearcreek, that's what I wanted—for you to stop dying inside."

She smiled. "You helped me a lot."

"I'm glad you listened."

The car fell silent again.

Eventually Rebecca turned back to the window, and for the next hour neither spoke. Instead the drive transformed into silent therapy, both lost in their separate, adjusting worlds. However, when he glanced over and saw her face scrunched into a recognizable position, he broke the silence. "You okay?"

She offered him a forced smile.

"For the next few hours, all I'm going to be doing is driving." John smiled. "If you want to talk, feel free."

She nodded and let more silent minutes pass. Then, finally, she said, "Sometimes I get worried about what's next."

He nodded. "That's to be expected. But know that we'll take care of you. Tomorrow you'll meet with Dr. Landersen, and he'll make sure you're in a good place. I promise you that."

She released a hurt laugh. "He didn't like me. Not at Clearcreek."

A tall cactus, cracked with age, caught John's eye. In the center was a large hole dug by birds that had stolen the plant's substance and left it to die. "Clearcreek had its problems," he said.

"What happened?" She looked at him. "Why did it close?"

A tense smile stayed on his lips while images of the past months exploded in his mind. The lies, the confusion, the fraudulent conduct that ensnared her, all his pain—and she was completely unaware. Oblivious.

Currently the public knew more about her present life than she did. Now it was her time to know. Feeling a bit hesitant, John began the tale of Clearcreek's demise, and detail by detail she learned of her role in the hospital's financial survival. When he finished, all she said was, "So it was Rick? Rick kept me in there?" Without needing an answer, she turned back to the window and watched the scenery. The cacti had given way to tumbleweed, which now kicked up dust and rolled across the wide wilderness.

Since Rebecca seemed lost in her thoughts, John gave her time to process the information. Yet there was still more of Downley's story to be shared. She needed to know of Downley's own destruction and the leftover inheritance that could have a huge impact on what happened next in her life.

Eventually he ventured forward with another detailed monologue, and she listened with no interruptions. When he finished, he asked, "So what do you think?"

"Rick's dead?"

"Yes."

A heavy sigh slipped from her lips. "Dr. Sanders, this is a lot to think about."

"I know."

"You said he killed himself."

"Yes."

For a while she remained still. Then her fingers twisted and contorted into painful positions. "What are my choices?" she finally asked.

"You don't have to do anything . . . but you could, if you wanted to. Dr. Steel, Dr. Landersen, and I all agree—it's your right, your choice."

The eager smile from hours before was gone; instead, a concerned scowl covered her face. Now she appeared troubled while she sorted through her memories and these new facts.

"I have a recurring fear," she said, "and it panics me late at night. I try not to think about it, but it's hard not to, especially since it's always there." She turned to study the vast, open wilderness. "I don't want to revert back. If ever I turned back to where I was, to that dark, empty confusion, I wouldn't have the courage to pull out again."

He wanted to tell her that she would have the strength if she needed to, yet he did not know what lay ahead. So John remained silent.

"There was a time when I cared about nothing," she said. "I held to that delusion because it kept me moving through time." She exhaled a pained breath, and her hands pressed against her face.

When she finally dropped her hands, her face appeared less strained. "I'm relieved I'm out. It's a miracle I'm here."

John nodded. "It is."

"I've often been afraid of returning to Clearcreek." Her voice changed to a sarcastic tone. "Guess I can stop worrying about that, right? No one goes back there."

He nodded again. "That's correct."

But when she remained silent, he tried to add something more. "As dark as your illness was, certain events at Clearcreek made your healing worse. It'll be better from here. Remember that you're getting stronger. Remember this when times seem hard. Remember where you've been and what you've overcome."

"That's what Dr. Steel says. 'Look at where you were six months ago. Think of where you'll be in another six months.' Always such a positive person. He made me feel like I could accomplish anything." She paused for a long time until John finally glanced at her. "What should I do? Should I fight for the money?"

He looked back at the road and heaved out a long sigh. "You can accomplish anything."

"So I should?"

"If you want your money, it's yours. You deserve it. But—" He paused, hoping to say the correct words. "The bigger question is, should you face a bunch of lawyers trying to convince the judge that you don't deserve what's yours?" He saw the expected tension and surprise in her face. "They'll rake through your life with Downley. Are you willing to go through that? Is the money worth it to you?"

She turned back to the passenger window. "I'd have to talk about him?"

"Yes."

"That's too hard." Her fingers resumed their awkward contorting. "It's been too much lately—too often I'm expected to talk about him."

"Perhaps that's part of healing. But being in a courtroom, surrounded by lawyers whose goals are to trip you up, who are being paid to confuse your brain . . . I'm not sure that would benefit you right now."

"You're right."

"I don't know that I am."

She released a long exhale. "I don't know either."

Right then the San Bernardino valley came into view—a place where people and pollution, dirt and decay, lies and life, awaited them. Almost as if the final minutes offered more time to prepare, the two finished their journey in silence.

CHAPTER SEVEN

Wednesday was a difficult workday. John kept stumbling over documents, pamphlets, and support manuals that addressed clients' critical transitions. First he touched a pamphlet entitled *Out of the Hospital and Staying Well*. "By choosing to take advantage of follow-up treatment, you begin a journey down the road to recovery. This road will have bumps and curves. In order to stay on the healthy track and avoid relapse you must develop good navigational skills."

Later, for a client, John opened up a support manual to the heading on acceptance. "Acceptance of your illness will come slowly but not steadily. One day you accept and the next day deny. This is a normal response. Talk about your feelings. Talk to your group members, therapist, doctor, family, and close friends. Don't let a relapse force you to get help."

By mid-afternoon, he saw a poster tacked to the clinic's wall. "It can be helpful to include a professional as support in your 'treatment team' if and only if that person believes in you and your recovery."

Each phrase, each warning, almost everything he touched, reminded him of Rebecca and beckoned him to check in on her. He chided himself for this abundant concern, and tried to stop thinking about her. He was no longer her protector. Landersen was taking care of her.

Yet throughout the day, the worries remained.

By the end of his shift, he succumbed and phoned Dr. Landersen.

"Rebecca left something in my car."

"What is it?" Landersen asked.

"A document." It was a scrap of paper, most likely a piece of trash. "I think it looks important."

"Okay. Do you want to drop it by my office?"

"Or I can deliver it." John held his breath and hoped that this paper could be his ticket to see her. "I'm close. I'm still at work."

"Great. By the way, I talked to her caseworker today. Sounds like she's in excellent hands. Already Dr. Webster's got her in day treatment and group activities, and they're talking about eventual employment."

"So she'll be okay?"

"Of course. Therapy sessions are daily. She has a variety of support at the complex, and Webster's good. It's the right leap for her, especially while she's deciding about the inheritance."

"What'd you tell Webster?"

"Exactly what you told me—Rebecca wasn't sure about pursuing it, and you advised we don't push her."

"Good."

Once the phone conversation ended, John rethought his need to visit her. Yet after a short inner debate, he determined that a quick hello was still acceptable. It would just be a simple act to show Rebecca she was not abandoned.

He found the complex with ease. When he knocked, Rebecca yanked the door open, mumbled a hello, yet gave no real sign of emotion—no surprise or indication that she was happy to see him. Nevertheless, she invited him in to her small apartment.

The place had cracked linoleum, spotted carpet, and sparse and dated furniture. John sat on a small couch which faced a thin bookshelf that supported a ten-inch TV set. Rebecca entered the kitchen and soon returned with two plastic cups of water. She handed him one, then joined him on the couch.

"Are you okay?" he asked.

She tapped her fingers against the cup. "I guess I am."

"Can I help?"

She shook her head. "I just thought it would be different."

"So are you saying you're not happy here?"

"Some parts are good." Again she tapped the cup. "But not all."

He noted her poor posture, lethargic motions, and discouraged words, and these signs of oncoming depression concerned him. "What's bad?"

"You told me what had happened. You told me how things were here. But I didn't understand."

"Can you give me specifics?"

She stopped tapping the cup.

"Talk to me about it," he pushed.

She released a heavy sigh. "Dr. Webster thinks he knows me."

"What does that mean?"

"I've met with him every day, and that's only been three days, but he thinks he knows me."

"What does that mean?" John repeated. "Give me an example."

"Every day he talks about Rick. I don't say anything, and he goes into uncomfortable details. He puts labels on me, and they're just things he assumes. It's like he doesn't need to get to know me." Her voice cracked with emotion. "It's like he's too confident—like he already knows who I am and what's best for me." Her voice picked up in tempo. "He wants details, Dr. Sanders. And it's disturbing how he approaches . . ." Her words trailed off. She looked down and resumed tapping the cup.

"Today he made me mad, and I think he did it on purpose. He wanted to upset me, like a trick, a stupid, hidden trick . . ."

"What did he do?"

She glanced up, and for a moment their eyes connected. Then she looked away, as if ashamed.

"What?" John asked again.

"It's about you." She bit her lip.

"You can tell me, Rebecca."

"He keeps asking about you." She brushed a tear away. "He says many unkind things."

"I'm sorry." She was being attacked from so many angles.

"It's uncomfortable. I hate it here."

During their journey from Tucson, she had needed to absorb so much unfortunate information. At that time, John had dismissed the pressure to forewarn her of the other circulating lies. Rather, he had hoped that this was one area he could protect and shelter her, especially since the recent news headlines had moved on to other current events.

Now John watched her, contemplating her situation and wondering what might help her, until an idea struck him. "I know what you need."

She brushed another tear from her face. "You do?"

"Dr. Blythe. Remember her?"

"Yes."

"She has her own practice, and she's incredible. As far as counseling goes, she's who you want. She'll help you in ways . . . ways that right now, you're not even dreaming about."

"Really?"

"If you aren't happy with other things, she'll help with that too. She knows people. She knows what'll be best."

"Okay."

"You want a decent life? Then Dr. Blythe can help you. You can become a person capable of those things. Of good things."

She finally shared her first real smile since his arrival. "That's what I want."

"Excellent. I'll make sure of it. We'll work out the arrangements."

"Wait." Rebecca looked at him, then bit her lip. "She's through the State, right?"

"No."

"She has to be. According to Dr. Landersen, my care comes from the State."

John groaned. "She's not State."

Rebecca frowned.

"Private," John whispered.

"Dr. Sanders, I don't have anything."

His neck muscles tightened.

"I have no money," she said.

"No." John twisted his body to look at her. "This is wrong. I was wrong about this. You can and should have the best care available."

Her eyes were full of insecurity. "You mean if I fight for my inheritance."

"We get you a good lawyer," he said, "and we make sure this doesn't go to trial."

"Would people still ask questions?"

"They would."

"That means I'd have to talk about Rick."

"You can do this."

"I hated that life. I hated myself."

He folded his arms and leaned against the couch. "Then tell me about Downley."

For a moment, they watched each other. Seconds passed. Then she dropped the gaze and examined her hands. Her fingers interlocked.

"Can you tell me about him?" he asked a bit softer.

"If you want me to." She twisted her fingers into a distorted shape.

"I do."

"Okay." The grip around her fingers tightened and her knuckles turned white

"Right now," he urged.

"Okay," she whispered.

"Good." A weird sensation shot through him. During his time at Clearcreek, John had attempted to learn about this man that Rebecca would not claim. Now, over a year later, this treasure chest crammed with Downley's garbage was finally about to open. John cleared his throat. "Tell me about Rick."

She glanced up at him. Fear filled her face and her hands began to tremble.

"Stop, Rebecca." John grabbed her wrist. "Don't give in to this." He released her hand and she looked at him with wide eyes. "He's gone, and this despair he brings can be gone, too."

She breathed rapidly. "Rick scares me."

"He's gone."

"Not what's left. Not the shadows of him that manipulate me."

"Look at who you are. Look at what you've pulled yourself out of."

"I don't want to go back to that," she said clearly.

"Then don't. Make your choice. Be stronger than this."

She shook her head.

"Rebecca, you can fight this too."

She nodded, closed her eyes, and chanted, "I'm good. I'm good. I'm good."

"You are good."

She paused, opened her eyes, and smirked. "Dr. Steel told me to say that over and over again." Her voice dropped to a whisper. "And to believe it."

"Because you are good."

She looked at him with an odd expression until her cheeks blushed. Then she turned away. "He said I needed to know that I'm okay—not bad or evil, not stupid or mean. I know I made mistakes, but I'm trying. I have to remember that. I'm trying." She rubbed her hands against her thighs and cleared her throat. "I just wish I was stronger, Dr. Sanders. I really do."

From the expression on her face, John knew she would not talk today. So he arose, walked over to a window, and looked out at the twilit sky. A strong breeze blew, shaking a small tree. But when the breeze subsided, the tree stood straight and still. "You can do this," John said, "but it's not my place to tell you that. It's your battle, and you're the one who will have to fight it, so only you can decide if you're ready to step into that pain." He turned around and stepped toward the door. "All I can ask is that you think about it."

"I am."

"Weigh out your options."

"I know," she said firmly.

"Good." He smiled at her. "It was good to see you again."

She gave him a half-smile and stood. "Thanks for seeing me."

He touched the door handle only to turn back. He owed her one final thing. "Before his death . . . Downley said some very unkind things."

"And they were about me." Her face seemed unaffected.

"He wanted to take away his negative press, so he turned it on you."

She stepped back and stared at the floor. "I'm not surprised."

"Gravers also wanted the focus off of him, so—" John drew in a breath. The words were awkward, but he owed her this. In haste, he proceeded forward. "He reported unkind things about us to the press."

Her face shot up. "Us?"

A sharp lump caught in John's throat.

"What did he say?"

He shifted his focus to a long tear in the linoleum floor. "He said that we were involved. That we were . . . that there was . . . a relationship between us." He glanced up to see a strange look cross her face, an almost quirky smile. "But we know the truth," he quickly added.

"Yes." Her eyes shifted to the door. "We know the truth." Then her gaze shifted to the window. "I know why you were there. Of course I know why you were there." Quickly she glanced at the couch, then back at the door. "And you did help."

"The media wanted to make more of it—lots more. They wouldn't have minded ruining me if it helped their circulation."

"It's really bad, huh? A relationship with me?" She looked at the floor. "I'm sorry."

"Gravers doesn't want to be alone. He doesn't want to be the only corrupt doctor out there, so he lit a match. The press fanned the fire and made the story spread. It's basically burned out now, but people hold judgments. That's why Dr. Webster said what he said."

"Oh."

"I'm sorry, Rebecca. Once again, it's not fair that you're in the middle of this."

"I'll be okay, right?" She looked near him.

"Yes. You will."

"Of course I will. I don't have another choice."

CHAPTER EIGHT

In less than twenty-four hours, John received a phone call.

"Sanders, it's Landersen. I just got through talking to Webster. He says Rebecca told him that she's getting a lawyer. And that when she gets her money, she's hiring a real therapist."

John suppressed laughter.

"Webster wasn't too happy. He says it's up to me to find her one. A lawyer, that is."

John grinned. He was proud of her. "Do you know a good one?"

"Of course I do—Ben Daniels. He specializes in clients with mental illness. I guarantee he'll be sensitive to her situation, which is good. Especially since, according to Webster, the press interviewed Anne Downley, and apparently the woman's furious that sympathies are being extended to Rebecca. The critics are saying that Richard humiliated Anne by never disclosing his association with Rebecca. Then he went and lost part of Anne's family money. And then of course he killed himself. So they speculate that Anne wants to redeem herself by making Rebecca her target. At least, that's what Webster said."

John drew in a steadying breath. "What do you think?"

"Daniels will do an excellent job. I'll take her in tomorrow. They'll meet. I'll make the facts clear. He'll take care of her."

"Keep me posted, will you?"

"You bet. But . . ." Landersen released a heavy sigh. "We've got to find her a new therapist. From what Webster shared, it sounds like those two didn't hit it off."

John's smile widened. "What about Linda Blythe?"

The phone line was silent. Then Landersen said, "I like that. I like that a lot. Excellent thought, Sanders."

"Would she work with Rebecca before the settlement's final?"

"You mean the fees? Of course. She owes me a favor—or two. Yes, we'll work something out."

"Good."

"Yes. Good idea. I like that. Like that a lot. In fact, I'll call her right now."

CHAPTER NINE

A week later, while at work, John received an urgent message from Dr. Landersen. The two needed to talk. The last John had heard, Rebecca had been welcomed into Dr. Blythe's clinic and the two had connected well. Now he hoped for more good news.

But once he stepped into Dr. Landersen's clinic and saw the receptionist's face, he knew he had been summoned due to trouble. Landersen had been waiting, with all other appointments canceled.

John headed down the hall to the office where Landersen sat at his cluttered desk rubbing his balding head. John tapped lightly on the doorframe.

"Good, you're here," Landersen growled. "Get in and shut the door. Have a seat." Then, hastily, he shuffled through a mountainous pile of papers, which caused a downpour of documents to flow to the floor. Landersen cursed, then struggled to the floor to clean up the papers. John bent down to assist.

But by the fifth sheet, Landersen stopped. "There it is." His stocky hands pulled John up, and he shoved a booklet into John's hand. "This is what you needed to see—why I asked you to come." He motioned John back to the wooden chair. "Sit. You must sit."

John abandoned the paper puddle and stared at the booklet. *California Department of Consumer Affairs Board of Psychology Update* Issue No. 11, January 1996. On the front was a yellow sticky note, and in tight scribbles were the words:

Merry Christmas, Gary
From Steve

"It's a mock-up," Landersen said. "From Gravers. He's telling us what we have to look forward to. Are you familiar with the BOP newsletters?"

"Yes."

"Well, all you should care about is page 21."

Dutifully, John thumbed through until he saw the bold title: DISCIPLINARY ACTIONS December 1, 1994–November 30, 1995. He read the boxed-in notice aloud. "The following decisions become operative on the effective date except in situations where the licensee obtains a court-ordered stay, which may occur after the preparation of this newsletter. For updated information on stay orders and appeals, please contact the Board Enforcement Analyst."

"I've already called them," Landersen inserted. "It's not released yet. But Gravers is trying to give us a glimpse of our future. Turn the page."

John read through the list of psychologists under condemnation. He turned the page and skimmed the rest. There, flashing out among the unknown names in red font, was his own: Sanders, John Harold, Ph.D. San Bernardino, CA. Then came the tight black paragraph of the accusation: Unprofessional conduct. Act of sexual relations with a patient or sexual misconduct contrary to the qualifications, functions, or duties of a psychologist. Repeated acts of negligence. Stipulated Decision effective November 29, 1995. License revoked.

John stared at the words until his eyes lost clarity and the black and red ink blurred into obscurity.

"There it is." Landersen cleared his throat. "Gravers has the pull, the influence, and the power. He knows he's at war. He mocked up a similar one for me and anticipates probation for me for three years. He charges me with repeated negligent acts and says that your problems—and any others at Clearcreek—were under my jurisdiction, so he blames me for their occurrence. He's creating scenarios and advertising other people's faults. It's ugly and it's excessive."

"I don't understand." John reread the words. "What's happening here?"

"If Gravers gets his way, your right to practice ends." Landersen swiped a collection of sweat drops from his forehead. "He's threatening us. He going to ruin your life and induce harm on mine."

"Can he do this?"

"Yes. He has connections and power in a variety of places. So this is our warning, our opportunity to reconsider our testimonies."

"He can do this?" John repeated.

"Ruin you? No doubt he will. This is your final out, your last chance. Otherwise, consider yourself dead."

John's fingers rubbed against the thick papers and his eyes stared at the words. Then he swallowed a familiar, tight lump. "What exactly does this mean?"

"You'll be under investigation. Since you've broken code, the Board will notify you. If your license gets revoked, you'll be ostracized from the field. Once this is filed, your days at the county are limited, and from there you'll be unable to work."

"If I was guilty." John offered a heartless smile. "But I'm innocent."

"You can contest. Yet from all the accounts I know of, contesting is ugly, long, and very painful. And you understand that finality rests in the Board's decision, right? So consider yourself on trial—a long, expensive road with fees, court fines, and therapy."

John's throat felt hot and dry.

"Or there is the other option."

"Okay." John dropped his tense shoulders. "What is it?"

"You surrender your license."

"No."

"Yeah, kid. Hard call. While charges are still pending, you turn in your license and walk away. The Board accepts your surrender, and your right to practice is done."

"I'm innocent."

"But you're not."

"I'm innocent, Gary."

Landersen became busy sorting through a group of files.

"You believe me, don't you?"

Landersen pulled out a manual from his stack of documents. "Well, Dr. Gravers pointed out some key things here. Are you familiar with this?" He raised a manual titled:

STATE OF CALIFORNIA
DEPARTMENT OF CONSUMER AFFAIRS
BOARD OF PSYCHOLOGY
SUMMARY OF CALIFORNIA LAWS
RELATING TO THE PRACTICE OF PSYCHOLOGY

John nodded his head while Landersen flipped through the manual.

"Gravers highlighted the Causes for Disciplinary Action, Business and Professions Code, Section 2960, 2960.1, 2960.5 and 2960.6." Landersen paused then wiped more sweat from his forehead. "And I figured you'd be just as interested in this as I was. Let me read you the pertinent part: 'The Board may refuse to issue any registration or license, or may issue a registration or license with terms and conditions, or may suspend or revoke the registration or license of any registrant or licensee if the applicant, registrant, or licensee has been guilty of unprofessional conduct. Unprofessional conduct shall include, but not be limited to:

Landersen tapped at the manual's page. "Okay, here are your parts: 'Impersonating another person holding a psychology license or allowing another person to use his or her license or registration."

"I never impersonated another therapist," John said strongly.

Landersen nodded but continued down the list. "Being grossly negligent in the practice of his or her profession. The commission of any dishonest, corrupt, or fraudulent act. Functioning outside of his or her particular field or fields of competence as established by his or her education, training, and experience. Repeated acts of negligence.'"

"I . . ." John rubbed his throat. He was unsure if he was breathing. "I am . . ."

"Sanders, it's a fact that you intervened in Rebecca's treatments. You lied to her and others in order to continue treating her. There are statements from nurses saying that you visited Rebecca's room after hours."

"You know why." John fought through a cough. "I had to. At the time, you didn't understand what was going on. I realize that. But you and Gravers kept me from helping her. She wanted out, and that wasn't being granted." His voice grew loud. "If I hadn't intervened, we'd never have learned the truth. She'd still be there, Clearcreek would still be in operation, and Gravers would still be manipulating innocent people's lives."

Landersen became preoccupied with shuffling papers into small piles of order. John shut his eyes. His career, which had taken years to build, was now collapsing. "What about you?" he asked, his voice softening. "How will all this affect you?"

An unsympathetic chuckle escaped Landersen's lips. "I'm better off than you." Then he offered a compassionate smile. "Sanders, it's the hard truth. You broke hospital regulations. You were in places and situations that were wrong. It makes you guilty on some of those charges, and it makes you look guilty on the others. It's a pity, especially with nurses being eyewitnesses. My situation doesn't compare. I've got the State backing me up. They support me and claim this won't hurt my job. But in your case, you've got nowhere to go."

The room was unbearably hot.

John drew in a breath. "Rebecca will tell them how absurd these charges are."

"Not a reliable source."

"That's ludicrous." John's entire body tightened. "She knows the truth but you're saying the Board doesn't want the truth."

"Sanders, you've infuriated Gravers." Dr. Landersen shook his head. "And the man knows how to fight. Look, the mere fact that he kept Clearcreek alive, hiding the truth even from me, shows his skills, so you need to understand that charges will be pressed." He smiled weakly. "Unless you negotiate with Gravers."

"What does that mean?"

"You take his deal. You change your statement or refuse to testify. He can be won over if you can."

The ventilation kicked on, which stirred warm air through the room. John looked at the ground and shook his head. "He's asking me to be a coward."

Landersen rubbed his forehead before looking at John. "Yes. He is."

In an effort to control a further outburst, John focused on his breathing. "Am I alone in this?"

"I don't want you to take Gravers' suggested way out," Landersen said, "but I'll empathize if that's what you choose."

John stared at him. "I shouldn't tackle this alone. We have a strong case together. Gravers knows that, so he's trying to scare both of us away."

Anguish covered Landersen's face. "I understand that."

"If I took the coward's road," John said, his tone softening, "what would you do? Would you testify against Gravers?"

Landersen wiped another collection of sweat from his face, cleared his throat, and fussed with a pile of paper. "The dilemma for me," he said, his voice turning bolder, "is not as much about testifying against Gravers as it is about testifying against you. At Clearcreek, you broke ethical rules. If Gravers files those charges, and if the Board comes to me, I'd have to validate those claims."

Again John focused on his breathing. "You would hurt me?"

Landersen cleared his throat and spoke strongly, but his eyes danced around. "I'd be honest in Gravers's trial. And in your own. That's what I'd have to do." Then Dr. Gary Landersen stood. "Sanders, it's all that's fair."

CHAPTER TEN

During the drive home, John fought a spectrum of emotion. But when he stepped into his apartment, loneliness astonished and overpowered him.

In the beginning, when he had searched for an explanation about Rebecca, when he had questioned Gravers and found clues about Downley, he had been alone. So alone he had not known how to combat Gravers. But Lisa had come, and then Landersen. They had offered support. They had shared the burden, the sadness, the pain. Then, with a team, John was able to expose the fraud and corruption.

But now where was this team?

In a quest to find comfort, agreement, or even understanding, John phoned Lisa. Weeks had passed since they last spoke, with their final conversation being a mutual decision to move on.

"John!" Her voice sounded happy, refreshing, even surprised, almost as if she had missed him. A sudden emotional surge caught him off guard.

He had missed her too.

At first they talked about her life, of her success and her joy in excelling at her dreams. Then John shared Landersen's betrayal, and Lisa was shocked.

He wanted her support. He wanted her to do something, but mostly he did not want to be alone. He searched for the right words, but while searching, she said, "Hold on, John."

Through the receiver, he heard Lisa unlock her deadbolt and then speak to someone. "Hey, it's Bill. He just got here, and I promised him dinner. We should finish this conversation, but later."

"Okay." His voice revealed the pain.

In response, she spoke softly. "Look, I'm sorry about Gary. I really thought he was after justice. I thought we all were."

"Yeah. Me, too."

"If I can help," Lisa continued, "with an article or anything, let me know."

In his desolate apartment, John smiled. "I wish an article could help."

There was an odd noise and Lisa giggled.

"Are you okay?" he asked.

"Bill's getting a little impatient."

"Is he nuzzling you?"

"I wouldn't use that word to describe it, but . . ."

"So you're seeing Bill?"

"He's good for me."

"Is he?"

"He shares my life." She released another giggle. "And my crazy decisions. Our lives are intertwined. Things are working well. Very well. Oh John, Bill's pulling me out the door. I'll call you later."

And the phone went dead.

CHAPTER ELEVEN

Saturday morning, John stood in the center of his apartment. It had been two years since his move there, and the place had served him well. But now, nothing kept him in San Bernardino.

Even his job, as hard as it had seemed, now appeared to be fleeting.

After learning of the potential destruction of his career, John had thrown himself into work. If the clinic were his only career option, he would accept it, live out his days there, retire at sixty-five, and be happy. But in truth, rumors already circulated that the county would dismiss him. If so, he soon would be jobless again.

Suddenly his apartment door swung open. "Howdy, Neighbor!" Randy called.

"Why don't you ever knock?"

Randy threw his brown suede jacket over a chair. "Why don't you lock your door?"

"I do. Sometimes."

"Do you know . . ." Randy curled his hands around the back of a chair while his voice mocked a scholastic tone. "Statistically, San Bernardino has one of the highest crime rates in the nation. In the nation, John." He nodded his head in contemplation. "You should lock your doors . . . and look into some serious deadbolts."

John approached the table and sorted through some scattered mail. "Next time I'm looking for criminal statistics, I'll be sure to ask an all-knowing Biology teacher."

Randy grasped his chest and, with a look of shock, said, "You doubt me?"

"Definitely."

"Fine." Randy pulled out a chair and had a seat. "What food do you have? I'm starved."

"Nothing."

"I came over here 'cause my fridge is a black hole. Of course, Shilo thinks the food's gone to my gut." He stood, raised his shirt up, and grabbed his stomach. "What do you think? Do I have a gut?"

John picked up an electronics warehouse ad. "Who's Shilo?"

Randy gasped. "Have I not told you about Shilo? I must have been so enthralled with her gun that I haven't seen you."

John looked up. "Gun?"

"Yep, you heard me." Randy eye's opened wide. "She's got a gun. She's in training to become a cop and carries a gun. I've never dated a woman with a gun before. It's cool."

John glanced back at the ad. "Lily's gone, huh?"

"Expired." Randy sat back down. "Shilo's why I know so much about the crime rate. In fact, she's frantic about the rising violence in the community. She wants me to be scared of my own face. But there's some crazy stuff out there. Just the other day, they had a gang shooting in a person's yard—a drive-by at four p.m. Four p.m., John. That's right in the afternoon, about six blocks from here. Now that's scary stuff."

John dumped the junk mail in the trash. "What do you want to eat?"

"Anything."

"I don't have anything."

"How about pizza? Let's order pizza and watch the Kings game."

"Fine." John handed Randy the phone.

After the hefty order was placed, Randy relocated to the couch, grabbed the remote, and began flipping the channels. "Shilo thinks it's 'over the edge' that I know you. She's dying to meet you."

"Great." John stepped over Randy's legs, which rested atop the coffee table.

"She's addicted to those stories that are circulating." Randy waited for John to look at him.

"I'm no longer in the news."

Randy offered a somewhat forced smile. "Have you seen yesterday's news?"

John slouched into the far end of the couch. When he spoke, he used no emotion. "I stopped reading the paper."

"Well don't worry, until yesterday, it seems only insignificant tabloids have been mentioning you." Randy chuckled slightly. "Shilo brought one over the other day. Crazy headline. Something like, 'Long-awaited Baby Conceived in Psychiatric Halls; Now Dr. Sanders Must Fess Up.'"

"How about a conversation change?" John shot his friend a tense smile.

"Yeah, I don't blame you." Randy flipped through a series of channels. "But if ever there was more to the story, you'd tell me first, right?"

"There's no story."

Then with a playful, sarcastic whisper, Randy added, "'Cause I could get a royal sum if I squealed."

John's neck muscles tightened. "What's with you?"

"Well, seriously, John." Randy's face turned sober. "Shilo insisted I ask. I told her there wasn't anything and that you're really boring. But she just wanted to know, was there ever any . . . ?"

John drew in a long breath. "Absolutely nothing."

"Yeah, that's what I told her." Randy turned his attention back to the television. "But . . . did you ever let any thoughts cross your mind?"

"Enough, Randy. Why would you ask that?"

"Come on, Johnny Boy." Randy looked at him with a boyish smirk. "There's nothing there."

"All right, fine." Randy turned back to the television and in a low voice mumbled, "But maybe there should be."

"You know nothing," John stated.

"I know you're good." A large grin covered Randy's face. "That's engraved in you. But I just wondered if . . . see, if it was me . . . I just wondered if you ever thought about—"

"Randy," John spoke sharply. "I can't afford to think like that."

"Okay, but let's just say, 'who cares what the press says?'"

"It's bigger than the press."

"Fine." Randy turned back to the TV and shuffled through several stations. "But she is hot."

"What?"

"Well, she is."

"How do you know that?"

"Well, if you'd have seen the news yesterday," Randy sighed as if slightly put out, "you'd have known."

John wanted to grab Randy by the shirt and force him to lose his silly grin. But instead, John breathed out the tension. "What was it about?"

"Last night Shilo and I were watching the news. We always watch the news together—ten o' clock, Channel 2. Don't think I've ever been so in the know. But she tells me it's good to be aware of the crime problems, and it's important to know what's taking place. It gives you things to talk about with other people, you know? Keeps you from being boring. In fact, it might be good for you to watch it a little more."

"You better give me the facts *now*."

Randy laughed. "You're tense, Johnny Boy."

"Randy! What was it about?"

"From what I remember," he said, shrugging his shoulders innocently, "it was in front of the courthouse. Beginnings of some trial she's involved with."

"What do you remember?" John stood up, his heart racing. "What did they say?"

"There were a lot of newscasters. A lot of people."

John headed to the front door and slipped on his shoes.

"Wait." Randy's mouth dropped. "Where are you going?"

"Out."

"No!" Panic filled Randy's voice. "Lighten up. You know my favorite pastime is to get you worked up."

John's hand was on the doorknob.

"Come on. We've got pizza coming."

"Call them back," John said. "Tell them not to deliver."

"But I'm hungry."

John opened the door.

"Wait." Randy jumped up and met his friend at the door. "I've never questioned your character. Ever. You know me. Please, just stay."

"Tell them I'll pick it up."

"The pizza?" Randy's face expressed relief.

"Yes." John checked his pockets for spare change. "After I grab a newspaper." Then he headed out the door.

When John reached the newsstand, he skimmed the exposed front headlines and saw that Rebecca's name was not there. But when he flipped over his purchased copy, he saw her face on the bottom corner—a small picture and a brief sentence, with more info on A13.

Unfortunately, A13 was a full spread. And, of course, Bill Harper had an article there. Lisa had one too, plus two additional articles by other reporters. John skimmed it, disgusted to see that reporters, photographers, and general spectators still hungered for the next installment of Rebecca's life.

In the reports she was called "Clearcreek's Prisoner," or, for an even stronger, unrestricted appeal, "Clearcreek's Mistress." There was even a small clip that mentioned the community's growing interest in this famous yet mysterious patient. But now, with the Brownell vs. Downley trial officially underway, the mysterious woman had at last shown her face.

Even though a snapshot had captured her look of surprise, Rebecca appeared elegant. Another picture featured Anne Downley with her cluster of lawyers. Then there was one of Attorney Daniels with his arm around Rebecca as they scuffled through the media.

John studied the pictures of Rebecca. She was a beautiful and fragile woman, too weak to be in the thick of this.

Yet she was.

AUTUMN 1996

CHAPTER TWELVE

John took his seat on the witness stand. Next to him, Judge Revere looked at him with soft brown eyes. With apparent Filipino descent, the man's round baby face expressed compassion mixed with honor, justice, and exactness. After months of wondering and worrying about testifying at Dr. Steven Gravers's trial, John felt a strange sense of safety, as if somehow being near Judge Revere meant that he was protected and that goodness and truth were valued and needed.

He felt that same security from the prosecuting attorney, Travis Brotherson, who had been hired by the California Department of Mental Health, the entity that had formulated the investigation and had now spent an extravagant sum of time and money on the case. Brotherson, clothed in his trendy dress shirt, tailored suit coat, pressed slacks, and shined shoes, conveyed youthful success. When he spoke, his words were confident, and his soft manner seemed to calm those summoned to the stand.

Brotherson questioned John for over an hour, spending most of the time recapping the events that had led John to discover the truth. Together they established the necessity for John to maintain a watchful eye on Rebecca while hunting for the secrets that would reveal the crime. In talking with Brotherson, John's worries lessened. His actions had been justified. He had a very clear reason for lying to Rebecca and pretending to still be her doctor even though she had been placed in another person's care. If he hadn't taken this vital step, the truth may never have been uncovered. For the past year, John's suspended license and inability to find solid work had humiliated him, but now he felt validated.

As the questions proceeded, guilt lifted from John's shoulders. No longer did he need to second-guess his actions. He had done what needed to be done.

However, once Brotherson sat and Hank Lester stood, the calming air ceased. Lester strongly resembled Gravers. Both were tall and trim. Both were gray and dignified. From their mannerisms, their speech, even their gait strides, these men exuded control.

Lester paced the courtroom and studied his prey with hungry eyes. John glanced down, only to meet the piercing glare of Steven Gravers.

John drew in a breath and reflected back on the conditions Brotherson had established. He lifted his eyes again to watch Lester. The baton had been passed, and now it was up to John to maintain the prosecution's lead.

But Lester knew how to pace himself. He started out slow, asking John to recite once again the events leading up to the disclosure. Throughout the replay, Lester remained steady while his eyes suggested an agenda, as if the repeated details were placing John in an extremely precarious position.

When the details lead to John's unauthorized visits, Lester grinned. Then his words sprinted forward. The questioning turned sharp, personal, and harmful as Lester sought to peek inside the darker corners of John's moral character.

Did John find Rebecca attractive? Certainly. But that did not mean he had acted on it or had even thought of doing so. Did he care about her? Most definitely. Such an answer appeared to give Lester what he needed. Suddenly Lester sketched a picture of a Dr. Sanders whose motives were evil and whose actions centered on personal gain. After this debasing, Lester concluded that Gravers did the only respectable thing possible and removed Rebecca Brownell from Dr. Sanders's care. But when Dr. Sanders took it upon himself to defy supervisors and conduct unauthorized visits, Gravers had no choice but to terminate Dr. Sanders.

According to Lester, none of Gravers's actions were wrong. Instead, John's unreasonable anger at his supervisor's just actions caused him to exaggerate Gravers's expectations over Downley's donations. Of course these donations were beneficial to Clearcreek's financial health; nevertheless, Gravers always had a clear grasp on the purpose of his institution.

As Lester spoke to the jury, John felt weak. He wished he could take back his answer, but instead he was released from the stand.

On returning to his seat, John reflected on the exposure, the ridicule, and the labyrinth of judgments, but he also cherished the grand realization that he was done. All those dragged-out months of this fiasco, and now his final moment was complete.

He resumed his seat next to Conrad Hooper, a former Clearcreek buddy, who gave John a thumbs-up while Judge Revere dismissed the group for lunch.

Soon former Clearcreek employees filled a large table at Diego's. John took his seat and dreaded a review of his testimony. However, other than occasional pats on the back mixed with some kind smiles, no one spoke of the court proceedings. Instead, the group sat together in tight quarters, and exchanged recent psychiatrist jokes over chips and salsa.

When the food came, conversation turned to their present lives, and a select few shared distant, jovial memories of times at Clearcreek. Overall it was a time of rejoicing and positive hopes with no talk of possibly losing this brutal game. John found the moment healing and safe.

After lunch, Brotherson called his next witness—Rebecca Brownell. When John spotted her, he caught his breath. She looked poised, collected, and more peaceful than he had ever seen her before.

To have her testify came as a complete shock to John. It was a possibility he had never considered. In fact, her appearance and demeanor were such a drastic change that, without Brotherson announcing her name, John would not have recognized her.

Her dark curls had been cut to her jaw line, her clothes were tailored to compliment her shape, her smile was strong, her eyes clear, and her voice controlled. This could not be the same woman. Yet throughout Travis Brotherson's simple questions about her treatments, her timeline, her associations with Downley, and her interactions with Gravers, this woman spoke clearly and with a comprehension that verified she had indeed lived Rebecca's life.

Then Brotherson approached the topic of Dr. Sanders and delved into the questions around the intent of his care. Such prying stirred John. It had been one thing to be the mouthpiece, to be able to testify about his own actions, but now, as a bystander, he faced the arduous task to sit mute and listen while Rebecca spoke of their association.

In some ways her words became a tribute to him—a recollection of a Dr. Sanders that John had forgotten. Since he had last seen her, he had toiled through a year of survival where life had hardened him. But now she refreshed his mind, touching something deep inside that revived a joy, an ecstasy of seeing her change. She was an example of how a seed he had planted could grow and transform into a vibrant, living being. He had indeed made a difference.

She continued to speak, expressing admiration and respect. For the past year John had suffered the pains of a suspended license, yet now he enjoyed the reward of having done the right thing. He earnestly recommitted himself to the service of others. He would complete any sacrifice necessary to once again strive to improve the value and quality of another person's life.

But this glowing warmth dispersed once Hank Lester approached the stand. John wondered how Rebecca would survive this standoff. Yet her arms remained poised, her body unmoved. When the questioning began, Rebecca's voice was clear, strong, and direct. Amazingly, she appeared ready to match the confidence of the dragon before her.

Nevertheless, John's ears still burned when he heard the words, "Did Dr. Sanders ever step outside of his therapeutic role with you?"

Rebecca paused and used the moment to look directly at John.

Each second she waited magnified the impact of her answer. Soon every pair of eyes in the courtroom shifted, and John felt as if he were back on the witness stand.

To avoid the sea of attentive eyes, John focused on Rebecca and prayed that the strained seconds would end. Finally, her soft, small smile gave way to her voice, which spoke with indelible strength. "No. Never." Her focus remained fixed on John's face. "He treated me with great respect and honored my opportunity for a second chance at life."

John's lungs worked again, and he breathed in the rich air. However, Lester moved on and acted as if the fireworks of the original question had never occurred. Instead, he launched into alternate questioning, addressing Rebecca's difficult conditions, her young home life, and the issue of her father's illness. With each question, Lester displayed a façade of respect, almost as if he had a sense of empathy toward her youthful hardships. He even praised her for how she'd handled the sudden shock of her father's suicide.

Yet only a fool could consider Lester thoughtful, because once he found her slight crack, a place where she still carried scars from her youth, Lester renewed his attack. He took her once again through the process, delving into the ugly hours that had erupted within the Brownell estate. At the death of her father, Rebecca had openly accepted Rick Downley into her life—Even though, before their marriage, Downley had abused her. Lester moved forward with the facts, alternately portraying Downley as either a devil or a saint, whichever cast the worst glare on Rebecca's life and character.

Time moved dangerously slow. However, Rebecca remained stoic. She admitted to her wrongs and mistakes, as well as the demons which had revealed themselves through her illness. And Lester smiled through it all.

Together they had created a picture; Lester drew the lines using professional craftiness and then allowed Rebecca to color in the details. Now through his cunning questions, Rebecca gave the jury a clear view of her condition upon entering Clearcreek She shared her unhealthy and intense delusion that she was a mother. During her six-year stay at Clearcreek, she'd continued to care for her "baby" Robert, letting no else into her illusory world until Dr. John Sanders helped her work through her condition.

Once she spoke of her healing, Lester took an approach which had clearly come straight from Gravers. John felt as if he had reverted back to his days in Gravers's office, when the dark-eyed man had used those same words to manipulate Rebecca's fate. "Did you have a family?" Lester asked Rebecca.

"No." Her face was solid, her frown concrete.

"Anyone to take care of you?"

"No."

"Then how could Gravers send you out with no support system to help you survive?" Lester turned to the jury and waited for his point to be absorbed. "How could he knowingly send you out into an environment where statistics claim you will fail?"

"Objection, Your Honor," Brotherson stated.

As Judge Revere sustained the hearsay statement, Hank Lester paraded back and forth. When he glanced at the audience, John caught those dancing eyes eager for a gain.

"But I did survive." The words filled the courtroom. "My life is rich." Rebecca's voice was strong, her face angry. "I currently work for a day care where the staff and children appreciate me. They love me. I have these people as well as my neighborhood friends."

The statement slapped Lester. He turned away from the audience to look directly at her and said, "Are those associations family?"

"They care for me and I care for them."

"Do these neighbors intend to be a long-term support team for the next time you are in psychiatric danger?"

John cringed. Lester attacked her the same way he'd attacked everyone else: he captured their fears and then preyed on them. Now he mocked Rebecca with implication that she would fail again.

Fortunately, she chose not to participate in his destructive game. "Dr. Blythe has given me the additional help I need. Through testing and other signs and expressions, she says I have the tools to maintain a good, solid life."

John's mouth dropped. She was more triumphant than he had ever envisioned her to be.

"In your opinion, Ms. Brownell, why did you remain at Clearcreek for over five years?"

"Steven Gravers wanted to rob me due to Rick's interference—"

"Did Steven Gravers," Lester cut her off, "see you capable and prepared enough to leave the safety of Clearcreek?"

"I don't know," she said honestly.

Then Lester took on a gooey tone. "I wish to congratulate you, Ms. Brownell, on your achievements."

For a brief moment, Lester paused. Then he shifted back to exploring Dr. Sanders's clinical practices with Rebecca. Carefully, Lester escorted Rebecca down a path that examined John's naïve beginnings, his mistakes, and his personal emotions. Meanwhile, John felt himself imploding. Finally, Lester wrapped it up by saying, "I ask you again, did Dr. John Sanders ever step outside of his therapeutic role?"

Although Rebecca's eyes burned with hate, Lester's tactics worked, and her tone weakened. "No. . . not that I am aware of."

"Did you ever want, or would you have accepted, him to act outside of his role?"

"Objection!" Travis Brotherson's body shot up, and John released a pent-up breath.

Meanwhile, Lester adjusted his tie and pulled his shoulders back, tight and high. "Did Dr. Sanders disobey orders to see you during personal time?"

"Not that I am aware of." She glanced at John, and her strong voice returned. "But I know he honestly cared enough about me to offer me the second chance I deserved. What he did was based on his concern for my welfare."

"And according to you, it was Dr. Sanders who acted in a way that led you to this second chance?"

"Yes. I deeply appreciate the great effort he made to bring me to the true knowledge of my condition and opportunities."

She smiled at Lester, then at John, and a bolt shot through him. With no forethought, he mouthed the words *thank you* to her.

John was in a daze as she finished her testimony. The only other thing he recalled was Rebecca's final statement.

"Dr. Gravers did not care about my progression. He never gave me the choices and opportunities that Dr. Sanders pushed me to have. But because Dr. Sanders and others valued me, I now have a life worth living."

Seconds later, Rebecca left the witness stand and Judge Revere adjourned court until the following day. A tamer, humbled Lester returned to Gravers's side.

Next to John, Hooper stood and whispered loudly, "Apparently Gravers wasted his time trying to destroy us, because that was the torpedo that will sink his ship."

Before John could respond, Hooper's linebacker body weaved through the crowd straight toward Rebecca. And while unsure and a bit reluctant, John followed.

Dr. Blythe hugged Rebecca, followed by a hug from a Dr. Maria Garcia, a strong handshake from Landersen, who had testified earlier in the week, and a series of ongoing pats and praises from Brotherson and a few others. Then Hooper jumped in for his introduction.

"Conrad Hooper," he said, stretching forth his hand. Rebecca accepted, which gave Hooper the opportunity to pull her into a half hug. "You were incredible." He kept his arm around her "Your strength, your caliber, your testimony—because of you Gravers will get what he deserves. You're a saint to all of us."

Rebecca looked at him briefly, "Thanks," she said. Then, with a small step, she removed Hooper from her space, which placed her in direct view of John. "Hi," she said with a large, lingering smile.

John wanted to hug her, to embrace her like the others had. But with all those eyes on them, as well as his ongoing internal debate of appropriateness, he held back. Yet in spite of the spectators, an emotion caught in John's throat. For a moment he could not speak. Rather, he extended a hand and in the midst of a solid handshake, he mouthed again the words *thank you*.

In return, her eyes sparkled with joy and pride. "Thank you," she said with emphatic richness. "Look at me."

"You look incredible." He had found his voice but now struggled to find the right words. "I mean, you're doing incredible . . . incredible things you're doing. That's obvious. You've done well. You look great."

"Well." She remained graceful and collected. "I'm trying."

"That's all any of us can do."

She offered him a beautiful, vibrant smile, and when he looked into her sparkling green eyes, John suffered a bolt of sensational and dangerous tingling.

Fortunately, the moment ended with Conrad Hooper placing his arm around Rebecca's shoulder. "Let's celebrate!" he called to everyone.

Dr. Linda Blythe stepped between John and Rebecca. "Good to see you again, Sanders." She placed her hand against his arm and turned to speak to everyone. "This has been a successful day," she said. Before stepping back into the crowd, she winked at John and her face beamed with pride.

"A successful day where the truth has been shared!" Hooper raised his fist in triumph. "Together we have paved a road whereon Gravers will rot like roadkill."

Landersen's eyes grew big. "Don't ruin my dinner. Where should we eat?"

"Champion's Bar and Grill," Hooper answered. "Seems appropriate, doesn't it?"

Landersen's face creased with concern. "I've never heard of it. How's the food?"

"It's excellent," said Dr. Garcia.

Dr. Blythe looped a sparkling red purse strap around her shoulder. "Sounds wonderful."

"If you don't know where it is, just follow me." Hooper took a step forward and placed his hand against Rebecca's back. In an affectionate way, he pushed her forward. "You in?"

"Me too?" she stuttered.

"Well, of course." Conrad released a rich laugh. "This day wouldn't have hit success status if you hadn't testified so courageously."

"Thanks." She glanced at John. He felt another uncomfortable rush of emotion. The hazard increased when Hooper said, "Do you need a ride? You're welcome to join John and me."

She kept her eyes on John while offering no answer.

"Why don't you come with us?" Hooper escorted her toward the door.

John watched but did not follow. Instead, he held back until Dr. Blythe ended another conversation and turned to face him. "You coming to Champion's?"

He nodded, unsure whether he should with Rebecca also going. "Rebecca's coming with Hooper and me." Perhaps Blythe would serve as the voice of reason.

Instead she smiled and nodded. "Good. That stubborn girl took a taxi here even after I offered to pick her up."

"Oh," John felt at a loss for words, and his heart beat a bit faster.

"That girl." Dr. Blythe's smile glowed. "She'll have her driver's license soon, and she's already looking for the car to spend some of that well-earned money on."

"The inheritance?" John asked.

"She's a special girl. A very special girl."

"She is."

"You know," Blythe grabbed John's arm to ensure his full attention. "She couldn't have made it through this today if it wasn't for her inheritance battle." Blythe exhaled a low whistle. "Those were grinding times. Anne Downley blames Rebecca for everything. She possesses a lot of anger, which she will forever direct at Rebecca. But the entire ordeal made Rebecca tough. That girl has been through the refiner's fire, and she is coming out a solid beauty."

John could only nod while Linda's swelling pride and happiness splashed over him.

"It's amazing to watch." They moved to the courthouse doors, and John pushed the exit open. When they were both outside, Dr. Blythe continued, "You know how a baby learns at an accelerated rate? Well, that's our Rebecca. It's like a rebirth or a starvation that's finally come to an end. Now she wants to participate in everything; she wants to glean all she can from the world around her. And she's one adamant, stubborn lady, absolutely determined to achieve all her goals."

"Which are?"

Dr. Blythe shot John a distrusting glance. "You know what they are."

Suddenly John could not speak. Instead, he feigned ignorance. "What are they?"

"That girl . . ." Dr. Blythe's eyes filled with emotion. "That girl is hungry for a family. She yearns for it. She sheds tears because she's so eager for it. Tells me she'll do whatever I tell her is necessary in order for her to have a family—a good, healthy one."

Dr. Blythe kept walking, but John did not move. Something took over his body, a glowing light that flashed within his mind, a craziness playing tricks on him. Dr. Blythe turned back. "You okay?"

He shook off the strange moment and hastily caught up to her. "Yeah, I'm fine. She's doing great," he said in a nonchalant tone. Then, for his sanity, he shifted the conversation. "You ever been to Champion's before?"

CHAPTER THIRTEEN

On the ride to Champion's, John's mouth failed him. He seemed unable to formulate educated sentences and converse like a comfortable therapist among friends. In contrast, Conrad Hooper owned the conversation. He kept Rebecca, who sat in the front seat, busy listening to his stories and laughing at his pointless jokes. In the back of the comfortable sedan, John sat helplessly listening to the charisma and ease of his colleague's mouth.

When they arrived, they found a packed restaurant. But Hooper had connections, and within twenty minutes the large group of twelve was seated and adding to Champion's rumbling chatter. The group had much to discuss: the current trial, the former shock of uncovering Gravers's deception, the struggles to find work, and the year of this drawn-out aftermath.

John had sat as far away from Rebecca as possible. Nevertheless, he found himself drawn to the conversation on his right, where Garcia and Steiner discussed early signs that, in hindsight, could have exposed Gravers. In listening to them, John kept Rebecca within his view. On occasion, he added to their conversation, but mostly he observed Rebecca's mannerisms and behavior as she interacted with those at the other end of the table.

After a rich round of appetizers followed by a full-course meal, the party slowly began to dwindle. Hooper, however, remained strong, recounting numerous stories and jovial memories of Clearcreek's valid days. Eventually, only Conrad Hooper, Rebecca Brownell, and John Sanders remained.

"Well," Hooper said after he finished off the last of his martini, "guess we should head out too." He stood, stretched his arms, and then patted his stomach. "Sure is good food here." He took the lead and weaved through the crowd as if this were his second home.

"Conrad." A voice called out through the fog of people.

Hooper scanned the display of faces, and the voice called again. Then a muscular, dark-haired man launched himself onto Hooper and yanked him into a bear hug. "Crazy to see you, buddy!"

"Gerry." Hooper returned the strong hug and shook his head in surprise. "I haven't seen you in years."

"What are you up to?"

"I missed your name with the pros."

The dark-haired man laughed. "I couldn't survive. It's now real estate, a lucrative business with fewer drills and injuries. You?"

"Psychologist."

"Whoa. *You?*"

"Surprised?" Hooper smirked.

"Did you officially make it through?"

"After a lot of caffeinated nights."

The man grinned. "Hey, let's get some drinks and catch up."

"Uh," Hooper said, motioning at John and Rebecca, "they're with me, and we were just heading out. This is John Sanders."

"Gerry Crandle." The man shook John's hand. "You got time, don't you?"

"And this is Rebecca Brownell," Hooper said.

Gerry Crandle looked at Rebecca, and in an instant his mouth drew up into a pleased smile. "Come and join us."

John watched Rebecca's eyes dart away from Gerry. Hooper glanced at the exit, the bar, and then back at Gerry. Meanwhile, Gerry kept looking at Rebecca. Then Gerry cocked his head toward the bar and gave her a subtle wink. "Come on," he repeated. "Drinks are on me."

Hooper turned toward the bar and grinned. "Excellent. Then count us in."

"We'll wait out front," John said to Hooper.

"Sure. Sounds like a plan," Hooper said with relief.

Gerry eyed Rebecca closely. "You sure? Conrad can be a lot of fun once I get him going."

In a stiff manner, Rebecca shook her head and turned to John. "You ready?" she asked.

"You won't be long," John said to Hooper, "will you?"

Hooper's smile seemed huge. "Not more than five minutes."

"If you change your mind," Gerry said while his eyes examined Rebecca from top to bottom, "the invitation still stands. Just come and join us."

Before Rebecca had time to respond, John stepped forward, placing his body strategically between Gerry and Rebecca. "Thanks," he said, as Rebecca turned around and headed for the exit.

But journeying out amid the craze of people proved challenging. In following her out, John felt a need to reach for her arm so as not to lose her, but he dismissed this desire.

Eventually the two made it out into the open air, and refreshing, clean coolness greeted them. On the east side of the building, tucked away from the continual stream of guests, an iron bench faced the entrance. John motioned Rebecca toward it.

Once they sat, he caught a whiff of her light and elegant perfume. "Are you okay?" he asked.

"Yes. I'm good." Yet she shook her head as if shaking off a lingering chill.

Something had bothered her, and John wanted to know what had happened back there. He searched for the right questions and finally said, "I'd imagine, in his younger days, that Hooper ran with an interesting crowd."

Rebecca studied John, and the firmness that she had carried all day returned. "His friend looked like Rick."

"Did he?" John thought back to Gerry Crandle. He had an olive complexion, dark features, a charismatic smile, an air of arrogance, and an expensive watch. She was right, certain similarities did exist. "You okay?" John repeated.

She nodded, but John was unconvinced. "Today has put you in a lot of awkward—"

"Dr. Sanders," Her solid tone, as well as the formality of his professional name, silenced him. "I'm okay. I've come a long way."

"You have." He found himself grinning at her strength. "You should be proud of what you've accomplished."

"I am."

Silence followed.

Followed by more silence.

While the two watched the Friday-night crowd head toward the restaurant, John wondered if Hooper's entire five minutes would be like this. But then Rebecca looked down at her hands and finally said, "Even though he's dead, he still lives inside my fears." The response was open, honest, and exactly how John preferred her to be.

But now it was his turn to respond, and he struggled with his obscure role. Finally, he casually said, "Downley wanted you out of his life. After he had your money and you became sick, he took further advantage of your situation. He used you to get what he wanted. It's odd, almost ironic, that once he left you at Clearcreek, he no longer thought about you, but now you keep thinking about him."

"You can't understand the memories he left me with."

"No, I can't."

From there, neither spoke. On a distant street, murmuring traffic droned past. Through their silence, John reflected back to his counseling days with her. Those were days when he believed he could teach her, could offer her counsel and hope. Yet those were other times. Now she sat there in her tailored suit with her short hair and her alert eyes. This was a special person who sat next to him, a refined person that was worlds past what he once knew. She was a person who no longer needed him.

"That's my last battle." Her smile returned slowly.

"What's that?"

"To conquer my nightmares." She leaned back against the bench and took in a tender breath. "Because during the daytime, I feel like a new person."

The streetlight rays touched her face and her soft features glowed.

John felt a joy in sitting next to her. He wanted to be close to her, and he wanted to learn from her. "So if I was to counsel someone, if I wanted to help move them in the direction where you are, what advice could you give me?"

She offered a warm smile. "You helped me," she said.

John's heartbeat increased. "I played a small part, but you've had exceptional help from many people."

"Yes, I have. For all the bad, I've also received much good."

For a long moment, he looked at her hands. Suddenly he wanted to touch them. Then he reprimanded himself, scolding himself for such a thought.

Instead he looked away and praised her. "Ultimately, it was you. You were the one who made the change. You took ownership of your destiny and placed yourself here."

"I finally saw the good," she whispered. Then she watched a young couple across the parking lot load their small family into a tight car. "I hope . . ." The tiny daughter started to climb into her car seat, then paused and pulled her father into a hug. Then the young father held the passenger door open for his wife. "He loves her," Rebecca said. She watched the father slip into the driver's seat and whispered, "He does." As the car drove away, she turned back to face John. "Rick was evil."

"Yes, he was."

"It's how he existed. It's all he knew how to be."

"But you're overcoming his influences."

"Dr. Sanders, you helped me understand that I needed to choose to *want* to live. And once I made that choice . . . once I did it . . . well, now I figure there has to be something more, and I want to find it."

"What do you mean?"

"When I think about Rick, I just know there has to be something just as strong, but the opposite of his evil."

He studied her face. "That's insightful, Rebecca."

"As I'm working to heal, I want to experience it. I want to find my answer."

"Then you will."

"Want to hear my quest?"

"Please."

"I have to believe that for all the fear, there has to be an equal amount of faith. For all the despair, there has to be an equal feeling of hope. And for all the hate, there must be an equal or greater portion of love. So I want to uncover those good things. And I want to become a person who lives those things."

Over the last year, in the midst of his suspended license, John's abhorrence toward Gravers had grown. During that time, John had claimed to be a victim, someone who had been hurt by the malice of a revengeful man. But the blow had only been to his career. For Rebecca, her very right to live had been attacked, and now she was rising above the hate, aiming to be stronger, and ready to face the future challenges of her new world.

"It's hard to release certain things," John said. "It's hard to depart from wrong beliefs and desires."

"Yes. It's a long process." Then she chuckled lightly, as if she knew a cruel joke. "One of the hardest first steps for me was boxing up that blanket and making sure it got into your hands."

"And it was a very triumphant day for me." He grinned at her, and she grinned back.

"What I desire is not bad." Her eyes watched him. "I want children. I want to love and to be loved. So I hope for such things, and those things aren't bad."

"No, they're not."

"But my old method—what I gave in to—and how I let those desires take over and shape me, that was an unhealthy outlet." She shifted her focus back to the active parking lot. "It was dangerous, and it almost destroyed me. Now I've learned, through therapy and watching others, that life's satisfaction comes from work. Dr. Blythe has told me that good things are not obtained through the illegal, unethical, or abnormal. She says at first glance, it may seem that we can grab and satisfy desires quickly and be as uninvested as we want, but all that's self-deceiving. A good family takes work. It doesn't just happen, and if I'm looking for easy solutions or short cuts, then I'll only find pain over a longer period of time.

"Those five years at Clearcreek, I binged on fantasizes. I've talked a lot with Dr. Blythe about this strange, contorted view I had of life. There were things I thought were acceptable. Things I believed I had achieved. It was odd—and scary—and I shudder to think I ever reached that point. But that twisted existence was because I desired something to the point that it strangled me. I was so lost. I saw no hope. My wants were out of reach, so I built my life on lies until I lost control of everything.

"Now I'm starting over. I'm building a real foundation, I'm full of hope, and I'm working hard. I'm improving myself and preparing myself to achieve certain things. Intense, good things that I have a right to—but only if I stay true to truth, only if I work as if my survival depends on this correct way of thinking . . . which it does." She looked back at John. "I died at Clearcreek, and thanks to you I was brought back to life. You gave me that extra chance to live."

As Rebecca had spoken, John had been studying her against the peaceful light, watching her face fill with fortitude as she expressed her goals. Now, as she looked at him, he nervously glanced toward the parking lot.

"You're so quiet," she said. "I want to know what you're thinking."

Something was happening to him, and it was either bad or extremely good. "I don't know you," he admitted.

In a different context, he would eagerly pursue her. But he could not act on such wishes. So he spoke in general terms. "You're an inspiration to others. Who you are today validates the worth of life, and because of this other people will want to be near you. They'll want to feel the hope that's radiating from inside you."

She blushed and looked at him with a tender smile. "Dr. Sanders, I'm not those things."

"Yes. You are."

"But I'm not."

"Right now, you're inspiring to others. Extremely inspiring. Today you were like a warrior, and you made all of us want to be stronger. You made us want to fight a little harder at improving our own lives. You made us want to find greater meaning and fulfillment in our own efforts. You made us want to pursue our own dreams." She still looked as if she questioned his statements, so he continued with greater conviction. "And it's your innocence, your ability to do all that you're doing while being pure and oblivious to how your behavior is affecting all those around you—that's what's so beautiful."

She looked down at her hands and then spoke in a humble tone. "Thank you."

"No," John said while his heart raced forward, "thank you." He looked at her one last time, enough to acknowledge to himself that these seeds of affection had grown too fast. Dangerous longings had crept in and captured the night. So against his sprinting heart, which pleaded with him to say more, John arose. He drew in a difficult breath and spoke with all the authority he could offer. "I believe Hooper's five minutes are up. I'd better go retrieve him."

CHAPTER FOURTEEN

Since Gravers's trial, John's life had changed. The Board had re-examined statements, investigated Gravers's Board representative, and reinstated John's license. Despite the fact that his flaws had been published, magnified, and even exaggerated, the psychiatric community now extended mercy, understanding, and respect toward him. He was a good man who had struck the match that had lit the dynamite inside of Clearcreek. As a result, Gravers's sentence involved a $2 million fine, a 10-year prison sentence, and a revoked license. In the words of Landersen, justice at last had been served "on a shiny silver platter," and John had been invited to the feasting. He savored every moment of it.

Now, with work options abounding, John could finally move on. Then, in the midst of decisions, an unexpected phone call came.

"Hello, Dr. Sanders." A strong woman's voice echoed through the phone.

"Hello?" John repeated, certain he recognized the formidable voice.

"It's Linda Blythe."

John caught his breath, suddenly concerned. "How's Rebecca?"

Dr. Blythe laughed. "She's fine. Doing marvelous. I see her only one or two times a month these days. And how are you?"

"Great."

"I'm not surprised." Again she laughed into the phone. "Your name's been receiving quite a bit of praise."

"It's been a nice change."

"Hasn't it, though? Glad your work's being recognized."

"Thank you." His cheeks burned to receive such praise from the reputable Dr. Blythe.

"Rumor has it you've recently taken work at St. Douglas Hospital."

"They offered me a spot in their psychiatric ward."

"You selected them over Kaiser?"

John drew in a breath. He had been procrastinating his decision for weeks. Both job offers were exceptional, yet John had been hesitant to commit to anyone. Instead, he had spent the last several months doing contract work for both hospitals, as well as a prison and a youth detention center, while watching job offers continue to pop up. Although he enjoyed this cushion of time to search and contemplate the best avenue for his career, time was running out. Soon he would need to stop stalling and make his choice. "I haven't decided yet," he said.

Again Dr. Blythe's laughter rang through the phone. "Excellent answer."

"Really?"

"Of course it is. Because you should come work for me."

"You?"

"I have a secret," Linda said with light humor. "I've been hoping to convert you over to private therapy sessions for quite some time now. You're young enough, so I believe you can be persuaded." Once again she laughed.

"You?" John repeated. "I'd be . . . I'd be honored."

"Great. Come see me tomorrow, and we'll get all the details squared away."

"Thank you," John repeated.

For the first month, John embraced his surroundings. The counseling sessions, the diligent clients, the brand-new office, the enjoyable interactions with the strong staff—all the details made the job great. Best of all, John found invaluable mentoring through the strong leadership of Dr. Blythe. Nevertheless, John knew he had a growing secret.

Although he had not yet seen Rebecca, he kept thinking of her, and kept searching for signs of her.

First, he spotted her name on schedules. Next, he paused regularly to listen to Dr. Blythe speak to others about this poster child of therapy. Finally, he sought any opportunity to prod Dr. Blythe with additional questions in order to hear even more praise of Rebecca's remarkable advancements.

The more he thought of Rebecca, the more he realized that, although her visits were limited, she did come. And this meant John would find a way to see her again.

During his fifth week, he saw her leave the building from a distance. For the remainder of the day, thoughts of her flowed freely. Two weeks later, he made certain that he had no appointments before her scheduled time. Instead, he stalled in the waiting area, visiting with the clinic receptionist, until he saw her enter the building.

"Hello," he said.

Rebecca's fingers combed through her dark curls. Her hair had grown longer since the last time he had seen her. "Hi," she said, and a priceless smile followed.

"How are you?" he asked.

"I'm doing really well."

"That's what I hear."

She smiled again. "How are you?" she asked.

"Excellent."

"Congratulations on the job."

He nodded. "Thank you." He smiled back at her, and a small, awkward pause followed. Then Dr. Blythe entered the waiting room.

"Rebecca." She spoke cheerfully, and John stepped away feeling an ounce of shame.

Yet over the next set of weeks he positioned himself again for more "coincidental" meetings in the hallway. This planning seemed to be paying off until his standard three-month review.

"Is having Rebecca here a problem for you?" Dr. Blythe asked.

"No." His answer came too quickly.

She clasped her hands together and leaned forward. "You told me in the beginning, when we went through the job offer, that you didn't see it being a problem. Your responsibilities are separate from her, and she's rarely here."

John nodded, aware that currently he scheduled all of his appointments around Rebecca's visits. "Sometimes I see her."

"Dr. Sanders," she said softly, "is it time for me to recommend her to another therapist?"

"Why?"

"Well, I'd prefer not to."

"Then I don't think you should."

"She and I have connected, and I believe the consistency has been good for her. She's very open with me." Dr. Blythe's studied John's face. "For that reason, I'd hoped that we could work around any awkward conditions."

"Of course we can."

"But the fact is, if she makes you uncomfortable in anyway, I don't want her here."

John smiled. "Thanks for your concern. And there's no uncomfortableness for me if it's not uncomfortable to her."

"Good." Dr. Blythe nodded. Then she moved on to discuss John's schedule. She wrapped up their session with an overall positive report, including praise from some clients.

When he exited, she stood near the door. "I'm not sure I ever shared with you why I wanted you to be a part of my team."

He paused in the doorway and waited.

"It's your integrity." She kindly squeezed his arm. "At Clearcreek, I saw your strength of character, how true you are to yourself and others, and I admired that." She stepped away from him. "I hope you always maintain that trait."

Throughout the next week, John could not shake off Dr. Blythe's words. Often, when he looked in the mirror, or when he tried to sleep, he found himself questioning what he wanted, what he cared about, and what he needed to do. After a week of introspection, John finally understood—and he knew.

At the end of the work day, he tapped on the door, entered Dr. Blythe's office, and laid an envelope on her desk.

"What is this?" she asked.

"My resignation."

"Sit down," Dr. Blythe commanded. She ripped into the envelope and scanned the letter, and as she read, her face turned from troubled to stoic. Finally, she set down the letter and said, "Is that right?"

He nodded.

She released a despairing sigh and refused to look at him.

Strained seconds followed.

John considered leaving. Or apologizing for the confession he had just shared. But he held no remorse; he was at peace.

Finally, Linda looked up. In place of her usual pleased smile, a troubled expression stained her face. "What, so far, has occurred between you two?"

John drew in a breath, then restated what he hoped she had understood from his letter. "I haven't done anything. But I'm currently considering my choices."

"Dr. Sanders." Although she spoke strongly, her eyes appeared weak, as if this conversation was physically hurting her.

"I'm aware of the concerns," John said.

She looked at the desk, then up at the ceiling. Finally, she exhaled and looked directly at him. "Are you really aware of the concerns?"

"I think so."

"Have you looked at the statistics, at the dangers, at the fact that you'll always hold this superior role over her?"

John had promised himself, regardless of her response, that he would be strong.

"You won't be equals," she continued. "You won't be able to build a solid foundation for a good relationship because of who you are and what her life is."

He was not naïve. He knew of the often-tragic consequences of patient-therapist relations. But their outcome would be different. Rebecca was different—she had already proved that. And he was different too. For this reason, with a steadfast voice, he stated, "The code of ethics says that after a two-year absence from a therapist/patient role a relationship can form between the two parties." He aimed to sound official, hoping Linda would validate his claim.

"Sanders, there's the letter and the spirit of the law. Do you understand me? Just because you've been out of that counseling role for some time doesn't differentiate the perimeters that have been set between you two. She'll see you in a light that you can't change, and you'll see her in a weaker role. You'll be unable to be partners in a long-term relationship."

He had to ignore her warnings. He already had considered the risks, the dangers, the concerns—but he had made his choice. Yet out of respect for Dr. Blythe, he had to say more. "I need to pursue this. But I need your help."

"My help?"

"If Rebecca and I both want the same things, then we'll both need your help. Work with us. Offer us joint counseling. Help us avoid the pitfalls and dangers that you're talking about."

Linda pulled her head back and closed her eyes. When she opened them again, her face softened. She brushed her hands across her head and looked at the east wall. Then a quirky smile crossed her lips, and she shook her head as if she'd participated in an ongoing joke with the room.

"I know too much, Sanders," she finally said. After a chuckle and another shake of the head, she added, "You've placed me in a hard spot, one in which I'd like to say you've given me no choices." Her ruby lips erupted into a huge smile. "Rebecca has shared things with me in this room, and . . . if you destroy her, I'll personally come and rip you apart, toe by toe."

"I won't destroy her."

"If you use her and then leave her, she won't recover. Do you understand that?"

"That's not my intention."

"Do you know how fragile she can be?"

"I care about her. I'll stay with her."

"Then you can't excite anything—you can't give in—until you've stated those vows."

"I'm promising you I'll respect her."

"Then don't—" Her words were like steel bars. Yet her face trembled, as if a mere softening of her voice would cause her to crumble. He had never seen her like this.

"Don't leave her. Don't humiliate her. Don't disgrace her."

He hoisted himself against the chair. "I'm not that kind of person. At Clearcreek, everything I did for Rebecca was based on pure motives. I've always wanted her to succeed. My desire was for her to find her life and live it to the fullest. Since then you've accomplished incredible things with her. You've shown her a fulfilling lifestyle, and she's happy. That's what I wanted for her. But what I didn't know, in all of this, was that she would transform into a woman whom I believe I can love, and I need to discover if that's true. And I need to find out if she has feelings for me, too."

Dr. Blythe leaned back in her chair and folded her arms against her chest. "Assuming she does, then what?"

"I want your blessing. I'm pleading that you give us that. But if you can't, I understand."

"I want to protect that girl."

"Then counsel us together. Help us build the best foundation."

Dr. Blythe rubbed her neck. "What if I say no?"

"Then I'll go elsewhere."

She shifted her body to regain her professional poise. "That's what I figured. So you tell me—do I have a choice?"

"You can help us, or someone else can."

"I want her to succeed. And I want you to succeed."

"Then will you help us?"

She picked up the resignation, released a heavy sigh, and again scanned the letter. "Has it really been over two years since she was under your care?"

"Yes."

"Then listen. Your resignation has been accepted." She set the letter down. "Your timing is right. I don't see a need to notify the Board, especially since you've already served your penance."

John gave her a sympathetic grin.

"I certainly wish things were different," she said. Then a mischievous twinkle shone in her eyes. "But curse my romantic heart. I like you, Sanders. That's why I brought you here. And even now, I still like you." She released a heavy sigh. "So I'll help you." Her brown eyes appeared gentle. "I'll offer joint counseling for both of you."

A large smile exploded across John's face. "Thank you."

Dr. Blythe's fiery stare returned. "Don't you dare hurt her," she commanded. "Be good to her. Prove my fears wrong."

"You have my promise—I'll always be good to her."

Linda's eyes softened. "Yes. Somehow I know you will."

CHAPTER FIFTEEN

That evening, John walked into his apartment eagerly planning his next step. He would contact her, share the truth of his feelings, and then learn her thoughts concerning him. With her number in hand, John approached the phone and drew in a deep breath. If all proceeded as he envisioned, his life was about to change in a drastic way.

Suddenly a high-pitched ring surprised him. He exhaled a pent-up breath and set down her number. The phone's shrill ring sounded again.

"John." It was his mother. "So glad we caught you at home. What are you doing right now?" She sounded full of energy.

John glanced again at Rebecca's phone number before slowly placing the slip of paper inside the end table's drawer. "Nothing."

"Great! We're less than a half hour from your place."

"Whoa!"

"Kilee and Cameron are with us too. Dan couldn't make it."

"Wow. What's the occasion?"

Cindy Sanders giggled with pride. "Your father's being honored by ASTEC."

"Aztec?"

"The American Science and Technology Educational Centers. It's a huge honor. They have their annual conference, which happens to be in LA this year, and they want to recognize your father for all he's done in helping children understand physics through his educational equipment."

"And you're telling me this *now*?"

"Tell him," John heard his father's gruff tone in the background. "Somebody canceled."

"Oh, Hal," his mom whispered. "John, he's diminishing the recognition because it came at the last minute. Do you remember Aurora Gomez?"

"She's a neighbor, right?"

"Three houses down, next to the Waltons."

"Yeah, I remember." Vaguely.

"Well, Aurora's on the board of the Santa Cruz Science Center as well as an officer for the ASTEC alliance. Every year they have this national convention with professionals from science and technology museums or special centers, and they all congregate to network and discuss the market trends and see what's available to advance their institutions."

"It was last minute," his father called out.

"I'm getting there," she said politely. "Anyway, last night Aurora called us. Apparently their keynote speaker, who was coming from Chicago, had a terrible family emergency. The whole alliance was scrambling to find someone to fill the spot. I mean, they'll have well over a thousand people in attendance."

"No," John heard his father's voice again. "She's exaggerating."

"Your father hopes I'm exaggerating. Anyway, Aurora recognized this as an ideal opportunity to focus on all the good your father's done both locally and nationally."

"Wow," John said. "This is a big deal."

"It's huge. It'll potentially increase his sales substantially. It's a bit risky for them to place a business in the keynote spot, but it's the best solution. And when you consider the referrals and increased test scores and all the AP successes due to how your father has helped high school physics students, I most certainly think he's the best candidate for this."

"He is." John echoed her pride.

"Anyway, your sister made some arrangements and is with us, and it's certainly last minute, but if you can, please join us."

"In LA?"

"Yes, tomorrow morning."

"Okay, I'll see what I can do. And you're coming here tonight?"

"Yes. We know it's a slight detour."

"Isn't it two hours out of your way?"

His mother laughed. "You're worth that extra distance . . . and Base Line High School is the only school in the state that has the newest model of your father's centrifugal force exhibit. They agreed to let us borrow it, and we're almost there. So once we pick that up, we'll swing by your place, take you to dinner, then head to the hotel."

"Wow."

"I know it's a long night, but it's very exciting."

"It is."

"They've already committed to doing an article about your father in their *Dimensions* magazine, which is such excellent exposure."

"This is great, Mom."

"It is. So we'll see you soon."

"Of course."

When John hung up the phone, he surveyed the room. It was not entirely messy but could certainly use a quick clean. In an effort to please his mother, he vacuumed the floor, gathered up a few dishes, and did a swift dusting through the room.

Within twenty minutes, as he wrapped up the last of his cleaning, he heard a knock at the door. He surveyed the apartment, smiled at himself, and headed toward the door. It had been over six months since he had last seen his family.

"Hey." He pulled the door open—only to freeze. On his porch, Rebecca Brownell tugged at a dark curl, and her green eyes stared at him. "Hey," he said, softer this time.

"Hi," she imitated his tone.

"How are you?" he asked, struggling for words.

Her hands twisted a ring around her index finger, and her eyes looked past him into the apartment. "Could I come in?"

"Uh . . ." John tried to process the situation. She was there, in front of him, at his place, in this precise moment. "Sure." He swung the door open and ushered her in.

"I just got through talking to Dr. Blythe," Rebecca said while John shut the door. Suddenly his head started to swim. This was not the setting he had imagined. He glanced at her face. Her eyes were studying him.

"Do you want to sit?" John motioned her to the coach. But after she sat, her face revealed no signs of what she thought.

"So you talked to Dr. Blythe . . . tonight?" John smiled and also sat on the coach while searching frantically for his next words.

"She called me."

"And . . ." He struggled for words while his mind juggled extreme emotions, his family's imminent arrival, and this inopportune timing. When the wordless conversation was interrupted by a knock, John felt some relief. "My family just called." He pointed at the door. "They're just stopping for a moment on their way through town."

"Oh." Rebecca stood, and her face appeared panicked. "Well, I will . . ." She pointed at the door. "I should . . ."

"No, you can—"

Another knock filled the room.

"Here . . ." John pointed at the door. "Let me just get this."

But before he could, the door opened, and Randy's buoyant voice greeted them, "Hello, neighbor!"

John stared at his friend. "What are you doing here?"

Randy's arms opened wide as if mocking the wish for a hug. "I haven't seen you in days . . . maybe even weeks. Thought you might have a little time to spend with your old buddy. Bet we could find a game, food, you know?"

John rubbed his face. "I've got family coming."

"Great!" Randy's face broke into a wide smile. "I haven't seen Cindy and Hal in years." He stepped forward, forcing John to step back. "You never met Bunny, but she and I are no longer, so a night with the Sanders family would be a perfect—" Randy stopped, stared at Rebecca, then quickly turned to John. "Family?"

"They're coming."

Randy stretched his hand toward her. "Hi. I'm Randy Case."

"I'm Rebecca." She shook his hand.

A gleeful smile spread across his face. "Rebecca, huh?" He grinned at John, then back at her. "Nice to meet you."

John's head pounded. He needed an immediate remedy for this colliding situation.

"So," Randy said to Rebecca, "John and I go way back, to our college freshman days. Yep, we're good friends."

"Oh." She smiled, then pointed at the door. "I was just on my way out."

Randy maintained his position near the door, thus blocking her departure. "How about you?" He smiled. "How do you know John?"

The statement caught John off guard. Randy was being cruel; he knew full well who Rebecca was—the humor on his face confirmed that. To help Rebecca escape, John reached for the doorknob, but she handled the moment with class.

"John and I," she paused to offer John a smile. Perhaps it was because she had just said his first name, or perhaps it was the flirtatious grin she offered, but John's heart was back to racing, fighting for attention over his pounding head. "We go back a few years too." Rebecca's voice remained composed. "He *is* a good friend, isn't he?"

John yanked open the door only to hear his father's voice. "Hey, there. We're here."

"Uncle John!" He heard his five-year-old nephew's high-pitched scream. Then Cameron's arms wrapped around John's legs.

"Hey there, big guy." John returned the hug only to feel his head pound again.

Before John knew it, his entire family enveloped him in hugs. Then they shook hands and offered hugs to Randy, only to stop in shock to see a woman there. Once John introduced Rebecca, the astonishment magnified. Everyone knew the history, the background, and the challenges that her case had brought to John's career. But no one understood why she was currently there. A quick scan of his family's faces, and John knew they expected a clarification.

But for now he offered them nothing.

To end the awkward moment, Cindy turned to Randy. "We're taking John to dinner. We'd love for you to join us if you have time."

Randy grinned. "Absolutely. And seems Rebecca timed it well, too." He winked at her, and Rebecca cast a glance at the door, which had been utterly blocked by the Sanders family.

"Come on," Randy encouraged. "An evening with the Sanders family—what a treat!"

Cindy beamed with Randy's praise while Rebecca gave John an urgent look. "Um, I'm really just on my way out," Rebecca said.

John nodded and reached for the door.

"Johnny Boy," Randy said in his teaching tone, "don't let this fine lady leave."

Against his will, a smile formed on John's lips, which turned all eyes toward him. His mother looked distressed. His father appeared waiting for John to dismiss the speculation that was going on in everyone's mind. And John's younger sister, Kilee, grinned at him as if pleased he was finally being proactive in his love life.

Perhaps for this reason, Kilee was the next to act. "Come join us, Rebecca. Although—" she raised her hand up before continuing, "here's your warning: My five-year-old's bound to make a scene. So if you're willing to share in communal embarrassment, we'd love to have you."

It must have been the instant acceptance in Kilee's eyes that made Rebecca smile and nod her approval. "If you're sure that's okay?"

"Of course it is." Randy offered a prideful grin at his accomplishment, but John caught the cautionary look his parents shared. He hoped the night was not heading toward disaster.

Fortunately, Kilee was an angel and took Rebecca under her wing. Throughout the evening, Kilee engaged Rebecca in easy conversation while Cameron demanded John's attention.

Other than only being able to speak to Rebecca in the midst of the entire group, John thought the evening proceeded nicely, except for one rough spot, when, during dinner, his mother grilled Rebecca. John heard the subtle warnings in his mother's tone—implications that this girl was not good enough for her son. In contrast, and perhaps to soften Cindy's heat, Hal displayed a remarkable gentleness toward the infamous girl. He helped her through Cindy's questioning and even answered taboo questions on Rebecca's behalf. Meanwhile, Randy found the entire night entertaining. It became a grand platform for his hints, jokes, and laughter, which were always followed by him shooting John a variety of obnoxious grins.

Once the entire clan had returned to John's apartment, his father focused on the night's remaining journey and hastened their good-bye scene.

"So we'll see you tomorrow?" His mother asked as she gave John another farewell hug, which felt tighter than necessary.

"Of course," John said.

"You should come too," Kilee said to Rebecca.

"Yes." Hal's eyes beamed. "I'd appreciate all the support. Please come if you can."

Rebecca looked at the group, then grinned, and John spied a slight sign of moisture in her eyes. But rather than reply to the invitation, she looked at John and waited for him to speak.

"We'll call you from the hotel with all the information." His mother inserted. Then she glanced briefly at Rebecca before looking back at John. "Unless, John, you'd rather come with us now?"

John reached back and rubbed his tense shoulders. "Let's meet up tomorrow."

"With Rebecca," Randy said, patting her on the back. "Nice to finally meet you."

"Thanks, Randy," she said, smiling at him. In spite of his quirky ways, Randy had won her over. John hoped he might also have such success.

"We'll see you both tomorrow." Hal smiled proudly as he herded the group out.

Then everyone was gone, and John realized he was alone with her. All alone in the quiet room.

"Do you want to come in?" John chided himself for sounding so foolish; seeing as she was already in. However, she still hovered near the closed door.

"Can we sit?" She pointed back at the couch.

"Sounds great," John said with relief. They had a plan, as short as it may be.

They sat, but they situated themselves with ample space between. Then Rebecca proceeded, "Your family seems nice."

"They like you."

She shared a guarded smile. "Some of them might."

Wise Rebecca, picking up on his mother's cautionary vibes. "She'll like you in time." The statement had been bold, so John hastened his breathing and added, "I know she will."

Warmth filled Rebecca's green eyes, offering him an expression he had never seen before. "I hope it's okay that I came?" she asked softly.

"Of course it was . . . it is . . . it'll be great to have you join us . . . with me and them tomorrow, too."

He had been smoother back in the eighth grade around his first-time crush. He paused, drew in a breath, and exhaled his pent-up anxiety.

Then he studied her soft face, her dark locks falling forward, and he listened to his heart. He wanted to reach out and carefully touch her hair, or her skin, or at least scoot closer.

But that seemed too bold, too rash of a beginning. Instead, he said, "I'd planned to call tonight, and arrange to see you . . . and talk with you, maybe share some things with you . . . about me."

She nodded and kept her eyes on him. "Yes. Dr. Blythe contacted me to share her concerns before you and I spoke."

All evening a question had been gnawing at his mind, and now he had to ask. "How did you know where I lived?"

"She gave me your address."

John struggled to suppress a laugh. "Dr. Blythe did?"

"She knows a lot about me."

"Like what?"

"She knows when I'm thinking straight and when I'm not."

John's heart sped forward. "So . . ."

"She told me a few things you said to her . . . and she asked me what I wanted." Gently, Rebecca smiled at him. "I told her I wanted your address."

John nodded. "She's worried about you. She wants to protect you from any other unnecessary hurt . . . and so do I."

"You both need to stop worrying." She shook her head. "I've been through hard things, and those are the things that have brought me here."

"Good," he said before thinking.

"Life is hard, but this is who I am. Although I don't like some of the memories, the past shaped me. It's why I am who I am. And if none of those things had happened, maybe I wouldn't feel okay about myself, and . . . then I wouldn't be here right now."

"You're very special."

"I have a choice. I can waste my life feeling cheated and robbed, or I can start living. And I choose to enjoy all that I have because I have a good life."

"You do." He drew in a breath, and then braved forward. "But Rebecca . . . is it time for you to have more?"

"If I find the right person," she said.

After years of fighting, he looked at her freely. She was beautiful. Together they exchanged a smile.

Then she spoke quickly, "Dr. Blythe has told me many times that if I stay focused and prepare myself, opportunities will come."

She still smiled at him, so he slid closer, touching her hand. "What if that opportunity is here now?"

She looked down at his hand touching hers, but did not say anything.

"Rebecca, I'd like to be that person. I want to be the person who can share your dreams."

She continued to look down at their hands.

"Is that okay?" John said cautiously. When she did not answer, he added, "Would you be willing to see if there's a future for us?"

She tightened her hand around his and finally looked up at him. Her eyes were wet with moisture. "John." She said his first name strongly. "I think you are that person."

His heart raced, yet his breathing became more still.

Then it became clear what he needed to do. He touched her face, and she tilted forward.

Tenderly, he drew her into a long-lasting kiss.

AUTUMN 1999

CHAPTER SIXTEEN

Early dawn broke through the heavy bedroom curtains and cast enough amber light for John to justify arising.

It had been an impatient night for him, with his quest for rest achieving only limited success. Still, he'd tried to remain quiet throughout the night so as not to disturb his wife. But finally, at 5:52, John slid out of bed and retrieved his running shoes. Surely a jog outside would release this nervous rush.

From their small house, he headed toward a local park. Barely three years since their first kiss, and now a baby was on the way. John could not think straight.

She had told him last night, and they both had rejoiced. As he ran along the trail, he felt nothing could be better. Her dreams were his dreams, her happiness his greatest joy. Life was truly grand.

Months later, during a peaceful evening, he sat on the bed reading. Rebecca sat next to him, rubbing her slightly protruding stomach.

Suddenly she giggled. "I think Robert kicked me."

"What?" John stared at her.

"He kicked me." She reached for his hand. "Tell me if you can feel it, if he'll do it again."

"What did you call it?"

"He. I know; I'm guessing. We'll know for sure soon, but I really think it's a boy."

"No, what name did you call him?"

She offered him a sheepish grin. "Robert."

"No."

"What?" She released a silly laugh.

"Absolutely not."

Rebecca's hands still rubbed her stomach. "Robert." She whispered and then giggled. "I think he's kicking again. See? It's his name. It's what he wants to be called." She pulled John's hand back to her stomach. "Feel it. Robert," she whispered.

He pulled away. "That's eerie."

"Could you really feel it?" She stroked her stomach. "Robert," she whispered again.

"Stop."

"What?"

"It's like conversing with the dead."

The words hit her, and the joy left her face. "It's in honor of my father. What's wrong with that?"

"Absolutely not. It's too disturbing." While at Clearcreek, she had carried around a blanket that she bundled up as if wrapped around a baby. For those years, she had cared for the imaginary infant she had called Robert.

Tears quickly surfaced on Rebecca's face. "It's after Father. This was always my plan. I already was caring for him in my mind; he just wasn't here." She grabbed a tissue box from her nightstand and blew her nose.

John hesitated to say more; instead, he tenderly touched her stomach. "Let's hold off on discussing this, okay?"

"I want you to feel him kick." Through the tears, Rebecca's eyes lit up. Extra happy in pregnancy, she seemed quick to forgive.

However, soon after the ultrasound, with the confirmation that a boy was on the way, the subject of a name returned. On a nice evening after work, John picked up Rebecca from her job at Kiddy Care. A special glow lit up her face.

"Everywhere today," her eyes beamed, "there were such adorable boys. So cute and precious."

"How are you feeling?" During the pregnancy, John felt disquieted about her health, more so than he wanted to be.

"I want him here."

"I know."

"But not yet," she said. "We still have lots to do. We need to decide on a nursery theme, buy the crib, the stroller, the car seat, the high chair, the clothes—lots of clothes. Oh, there is so much to do." Even amid feigned panic, her voice revealed great delight, until her demeanor shifted. "John, all the aides keep asking what we're calling him."

He nodded and prepared himself for this difficult topic.

"Bobbie, Robbie, or Robert. A few suggested Rob or Bob." She gave him a hopeful grin. "What do you think?"

"No."

"Please." She kept her eyes on him.

"Only if you follow these conditions." John counted the specifications on his fingers. "His first name can be anything else. Hal, or Harold if you want. Middle name Robert, with the understanding he never goes by it."

She mocked him through laughter. "Your father's not dead yet."

"That's not a rule." John grunted. "My father's a great man. It'd be a privilege for him."

"Whose privilege?"

"Our son."

"My father was a great man too."

Her words led him toward dangerous ice. The thought of naming their son, born with a clean slate, after a man of her father's history seemed an enormous insult. Yet any word that remotely revealed John's true feelings would devastate his wife. In a quest to maintain peace, John calmly smiled and said, "Good thing we've still got more than four months."

"Unless he comes early."

"Well, we still have time."

"We need to discuss it." Her stubborn side was emerging.

"Let's make a list." John said, hoping to cling to peace. "Let's explore more options. Certainly there are millions of names that we haven't even considered."

"Robert," she persisted.

"What if he's not a Robert at all? Have you thought of that?" He glanced at her, hoping to see some concern in her eyes. But there was none. "Just in case," he pushed forward, "we'd better be prepared."

"He will be."

"Better be prepared," he repeated.

"He's a Robert."

"Robert can be on the list, but we need twelve other names. We need some more options of what he could be called."

"Why twelve?"

"It's a safe number."

"I'm hungry. What do you want for dinner?"

The conversation shift relieved John. He had four months to convince her that Robert was not an option and then give their son a safe name—one that did not have ties to a delusion that Rebecca had believed in for six years. "What do you feel like eating?"

"There's nothing at home." She rubbed her enlarged stomach. "Either take-out or we shop."

"You want take-out?"

"Take-out sounds good," she said.

"Take-out it is."

"Can I choose?"

"Sure."

"I've been craving tacos," she said, "for weeks now."

"Tacos are fine."

"Actually, I think the baby wants them—certain tacos, too."

"So not Speedy Taco, huh?"

"No. More like that one place, you know?"

He looked at her and shrugged.

"They make really good tacos. We had them a couple weeks ago."

John maintained a puzzled look.

"The baby really wants it," she said. "Its name is . . . um . . . its name is . . . I believe it's Roberto's." She looked at him and smiled. "Can we have Roberto's?"

John chuckled. "You're awful." Nevertheless, she grinned all the way to Roberto's.

Weeks continued to pass, and the baby's due date drew near. With two months left, most things were falling into place, except for the looming subject of the infant's name.

A desperate John turned to Dr. Blythe.

She had been their lighthouse through their dating, courtship, and first year of marriage. She loved them both and was committed to seeing their marriage succeed, so John felt comfortable confiding in her. Upon hearing of Rebecca's Robert obsession, Dr. Blythe expressed her concern.

"Due to the pregnancy, her medicine has been altered," Dr. Blythe said as she tapped her long, red fingernails on the office desk. "That could be adding to the issue."

A framed wedding picture of John and Rebecca rested on Dr. Blythe's bookshelf. Rebecca's smile was beautiful. "Maybe that's what it is."

"We need to get her back to where she was as soon as possible."

Against his will, he rolled his eyes. "The baby will be here before then."

Dr. Blythe gave John a humorous smile. "Well then, you're in trouble, aren't you?

"Yes, I am."

"That girl's stubborn." She shook her head, but her eyes revealed her affection. "So it sounds like you may have an unnamed child for eighteen years."

John sighed. "Exactly."

The final countdown had arrived. Rebecca was on her last month, and according to her, a decision had to be made. However, if necessary, John was prepared to call the baby "Boy Sanders" before giving in.

Then he arrived home one evening to find her note.
I'm picking up things for the nursery. Be back soon.
R—
John shook his head and chuckled. This "nursery run" had turned into her weekly ritual. Even before its birth, the baby was spoiled.

But then next to her note was an open book—her father's journal. On top of the open pages was a list titled *Names for our Baby*:

1   *Robert*
2   *Robbie*
3   *Bobbie*
4   *Bob*
5   *Bobby*
6   *Robby*
7   *Rob*
8   *Roberto*
9   *Bert*
10 *Obert*
11 *Ro-bert*
12 *Trebor*
13 *Hal Robert* *

* Since the #13 is unlucky, it would be best to disregard this last one.

John smiled. She was funny, clever, and stubborn, and now the countdown was on. Why did he already fear the outcome?

The journal had been opened for him to see. She wanted him to read it and connect with her father. He sighed, and, against his own personal wishes, he picked up the book and read the selected entry.

December 9, 1967
   A son? Or daughter?
   Mia believes she knows
   She dreams of a little boy with brown eyes

A boy, and she wants his name to be mine
Robert—my maternal grandfather's name
Before him—his father's
Chosen name for eldest male
Tradition?
Honor?
To be like my grandfather—Yes
To be like me—No
Such would carry disgrace
But I smile at Mia
Please—I tell myself—make her happy
Anything for her smile
Make her believe I am good
She says the child should carry my name
She supports me
Only sees the positive
So I hide pain
She wants posterity to be like me
Let them connect with their ancestors—I say
We settle
Name will be Robert
Perhaps this boy can carry the name past me
Make right my wrongs
Let him be a gift for us
All of us
This is my prayer
My request of thee

John flipped the page and continued reading.

March 23, 1968
Mia sleeps
Baby sleeps

Rebecca Ann Brownell
Born early this morning
4:23—her birth. My little Becca
I feel guilty
Too happy
Too overjoyed
I don't deserve this ecstasy
She is beautiful
Tiny
Small
Very innocent
Mia is beautiful too
Love them
Wish to make them proud
Pleased of my soul

John heard the front door open. Two lines remained. Quickly, he skimmed the words:

I will try
For them, I need to try and be

He shut the book and looked up to see her smiling at him.

"Please," she whispered.

The look on her face obliterated his last ounce of willpower. "Close your eyes," he said. She did. "Tell me." He paused, afraid of what he was opening himself up to, but he continued nonetheless. "What do you see? What is the image when you hear . . ." he drew close and whispered, "Robert?"

Her mouth broke into a smile, and her entire face glowed. Her hands caressed her large stomach. Then, with her eyes still closed, she said, "Our little boy, and he's happy. I've wanted him for a long time, and he's special." Tears of joy came to her eyes. "We will love him, and we'll make him happy. We'll do everything to protect him, and we'll watch him smile and grow."

He was a fool if he thought he could still win. She had a way, a beauty about her, and when he saw that his actions and his choices might actually increase her genuine joy, he melted into a passive fighter.

John did not understand Rebecca's father, his ways, or the depth of the sickness that trapped him. Yet it was his profession to support those afflicted with illness. Therefore, it was time for John to offer that same level of respect to this deceased man.

Above everything else, he wanted to please Rebecca. "Robert Sanders," he said. Her eyes opened and her face beamed. "How does that sound?"

"Thank you." Her hands covered her mouth while she released jubilant laughter. "You're wonderful!" She grabbed his arm, offered him a joyous smile, and leaned into him. "Absolutely wonderful."

WINTER 2002

CHAPTER SEVENTEEN

John fired up the Jeep's engine and glanced over at Rebecca. She was beaming.

"Almost makes all of it worth it, doesn't it?" he asked. The house of their dreams lay in front of them—a magnificent mountain home situated against the handsome ponderosa pines. For the last month they had hunted and searched until they wound along the path of Chimera Lane and dipped down into the private drive. The home's secluded location, heavily treed lot, and spectacular mountain view had immediately drawn them in. Inside, the house was spacious, modern, and inviting. John noted the artistic rock fireplace, the den area, and the open floor plan. Rebecca commented on the breakfast nook, the bar, and the secluded laundry area. Both fell in love with the grand deck overlooking the forest outside the master bedroom.

"She really put up a good fight." Rebecca avoided using Anne Downley's name. "There are some days I really feel sorry for her."

John looked again at the house in front of them. In a matter of hours, it would officially be theirs. "But not today?"

She grinned. "Is that bad, John? I can't think about her today; I'm so terribly happy."

He chuckled softly, then shot their future home one last glance before pulling out of the drive. From a neighboring car, their real estate agent, Elle Gray, waved at them.

"I really like Elle," Rebecca said.

"You two really hit it off."

"She's been a tremendous help."

"Yes, she has."

John glanced in his rearview mirror.

"Is Robert already asleep?"

Rebecca turned to confirm. "Yep."

They both grinned. Minutes earlier, their active two-year-old had been running through the empty house, eagerly exploring and offering his own approval of their new abode.

"I'm glad you suggested we look on the mountain."

"I certainly didn't need to twist your arm or anything."

John reached for her hand briefly. "You sure you're fine being here?"

"Of course. I love it here." They had already talked about it. John had shared his concern about Clearcreek being on the other side of the mountain, but Rebecca saw no issue with the location. Clearcreek was a different place from an entirely different era in their lives.

John gave her a quick grin. "Me too. It's beautiful here."

They passed the few shops that made up the unincorporated town of Sky Forest. A sprinkle of snow began to fall. The windshield framed a scene of magical flakes descending down among the majestic pines.

For a few minutes, the two enjoyed the enchanted view.

Then Rebecca said, "I hope, after the sale is final, that Elle still stays in touch with us."

"We can invite her over once we get settled."

Rebecca nodded. "I'd like that." Then suddenly she giggled. "Maybe we could invite Randy over, too."

John shot her a quizzical glance. "At the same time?"

"Sure, why not? She said her divorce has been final for a year, and she's had a difficult time meeting new people."

"I don't think so."

"Why not?"

"She's not his type."

"Sure she is."

John raised his eyebrows up and shook his head.

But Rebecca was firm. "Do you mind if I ask him?"

John chuckled. "Be my guest."

"Thanks." She smiled proudly at herself and stared out at the falling snow.

A few evenings later, John sat in bed, a psychology manual resting on his lap. But rather than reading, John leaned against the headboard and focused on letting his mind unwind from the day. The move was underway, and many aspects of their lives were in the process of change.

When he opened his eyes, his wife stood above him with a furrowed brow.

"What's wrong?" he asked.

"I can't find Robert's pajamas." She shuffled through an open box. "I left some out, but I can't find them."

John leaned forward. "Do you want help?"

"No, I've already put him to bed." She shut the box and looked through another. "It just upsets me. I've tried to have a system, but since yesterday its all become chaos." She shut the second box, and with her foot pushed both boxes into a corner.

John settled back against the headboard. "Let's slow down the move."

"No." Her voice was firm. "I can't. We promised we'd be out of here this week. So at this point, it'd make everything worse."

"Then how can I help?"

Her face held a scowl. "From now on I have to think clearer." She looked around the room and rubbed her eyes, then her head, then her neck. "We'll be in the new place soon."

"Is this move an unwanted chore?"

"Of course it is."

"Is it too much?"

"No." She released a long sigh. "I'm fine."

"With classes starting . . ." he paused to recall how soon they did begin.

"Tomorrow," she said.

"You're sure this isn't too much?"

"I'll be fine."

"It is tomorrow." He confirmed this reality to himself, then glanced at the open book on his lap. After Robert's birth, Rebecca had experienced one scare with her illness. The event had been minor, but it had sent her into a search for balance. The result was an evening class at the local community college. Now, two years later, her education was both a routine and a goal. This January she was transferring to Cal State San Bernardino and doubling her class load.

John was also in the midst of change, his a professional one. Recently he had secured the position of the Assistant Director at Second Chance, a new outpatient treatment center for adolescents and another brainchild of Dr. Linda Blythe. The transition to administration was a new and exciting stretch for John. "A lot of good things are happening right now," he said.

"Yes, they are. Now . . ." She looked around the room. Boxes were everywhere. "If I can find my pajamas. . ."

John glanced at his book and waited, wondering whether he should assist. When she attacked a box, he said, "You sure you don't want help?"

She looked up at him, shook her head, then disappeared out of the room. Ten minutes later she walked back in, this time dressed in flannels.

"Guess what?" Her hands remained behind her back. "During all this packing, I found something. I just spotted it again now." She pulled out the blue baby blanket from long ago.

John stared at the forgotten object that lay cradled in her hand. The memory came back in a violent rush. At Clearcreek, her entire

life had been absorbed in this blanket and the delusion it represented. Swiftly he set the book aside while Rebecca's hands caressed the
fabric.

She pulled down the sheets on her side and climbed into bed,
still clinging to it.

"I was surprised to find it. It feels odd to see it, to hold it again."

"You were a different person then." He wrapped his arm around
her, and she leaned into him, yet the blanket remained between them.

"Why was I such a different person?" Her fingers stroked a worn
section.

John looked down at the object. A large cluster of dust rested in
one of the folds. "It's filthy, Rebecca."

"That's because I found it way back in the closet."

John clutched the fabric. "It really doesn't belong here."

"I know."

He pulled it from between them and tossed it across the room.
"Rebecca." His tone was more intense than intended. "I don't want
this to sound harsh, but some memories can be toxic if you hold on
to them for too long."

"You're right," she said calmly. "I know it's time to get rid of it."

"Yes, it is."

He pulled her close, but she did not succumb to his kiss; instead,
she pulled back slightly. "That person I was—that person scares
me."

"Me, too," he said softly.

"Why was I so different?"

He touched the dark curls that draped against her soft neck.
"Polar contrasts." He paused. "A sort of beast and angel."

"Am I that?" Her face scrunched up in fear.

"Everyone is." His fingers ran along her neck, her shoulders,
her back. That blanket held many memories, most of which John
preferred to forget. Yet the blanket's sudden presence stirred his

memory of the first time he had met Rebecca. She had been a woman who no longer lived in reality, whose entire life had been confined to her crippling delusion.

"My beast is worse than others," she said.

"No, it's not." She smelled fresh and desirable, and John wanted to hold her close so that the other image of her would slip from his memory.

He glanced at her face and saw her eyebrows scrunching in a concerned scowl. He brought his fingers up toward her forehead and touched the wrinkled glare. "We all make choices. And you've made some very good choices over the years."

"Thanks for your patience with me."

His fingers ran down her cheek, and her scowl lessened. "You're so worth it." He pulled her next to him, and she smiled. This was the Rebecca he knew and cherished. He drew her into a kiss, and this time she responded.

Hours later, a noise outside caused John to stir. The clock on the nightstand read 4:20 a.m.

He sat up. Rebecca was not in bed.

He turned, looking for her, and saw her silhouette on their small deck. He released a tired sigh and lay back down. But his mind remained awake.

Five minutes later, he put on a thick robe and joined her outside.

"Aren't you cold?" he asked.

"I woke you," she apologized with a soft smile. She turned toward the trees.

"You okay?"

"It's nice out here."

He wrapped his arms around her, and she leaned into his chest. Together they looked out into the dark night. "It's warm tonight," he said.

"It doesn't feel like winter."

A gentle breeze swept by them, and John's hands glided along Rebecca's arms. "You okay?" he asked again.

"I'm just thinking."

"I didn't hear Robert."

"He's not what woke me."

"Do you want to be alone?"

She turned to face him. "Do I ever scare you?"

"Scare me? What do you mean?"

"I don't want to be a burden to you."

"You're not."

"Ever." She said firmly.

John released a loud yawn, then shook his head. "You're fine."

"I need to know I won't be."

"You know you're not."

"I scare myself."

He closed his eyes and chose his words wisely. "What scares you?"

"That I'll let you down."

"You can't. You know that."

"But—"

"You're amazing," he said. "To me. To Robert. So believe me and stop worrying."

"I still have weaknesses."

"Good. I'm glad we can still claim you as human." He closed his eyes and listened to the soft wind.

"You talked about being part angel, part beast."

His eyes remained closed. "Yes."

"Do you know what it reminded me of?"

"No."

"My father. You quoted him, from his journal. Did you say it intentionally?"

He rubbed his eyes. "Probably not." Against his arms, her body twisted slightly. He opened his eyes to see her looking at him.

"Rebecca, what I said was a compliment to you. Clearcreek was a dark time, the worst you'll ever endure."

"I hope."

"You've come a long way, and what you've done, your hard work to get here, has blessed you and me and Robert. I can't thank you enough. My only wish is that you would believe me. I hope you know I appreciate you," he whispered, "and all that you do for us."

Her arms tightened around him. "This move scares me."

"But you're excited. You want this."

"I do."

"Then be happy about it. Enjoy your father's gift and my new job. Our fresh start, our new home." He paused, and then spoke softly. "I love you. You're magnificent. You truly are. I should tell you that more." His words turned the strain in her face into a smile. "Everything will be fine," he added.

"It will." She loosened her grip and widened her smile. "I love you, John." Then she stepped away, took his hand in hers, and led him inside.

CHAPTER EIGHTEEN

The first night in their new home and boxes were everywhere. The following day, the stress of moving in escalated to the point of overwhelming Rebecca. John tried to do everything he could to calm her, but she appeared urgently committed to restoring order, almost in compulsive, haphazard haste.

Early the next morning, an hour before his alarm would ring, John heard her up. Outside, heavy darkness still covered the sky, yet he arose. A light was on in the den, which was filled with open boxes. Contents were pulled out everywhere, and Rebecca's recent ransack added new height to the clutter. Almost hidden in the middle of the disarray, she sat hunched on the couch.

"What are you looking for?" he mumbled through a yawn.

"I found it," she said.

"Wow," he motioned at the clutter. "What was so urgent?" He rubbed his eyes and approached her. Then, to his horror, he saw the blue blanket clutched in her hands. He reached down, touched it, and chuckled in disgust. "We moved *this* with us?"

"I needed to find it." She tugged it from John's hand.

He watched her closely. "Didn't you decide to get rid of it?"

"No." She tucked it against her chest. "It's part of me."

He removed a box from the couch and sat next to her, all the while chiding himself for not throwing the blanket out ages ago. "Do you want me to get rid of it?"

"It holds memories."

He gripped his hand around it. "Yes, it does . . . for both of us."

"It's part of who I am."

He released the blanket. "It's only an inanimate piece of cloth—that's all. And yet it sends both of us back to a very difficult time."

She stroked the blanket. "It's a necessary reminder."

"Rebecca, it's time. We need to get rid of it." Carefully, he locked his fingers around it and pulled it from her grasp, then dropped it onto the coffee table and reached for her hand. "We don't need it."

She looked up at him, and a tender smile formed. "I'm sorry, and you're right." Her eyes glanced at the blanket, and then she shook her head. "Of course you're right." She clutched her chest and released a very high sigh. "I just need us to get moved in, and then I won't feel overwhelmed."

"The timing for this move was bad."

She glanced over at him. "No, we'll be fine. We just need to get settled. Hopefully, when you get home tonight, you and I can—"

"Aren't you going to class?"

She rolled her eyes. "I should, but how can I?" Rebecca pointed at the mound of boxes. "I have to stay here and get this done. Otherwise, I'll never be able to think clearly."

He touched the collar of her soft, flowery pajamas, then massaged the tension in her neck. "I wish I could ease some of the things you demand of yourself. We've only been here a couple of days. Give us some time."

"I can't seem to concentrate." Yet her breathing slowed in response to his touch.

"As soon as the weekend's here, we'll get moved in. Meanwhile, we both have busy agendas, so let's let it wait."

"We can't."

John surveyed the room. It truly was a disaster. "We can survive a little chaos."

"I want to be done." Her fingers pressed into her temples. "I want to enjoy this place."

"You little perfectionist," he teased. "What if we grow old in this place? Then you'll have years to enjoy it."

She leaned forward, which ended his effort to relax her tense muscles. "I need it livable." Her face looked determined. "And soon."

"Okay, but for today, why don't you and Robert get out of here? Go play somewhere. Explore the area."

"I can't."

"Try."

"I want this done."

She did need routine and stability, which meant she needed to establish order in her new home. After a quick mental check, he said, "Let me verify my appointments, but I should be able to clear up a few things. What if I was back here by two?"

"Really?"

"We'll make progress together. Then you can go to class, and I'll keep moving us in."

She took in a deep breath, and her shoulders dropped. "That would help."

"Good." He touched her face. "Life will return to normal."

He pulled her into a kiss only to hear the scuffle of small feet.

"Hungry," Robert said.

John smiled at their son, dressed in dinosaur pajamas, standing in the doorway. "Looks like an early morning for us all."

"Food," he urged.

Rebecca sighed. "New house. New toddler bed. New freedom."

John stood up. "I'll help him."

Hours later, John was lost in the demands of his new work responsibilities. But during a break, John remembered the blanket. He had left it there on the coffee table. Why had he not taken it? At two in the afternoon he was home, working alongside her to restore order. He shuffled through boxes, unpacked contents, and causally searched for the blanket. But he found nothing.

Once she left for class, he searched harder, but he still could not find a trace of it.

At three in the morning, Rebecca crawled out of bed, and John sensed the item resurfacing.

He waited for several minutes until he felt adequately prepared. Then he arose and joined her in the living room. Sure enough, the vice was twisted around her arms and pulled up against her chest. Her eyes stared at a bare wall.

He sat next to her and touched her leg. "What's up?"

She shook her head but still watched the wall. "Just thinking."

"About?"

"Clearcreek. Rick." She then looked down at the blanket. "This."

John placed his arm around her. The words he repeated to his own patients as they maneuvered through their roads of recovery rang in his ears. *Keep regular sleep patterns. Stay away from drugs. Take your medicine. See your therapists. Check with family members to see how they think you are doing. Be aware of your symptoms.*

That was it. He said the words slowly to her. "Be aware of your symptoms."

"It's powerful." She softened her grip, and the blanket fell to her lap. "Controlling." Her hands slid up her arms. "I'm like a slave, willing to let this be my master." Her long fingernails pressed into her arm.

John cleared his throat and took her hand in his. "Rebecca."

But she pulled her hand away from his, looked back at the wall, and rubbed her arms. "If I look at it, I see that dark hole. I hear him calling, screaming, trapping me." Her eyes remained fixed on the wall, as if viewing tortuous scenes.

"Rebecca," he said again.

But she appeared unable to look away. John's heart raced.

"I'm not free," she said.

He drew in slow breaths, and aimed to sound calm. "At Clearcreek? Right? That's what you mean?"

"Trapped terribly." Her breathing appeared shallow. "Freedom's not an option." Then she clutched the blanket in one hand and supported her head with the other. "This headache—I want it to go away."

John tried to pull the blanket from her hand, but she held on tight.

When he looked at her, she was oblivious to him. "Rebecca." He touched her arm. "Let's go to bed."

Eventually she focused on him and surrendered the blanket to him. Tenderly, he placed it on the far side of the couch, then stood and drew her up to join him. "You need your sleep," he insisted.

Slowly, she nodded. "Maybe sleep will help."

He escorted her to their room, yet his mind remained on that blanket resting on the couch. First thing in the morning he would remove it—definitely.

But hours later, when he returned to retrieve it, it was gone. Rebecca had been asleep next to him the whole time, but it was missing, and after a quick search he found nothing. Unfortunately, time was short. He left for work with a determination to find it that evening.

After his fitful night of worries, work seemed long, and the hours dragged on. When he returned home, his spirits were low.

Then, the moment he walked in the door, everything became worse. Robert held the blue blanket. In horror, John watched his little son drag the article around. John instantly snatched the item away. The swift move startled Robert. He began to cry, and Rebecca ran into the room.

"He had this." John's explained loudly.

"I gave it to him." She reached down to hug her upset son.

"I want my blanket," Robert cried.

"He likes it," she said. "Let him have it."

John rolled it into a ball. "We'll get him a new one."

"But it's special." She smiled. "It'd be nice for Robert to have it."

John's hand tightened around the poison. "No."

"You're being ridiculous." She looked at him and smirked. "Let Robert have it."

John pointed his finger at her. "We will not forget the promises we made for this family." He turned toward Robert, who stared at him with hurt in his eyes. "This is bad for you, Son," John explained.

Rebecca's arms shielded Robert. "What are you talking about?"

"No one will have this blanket." John turned and marched out the front door, slamming it louder than intended. In a sense of fury, he opened the back of his Jeep and threw the blanket inside. When he reentered the home, his wife glared at him.

"Daddy's mad," Robert said.

Rebecca scooped the little boy up. "He must have had a bad day."

"Yeah," Robert whispered. "A big, bad day."

CHAPTER NINETEEN

The rest of the evening, Rebecca remained busy with Robert while John engaged in urgent reading. Both parties made their conversations cautious and quick.

But before they went to bed, Rebecca hugged him. "I'm sorry," she whispered. "You were right." She leaned against his chest. "It was foolish."

"It was."

"It was silly of me." She pulled away to look at him.

He kept his expression guarded, offering only a solemn nod.

"It's because I wrapped him in it last night." Rebecca turned away and pulled down the covers of the bed, then fluffed her pillow and crawled in. She lay on her side and looked across the room at him. "At the time it seemed like a good idea."

"It's wrong, Rebecca." His tone was sharp.

"You're right." She hoisted her body up and leaned against the headboard. "It was a mistake. I helped Robert curl up in the blanket last night. And then today, for his nap, he got attached to it. I thought it was sweet. I saw the blanket differently. It just made sense to me. It was cute."

His neck muscles tightened. He needed to calm down, but he did not want to. The image of her from years ago was at the forefront of his mind, and terror had attached itself to this memory. "Rebecca, what you did was wrong."

"I know." She looked hurt. "I'm sorry. What else can I say?"

"I don't want it in our home."

"It won't be."

"No, it won't."

"I was just explaining what had happened. Good night." She gave him one last look before sliding her head back onto the pillow and closing her eyes.

After a long, quiet moment, John touched her shoulder. "I'm sorry, too. I overreacted." Fear had controlled him.

"We both did," she whispered.

"Are we okay?"

"Of course."

"Okay." He kissed her cheek. "I love you."

She offered him a soft smile. "I love you, too."

Later, in the middle of the night, John lay awake. He could hear Rebecca's light breathing, and he envied her blissful rest. He longed for such peace, but the day's events had trapped his mind in a vicious analytical cycle. In another attempt to induce sleep, he twisted onto his side. His movement stirred Rebecca. She panicked in fits of fast, quiet whimpers.

He reached for her. "You're okay."

"No." Her body shot up. "Please don't touch me." She released a sudden, stark scream. "Don't touch me!"

John grabbed her. "You're okay!"

Her eyes fluttered open. "What?"

"You were dreaming."

She shook her head before falling into his arms. "Am I okay?"

"Yes. You're okay."

She clutched her neck. "My throat hurts."

"Of course it does. With a scream like that, you've most likely frightened everything that moves."

"Was I having a nightmare?" She asked as she leaned into him.

"Do you remember it?"

In the next room, Robert broke into cries; Rebecca flung the covers off and hurried out. Soon Robert's cries subsided, and when

Rebecca returned, Robert was with her. The little boy climbed into bed between his father and mother and then smiled. Within minutes, both he and Rebecca were back asleep.

But John's thoughts were still too active, and sleep continued to be his unobtainable night's dream.

Through the nights that followed, John's thoughts refused to rest, and deep sleep became a rare joy.

One night, around eleven o'clock, he read in bed a recent research article about teenage depression. He was searching for additional understanding and fresh insight into some of his current patients' lives. For one suicidal teenager, hospitalization had been presented as the next logical step. But since their son had not acted on any of his threats, his parents felt that hospitalization was a hasty reaction. John felt divided—eager to supply hope and motivation for the young man while balancing the concerns of a family still struggling with denial. If things did not change, a long, painful road might lie ahead.

John looked over at Rebecca. His wife was fast asleep. The dim reading light slightly illuminated her face. He, too, needed to attempt sleep soon.

But before he could turn off the lamp, Robert's whimpering cries broke the silence. In that same instant, Rebecca's motherly instincts kicked in and she jumped up. Tonight the crying took longer to subside, but when she returned she was alone.

"Next time let me help him." John said.

"He wants me."

"I know." He reached over and turned off the lamp. "But maybe if you gave him a chance, he'd accept me."

"Maybe," she said. She slid her body back into its previous position. "Good night." In a matter of minutes, her breathing flowed softly. John focused on his own breathing. Once he had established a steady rhythm, his mind finally began to unwind. The comforts of sleep seemed to be closing in.

However, Robert's nightmare proved foreboding. Hours later, cuddled in the depths of a REM cycle, John awoke to horrific cries. Next to him, Rebecca was screaming.

In frantic state, John flicked on the light. In dazed awareness, he surveyed the room, then turned back to his wife. She sat upright, still screaming, but her eyes remained closed.

John grabbed her. "What is it?"

She pressed her palms against her eyes. Then her head leaned against John's shoulder. "A man."

"What was he doing?" John asked.

"I don't remember." Her body relaxed against his chest.

"Can you remember anything?"

Her eyes stayed tightly shut while she mumbled, "His face, just his face." Then her breathing resumed its normal progression, and in time John assumed she had fallen asleep. He gently slid her back onto her pillow, yet with her eyes still closed she spoke clearly. "They were Rick's eyes."

"You saw Rick?"

"No." Her eyes opened and she stared at him. "Today at the grocery store, clear on the other side, a man reminded me of Rick."

"How?"

"I don't know." She shut her eyes. "Nothing really. He was heavy, had long hair, a beard, even had boots on, and none of that was Rick. But when I looked at him, I felt afraid—the same way I did around Rick. It must have been his eyes." Her breathing softly cycled. "They were Rick's eyes. They held that same darkness in them."

Minutes later, she was asleep.

Once again, however, John's mind was too alert for peaceful slumber.

In the passing week, the night terrors continued. Each one seemed to build on the fears that Rebecca associated with Downley. Soon these fears not only haunted her sleep but invaded her waking day. In fact, one night while still half-asleep, Rebecca informed John that men were following her—out to get her—and she was in great danger.

For John, visiting Dr. Blythe became urgent. Through a series of tests, Rebecca's health was reevaluated. Then, after the diagnostic procedure was complete, and after Rebecca and Robert went home, Dr. Blythe asked John to join her.

"In the category of poor concentration, she tested high." Dr. Blythe skimmed through the list. "Extreme distraction, irrational decisions, thinking visionary thoughts. When I hear her talk about her schooling, the move, Robert, even you, she hints at anxiety attacks, panic attacks, and paranoia. It's as if the line between her subconscious fears and reality is fading."

At first, John objectively processed the situation. He removed himself from his feelings and listened to the news as though this was another patient that had caught their attention. But when he spoke her name and thought of who she was and how this information impacted his personal life, John felt a need to protest. Certainly Dr. Blythe remembered how they had discussed Rebecca's phenomenal advancements, how her willpower had moved her toward conquering her mental struggles. She was a success story. Dr. Blythe knew this, which made John want to ask if she had made a diagnostic mistake.

Instead, he calmly said, "Then we need to get things under control."

"She wants a new psychiatrist." Dr. Blythe twisted a sapphire bracelet around her wrist. "Apparently, she didn't like Dr. Haden, who was the last one I'd recommended. But he is very good."

John rubbed his head like it had just been hit. He had a confession to make. "I don't know if she's still taking all of her prescriptions."

Concern drifted over Dr. Blythe's eyes. "That's not good."

"I could have prevented this."

"How?"

"Linda, I know better. And you warned me about her attending school." He took a deep breath, hoping to free up the tightness deep in his chest. "But she seemed happy."

"Many things have placed her here. It's a chemical imbalance, a disease. You of all people know this."

He did know. The patient's dopamine, serotonin, epinephrine, and norepinephrine levels were unbalanced; the way in which the brain responded to these neurotransmitters was off. He understood this. He had spent years learning and preaching this. But now his mind struggled to communicate this clear fact to his heart. He ached to respond differently. "I should have seen the warning signs."

"It's out of remission. These things happen. And *you know* blame is self-destructive."

John nodded solemnly. "Then what's next?"

"You know." Her eyes softened, revealing the love she felt toward his family. "You know what to do, John. She's lucky to have you," Dr. Blythe said. "You can support her correctly because you understand. If you go back to Dr. Haden, he'll get the meds sorted out." She offered an encouraging smile. "He'll help. We'll all help."

"Thank you," he said sincerely.

"It's not possible for Rebecca to fall to where she once was."

John nodded again. That was the answer he needed to hear. He would support her, help her, reestablish reality for her—and she would be okay.

Of course she would be okay.

CHAPTER TWENTY

That evening, on his way home, John made a deliberate detour to the back side of the mountain. With each switchback, the memories of his daily routine from years past returned, especially as he drove down the long, private road, past the deserted security gates toward the dark red building nestled among the pines.

He parked in the once-honored spot of Dr. Steven Gravers, and more memories flooded John's mind. From his window he could see the bridge, the small stream, and the grand psychiatric hospital. Clearcreek had been Steven Gravers's masterpiece.

But it had come at too high a cost.

Now Gravers was confined to years of prison and a lifetime of disgrace—and Rebecca was free.

To compare Rebecca's recent symptoms of distress with those of her full-scale illness at Clearcreek was wrong. Outside forces had controlled and limited her then. Variables were different now. She had a strong support group, a life to live for, and a previous courageous victory. This time around, John and Rebecca would quickly and successfully regain control of her health.

With renewed hope, John retrieved the necessary items and approached the grounds. The place seemed smaller than he remembered. From the wild lawn, John read:

CLEARCREEK MENTAL CARE CENTER
An Oasis for the Mentally Ill

The marble sign etched like a tombstone showed little evidence of age or decay. John glanced up at the tall building. Vacant for years, it now looked like a haunted estate.

John exhaled a heavy breath. He climbed the cobblestone steps and felt the demons of the past, as well as the memory of his former innocence, swirling around him. Then there were other flashbacks of his younger life, when he had been hopeful and eager to make a difference. But when he had left this building on that final day, he had lost that innocence. He had never come back until today.

Now, in a full circle, John returned to rediscover what he had lost. He came seeking a renewal of hope, a restored confidence in Rebecca, and a reassurance in his abilities.

At the top of the steps, near the golden door handles, he found his safe spot. He looked out over the grounds, drew in a courageous breath, then lit a match and held it close to the blue blanket's soft fibers. First, the yellow flames danced around. They leaped and laughed, only to leave a small black mark, a silly mock at his attempt.

But patience prevailed, and eventually heat took over. The blanket, which he had since hid in a dark, safe corner of his office, now accepted the flames and slowly disintegrated.

In a state of tranquility, John took a step back and watched.

It was a cleansing act, one in which the purifying smoke served as a balm for recent events. In exchange for the blanket's existence, reflections from the past weeks no longer carried such weight.

As he watched the final pieces whither in the heat, he felt peace. The past was gone. The move was almost complete, the school routine was underway, Dr. Blythe's counseling sessions were back, and Dr. Haden was sorting out the meds. Things would improve.

Rebecca only needed reminders that she was a fighter. She would survive this bump. She would pull out of this and be healthy once again.

Only a few scraps of flaming cloth remained. He watched the fire consume them, then used a gallon of water to extinguish the flames. Afterward, he kicked at the ashes, ensuring that the burning had ceased.

Following the ritual's completion, John took a final look at the place, but nothing was there—only a building heavy with age.

John climbed into the Jeep, and with the burden lifted, he fired up the ignition and drove away.

CHAPTER TWENTY-ONE

A few nights later, Rebecca gleefully prepared for the evening's events.

"Randy's here!" she called out.

John wanted to support his wife, but he did not have the same enthusiasm for what lay ahead. Nevertheless, he headed toward the door just as the knock sounded.

"Hey, hey," Randy said.

"You ready for your blind date?" John teased.

"Certainly."

Rebecca gave Randy a hug. "John told me that you weren't happy with my meddling."

"Johnny told you that?" Randy grinned. "No, it was sweet."

"Have a seat." John pointed to the couch.

"Not until I have the grand tour of the Sanders' cabin."

"It's not really a cabin," Rebecca said.

Randy raised his eyebrows at her. "Excuse me," he said in a teasing tone, "anything positioned in the mountains is a cabin. Look, it's got some wood and it's homey . . . and it looks nice."

"Why don't you come see the best part?" John led Randy straight to the entertainment area. Randy was full of praise—and quick to plan future sport-watching events.

"Elle," Rebecca said from the den doorway, "just drove up." She shot Randy a quick wink. "You nervous?"

"Who, me?" He laughed. "Never. Hadn't even crossed my mind. Just don't be disappointed, though, if Cupid's arrow accidentally misses me tonight."

"Yes." John stepped toward Rebecca. "I told her Elle's most likely not your type."

Randy appeared concerned. "She's not?"

"Seeing how she has a brain and all." John grinned.

Randy gagged on a sarcastic laugh, but a knock at the door brought him straight to a hanging mirror. He rustled his thinning hair, checked his teeth, and smelled his breath.

"You ready?" John asked.

Randy chuckled. "Don't I look ready?" However, he kept clearing his throat as he followed John to the door.

"Come in. Good to see you again, Elle." John ushered her in. "This is Randy."

Elle wore tight jeans, a tailored blouse, and a scent of sweet perfume. With a nervous smile, she held out her hand. "Nice to meet you, R—" but before she could finish, Randy brought her hand up for a kiss.

"Truly a blind date," he said, speaking deep and low, "for I have been blinded by your beauty."

She pulled back her hand and ran her fingers through her thick dark hair. Then she released a nervous laugh. "Nice to meet you."

"You're pathetic," John whispered to Randy.

Randy shut the front door and laughed softly at himself.

"Come in, Elle." John led her toward the kitchen. "I think the food's almost ready."

"Wow," Elle said to Rebecca. "You've made the place extraordinary. I love the cabinets."

"All I did was replace the handles."

Elle's fingers ran down a cupboard's handle. "They're beautiful."

"I wish I could've done more," Rebecca said.

"But she started school while getting us all moved in." John reached for Rebecca's hand and squeezed it softly. "She's done a lot."

"Mostly moved in," Rebecca sighed. "There are still a few boxes."

"There always are," Elle smiled, and the two women continued to chat about the house, the details of settling down after a move, and Robert being off at a babysitter's tonight.

Finally, Randy cleared his throat. "So when do I get my tour?"

"Oh." Rebecca looked slightly surprised, as if chatting with Elle had made her lose focus on her evening plan. "Elle can give it to you. She's a great saleswoman."

"Thanks, but the place spoke without me." Elle started down the hall. "Still, I'd love to see what you've done."

Close behind her, Randy followed. "Go ahead—wow me, Elle."

Meanwhile, in the kitchen, Rebecca grabbed John's arm and whispered in his ear, "Is Randy nervous?"

John shrugged his shoulders.

Elle's laughter rang through the house, and Rebecca breathed a sigh of relief. "I want this to go well."

After some time, Randy reappeared. "I love this place. In fact, after this, my apartment will feel like a lonely suite at Motel Six."

Elle's loud laugh filled the kitchen. Nervous energy seemed abundant.

With a silly grin on his face, Randy patted John on the shoulder. "If you need a house-sitter, you know who to call."

"Let's eat," Rebecca announced, shooting John an anxious glance.

He reached for her hand, then lightly squeezed it again before whispering in her ear, "Some things are out of our control." Then he directed the group toward the dining room table.

With the meal underway, Elle kept the conversation moving along. "Have you explored around here yet? Yesterday, Jade and I went on that nature walk right off Hwy 18. It's an excellent spot. You should take Robert there."

"Jade?" Randy asked. "Is that your daughter?"

Elle set down her fork. "Want to see a picture?" She stood up, located her coat, fished through the pocket to retrieve her key chain, and returned with a picture of Jade. In the photo, the girl's blond hair was pulled up into pigtails. She wore a light blue dress and clutched a stuffed frog against her chest.

"Robert and I have played with her," Rebecca said. "She's very cute."

"What a surprise." Randy pointed at the picture. "We're a match—there's a twin picture of me with that exact same pose in last year's yearbook."

"Really?" Elle gave him a puzzled look. "She was three in this picture . . . and she's five now."

"No, honest." He returned the key chain. "Faculty pages. Same setup."

"You were holding a frog?" She gave him a bewildered look.

"Yep." He grinned. "Only mine was the real deal."

"Really?"

"Freshly smelling of alcohol and ready to go under the knife."

Since Elle's smile seemed slightly distressed, Rebecca jumped up from her chair, "Did everyone get potatoes?" She pushed the dish at Randy. "Let me get you some sour cream. Because we have sour cream." She looked at John. "And could you check on the dessert?"

Due to the non-subtle request, John stood up and followed her to the fridge. There, away from their guests, she flashed him a concerned glance. "Did you see her look?" Rebecca whispered. "She thinks he's odd."

He placed his hands on her tense shoulders and massaged the muscles. "Relax. He is odd—and nervous."

"Well, he's making *me* nervous."

"Well, he's nervous enough for all of us—so that means you can relax."

"I just didn't expect him to—"

"She's different for him. She's not like what he's used to."

"Well, I feel responsible."

"Elle's okay. Relax."

When John and Rebecca returned, Randy roared in laughter.

"You okay?" Rebecca asked.

He wiped his eyes. "Elle's been holding out on us. She's got hilarious stories."

"No," Elle said. "It's not that funny."

Randy continued to laugh, "I think it is." But Elle looked embarrassed.

John heaped sour cream on his potato while Rebecca stared at Randy.

"Can I tell them?" Randy asked Elle.

She shrugged. "It's not that funny, but go ahead."

Randy cleared his throat. "This is good. Last week, late in the evening, Elle remembers she has something to do at her office. And it's deathly urgent."

"It wasn't urgent," Elle said. "I was just stupid and thought it was urgent. I thought I had listed a house for the wrong price."

"Even though it's past ten," Randy continued, "she dutifully desires to be the star realtor that she is. So she returns to her office with great determination to correct this error before it mounts into further disaster. Jade has been sound asleep, but she wakes up to follow her mother because no matter what, this late-night correction will be made. On the way there, Elle stops to get gas. And to make the trip pleasant for young Jade, she buys ice cream. Soft-serve, right?"

"Yes." Elle smiled.

Randy nodded his head in approval. "What I love about soft-serve is that you can build masterpieces as high as you can hold it. If you're a real architect you can get two servings in one—though you've got to be careful, because it takes position and skill." He cleared his throat. "Okay, so back to Elle and Jade. They have their soft-serve and are making their way to Realtor World. But when they get there, Elle discovers . . ." Randy paused, taking a moment to look at each listener. "That the door is not completely shut." He whistled an eerie song before continuing. "So she's worried. Now, being braver than I would have been, she proceeds into the dark office and holds tight to her daughter's hand—and, of course, the soft-serve in the other. But then what does she see?" Randy froze, his eyebrows lifted. "The filing cabinet door is wide open." He whistled another eerie tune. "Then she turns to hear the humming of . . ." He paused, making sure everyone's eyes were on him then said, "the humming of . . . the copy machine." He quickly released a sinister laugh. "She's terrified and hustles Jade out the door, yet when she departs, she forgets that when turning on the lights, she'd set down . . ." He exaggerated a dramatic pause. "The soft-serve." Elle offered him an amused smile. "Poor, beautiful woman is spooked, not to mention without her chocolate swirl." He winked at Elle, "It was chocolate swirl, wasn't it?"

"Yes."

Randy released a magnified sigh of relief. "Good." Then he cleared his throat and continued, "She jumps back into her car, grabs her cell phone, and calls the police. Now, with the car door locked, Elle and Jade wait. And watch. Wait. And watch. Meanwhile, mind you, Jade is contently licking her soft-serve—but no, not Elle. Hers is abandoned in the office, slowly melting away."

"Wait," Elle interrupted. "Just to lessen some embarrassment, you have to know that I'm meticulous. Especially when it comes to the office. I want clients to know they can depend on me. A customer called to make an urgent change to his listed price, so when he gave me the new price, I thought I'd already made a mistake listing it for thousands less. I know it's stupid, but the ads were coming out in the next day's paper. Since I thought I'd made a mistake, instead of waiting until the morning, I had to fix it then. Silly of me, I know."

Randy looked at her and politely asked, "May I proceed with your trauma?"

"And," Elle said, raising her hand to continue, "usually I keep everything in order, especially when I leave. I shut off the copier, I always close and lock the filing cabinets, and I definitely shut and lock the office door. So it all seemed strange, and I was just taking precautions."

Rebecca nodded her head. "It sounds scary to me."

"Now," Randy cleared his throat, "back to Elle and Jade's Night of Terrors." He released another sinister laugh. "The cops finally arrive. One, of course, had a doughnut in hand. The other had a cup of coffee."

"Really?" Rebecca laughed.

Elle shook her head and rolled her eyes.

"Slowly they cover the building and then proceed in. Then Elle, who's braver than any woman I've met, can't stay put. She hovers near the entrance, and as soon as it's clear, she's back in the building—just in time to see the doughnut cop stick his finger right into Elle's soft-serve."

"What?" John asked.

Randy demonstrated by using his index finger to poke at an imaginary ice cream cone. "Squish," he said.

"Why'd he do that?" John asked.

Elle released her trademark laugh. "Because I'd been gone long enough that some had melted—at least enough that the puddle beneath the cone looked exactly like those plastic play foods. At home we have a play kitchen where Jade has a plastic ice cream cone that looks identical to what mine looked like—the puddle and all. The officer thought it was a plastic toy. He stuck his finger in it to see if it was real."

"He just wanted to eat it," Randy said.

"The cop thought someone had broken in," Elle said, "and left their cone."

"This guy was brilliant," Randy laughed. "For sure, if I ever break into a building—first of all, why would anyone want to break into a realtor building?—but anyway, if I ever did, I'd make sure I had a chocolate swirl soft-serve to leave for evidence."

"So what did they find?" Rebecca asked.

"Nothing." Elle's smile revealed her chagrin. "They looked for a little while, but such emphasis was placed on the ice cream . . . I was embarrassed. The cop was embarrassed. We just wanted to be done with each other. Anyway, it was nothing, a false alarm. I must have left too quickly to pick up Jade that afternoon. It was silly of me, especially to turn it into something more. Anyway, it was late, and I guess I spooked myself."

"So what happened?" Rebecca asked. "With the ad in the newspaper, I mean?"

Elle laughed again. "Of course, with all that hype I forgot to check. Can you believe it? And, of course, after I drove away, I remembered." Another laugh. "But I wasn't going back then. Lucky for me, it was a different house; the numbers did match up. Everything worked out fine."

"And your office was fine." Rebecca restated.

"It was a relief," Elle sighed. "The cop said my type of lock tends to have problems. I'd never had any trouble until that night, but he recommended I replace it."

Randy raised his hands up and examined them. "See these hands." He brought them closer to Elle's face. "These hands can perform magic. Give them a new doorknob and a screwdriver, and you would be amazed."

Elle smiled. "I'll keep that in mind."

Then Randy gasped. "Look at me. All you eating while I'm busy retelling soft-serve splats. I'd better clean up my plate." Quietly the group watched and waited as Randy shoveled in bites. In between chews, Randy asked, "So how long have you been divorced?"

"A year and a half," Elle said. "Two this summer."

"Are you friends?" Randy shoved in a large piece of meat.

Elle nodded. "Because of Jade. Otherwise, it'd still be ugly."

Rebecca stared at her and slowly nodded. "I was married before John."

"Oh." Elle's eyes opened wide. "I didn't know that."

"Long story." Rebecca looked down at her plate. "But I understand. Things can get bad."

Underneath the table, John's placed his hand on Rebecca's thigh. He felt her leg jitter nervously. The statement had been hard to share, especially since she rarely disclosed the past. And now Elle was staring at her. But Rebecca appeared preoccupied—busy smashing cooked carrots into her plate. Meanwhile, Randy looked back and forth, knowing more than he should. The moment felt stiff.

Finally, Rebecca stood up. "Are we ready for dessert?"

Once chocolate cheesecake was near, the previous conversations was forgotten. For another hour, the group talked and laughed. Finally, Elle stood. "I better get going."

"Is Jade also at a babysitter?" Rebecca asked.

"No, it's Keith's weekend. But I've got homes to show in the morning."

"Oh." Randy stood. "Let me walk you out."

Rebecca and John also stood and joined them at the door, where a round of thanks was exchanged. Then, right as Randy reached for the knob, Rebecca said, "Wait, Elle, before I forget." She walked into the kitchen and pulled some mail from above the microwave. "Strangest thing. Since we moved here, two of these have been in our box. Here." She handed over the letters, which were addressed to "Elle Gray or Current Resident."

"How odd," Elle said. "Your P.O. is 222?"

Rebecca nodded.

"Remember me saying I lived near here?" Elle laughed. "It's been over a year, but how funny. Sky Forest is such a small Post Office, but it's still crazy you'd get my old box."

"Actually, I requested it. How can you forget 222?"

"Oh, Rebecca," Elle laughed. "We're so alike. I scoped out the numbers too. I had, like, six choices, but when I heard 222, I thought the same thing."

Randy batted his eyes playfully and clapped his hands. "Oh, girls. This is too fun. Let's do tea sometime and discuss how to get the zip code changed to 4-5-6-7-8."

Rebecca scowled at Randy, but Elle released her signature laugh. Then Elle glanced at the mail. "Please, don't pass it on. At this point, it could only be junk."

"You sure?"

"Well . . ." Elle shrugged. "I guess you're right. If it looks important you can pass it on, but otherwise just toss it."

"But I'd be happy to give it to you," Rebecca said. "It'd give me an excuse to say hello."

"You need no excuse," Elle chided. "In fact, let's do this again."

"I agree." Randy smiled, but then stifled a small yawn. "Maybe I'll head out as well. But thanks for dinner, you two."

After exchanging good-byes, followed by the shutting of the Sanders' door, Rebecca's face held a slight pout. "I wanted Randy to come back and tell us what he thought."

"Believe me, if he likes her, he'll tell us," John shrugged his shoulders. "It seemed like they had fun."

"I hope so." Rebecca released a chuckle. "Should we peek through the window and watch?"

"You're pathetic." He went into the kitchen and picked at the leftover cheesecake. "Let's hope they don't linger too long. I need to go retrieve our son."

She joined him and forked another small piece of cheesecake. After two bites, she suddenly set her fork down. "John, I need to ask you something." Her face was somber.

He also set his fork down. "Sure."

"I need you to promise me something."

"What?"

"Don't tell Elle about my past, okay?"

John nodded. "If that's what you want."

"I really like her, and I don't want her to treat me differently." She glanced at the shaded window. "And she might if she knows."

He reached for her hand. "She may, or she may not—but it's your story to tell."

"Really, she doesn't need to know," Rebecca said, almost to herself. "She doesn't need to know about my family, my youth, Rick, Clearcreek, any of it." Then she looked directly at John. "Okay?"

John nodded again. "I understand."

"Promise?" She pushed.

"Yes, I promise."

CHAPTER TWENTY-TWO

Progress had been made with the suicidal teenager—great progress, in fact. The client's parents had turned proactive. They listened and learned, and the situation now moved down a promising path.

As his Jeep descended down the drive, John felt grateful for his good fortunes. He truly had so much. He approached his new home and thought of his lovely wife and his precious son, and joy embraced him.

Robert was already waiting for him at the door. John gave his son a big hug, then tossed him in the air. But rather than making his traditional request for more, Robert only smiled cautiously. John set him down and asked, "Where's Mommy?"

Robert said nothing, only latched his hand around John's finger and pulled him toward the master bedroom. Something was not right. Once John saw Rebecca, he understood Robert's mood.

Rebecca was rolled up into a ball on the bed, sobbing, with piles of used tissue scattered across their purple silk comforter.

John lifted Robert into his arms and quickly sat near Rebecca. "What's wrong? What's going on?"

"No." Through the sobs, she spoke sternly. "I don't want him to see me like this."

John looked at his son's face and saw the concern. He set Robert down, but the boy did not move. He watched his parents intently.

"Can you go play?" John asked. "While Daddy and Mommy talk?"

"Go feed him." Her fingers pressed against her eyes. "He hasn't eaten. There's hot dogs and ketchup, and there's soup for you."

John pulled her fingers away. "What can I bring you?"

"Nothing."

"I need to know you're okay."

"Go feed him."

John reached for Robert's hand, but the child appeared preoccupied with his mother. However, after some nudging, Robert finally allowed John to lead him into the kitchen.

Robert waited in his high chair while John prepared the hot dog and soup. A quiet meal followed.

Finally, John asked, "What happened to Mommy?"

Robert's big brown eyes stared down the hallway. When he looked back at John, his face was tense, and his eyes appeared ready to cry.

"Hey, hey, big guy. It's okay. You're okay. She's okay, too."

Robert looked down at the last hot dog piece. His round fingers pushed it across the tray.

"Pop it in there," John said while Robert fumbled it around in the ketchup. "Do you have milk left?" He shook the toddler cup. "Why don't you drink it in front of your movie?"

After wiping the small hands and face, John released the boy from his high chair. Then Robert pulled John by his fingers to the video library.

"I want Simba," he said.

John chuckled. "Bet I could have guessed that."

With the video underway and Robert snuggled under a blanket and appearing sufficiently engaged, John went back to Rebecca's side.

"What is it?" he asked her.

Tears clouded her eyes. "I can't tell you."

"You know you can talk to me."

Pain covered her face. "I'm scared to tell you."

John joined her on the bed, and she fell into his arms. He stroked her back and waited for a response.

Finally, she spoke in a choppy voice. "Robert and I, we went out on the deck for a moment today. It was cold and foggy. But when I looked out, when I looked through the trees, I saw it." Her small body tightened. "It was a bright flash of light. Out of nowhere."

"In the sky?"

"No. Through the trees."

"Probably the sun reflecting off something."

She pressed her lips together, then shook her head while her fingers squeezed his arm. "After the flash, I thought I saw a man. He was far away, but he looked at me—for a long time. Then pointed at me, and I thought I heard him speak. Then he left."

"What did he say?"

"I couldn't have heard him," she stated. "He was too far away." She buried her head into his chest and resumed crying.

Patiently, John combed his fingers through her hair and waited.

Finally, she looked up at him. "What are you thinking?"

"What are *you* thinking?" he asked.

"I don't want to say."

"You're sure you saw someone?"

"I don't know."

"You could have, Rebecca." He tried to sound safe. "The area's pretty secluded . . . but maybe. We don't know—maybe there's even a trail around here."

Her body relaxed slightly. "You think someone would be on it . . . on the trail?"

"What do you think?"

"I know what you're trying to say." She looked up at him, and fear drifted back over her face. "No one would be out here—nothing was there, but I thought there was. That scares me. And it scares you, too."

John took in a deep breath. "I didn't say that."

"But you know you're thinking it."

"Rebecca, I'll think it's whatever you tell me it is."

"I looked at him for a long time. I thought it was real, that he was real."

"Then maybe he was."

"But he was gone. Nothing was there. No car, no man, nothing. It doesn't make sense."

"I don't know, Rebecca."

"There's something else."

His fingers rubbed the tenseness in her neck. "Yes?"

"But I've been scared to tell you."

He found the pressure points that carried her strain and massaged them.

"I'm still being followed."

"Where?" His words remained guarded.

"At stores. While Robert and I do errands. Just around town."

He pulled in a deep breath and let the exhale release all the pressure he felt. Then, almost too calmly, he said. "Is it a certain person?"

"I don't know. I couldn't see anything. It's just that feeling." She heaved out a long sigh and then wiped her eyes. "It's not important. I shouldn't have said anything."

"No, it is important." The collection of discarded tissue scattered across their bed proved that.

"You know what it means," she said solemnly, "and so do I." For a moment, the music from Robert's video rang through the house. Notes of joy contrasted against the perilous stress in Rebecca's eyes. "Dr. Blythe wants to see me more. Did she tell you that?"

"Yes."

"Should I?" Rebecca rubbed her head. "What should I do?"

"You should see her."

"I don't know."

John waited, listening to more of the movie that echoed through their home.

Finally, when she spoke, her words were stable, emotionless. "Two years ago, I decreased some of my medication."

John shook his head. This confirmed his fear. He wanted to say more, wanted to reprimand her, but he refrained.

"And lately . . ." She looked at him with cautious eyes. "Because of her schedule, and the holidays, the move, your job, and getting ready for school, I pushed Dr. Blythe's appointments back. Prior to this last visit, it's been almost six months since I've seen her."

"That's unfortunate," John said carefully.

"But now," Rebecca shook her head. "Seeing her doesn't help. Not like it used to."

"Give it time."

"She used to agree with me and say I was fine." She exhaled a tried sigh. "But she doesn't trust me now."

"She does." John chose his words wisely. "But she's concerned."

"I know."

"Look at the stressors," he said calmly. "Changes agitate your health." He touched her hair. "Look at what you've been up against: first this move, then taking two classes. Schooling is your act of independence; it's the boldest thing you've ever done."

"No. That evening five years ago—when I came to your apartment—that was the boldest thing I've ever done." She grinned, and John grinned back.

He brushed a strand of hair away from her face. "True. But you're at a new campus, and it's bigger than Valley. You don't know anyone. These are larger classes, and you're surrounded by younger people who appear more confident and more familiar with the place." He felt her body relax. "Rebecca, what's happening isn't a surprise. We should've seen this coming. Of course you'd have a slight setback; your mind's trying to adapt, but in a maladaptive way. It's a warning—so let's listen."

For the first time that evening, he heard hope in her voice. "You're not worried?" She watched him closely.

"You'll be fine—if we heed the warnings."

"I don't want to see Dr. Haden again."

"I know," John said. "Dr. Blythe told me."

"I don't like him."

"Dr. Blythe says he knows his medicine."

"I'd say so. He likes them all so much that he thinks I should take them all."

"He will be able to help us through this bump."

She rubbed her eyes, took in a deep breath, and then looked at the tissues scattered on the bed.

"You know that you don't have to take two classes this term," he said.

"I know." She picked up a few wads of tissues.

"It was a bold step, but your health is more important than—"

"No." She pulled away from him and continued to pick up the physical remains of her emotions. "I want to do this, and I can. I know I can."

"And you will."

"Okay." She looked down at the large collection of tissues in her hands. "I know I'll be okay."

"Yes. I know you will, too."

"Thanks." She gave him a quick kiss, picked up the last tissue, and proceeded to the trash.

CHAPTER TWENTY-THREE

For the first time since the clinic's opening, John had finally achieved a definite administrative success. Today he had facilitated a professional development session for his staff on how to effectively engage adolescents considered at risk of suicide or prone to serious self-harm. Driving home, John reviewed the session, the guest speaker, the follow-up discussions, and his staff's feedback. Their comments had been genuinely positive. Some had shared extraordinary success stories, which opened up additional discussions. During the conversations, John reflected on how small differences truly could change an individual's life.

By the time he turned onto Chimera Lane his thoughts turned to Rebecca. He reviewed the past manifestations of her illness, her current symptoms, and her responses to different types of treatments through the years. The most important thing John knew was that she was a fighter, and he believed in her.

When he walked in the door, he saw her sitting in the front room rocking their son.

"How was your day?" she asked.

"One of my best yet." He approached her and gave her a kiss. "The staff really enjoyed the training."

She smiled at him. "Good."

"How are you?"

"Robert's tired. We didn't get a nap today."

John patted Robert's head, but the boy turned away.

"Mom's been busy with schoolwork," Rebecca admitted. "And cleaning, and getting dinner ready."

"Rough day, huh?"

"Only because of a project. It threw us off our routine." She arose from the chair and gave him a quick hug. "I didn't get to run any of our errands, didn't even make it to the post office. Huh, Robbie?"

"Hey, Son. Why don't you come to Daddy?" He reached for Robert, but the little boy kept clinging to Rebecca's neck.

"I think he's felt neglected." She carried Robert into the kitchen, opened up the fridge, and pulled out some lunch meat. "Are sandwiches okay?"

John followed, pulling bread out of the cupboard. "Sure."

She grinned. "Okay, so I'm caught in my lie. I haven't started dinner yet. But I did think about it."

From the fridge, he removed lettuce, tomatoes, and a jar of pickles. "Sandwiches are fine. Is it a big project for school?"

"I want an A in both classes—so yes, it's important to me."

He placed the vegetables on the counter. "Anything I can do to help?"

"No, I'm fine." She placed Robert in his high chair.

"What about Robbie? What can I do to help with him?"

Rebecca walked away from the high chair, and Robert started to cry. He flung out his arms to be held. John set down the cutting board and went to pick up their son, which caused the screaming to intensify.

"He doesn't want you," Rebecca said.

John pulled the boy out of his chair. "You're sure grumpy, Son."

Once Rebecca stepped close, the crying subsided. "Do you want to eat, Robbie?" He shook his head.

"What do you want?" John asked, only to watch Robert shake his head and rub his eyes. "Do you want sleep?"

"John, he should eat first."

"Will he?"

Rebecca tore off a piece of bread and brought it to the boy's lips, but Robert pushed her hand away, rubbed his eyes again, and this time nestled into John's shoulder.

"Sleep wins."

"You should feed him first."

"He's not going to eat." John waited as Rebecca attempted to offer Robert more bread, but once again she received the same response. "I'll go put him down," he said, and against Rebecca's protest, John headed down the hall.

Inside Robert's room, John was greeted by a trampling of magazine pages and clippings. Pages and scraps were strewn across the room like confetti. Little scissors hid among haphazard clippings. John sat at the edge of the bed and watched Robert fight sleep and eventually give in. He kissed his son softly on the forehead. Then John stood up and took another scan of the glossy pages scattered across the room. When he returned to the table, Rebecca was finishing her meal.

"What's with those magazines?" he asked. "There are pieces everywhere."

"Oh, it's Robert. He's finally old enough for those little scissors."

"Did you want him shredding all that? The room's a disaster."

"I gave it to him." She smiled. "And it kept him busy for most the day."

"It's a paper explosion in there."

She grinned. "So he didn't learn to cut. But he caught on to tearing the pages."

"I'd say." John sat and examined his food options.

"I should have cleaned it up—but there's always tomorrow, right?"

"Sure." He pulled out two slices of bread and began building his sandwich.

"So Kim suggested a collage for our project."

"Who's Kim?"

"That woman I've been telling you about."

"At school?"

"Yes, remember?" Her voice held a slightly agitated tone. "She's super easy to talk to, and she makes school a lot of fun." John quickly nodded, although he was unsure if he truly did remember. "Which means," Rebecca said in a teasing tone, "you'd be proud of my social progress, Dr. Sanders."

"Good." He bit into his meal.

"She's a little older than me—which is nice, especially since most of the students are ten years younger. Plus, she's in both of my classes. She's going full-time and works full-time. She doesn't have any children, but she says she wishes she did. She would be a great mom. She's amazing. I wish I was as smart as her. She keeps asking what my major is."

"Do you know yet?"

"It seems too confident to declare a major. Like I'm actually seeking a degree."

"Well, are you?" He took another bite. A tomato slice fell from his sandwich.

"You don't want me to, do you?" Her question came out sharp. A hint of anger hung in her tone.

"No. That's not it." He heard his own defensiveness. Rather than look at her, he pulled a fork from the pickle jar and began stabbing at the fallen tomato. "I want you to be happy, Rebecca."

"Well, I am."

"Good." He gave her a quick smile.

"Then what's the issue, John?"

"I didn't say there was an issue." He was being attacked and he wasn't prepared for this.

"I can tell you have an issue with something with school. What is it?"

Her eyes would not leave him.

"Well . . . I just wonder if, lately . . ." he pierced the tomato with his fork and looked at it, "if certain things have been extra difficult on you." He popped the tomato into his mouth.

"Of course not."

"On Robert?"

"No."

"On us?" he asked.

"Do you think so?" She gave him an angry look.

John decided not to speak.

"Look, John. Two assignments had to get done. Today was a busy day. That's all. Robert's fine. Usually he gets his nap, and I don't always give him the chance to destroy his room. He's fine."

"That's not the issue."

"Then what is it?"

"Nothing." John pulled out two slices of bread and began building another sandwich.

"What?"

"Maybe next semester we should go back to one class."

"Why?"

He piled the turkey meat on. "It's just a suggestion."

"Then I'll never get done."

He focused on smearing mayonnaise and mustard onto a slice of bread. "So you're doing this for a degree."

"Of course I am. Seems rather pointless not to … don't you agree?"

He remained busy spreading out the mayonnaise and weighing out his options. He could turn school into an issue, or he could share the real problem. "Rebecca, you know I support you. I'm proud of you with your schooling, but lately, how are you feeling?"

"Fine. Don't I seem fine?"

John added salt and pepper. "This week you have." He bit into his meal.

"Is it too much for you to be with Robbie?" Her voice hardened. "For two evenings a week?"

"No," John muttered between mouthfuls. "Of course not. I enjoy that time."

"Then what's wrong?"

He chewed through his bite, then took another. And another.

"What is it, John?"

He used a napkin to wipe his mouth, only to see her still waiting for a reply. "I'm concerned about the stressors. And I don't want you to get sick again." He shoved the last large bite into his mouth.

"That's what I thought." She gathered up her plate. "But I know I'm fine." Without looking at him, she left the table and placed her dish in the dishwasher. Then she returned to pick up the bread bag.

"Hey, what if I want another sandwich?" he asked.

She gave him a skeptical look. "Three sandwiches?"

"Maybe."

She tossed the bread back on the table and picked up the bottles of mayonnaise and mustard.

"Whoa. I might want those, too."

"Fine." She set them down and left the room.

CHAPTER TWENTY-FOUR

Late the following Monday evening, John retreated to the back deck. The new workweek had begun with an emotional verbal conflict between one of the clinic's therapists and a client's mother. John had quickly been pulled in to mitigate the tender situation. The mother was in tears; the therapist was fuming. Neither would recant their strong words. John had pacified the situation by assigning the client to a new therapist. Nevertheless, the outburst had cast a heavy cloud over the clinic.

Plus, there were increasing financial concerns. Although the clientele list was expanding, the clinic's expenses appeared to be growing almost twice as fast. John felt trapped between projected commitments and budget constraints, and for the first time he felt sympathy toward Dr. Gravers. The fraudulent conduct had been inexcusable, but now John understood why Gravers had compromised his ethics.

Dusk softened John's thoughts. He remained outside, silently enjoying the soft breeze, until he heard the sliding glass door and felt Rebecca's hand against his back.

"Is Robert asleep?" he asked.

"Yes."

He wrapped his arms around her, and they both listened to the serene night.

"It's beautiful here," she said.

"It is."

"I'm glad we made the move."

"Me, too."

In silence, they both looked out into the vast woods and watched the bright moon cast alluring shadows through the pines.

Finally, Rebecca spoke. "Do you want to hear something strange?"

His arms tightened around her. He took in the soothing scent of her hair. "Sure."

"Today I was at the corner of Pine & Chimera Lane. You know where the stop sign is?"

For a brief moment, he closed his eyes and felt the tender breeze glide through the air. "Yeah."

"A man was begging there."

"Oh."

"Don't you think that's odd?"

He glanced down at her. "Yeah, I suppose so."

"I mean, if he was near the Village, it would make sense, maybe. But I don't know. Even that's not a place where it seems like a beggar would be. At the bottom of the hill—right when you exit the freeway, at Watermen—I've seen homeless people begging there. In fact, once, on my way home from school in San Bernardino, I was at a gas station, and a guy who'd lost an eye was asking for money." Her words stumbled out as her body stiffened. Then she paused and spoke in a composed tone, "But today, it just seemed odd. I mean, there are only houses around here."

"Did you stop?"

"No."

Her effort to appear casual only intensified the oddness of her story. "How'd you know he was begging?"

"He had a cardboard sign that said, 'Look at me.'"

"'Look at me'?"

"I know. I told you it was strange."

John turned Rebecca around to look into her eyes. "Maybe he was there to make a statement?"

"He was a big man with really long, dark, dirty hair."

He searched her face. "What else do you remember?"

"I don't know." She left his arms and leaned against the deck to look up at the moon. "There was a little bit of fog," she said. "Not lots, but a little. It was hard to see."

"But you saw his sign?"

"Well, he yelled at me. I think." She avoided John's eyes. "That's how I saw him." Her tone was strained. "He pointed at the sign and then smiled at me. I think he even had a gold tooth." She released a nervous laugh. "Maybe I'm making that part up; he just seemed like the kind of person who would have a gold tooth, you know?"

John stepped closer. "You okay?"

She glanced at him. "Of course."

"When do you see Dr. Blythe again?"

"I don't remember. Why?"

"Is it this week?"

"I think it's in two weeks. It's written down."

"Could you reschedule? Could you move it up?"

She shook her head. "I just saw her. Besides, with all our changes, there's been enough shuffling."

John took in a deep breath. She was on the defensive, which meant he had to pick his battles. "Will you mention this? And the other . . ."

"John, it was a man, that's all. I just thought it was strange."

"It is."

"I'm fine." She shook her head. "Don't . . . don't turn this into something it's not." John kept his eyes on her, which caused her face to scrunch up into an angry stare. "Please don't," she said.

He drew her into a hug, but her body did not soften.

Instead, she pulled away. "I'm tired. I'm going to bed."

CHAPTER TWENTY-FIVE

The next day, the weather was muggy. Rain wanted to fall, but instead only sputtered through a few false starts. Darkness seemed to creep from the overcast sky into the Sanders' home.

"You boys will be okay with dinner?" Rebecca asked as she sorted through her book bag.

"Yes." John placed his hands on her shoulders and massaged the base of her neck. "Randy will be here soon, and he'll have pizza for the game." His fingers pressed down until her body softened. "Relax, okay?"

She stopped shuffling through the bag and dropped her hands to her side as John hit a tight muscle. "Don't forget about Robbie," she mumbled, "while you're watching."

"How can we? It was his idea to watch the game."

Rebecca pulled away to offer John a bemused look.

A long series of honks erupted outside. John opened the door to see Randy unloading two large pizza boxes.

"Hey there, Becky Boop," Randy called as he entered the house.

Rebecca glared at him. "Randy, you know I absolutely hate it when you call me that."

"That's exactly why I do it." He grinned.

John took the pizza boxes. "Think you got enough food?"

"As long as you got the drinks."

Rebecca closed her bag. "Can I steal a piece?"

"Please do." Randy motioned at the boxes.

"Thank you." She stepped toward the pizza.

"Any person who refers to me among their friends as 'the beloved biology teacher' certainly deserves a slice."

"Oh?" She paused.

"For that matter, a whole pizza, if you'd like."

"So . . .." Rebecca smiled. "You and Elle talked?"

"More than just talked." He winked at her.

"I knew it!" Rebecca clapped her hands together. "And I'm very glad."

"Thank you." Randy opened the pizza box.

She grinned with pride. "You're welcome." Then she looked inside. "Oh. What kind is this?"

"Meat, meat, and more meat."

She grabbed a piece. "Guess I probably didn't need to ask."

"Other than the cow's tongue, the whole beast should be there. Plus his friend." Randy imitated a pig snort.

John approached the pizza. "You're dissecting in class again, aren't you?"

"Yep." Randy raised his eyebrows to imitate a psychotic look. "The power of the knife."

"Leave now," John said as he handed Rebecca her bag. "Otherwise Randy will reveal details that will ruin your meal."

"Thanks." She smiled at both of them. "You boys have fun tonight." She kissed John, and then went into the den to hug Robert.

Five minutes later, pizza, snacks, and drinks were within easy reach. Robert's high chair had been moved to the den, and discarded pizza pieces were already scattered on the tablecloth laid out below.

"Does he always make a mess?" Randy asked as the boy wiped more sauce against his check.

"When I give him a piece like that . . . without cutting it up . . . yeah. Especially since he just wants the toppings."

"Wow. Do you realize that within a few months, you could be driving a minivan?"

"Huh?"

"One day Rebecca could show up with a minivan, and then you'd be stuck."

"What?"

"Then you'd have enough seatbelts, so there'd be no excuse to stop the Sanders family from exploding."

John started to laugh. "Thanks for the warning."

"You'll lose your hair, your stomach will expand to a full-fledged father gut, you won't buy toys for yourself, and then, because of the vanload of kids and that big gut, you won't come on our camping trips anymore. Your life will waste away to nothing. All you'll have left is fixing the van's engine, because with all those kids and that huge gut, you'll put too much weight on that van, and that's the end of your play days."

"You're disturbed."

"Do you think I could be like you?"

"Do I look miserable?"

"I've never driven a van."

"I drive a Jeep."

"Not for long." Randy released a dramatic sigh.

John arose to pick up the pieces Robert had thrown on the floor. "You're even more abnormal than normal tonight, Randy." John shot his friend a humorous grin.

"More . . . please," Robert said, and John handed him another small piece.

Meanwhile, Randy kept watching Robert. "Elle drives a van."

"Oh?" John raised his eyebrows. "Well, you're already losing your hair, so you might as well go for the complete package."

"I know." Randy stroked his head. "I'm in trouble. For each hair that falls out, I lose options. I'm slowly having to accept the horrible fact that a few select girls might become resistant to my charm." His fingers caressed his scalp. "But really, take a look; it's not that bad, is it?"

"Better get what you can now." John smiled. He walked into the kitchen, got a wet dishcloth, and returned to the den. By the time he reached his son, more small pieces of pizza were scattered on the floor. After wiping up Robert's hands and face, John released Robert from his chair. Then John gathered up the last of the discarded pizza slices.

"You missed a spot." Randy pointed at a splatter of red on the wall.

John sighed and turned to wash the sauce off, only to hear Randy say, "I couldn't be like you."

John turned back to look at him. "It's different when it's your own kid."

Randy released a giant sigh.

"What's wrong with you?"

"I talked to Elle on the phone. I told her I was coming up to watch the game, and she told me when it was over to come by and meet Jade."

"Randy, the game's just about to start, which means it'll probably go past ten. You're not meeting the kid tonight."

"I'm not?"

"She'll be asleep."

"Oh." Randy focused on the commercial. "Should I invite them over here?"

"Do you want to meet Elle's daughter?"

"Sure . . . when she's in seventh grade." Randy looked over at Robert, who had wandered over to John's plate. "When most of her brain's developed."

"Does Robert scare you?" They both looked at the two-year-old busy finishing off the cheese from John's half-eaten pizza slice.

"All done." Robert raised his hands, which were once again covered in sauce.

Randy and John both grinned.

"Nice work, Robbie," Randy said.

John laughed. "Go wipe those all over Uncle Randy. He'd love that."

In an instant, Randy shot over to the far end of the couch. "Not funny."

John paused and studied Randy's face. "Wow. I think you're scared of kids."

Randy eyed Robert cautiously. "No, I'm not."

John squatted down to Robert's level, then proceeded to clean off his face and hands again. "You sure?" He glanced briefly at Randy before pulling out the box of toys, which Robert sorted through until he found a truck.

"I'm not scared of kids," Randy said defensively. "Besides, it doesn't matter if Robert doesn't like me; you and I are still friends. If Elle's off-spring dislikes me, I'm dumped. I'm trash food, rotten rubbish."

"Elle's making you sweat." John grinned. "This could be enjoyable."

"I saw her a lot this weekend, and she's different than the others." Randy's face held a perplexed look. "I still can't decide if that's good."

"What's she like?"

"She's an adult."

John chuckled. "Okay."

"Everything's adult. She drives a van, has a real job, talks responsible, acts responsible, and is responsible. What am I supposed to do with that?"

John shook his head. "So she's not your type. I told Rebecca she wasn't."

"No," Randy jumped in. "I don't know that she's not. She's just a . . . a woman, and the whole thing's so . . . so adult."

"She seems like a good person." John proceeded to wipe down Robert's chair.

"So should I ask her to come over to watch the game?"

John gathered up what was left of his pizza and set it on Robert's tray. "Either go meet Jade or stay and watch the game, but don't do both."

"Okay," Randy drew in a big breath, then pulled out his cell phone. He looked at it for a long time. "Okay," he pushed a number, then rubbed his head. "Elle—Game. Elle—Game." He took in another deep breath. "It's not a big game, right?"

In ten minutes, Randy was gone. In another ten minutes Robert lay asleep next to John.

Eventually, John took Robert to his bed. Then he returned, turned up the volume, and enjoyed the game alone.

During the post-game, John heard the front door creak open. Rebecca's light footsteps moved across the wood floor. Soon she was standing in the doorway. "How is he?"

"Fine. He fell asleep early on; I put him in his bed about an hour ago."

"Is Randy gone?"

"Yeah. He went to see Elle."

Rebecca smiled. "Good. I'll be back." She headed down the hall to check on Robert. When she returned, she handed John a dish of ice cream.

"Thanks," he said.

"How's the game?" she asked.

"It's over. The Lakers had a bad night."

"Can I?" she picked up the remote from the table and pressed the mute button. "Can I talk to you?"

"You can shut it off."

Instead, she took off her shoes and placed her feet on his lap. "How are you?"

"Fine." He looked at her. Her face was tight. "How are you?"

"I don't know. Something strange happened tonight, but I'm trying to be calm."

"Calm is good." He smiled at her, but her face did not soften. "What happened?"

"When I drove to school . . ." Her tone signaled she was about to share something connected to her illness. "I drove into the same parking lot I always park in, but today it was different."

"What?" John prodded.

"Today there was a man at the entrance standing in the rain."

"Okay?"

"He acted like a parking attendant, and he had a sign." She paused, took in a deep breath, and said, "It was made out of cardboard." She looked down. "And it said, 'I want you to park near here.'"

"'I want you to park near here'?" John repeated.

"Yes." She avoided his eyes.

"Did you park where he directed?"

"No."

"Why?"

"I felt uncomfortable, like he was waiting for me, like he knew what kind of car I drove and was waiting."

John's mind worked like an encyclopedia, flipping through pages that detailed the signs, dangers, and manifestations of her illness. Her early diagnosis of schizophrenia had revealed an impaired ability to distinguish fantasy from reality. If she was entertaining delusions again, then these mood swings and hallucinations were more expressions of her illness.

Last week, a client's mother had told John that as the symptoms took over it was as if her teenager seemed to gradually slip away. The thought of this now happening to Rebecca sickened John.

If she could accept that she had a problem, there was still hope. Without that key insight, she would become another research statistic, another mental health client who refused treatment because she saw no problem. The most critical thing John could do at this moment was help Rebecca acknowledge her problem.

He chose his question carefully. "What made you think that?"

She looked at the muted television set. For some time her eyes took in the scene, then she spoke calmly, "The top of the sign said 'Brownell.'"

John drew in a long breath. Rebecca watched him and waited. Finally, he said, "Did he do anything when you drove by?"

"He looked at me the whole time. From the time I slowed down until I passed, he kept watching me. I circled the parking lot, and when I drove out, he was still watching."

"Did you park somewhere else?"

"I drove around another parking lot, but the sign upset me, so I drove back."

"And he was gone?"

"He was."

John watched figures on the silent TV. "So what do you think?"

"Maybe . . ." She heaved out a tense breath. "Maybe he was in my mind."

He nodded, feeling relieved. She was en route to acknowledging her problem. "Maybe."

She grabbed his hand and looked down at his fingers. "It was, John."

Again he nodded slowly, listening carefully to her words.

"Do you want to know how I know?"

He nodded a third time.

"It was the same man," she said. "The same one begging at the stop sign, the man with the dirty hair, the smirk . . . it was all the same."

Rebecca leaned against his chest. He placed his arm around her, closed his eyes, and listened to the hum of the television.

Holding her, he could feel her deep breathing and her fast heart-beat. She would be okay. She was strong and committed.

"I didn't go to class," she said.

Carefully, he glanced at the clock. "But you didn't come straight home?"

"I drove by Dr. Blythe's office."

"I'm sure she wasn't there."

"I know." She clung to his arm. "And I knew it at the time. It just seemed safe, like a good place to be."

"Are you trying to run from your mind?"

Her eyes teared up. He quickly tried to lighten the mood. "You know what this means, don't you?"

She shook her head.

"It means that the beggar found a job." He gave her a playful squeeze.

She sat up and gave him a sympathetic smile, but it was not genuine.

"You're going to be okay, Rebecca."

"You're not worried about me?"

"We'll deal with whatever this is."

She expressed a small flicker of panic. "It won't interfere with school. I'll be behind, but I have Kim's number. I'll call her, and I'll get caught up."

John glanced at the television to see the postgame ending.

"Did I tell you she's bipolar?" Rebecca asked.

John reached for the remote and pressed the power off. "Who?"

"Kim. She's also had an anxiety disorder—had it real bad for a couple of years. Because of it, she understands me, and it's been nice to talk to someone who can relate to my challenges. I know she'll help me. Don't worry, I'll get caught up."

"I'm not the one concerned about you getting behind or missing your class."

"But you'll say that school stress is causing these problems."

"Do *you* feel like school is stressful?"

"I don't want to quit." Her tender eyes searched his face, as if working to understand his current thoughts. "I'll take care of things."

"How?"

She hunched her body over and rubbed her eyes.

John set his dish on the coffee table, then placed his hand on her back. "What do you want to do, Rebecca?"

When she lifted her head, tears were falling past her checks. "I want this to go away." In haste, she wiped at her face. "Why can't it leave me alone?"

"Let me talk to Dr. Blythe tomorrow."

"She can't help me." She paused to wipe away more tears. "It's going to be my medicine. The dosage will go higher. I'll be sick. It'll take months to get everything in order. And we both know the process turns me into a different person."

"Talk to Dr. Haden. He'll work with you."

"I'm not going back to him."

"Are you sure that's the best choice?"

"I'll go through Dr. Blythe to get another referral." She pressed her fingers against her closed eyes, then made one last brush at the tears and stood up. "I'll call her in the morning. Good night."

CHAPTER TWENTY-SIX

The next evening, when John walked through the front door, the aroma of his favorite meal filled the air—sweet and sour pork.

"Smells good." He entered the kitchen and gave his wife a kiss. "How was your day?"

"Great. Really good." She avoided his eyes. "Robert and I have had fun."

"Daddy! Come see!" Robert ran into the room, and John lifted his son up. Robert smothered John with a hug and a kiss, then wiggled to be set free.

Rebecca turned back to the stove. "After dinner, he'll want you to come play in it."

Robert pulled John into the den. Four chairs were strategically positioned near the old couch, and a large blanket lay across the furniture to form a play fort.

"My tent. My name is Chief Bert!"

"Chief Bert, huh? Did Mommy give you that name?"

"Yep. And you're War-your Wig . . ."

"Out." From behind, Rebecca's voice completed the sentence.

John smiled. "Warrior Wig-out, huh? And what's Mommy?"

"Princess," Rebecca said.

He turned around. She stood in the den's entrance. "Princess what?"

"Princess Pamper. You must pamper me all night."

"Really?" He reached out to pull her close, but her hands held him back.

"First, Warrior Wig-out, we must eat."

He followed her into the kitchen. "Thank you for dinner."

She offered him a flirtatious smile. "You're welcome."

"It looks like Robbie had a lot of fun today."

"He did."

"And you did too?"

"I did." Her large smile confirmed it.

"Did you call Dr. Blythe?"

Her smile faded. "I didn't get a chance. But I'll talk to her soon."

John took in a strong breath. "I had a chance to talk to her today."

"Okay. But I was going to see her soon."

"I know," he said cautiously. "She said your appointment is this Friday."

"Of course. It's written down on my calendar." Rebecca turned toward the stove. "Would you set the table?"

John reached in the cupboard and pulled out the plates. "She's concerned, too." From the corner of his eye, he could see Rebecca biting her lip.

"I'll see her on Friday," she repeated.

"Yes. After that she'll be out of town for two weeks. But she says that if you need to, you can meet with someone else during that time. And she gave me the list of her recommended psychiatrists. If you choose not to go back to Dr. Haden, she'll write you a referral for anyone you want. But she recommends you get in to see someone soon."

Rebecca threw a hot pad on the table, yanked a pot from the stove, and dropped the pot on the pad.

"You're okay," John whispered.

The words touched an exposed nerve. Rebecca paused. "You'll come with me," she said.

"Of course."

He approached her and carefully wrapped his arms around her. "Linda thinks it'd be best for you to go back to Dr. Haden."

"No." She pulled out of his embrace and moved across the kitchen to lift the rice cooker's lid. "He's too medicine happy. He wanted me on four different things."

"But if you need them, will you take them?"

She was too busy investigating the rice to respond.

"Rebecca," his voice was stern, strong enough that she turned around. "Please."

She stood taller and cocked her head in defiance. "I don't want to be taking all those pills."

"No, Rebecca," John kept his voice stern yet calm. "What you don't want is to fall further into your illness. We've talked about doing what's needed, which means you have to keep ahead. You have to control this."

"I don't like the side effects. I don't like what he prescribes; I don't like how they make me feel."

"But right now we need to get the upper hand on this."

"It's not that bad."

"Not if we take preventative care."

She walked over to the table. "Let's eat."

John held back. "What's your next step?"

Her hands tapped against the chair's back. "The food's getting cold."

"Do you want to call Dr. Haden or find someone else?"

She lifted the lid off the pot and huffed out an angry breath. "I'll call."

He stepped toward her, touched her arm, and beckoned for her to turn and look at him. "Will you?"

"Let me talk to Dr. Blythe," her voice was agitated, yet soft. "Then I'll set up an appointment."

"Okay." He kissed her cheek. "Thank you."

CHAPTER TWENTY-SEVEN

After her appointment with Dr. Blythe, Rebecca said little, but through the weekend she appeared to be in a dark cloud of despair.

John opted not to ask much, especially after learning from Dr. Blythe that Rebecca had agreed to call Haden's office on Monday. This satisfied John, and to maintain peace through the weekend, he refrained from mentioning any concerns about her health.

However, during that time, John watched every movement she made. Sunday morning, she poured milk in her bowl before pouring the cereal. John found the behavior odd, which caused him to ponder the action until he worked himself into an analytical tangle. He observed Rebecca like she was an organism trapped under a microscope. He looked for signs of peculiarity, abnormality, or irregularity in the gestures she made and the words she spoke. This only increased the stress on both of them.

When Monday arrived, John was relieved to get away, to be back at the clinic and dealing with patients in an environment where it was acceptable to analyze and advise. Other professionals—ones who were not deeply connected to Rebecca—could separate their knowledge from their emotions. They would find the answers. They would help John's family.

During dinner that evening, John waited until their son was done, away from the table, and too busy playing to hear the tones that would be connected to his parents' conversation.

"When's your appointment?" He watched her face closely.

"My what?"

"When do you see Dr. Haden?"

"That's right." An embarrassed grin crossed her face. "I planned to call this afternoon. I really did. But Elle invited Robert and me to play with her and Jade. I got busy and forgot. I'll call tomorrow."

She needed to call Dr. Haden, and she hadn't. He did not want to dwell on her situation, but this red flag made him more anxious than ever. John gritted his teeth, and to maintain peace he made his own promise—tomorrow, he would make the call. He looked down at his meal and kept eating, determined to drop the subject for the night.

His moment of silence must have relieved her, because she lowered her fork and began recapping the day. "Originally, I thought Elle would be a good friend for me. And Robert and Jade get along great. Everything seemed to be going fine. But I might be wrong about her."

John didn't answer immediately. He was still thinking about Dr. Haden, but he pulled in a breath and tried to refocus his thoughts. He pierced a piece of meat with his fork, and although only half listening, he said, "Really?"

"Today she picked us up and took us to a gorgeous daffodil garden in Running Springs. I'll have to take you there. She says in another week it'll be even more spectacular."

John nodded, chewing the tough beef.

"Afterwards, when she was driving us home, she asked if she could run a quick errand. She needed to drop something in the mail and wanted to stop by the Running Springs Post Office. But I asked her to go to Sky Forest because I hadn't picked up our mail. So she did. She sent her package while I got our mail, and there was a letter that had a strange envelope with my first name typed on it. As I was opening it, Elle noticed it." Her voice fluctuated. "It had letters cut out from magazines and newspapers, and there were words typed along the side. But I didn't get a chance to read it because Elle snatched it out of my hand."

John stopped chewing. "She did?"

"I know. I was shocked. All I could do was stare at her."

"Did she say something?"

"She said she was sorry. So I asked her why she took it. But then she turned weird and started tripping over her words."

"What did she say?"

"That it was hers."

John studied Rebecca's face, and again began analyzing her. "Why did she say that?"

"Well, I showed her the envelope. It was addressed to me, and all Elle said was that her middle name is Rebecca, and she thought she'd mentioned that. But she never had. I think she was lying. Then she said that over a year ago, while she still lived in Sky Forest, she dated a guy who always called her Rebecca. Sort of like a pet name thing, meant to be endearing. But then when they broke up, he started sending letters like that."

"Like what?"

"She said they're horrid and mean. They stopped right before she'd moved, and she'd thought that was the end of them. She apologized and said she hoped they hadn't upset me. But how could it have? I didn't even see it or read it. Then she stashed the letter in her pocket, took the envelope from my hand, and said that she hoped he didn't send any more. She walked to her car and acted like it was nothing. But it was strange, John. She was strange, and the entire thing was . . . just odd."

John said nothing but kept his eyes focused on her face, observing each movement she made.

"What?" she asked. "Do you think I'm acting paranoid? I'm telling you she was the strange one. After what she did today, I don't think she'd be good for Randy. Of course, I feel responsible, but I didn't know she was odd until now." She looked at John for a response, but before he could answer, the phone rang. Rebecca let out a sigh and left the table to answer it.

"Oh, hi." She turned to face John and mouthed the word 'Elle,' then rolled her eyes. "We're eating dinner right now. Yes, I was about to tell him, right before you called. You sure it has to be tonight? Okay. Let me ask." She lowered the phone and shook her head in disgust. "John, it's Elle. She says there are some papers regarding the house that were never signed. Nothing that will affect us—just stuff she needs for her records. I signed my part today, but she wants your signature tonight."

"Tell her I'll be there in a half hour."

"You sure?" She rolled her eyes at the phone.

"Yes."

"You heard that?" Rebecca said into the receiver. "Okay, no problem. Good-bye." She returned to the table and said, "See? She's odd. Really, how important is this? So anyway, after the post office, she told me about these papers. I gave her my signature, and then she asked me to have you call her. Then, about ten minutes before you got here, she called, and now again. Does she think I can't give a message?"

"She probably just wants to wrap things up, especially since it's been a few months."

"Well, if it's her error, it should be her inconvenience, not yours. She should bring them here or find a time that's good for you, not tell you to come over right now. You just got home."

"It's fine."

"Just because we've done things outside of her office, she thinks she can inconvenience us now. She shouldn't expect this from you. Call her back. Tell her you'll come by her office next week."

"It's probably a few quick signatures. Not a big deal." John finished the last of his meal, then loaded his dishes into the dishwasher. "Thanks for dinner."

He grabbed his keys and then bent over to kiss her forehead. "And don't worry about it. I'll be back soon."

CHAPTER TWENTY-EIGHT

Elle's A-frame house blended in with the trees; only the bright white door broke the camouflage-green paint. John parked to the side of the busy highway and climbed down the inclined steps. When he knocked, Elle opened the door to reveal a frightened face.

"Come in, come in." She motioned him into the poorly lit room. "I'm so glad you came. I've been anxious about this all night."

A burgundy couch, shaped like a fat *C*, engulfed the area. Although there was a lamp in the corner, it seemed only to throw shadows across the room. Elle signaled John to sit, yet in the uncomfortable darkness, John remained standing. Elle's nervousness concerned him. "Rebecca said you had papers—something I needed to sign."

"That's not why I wanted you here." Her eyes were open wide. Her teeth clenched together as she watched him. Finally, she said, "I only did this to protect her."

"To protect Rebecca?" John felt a throbbing inside his ears.

"Sit down." Again, Elle motioned at the couch.

Something was not right. John sat, but the large coach made him feel small and disoriented. The room's darkness made the moment feel heavy. He wondered what had actually happened today. From Rebecca's account, it seemed his wife had displayed signs of paranoia, and depending on what symptoms Elle saw, this would explain her uneasiness.

Elle sat close and waited for him to look at her before she spoke. "I had to make up a story," she said, looking him directly in the eye, "and it had to be quick."

John clasped his hands together and felt the sweat. He rubbed his palms against his pants. He had promised not to speak of Rebecca's private battle, but he feared the conversation was headed in that direction. To protect himself, he stood. "Do you have papers for me?"

"Wait," she commanded. "Stay here."

Slowly, he sat again while Elle stood and disappeared into the kitchen. In the silence, John took in a deep breath and focused on selecting the words he could share that would not violate his wife's trust. When Elle came back, she handed him a crumpled envelope. "Look."

He unfolded it to read:

REBECCA
P.O. Box 222
Sky Forest, CA 92385

The envelope was typed, but when he pulled out the letter he saw alphabet pieces from magazines and newspapers that had been cut and pasted to form a message.

LoOk At mE
LoOk
LoSe
At
ANOther
mE
moTHER
LoSe ANOther moTHER

John clutched his forehead. A footer, typed in Courier font, lined the bottom with the word good-bye typed over and over again. He stared at the letter until the words blurred.

"John, I've seen this before, or at least this type of thing. It happened to my youngest sister when she was in seventh grade. A psycho sent her letters with obscene, vulgar drawings. Horrible stuff.

My family lied to her—told her they were intended for me—and then we hovered over our mailbox like hawks."

John touched the magazine scraps, his fingers feeling each individual piece. Then he felt as if he had just been punched in the gut.

"We couldn't let Ashlee near the mail, at least not until we'd checked it. And we never let her walk anywhere by herself. Someone always had to be near her." Elle paused to bite her lip before continuing. "My sister's the super-trusting type—worse than me. But in this instance, that was good because we had to keep lying to her. We had to keep her oblivious to what was really happening." She bit her lip again. "I'd like to say there was a happy ending to this, that we finally caught the pervert and sent him to jail. But we didn't. In the end, my family moved, and that stopped the filth."

John said nothing. Instead, he focused on the first line of the letter: *Look at me.*

"My point is that you need to protect Rebecca," Elle said.

John stared at the cut-out letters. He thought of Rebecca's collages. Could it just be an extraordinary coincidence? It seemed extremely unlikely, but the alternative was even more painful.

Either a sick, disturbed individual had sent a letter to his wife that just happened to contain the same phrase she'd seen on an oddly located homeless man's sign, or, more likely, the sick individual sending this letter was his own wife.

"You understand," Elle stood up and turned on another lamp. The light further illuminated the letter. "Mail stalkers' entire purpose is to stimulate fear. It's the whole reason why this psycho's doing this. There are crazy people—real sick ones out there—who get off on doing this type of stuff." John looked up at her, and she offered him a sympathetic smile. "I mean, none of it makes any sense. Obviously, the person's crazy . . ." she released a nervous laugh. "I imagine, being in your profession, you understand that."

John slowly nodded.

"Far more than I do," Elle continued. "But I wanted you to know. And please . . . please know that I'm here to help."

John offered her an empty smile.

"If you want me to," Elle said as she sat back down, "I can swing by your box before Rebecca goes to the Post Office . . . if that would help."

"Thanks," John said softly.

"We can't let her see it; we don't want this person to win. We don't want him to terrorize Rebecca. Oh, it just makes me sick and angry."

He wanted to embrace Elle's words. He wanted to believe in what she was saying. But the tight, awful pit in his stomach would not allow it. John stood up. "I appreciate you watching out for her."

"I just wish I could say something encouraging." She stood up next to him, her fingers touching the letter. "But it's ugly stuff. With my sister, my parents complained to the postal service and the police. But since they couldn't track it, and since her life didn't seem threatened, there was nothing they could do. It's frustrating having people not care. Oh, the memories fire me up again." She drew in a hasty breath.

One last time, John glanced at the letter. Then he folded it up and slid it into the envelope.

"But maybe," Elle said, "with you having a post office box, they can do more. Maybe they'll even toss it for you. That way you wouldn't have to worry about it. It's just a hopeful idea, but talk to them. See what advice they give."

John headed toward the door. "Thanks, Elle."

Swiftly she moved to the door and placed her hand on the knob. "Be glad it's a post office box. Certainly, you must feel safer. This psycho doesn't know where you live. And most likely, he's only trying to cause her—and you—a lot of fear."

She pulled the door open then said, "Or maybe this was a one-time thing. Let's hope that's all it was. But you just need to keep an eye on it, okay? So Rebecca doesn't get scared."

"Thanks, Elle," he said again.

"I'm sorry, John." Her voice softened. "I hated to share this with you. It's a terrible thing, but I didn't know what else to do."

He nodded. "I needed to know."

"Keep me in the loop, okay?" She stood in the doorway to watch him leave. "Remember—I'm here to help. Call me anytime."

He forced himself to smile at her. Then, with heavy feet, he walked to the car.

CHAPTER TWENTY-NINE

That night, John did not sleep well. His thoughts ran in circles, thinking of Rebecca, of Elle's words, of the seriousness of the situation. Elle's great concern only highlighted the fact that John's family faced an extremely sick issue.

He wanted to believe Elle and convince himself that this was a mail stalker. But no matter what he hoped, he knew that if he denied the facts, it wouldn't change the outcome. One's beliefs could not change the truth. And the truth he could cling to was that he loved Rebecca and needed to protect her.

The following afternoon, John spent most of his hours testing and processing a set of twins with bipolar symptoms. After a restless night and an intense work day, John longed for an evening of peace. But when he turned down their drive and saw Elle's van parked near the house, he groaned audibly. He was not in the right frame of mind to repeat the previous evening.

He entered his home to see Jade helping Robert do a puzzle and heard Rebecca and Elle busy talking in the kitchen.

"Hey," John called out.

"Daddy." Robert came running.

John lifted the boy into a hug as Rebecca entered the room. Once John embraced Rebecca, Robert wiggled to be free and then ran back to his puzzle.

After a quick peck on the lips, Rebecca grabbed John's hand and pulled him into the kitchen. "How was your day?"

Eye contact with Elle made John's day feel longer. "Fine," he lied. But Elle's glance revealed an uncomfortable urgency that instantly put John on edge. He was not ready to hear more of her worries, her experiences, or her conclusions. He needed time to think through how to handle what was truly taking place.

Then, within a second, Elle's face shifted to an innocent, friendly smile, which was all Rebecca saw of the exchange.

John returned the smile. "Hi, Elle." Then he turned to Rebecca. "Are you ready for your class tonight?"

"Oh, no." Elle offered him a forced grin. "I've been talking with Rebecca for way too long. I forgot you have class tonight." She rose and looked at the door. "We'd better go."

Rebecca also stood. "Thanks for all your help, Elle."

"Anytime. I mean that." She grabbed her purse from the table then walked into the front room. "Jade, time to go."

"Not yet." Jade hovered over her pieces.

"Pick up your puzzle." Elle forced another smile.

"No." Jade pressed a piece into the emerging image of a duck.

"Jade." Elle's voice was firm. "You can play more with Robert another day." She abruptly hastened the clean-up process, which only intensified Jade's refusal. Within seconds, a battle between mother and daughter erupted.

Rebecca pulled Robert from the puzzle, and in an effort to be oblivious to the squabble, she shifted her eyes to John. "It's been quite the day."

"Has it?"

"You know how I thought Robert was ready to be potty trained?" Her eyes stayed focused on him. "Well, I was wrong."

"Really?" John smiled, also trying to shut out Elle's rising scolds and Jade's angry protests. "Robert's not ready, huh?"

"This afternoon I went out to run errands," Rebecca said. "I did some shopping, dropped off a few things, and then had some bills to mail. I had them in one hand and Robert in the other. Huh, Robbie?"

But the little boy's face was focused on Jade. "Then I set him down to get the mail. I only turned my back for a brief moment, but it was enough time for him to pull down his pants."

John shook his head, but he could feel himself starting to grin.

"I screamed," she said, almost in unison with Jade's present scream. "I pulled up his pants and ran him back to the car. Since that's what the Pull-Ups® are for, right?" Jade began to cry, which caused all the Sanders to glance at her, but then Rebecca quickly made eye contact again with John. "Could you imagine? Right there on the Post Office floor. Good thing I caught him in time."

"Did you?" John struggled to keep his eyes on his wife.

A sheepish grin crossed her face. "I was too embarrassed to go back and see."

John chuckled. Jade turned quiet.

"Wouldn't that be embarrassing?" Rebecca glanced at Robert who was still watching Jade.

"Especially," John said with a smile, "if the whole town knew where the puddle came from."

"Well, I have a hunch that it couldn't have been too bad, because when I got home, Elle was here. She'd come by to say hello and ended up helping me take in a huge load of groceries." Rebecca glanced at Elle, who was busy shoving puzzle pieces into a bag. "Of course I got caught up with that and talking. When I turned around, there he was again—pants down, accident in progress. I rushed him to the toilet, but we left a trail the whole way. So as a conclusion to this day, I've decided that this over-eager mother is going to leave you in diapers." Rebecca tickled Robert's belly. While he laughed, she had his full attention, but when she stopped he squirmed to be free.

"I think that's a wise move," Elle said, joining them, a subdued Jade by her side. "Don't push Robert if he's not ready. I told Rebecca about my nephews," she said, facing John. "Both her boys gave my sister an extended headache, but personally I think she deserved it because she tried to potty train them far too early. I'm a firm believer in letting the child tell you when he's ready." Elle glanced around the room. "Did I get everything?" Then, once again, she looked straight at John. "Oh, last night, I forgot one more form, one more that I need you to sign. It's in the van, why don't you come out with me?" Her smile turned tense.

John held in a reluctant sigh. Most likely she was leading him into a conversation similar to last night's. But Rebecca's curious look forced John to agree. "Sure," He held the door for Jade and Elle and followed them out.

The sky was overcast and bleak. John's eyes adjusted to the evening darkness while Elle opened the van's side door and Jade climbed in. Then, as the little girl was busy buckling herself in, Elle turned to John.

"I thought you understood what I was telling you, but I'm not sure you did." Elle's eyes seemed to shoot bullets. "If I hadn't come over today, it would have been a disaster. I came by just to see how things were, and it's a good thing I did, because while I was helping put groceries away I found the mail inside one of the bags. I'd been worried all day, so I sifted through, and there it was. Another one, John! If circumstances had been different, she would have opened it." Her voice was panicked. "This isn't fair to her. She doesn't need to be a victim of some lunatic's hobby. Did you speak to the Post Office today?"

He glanced over at some loose gravel that covered the drive and debated his response. "I couldn't today."

"This is serious!" Elle's voice squeaked. "You're concerned, aren't you?"

He nodded and looked up at her earnest face. "I'm very concerned."

"Then what are you going to do?"

"It's being taken care of on Thursday."

"Thursday? What do you mean, *Thursday*?" A small vein protruded from her forehead. "You're not going to do something until then? What about tomorrow?"

John released a heavy sigh. He did not want Elle involved in his family affairs, but after another quick internal debate, he aimed to assuage her concern. "Tomorrow . . . would you mind going through our mail?"

"Not at all." Her voice was urgent. "If that's what you want me to do, absolutely. I'd feel much better about that than letting her find this trash."

He pulled out his key chain and unwound the Post Office key. "Just for tomorrow. Then I want the key back."

She looked hurt. When she reached out her hand, she spoke in a subdued tone. "I'm just trying to help you . . . and her."

"Thanks. But after tomorrow I can take care of this."

"I'm hungry," Jade called.

"We're leaving, dear." Elle handed John another envelope with the same eerie type:

REBECCA
P.O. Box 222
Sky Forest, CA 92385

"Don't leave yet," Elle said to him. Then she reached into the passenger seat and shifted through some documents in her briefcase. "I was serious; I have papers for you to sign. I had them there for you last night, but in telling you about that . . . stuff, I forgot. Here they are." She handed him the sheets. "Nothing terribly important—in fact, I thought you'd already signed them with the rest of the stack. But I can't find them."

John skimmed through the pages. It had his prior address, along with his recent address, and a few legal notes. "I thought we'd signed this too."

"Sorry. I'm not sure if this one slipped through the pile or what."

"Yeah. Maybe I didn't; there were a lot. I could have confused it with another." He scribbled his name, then handed it back.

"Thanks, John." She shut the van door and marched over to the driver's side.

He stepped away from the van, but before she slid onto her seat, he added, "Thanks for your help with Rebecca."

"Well, this is serious, and I just hope you realize that."

"I know. I do."

After her van drove away, John looked at the typed envelope. Then he ripped it open and read:

BROwnELL i wAnT yOu tO pARk nEAR HerE

BROwnELL

BuT

i

i

wAnT

wAnT

yOu

yOu

tO

tO

pARk

pAy

nEAR

nOT

HerE

HiM

BuT i wAnT yOu tO pAy nOT HiM

John folded the letter and placed it back in the envelope. This was the final evidence he needed.

He shoved the envelope in his pocket and walked back into the house.

CHAPTER THIRTY

The following evening, Randy veered his Mazda RX-7 into the Interstate 10 carpool lane and hit the accelerator. "Johnny Boy, I can't believe you almost backed out on me." They began passing decelerating lines of trapped cars. "Especially since we've had tickets for months."

John nodded, watching the flash of people in their automobiles.

"Remember how thrilled I was when my hot little fingers held those tickets for the first time?"

John watched a woman dab at her cheek as if crying, and then she was gone.

"It's not every day we get to see the Kings take on the Lightning, you know?" Randy glanced at him, "This game decides who plays in the Stanley Cup."

A man talked on his cell phone, another man banged his fist against the steering wheel, a young teen's bass rocked the freeway. Randy sped past them all.

"You okay, Johnny Boy?"

"Sure." He shot Randy a hasty, reassuring smile, then turned back to the window.

"Just so you know, I did try to get someone else to use your ticket. But Tom's out of town, and Jeff wanted to attend some monster truck rally. I don't see the comparison, but in his opinion, it was more important than the game. And Elle couldn't find a babysitter—besides, she'd already agreed to watch Robert while Rebecca's studying for a test. But let's be honest, she didn't want to come. So, really, did I have a choice?"

"It's fine," John said. They passed a "Just Married" car with a couple exchanging quick kisses amid the stopped traffic.

"Well . . ." Randy's voice turned serious. "Elle's worried about you."

"I know."

Across the freeway there was a concrete wall, a dull gray barricade blending in with the polluted sky. John watched the fortress wall for several yards. Then his eyes returned to the lives passing by him. A heavy sigh slipped from his lips.

"I knew it." Randy shook his head. "I knew it was impossible, but what could I do? She gave me strict orders."

"What?" John looked at him.

"Yeah," Randy growled. "Elle told me about those letters."

John released a frustrated sigh.

"She's worried. She told me she spent two days tormenting herself, stressing over Rebecca and those letters. But today she's worried about you. She claims that no matter what she tells you, it's as if you don't care."

"That's because she doesn't understand."

"Well, isn't that ironic? Because according to her, she thinks you don't understand. At first she was opposed to you going to this game. She didn't think you should leave Rebecca right now. Then she changed her mind because she figured that maybe I could talk some sense into you and help you see that you need to do something."

"Can we talk about this later?"

"She wanted me to ask you if you were concerned about Rebecca being at school."

"Not at the moment."

"Well, she wants you to intervene."

John clutched his forehead and took a steady breath. "I don't think you or Elle really want to be involved with our family's issues."

"She sounds like she knows about this type of stuff. She thinks the threats are most likely just through the mail, but that you can't be sure—you need to do something, Johnny Boy."

"I know she's trying to help."

"Before I came to your office, I'd just finished talking to her." Randy shot him a quick glance. "She had a message that I'm supposed to give you."

Once more, John rubbed his forehead. Talking about what Elle thought was pointless; and her actions, though kind, were dangerous. They would only build on Rebecca's mounting confusion. He needed Elle to step away from this precarious situation.

Randy interrupted John's thoughts. "You do want to know what Elle said, don't you?"

"Sure."

"Elle wants you to know that there was nothing. No letter in the box."

"Thanks."

"And tomorrow you can stop by her office to pick up the key."

"Fine."

"But she wanted you to know she'd hold on to it." Randy shot John a fast raise of the eyebrows. "Would that help?"

"I don't want her to get involved."

Randy's voice was low. "She's upset with you. She says she can't understand why you don't care. You have her cell number, and you could've called anytime today. At any time today you could have found out if something came, but you didn't."

John tried to laugh off the accusation. "That sounds like Elle."

"She's very concerned . . . which has me concerned. This isn't like you."

"Randy, what good does it do if I'm upset about this?" Suddenly the pent-up frustration surfaced. "Huh? Elle's suspicious that someone's out there creating terror for Rebecca. According to Elle, my job's to protect Rebecca, to ensure she doesn't feel that horror. Yet, she's frustrated with me because I'm not panicking? Is that what she wants from me? Instead of Rebecca feeling the terror, I'm supposed to feel it for her? I'm supposed to react to all this, so Elle knows that I care about my wife? That I'm scared for my wife? Is that what she needs to know? Well, I am, okay? Make sure you take that message back. Tell her I'm horrified, absolutely horrified, about what these letters mean."

The car sped forward in silence while John's fury at life slid deeper into his heart. To distract himself, he looked out at the hundreds of motorists' mystery lives and then watched them all blend together into one congested freeway.

Finally, Randy broke the taut silence. "So does Rebecca have enemies?"

John chuckled. "We've had our share."

Randy lit up. "So what do you think? Who do you think's sending them?"

"I know who's sending them."

For a split moment, Randy paused. "You do?"

"Yes."

"Does Elle know that?"

"No."

"Have you gone to the police?"

The conversation was headed exactly where John did not want it to go. He spoke slowly, delaying the inevitable. "They can't help."

"Did they tell you that?"

John pressed his forehead against the palm of his hand. He drew in a long breath and thought through his sparse options. Then, in a calm breath, he spoke the facts. "She's seeing things."

"Who?"

"Her visual hallucinations are back."

"No." Randy denied it too.

John closed his eyes, and in a tranquil voice, said, "Did you know that only 40% percent of schizophrenic hallucinations are visual?"

Suddenly, he released a sarcastic chuckle. "Imagine that?" He looked out at the dull sky. "Somehow she's in the minority, caught with that lucky bunch of limited hallucinations."

Randy gave John a perplexed look. "So . . . she thinks she's had another baby?"

"No."

Randy looked ahead; his face was somber and confused. "Then what?"

"It's happened twice. At least that she's aware of. A man appears in random spots carrying a message for her."

Very slowly Randy nodded his head. "That's eerie."

"Yeah." John looked out at the other cars, the other lives, the other tragedies all self-contained within their cars. Then he looked again at the solid concrete wall.

"She's receiving messages?" Randy's voice turned timid. "Like what?"

"'Look at me' or 'Brownell, park near here'." He drew in a stabilizing breath. "Nonsense, basically."

"John, you're sure they're hallucinations?"

Straight from his heart, John released a sad chuckle. "My wishing they weren't doesn't change the facts."

"I'm sorry."

"The truth is, I've been in denial for too long. I've been living in my own fantasies, believing she was okay. But it's clear that she's not. Yes, it's serious—believe me, I know it's serious. I don't need Elle to tell me that."

"Elle?"

"Yes."

"I don't get it," Randy said. "What does Elle have to do with Rebecca's hallucinations?"

John closed his eyes. "I promised Rebecca that I wouldn't share her health issues with Elle. And you know because . . . because you know everything about me."

"Okay. So we keep this from Elle. I can do that."

"But now with these letters," John said, rubbing his forehead again, "Elle's pulling herself in."

"Because your wife has a mail stalker . . . how does that . . .?"

"Because everything's out of control." John drew in a sustaining breath. "Randy, the letters are from Rebecca."

"What?"

"She sent them."

"What? To Rebecca, from Rebecca?"

"Yes."

"And you know that how?"

John drew in another concentrated breath. "Lately, she's had this recent fixation with collages. She's shown this absorbing behavior of cutting things up, and every school project seems to be connected to a collage. She even has Robert engaged in it."

"Really?"

"The worst part is . . . I don't know what I'm supposed to do. That's the hardest part—I don't know what I should say, or how I should act. I don't know what she's accountable for."

"Aren't you trained for this?"

"No. I'm trained to help patients, not my wife." John turned back to the window and stared out at the passing cars. "In time, I come to understand patients. I recognize their struggles. I try my best to show patience toward their behavior. But with her, it's different. To be honest, I'm angry."

"Angry?"

"Yes, for putting us through this. Somehow I can't seem to excuse her for letting this happen."

A long silence followed until Randy finally repeated, "She's sending herself those letters."

"Yes."

"So what are you going to do?"

"Tomorrow afternoon we meet with her psychiatrist, and we get her on the correct medication. Then, in two weeks, her psychologist will be back. We get to the bottom of this. We discover what's happening, what stressors brought this on, and how we can prevent this in the future."

"And that will take care of things?"

"It's a start, which is good."

Red taillights flashed ahead, and Randy eased down on the brake. "Are you okay?"

The vehicle slowed to a crawl and joined the congested mass. "I don't know. It's hard to be confident about much."

Ahead, the carpool lane was blocked off, and cars were merging into other lanes.

"All I'm certain about," John said, "is that we have a long journey ahead."

CHAPTER THIRTY-ONE

Finally, Thursday arrived. John watched the clock in his office. They would met with Dr. Haden at four, Rebecca would be reassessed, and the issues around her medication would be sorted out. All John's hope resided in the outcome of this appointment.

Until the phone rang, directly after his last scheduled session. It was Rebecca.

"Robert's sick."

John rubbed his forehead. "You've got to leave. If you don't leave right now, we'll be late."

"Robert's sick," she repeated. "I can't leave him with anyone while he's like this. He feels hot, like he has a fever, and I think he might throw up."

"Bring him down here." John tried not to yell. "I'll watch him here while you go."

"No." Her voice was firm. "The drive down the mountain will make him worse. Besides, what if he throws up in the car or in your office?"

"Then I'll head out right now." He glanced at the clock. "If you leave as well, we can meet at a turnout. Let's meet at the one near Crestline. I'll take Robert home, you go to the appointment. But we both have to leave *right now*."

"We'll have to reschedule," she said calmly.

"Why didn't you call me before?" He said, letting his anger bleed through. "We can figure something out. Just call someone to watch Robert. I'll head over to Dr. Haden's. You'll be a little late, but we'll get you in before he leaves for the day."

"No. I'm not taking Robert somewhere when he says his tummy hurts and he's acting like he's going to throw up."

"Rebecca, we can't keep putting this off."

"I'm not. Robert's sick!"

"Fine. I'll see you tonight." He hung up the phone and threw his pen across the room. Then he punched in Dr. Blythe's private cell number.

Although in the midst of her vacation, Linda Blythe was kind. She told him to keep the appointment with Dr. Haden. In fact, she asked him to call her during the visit so that all three of them could discuss the situation together.

John followed her instructions and soon sat across from the reputable Dr. Haden, who was, as always, full of judgments and opinions. His office had a shrine dedicated to Harley-Davidson motorcycles, and he had already slipped into his leather pants in anticipation of his ride home after this last appointment. He was not impressed by Rebecca's absence. "What did you think would happen?" he asked as he retrieved his riding jacket. "I put her on Prolixin and Navane and highly recommended Trifluoperazine and Haldol, but she refused to take them. There's only so much I can do."

John nodded. "I understand, but—"

"People think I'm a miracle worker." Dr. Haden reached for a leather glove and slid his hand through it. "But if she doesn't want the meds, I can't force them on her. With her not here, I'd simply recommend getting her back on what I've already prescribed, especially Haldol. See how that does." He lifted a paper to locate the other glove.

John grabbed the moment. "Dr. Blythe said we should call her right now to discuss a few things."

Dr. Haden lowered his shoulders. "Fine."

Soon Linda's soothing voice rang through the speakerphone. After hearing the details, she was optimistic. "John, do what Dr.

Haden has said. Get her on the Haldol. I'm back a week from Monday. It'll be a packed day, but I'll make sure we squeeze her in."

"Thank you," John said.

"It seems she's trying to interact with her delusions through those letters. Let her find them," Dr. Blythe advised. "Don't intervene. We need her out of denial, and the sooner she accepts that she has a problem, the sooner she'll be receptive to our help."

"What if she won't come meet with you?" This was John's most pressing concern. "Or what if she still refuses to take the medicine?"

"Is she defiant?" Dr. Blythe asked.

"No. Not exactly."

"Do you feel like she, or you, or your son is in danger?" she asked. "No."

"Well, if there are no threats, then don't worry. Give this a little time, and we'll get things under control."

Dr. Haden's pen tapped against the desk like steady rain on a tin roof. When John paused to look at him, the man set the pen down and said, "Okay. Sounds like we've got this situation solved."

John glanced up at a large, elegantly framed portrait of a red vintage Harley and then turned back to the phone. "Thanks, Linda . . . and sorry to disturb the vacation."

"John," she said with authority, "you're as qualified as any of us. You know her better than we do. You know what your options are. So weigh them out and trust your inner feelings. We're here to help, but if you think this is more serious than what it appears, by all means take action. Be proactive, Sanders. It's better to act safely now than to have regrets later."

"I know," John said. "I'm considering all the options."

Rebecca was at the door when he arrived home that evening, her book bag clenched in her hand. "Where have you been?"

"You know where I was." John stepped past her and into the kitchen. "Where you were supposed to be."

She marched into the kitchen, her eyes cold. "I told you. Robert's been sick."

"How is he?"

"Asleep."

"And you?"

"I thought you were mad at me. I thought you weren't coming home just so I'd have to miss class."

"I had to stop and pick this up." He raised a small pharmacy bag and watched her eyes shift from him to the bag's label.

"Leave it on the counter." She gave it a final, vehement glance, then turned to leave. "I have to go."

"You have a meeting with Dr. Blythe a week from Monday."

She paused. "That's fine."

He set the bag on the counter. "I don't know what time yet."

"Fine." She still hesitated at the door. "So what's in there?"

Slowly, he opened the bag and set the bottles down one at a time. "Prolixin, Navane, Trifluoperazine, and Haldol."

She turned around and stepped back into the kitchen. Another few steps and she saw all John had laid out. "I'm not taking all those."

"Dr. Haden recommends all of them. Especially Haldol."

"I'm not taking them."

"We'll talk about it when you get home."

She folded her arms against her chest and shook her head. "I'm not, John."

He chose to respond calmly. "It's your life. It's your choice, and you can choose what you'll do to take care of your illness. But the consequences of your choices are going to affect all of us."

"I'm going to be late." She shot the pills another disdainful glance, then retreated out the door.

CHAPTER THIRTY-TWO

John knew he was dreaming. The images were hazy and unclear, yet, subconsciously, he accepted where he was. John was standing near his father in a granite fortress. Both were armed in medieval battle gear, and John was confused. He turned to his father.

"Get to your post," his father said, adjusting his breastplate. "Don't leave your spot."

Then his mother stood in front of him too. "We'll support you, John. We're here to encourage each other." She secured the strap on her helmet. "But we have our own spots to defend."

"So stay focused," his father said.

At that moment, a rock the size of John's head zoomed past his ear. His heart raced. The rock had been aimed at him.

"Use your shield!" his father called, pointing towards John's feet.

As John picked up the steel shield, he noted the empty post next to him. A huge rock crashed through the vacancy and granite chips sprayed everywhere. The fortress's foundation shook. Below, John saw the source. A besieging army set another rock in their catapult. He needed to raise his shield and be in position for the next attack, but then he saw her—and froze.

Rebecca was there, mixed in with the enemy. She must have been captured, yet it was she who launched the rock at John.

"That's what we're fighting for!" his father shouted.

"We can still get her back!" yelled his mother.

But Rebecca's eyes said otherwise. They were demonic, hateful. She sprang the catapult, and the missile arced high through the air, straight toward John.

He watched it plummet directly toward him, and then he awoke.

CHAPTER THIRTY-THREE

The following day, between counseling sessions, John listened to his phone messages. One was from Rebecca. She needed him to call back as soon as possible. There was panic in her voice.

He took a deep breath and called home. On the third ring, Rebecca picked up. Once she heard his voice, she said, "Where'd you put it?"

"Put what?"

"The Haldol."

"In the medicine cabinet. With the rest of them."

"I'll take it, John. If that's what you want, I'll take it."

"All four of them?"

"All four," she whispered.

He paused, trying to determine the best way to respond. "Thank you," he finally said. He heard a sob through the phone, and his voice softened. "You okay?"

"No." The sobs intensified. "You were right. It came again."

"The same person?"

"I can't . . ." her voice cracked. "I can't talk about it."

"Where did you see him?"

"It doesn't matter. I'll get on the medicine, if that's what will help."

"We're testing all the options," he said carefully. "What did the sign say?"

"He was selling toys."

John waited for more, but heard only silence. "You still there?" he finally asked.

"I'll see you tonight."

He heard the click, but he stayed on the line until he heard the dial tone.

A family picture on the desk caught his eye—smiling father, joyful mother, and energetic son, all dressed in black and red for their holiday photo. His own beloved family, yet it was hard to believe it had only been four months since they'd taken that picture. The thought made John's eyes burn.

He missed who they had been. Now their laughter had been replaced with anger, their loving companionship with suspicious distance, and their open talks with strained conversations.

At least today he hadn't lost his temper. And Rebecca had finally agreed to take all the medicine. All of this was good, but instead of taking joy in his victory, a strange, guilty sadness settled over him.

Nothing made sense.

After a hopeless hour of trying to refocus, John gave up. He had no remaining scheduled sessions, so he closed his office door and headed home, only to find that Rebecca still refused to share the details of her hallucination. It was private—her own demon to absorb—and for his own sanity, John decided not to push the issue.

CHAPTER THIRTY-FOUR

When John left for work the following Monday, Rebecca hardly stirred. When he called before coming home that evening, her voice broke up over the phone. "I'm not feeling well," she said. "It's been a long day."

"All day, huh?"

"Yeah. Robert's grouchy. We've been fighting a lot."

"About what?" he asked softly.

"He just doesn't want to listen to me, and I don't feel well. I've been in bed most of the day. I don't feel like myself."

John rubbed his forehead. Reluctantly, he asked the dreaded question. "Is it the medicine?"

"Probably."

He sighed into the phone, then said, "Do you want me to pick up dinner?"

"Yes. And can you pick up some milk? We need milk for the morning."

"Anything else?"

"No."

"Did you pick up the mail?"

There was a slight pause. "No." Then she added, "I haven't been out today."

"Okay."

By the time John hung up the phone, his head was pounding. He already knew what he would find once he retrieved the mail. An hour later, when he opened the box, it was there. He set the stack of bills on the post office counter to study the baleful envelope. It breathed a life of its own. John ripped open the envelope and unfolded the letter.

NIce HELIcopter CaR TRain
NIce
No
HELIcopter
He
CaR
CaN
TRain
To
No He CaN Too

On the bottom right corner was the typed word *suffer*.

When he walked into the house, he tossed the bag of cheese-burgers, fries, and Robert's happy meal on the table.

"John?" Rebecca called from the bedroom. "Is that you?"

"Yes."

"Daddy." Robert appeared in the hallway. "Mommy's sick."

"Yeah, I know." When he lifted his son, he could feel the heavy diaper, and he quickly pulled away from the strong odor. "Whoo! You stink."

"Robbie stinks," the little boy laughed. "Robbie stinks!"

"John, could you change him?" Rebecca called again. "I feel like I've been ignoring him all day."

He walked into their room. Other than having her hair pulled back into a messy knot, Rebecca appeared as if she had not moved from the bed all day. Her face appeared colorless and drained. "How are you?"

"Strange." She pulled her hair back and then tucked it behind her ears. "I don't know what it is, but everything's strange. I really don't feel like myself."

John nodded at her statement. The letter's typed word *suffer* played through his head.

"My midterm's tomorrow," she said. "I tried to study some, but I felt like I was having an anxiety attack."

He spoke in a callous tone. "We need to talk."

"Ketchup," Robert said, pointing to the kitchen.

Rebecca looked at their son. "He's hungry."

John nodded. "I'll take care of him. There's food on the table if you want it."

After Robert had been changed, fed, read to, changed again, and tucked into bed, two hours had passed. If John could have procrastinated longer, he would have, but he was out of distractions. He moved slowly back to the bedroom. Rebecca sat in bed, her child development book on her lap, but she wasn't reading. She was crying.

"I'm sorry, John. I don't know what's wrong."

"No." He stood near the bedpost and watched her. "We do know."

"I'm scared of this test." She tenderly wiped a tear from her cheek. "Professor Scott says we have to get 70% or better or we won't pass the class."

"Your test—" John drew in a breath, only to feel a hurricane circulating, preparing to hit their home. "Even if it's a midterm, it's not that important."

"I called Kim today. She asked me to go study with her. She said she'd take off work this afternoon. Wasn't that nice?"

"Rebecca," he said, his voice stern, "some things are more important than this exam."

"I know." Rebecca closed the book. "I told Kim I was so scared I couldn't get out of bed today. I asked her if she ever gets like this, and you know what?" Rebecca looked down at her hands. "Kim thinks my sickness is getting worse."

"It is."

"She told me about a panic attack she'd had. It was on a business trip, and she was alone and starving. She went looking for food but panicked. She felt like someone was there to get her." Rebecca interlocked her fingers and began twisting and contorting them. "She said she only felt safe if she kept walking. So she walked for two miles and almost fainted from exhaustion before she could stop. But she still felt its presence on her skin, so she dropped her food and ran to her hotel. Then she locked the door, moved furniture against it, sat in the corner, and listened. She waited all night. She never slept." Rebecca's fingers were locked in what appeared to be a painful poise. "After I heard her story, I crawled into bed and cried. I can't do this anymore, and I know that now."

Dr. Blythe had promised that Rebecca would recognize the dangers of her illness on her own, which would motivate her to seek help. It was finally happening, so John proceeded in an even tone. "Then what are you going to do?"

Her eyes searched John's face for sympathy. He needed to be strong, and she needed to be proactive in her recovery. But what lay ahead for her still terrified him.

Tenderly, he approached her, sat on the bed, and freed her trapped hands. "You won't give up. You know that."

"Kim asked if I was still seeing people."

"What'd you say?"

"I told her about the last one."

He searched her face, trying to sense if she would let him in. "Did you tell her more than you told me?"

"I told you," she said.

"You told me it was the same man, just selling toys."

"I told you enough."

"Do you want to tell me the rest now?"

"All that matters is that it doesn't make sense. It's just a scary delusion."

John paused. It had to be done. "Helicopters," he said. "Cars and trains."

"I didn't say that," she said in defense.

John drew in another breath, sure that he was about to unleash the hurricane. "You shared it in your own way."

"No." She shook her head. "That's what the sign said. On his sign it said, 'Nice Helicopter, Car, Train.' But that's not what he was selling."

John watched her eyes, her hands, her mannerisms; anything that would give him a clue to understanding her. "What was he selling?"

"Dolls."

"Dolls?"

She exhaled a short breath. "Babies with no heads."

He used his counseling voice to restate. "They didn't have heads?"

"Their heads were at his feet."

"Tell me why."

"I don't know why." Her voice rose to a flurry of panic. "He dropped the heads when he saw me. Then he took a blue blanket from around his shoulders and covered the bodies with it. Then he laughed. He walked through the trees, and I couldn't see him from there."

"What about the dolls?"

"I don't know. I was shaking. I was crying. I don't know how long I was there, but a car suddenly was behind me and it was honking. I turned around and drove home." She took in a loud breath. "I hate this, John. They're scary—and to me, they're real."

"I can understand that." She had no idea how much he truly did want to understand.

"I can't tell the difference."

"I know." He pulled her into a hug. "But we'll win this," he whispered.

"None of it makes sense," she muttered into his shirt.

"I know."

"Except," she spoke slowly. "You know I'm crazy."

"No." He felt her body collapse into his arms. "Your mind's working against you. But you're fighting. You're using rational thinking to remind yourself of what's real and what's not. That's good—it's progress."

"It's not. The images keep coming." She broke away from his arms and reached for a tissue.

Slow seconds passed as she cried.

When she didn't stop, he softly touched her, and she fell into his arms. He tried to soothe her by whispering soft, reassuring words in her ear, but he couldn't keep his mind off the hurricane that was still approaching and expanding. It would strike. No matter what John did to deny, or prevent it, the storm would strike. They had lost control of her life, and he had to accept it. He took in a final breath and said, "You've been corresponding with them, haven't you?"

"What?"

"You've been writing to them."

She gave him a puzzled look. "Do you think I should?"

"Have you been?"

"No."

"Not at all? You haven't done anything?" Against his will, his voice grew louder. "Are you sure you've done nothing at all to correspond with these hallucinations?"

She pulled back. Her face wore a look of complete perplexity. "I don't know what you mean."

"I know this is hard on you." He paused to compose himself. The letter was in his back pocket. He could pull it out, use it to prove the extent of her illness. But Dr. Blythe's analysis was that Rebecca was using the letters to communicate with herself, so John knew that Rebecca needed to bring the letters to him, not the other way around. She needed to identify the severity of the situation, not because he told her it was severe, but because she recognized that it was. So John held back. Instead he spoke in a softer tone. "This is hard on all of us."

Her eyes glanced down at the textbook. A small child's image smiled up at her. "What do you want me to do?"

"Do you agree that we can't do this anymore? That something has to change?"

"What?" She set the book on her nightstand. "You tell me. I'm scared, and I want this to stop."

Carefully, he reached for her hand. The hurricane would strike, but eventually it would cease, and they would rebuild their home. It would take time, but they would succeed. For now, all they could do was prepare for where they would be hit the hardest. "I don't want Robert to suffer."

She shook her head adamantly. "Neither do I."

"Then is hospitalization the answer?"

She ripped her hand from his grasp. The hurricane had hit land.

Rebecca slid out of the bed and walked over to the window. She looked out over the pines. John arose and joined her. He looked out at the dark night and thought of her raging storm. How long would she suffer?

In time, she turned away from the window, and briefly looked at him. Then she rushed into his arms. "Whatever you want, John. I'll do whatever you want."

CHAPTER THIRTY-FIVE

The next morning, John hunched over the kitchen table and looked at facility names, phone numbers, and figures. Information scrawled across this notebook's pages like graffiti. His mind reviewed the formulas, locations, contacts, and referrals, hoping to compartmentalize the emotion attached to the scribbles.

Eventually he heard their bedroom door open. "Won't you be late?" Rebecca asked as she walked into the kitchen.

"I'm not going in today."

Tenderly she draped her hands across his shoulders. "Don't you have appointments?"

"I'm having them rescheduled."

She sat next to him and glanced at the notebook. Sudden fear covered her face. Then, in a slow, cautious manner, she stood up. "Have you eaten? I'll make you some eggs."

"I've eaten." He scribbled around the notes, equations, timelines, and then slowly rewrote the chosen facility's name. "I've been up for awhile."

She pulled items from the fridge and cupboards and then cracked an egg into a bowl. "About five this morning, wasn't it?"

"A little earlier."

"I'm surprised I slept in this late." She mixed the eggs with a fork. "Maybe I'm getting sick. That's probably why I've felt strange. I haven't thrown up, but I must be getting what Robbie had."

John rubbed his tired eyes. "How soon can you pack?"

"What?" Her voice was light.

He took in one long deep breath. Exhaled. Then turned to look at her. "Pack? When can you pack? The sooner we move on this, the sooner you can be home."

The bowl thumped down onto the counter. "You're serious?"

"We agreed on this."

"Not for today." She opened the fridge and lingered behind the door until she pulled out the milk.

"Why put it off? Delay only hurts all of us."

"No." She turned back to the counter and studied the eggs.

"Rebecca."

"Not now."

"We've talked about this."

"I'm not." She poured the milk and again studied the bowl. "I have a midterm today."

"You won't be finishing the term."

"No." She picked up her fork and began banging it against the eggs. "I have Spring Break coming up, then another three weeks, and then I'll be done with classes."

"Rebecca, in the state you're in, you won't complete them."

"I will."

John drew in a stabilizing breath. "Let's talk to your instructor and explain what's happening."

"That's just it." She dropped the fork and clutched her head. "I don't want people to know. They don't need to know I'm sick."

"You've already talked about it."

She turned to face him. "With Kim? Is that who you mean? She understands."

He tried to soothe her. "Your instructors will understand, too."

"She knows what this is like. Others don't, and they don't need to know." She dumped the bowl's mixture into the frying pan and stood over the stove.

He needed her to know he was her ally in this war. "You don't need to be ashamed," he whispered.

Once again, she spun around to face him. This time her hands were pressed against her hips. "Of course I do."

"Fine. Don't tell your professors. Leave without an explanation."

"I've put in hard work. I'm not losing this term."

John shut the notebook. Extending this confrontation would do neither of them any good. He arose from the table and spoke matter-of-factly. "Leaving won't hurt you. By getting help, you'll be more equipped to retake the classes."

"You're lying." She turned back to the stove. "I'm doing well in my classes, and I'm not going to lose that. I'll finish. Then we'll talk about it."

John leaned against the table, lingering to watch his wife move stiffly through her breakfast goal. Finally, he said, "Your health is more important than your education."

Rebecca slammed the frying pan against the stove. A small portion of egg flew through the air and bounced across the floor. "It's my choice," she said. "Voluntary admittance." Their eyes locked. He saw her anger, but even more so he saw her pain. "Last time, I made the mistake of not refusing. Compared to Rick, I thought it was my best option."

"And it was—"

"Don't." Her eyes turned fierce. "How can you?"

"Good things still came from—"

"After what they did to me . . ."

A tension headache exploded inside his skull. "You needed help."

"It was wrong."

"Of course it was. It was horrendous. But it won't happen again."

She folded her arms against her chest. "It could."

"No. It won't. We're in this together. You're not alone. We will fight this together."

"I know what'll happen." She paused. "More time wasted. More life confined." Her voice wavered. "It didn't help before—why would it now?"

"It did help. Look at these past few years. Look at all the good you've had."

She released a painful laugh. "It didn't help. I spent over five years trapped there, and now you're saying I'm back to where I was."

"I'm not saying that."

"It's a waste." A few tears slid down her face. She wiped them away. "Nothing good will come from it."

John wanted to reach for her, but a wrong move at this moment might push her farther away. He tried to speak calmly. "Rebecca, listen to me. Don't diminish what you have. Look at your life. You have me, and you have Robert—two people who care about you, who love you. We need you. If you won't do it for yourself, do it for us. Help us be a family again."

More tears streamed down her face. "We're not a family? Because of me, we're not a family?"

John shook his head. The situation was spiraling out of control. "That's not what I meant."

"Then what?"

"That we're in this together, and we have a slight bump to get over. That's all. This'll take three weeks."

Instantly, her face changed. "Three weeks?" She asked skeptically. "You know that?"

"Most likely." He offered her a hesitant smile. "A short detour compared to all that's ahead."

"What if it's longer?"

"Go now, and you'll come back stronger—better equipped to face future hard times."

"Stronger! I hate that word. I hate how you use it. Stronger. Like I'm so weak."

"You're not always." He stepped toward her, softening his voice. "But maybe right now you are. That's why you'll go and get some mental muscles to wrestle this beast." He reached for her hand.

But she turned away. "I'm not going. After I finish classes, if you still feel there's a need, we can talk. And not until then." She thrust the frying pan toward him, then marched into the bedroom and slammed the door shut.

He grabbed the notebook and threw it across the room.

Ten minutes later, he tried the bedroom doorknob. It was locked. He consciously relaxed his shoulders, then knocked lightly. "Robert's up."

"Well, take care of him!" she called back.

The door remained locked for two hours. Finally, Rebecca emerged. She hugged her school bag against her chest and wiped her red, puffy eyes. "Since you're home, I'm leaving. I called Kim, and she offered to take off work so we can study at the library."

John hunted for the right words, but nothing was appropriate. Finally he said, "Well, then I'll see you tonight."

CHAPTER THIRTY-SIX

Wind blew through the trees outside. Rain had been forecast for that evening. Inside, a brilliant fire danced in the fireplace. John sat near it, reading a book, while he waited for Rebecca to return. Gradually the pages seemed heavy and his eyes drooped.

When Rebecca's schoolbag finally hit the floor, John rubbed his eyes and glanced at the clock. It was just after eleven. "What took you so long?"

"Aren't you going to ask about my test?"

"How was it?"

"Kim's amazing. She spent two hours reviewing with me. By the time the test came, I was thinking clearly again."

"Good." He glanced down at his watch to confirm the time. "Where have you been?"

"Once the test was over, Kim suggested we celebrate. So we went to Denny's."

"You could've called."

"Why?" An unhappy face stared back at John.

He pressed his lips together and looked at the fire. The flames arched and leaped.

"I'm still angry." She unzipped her jacket, then pulled a hanger out from the coat closet. "I told Kim everything, and she thinks you're insensitive." From his seat, John caught a pause in her action, as if she were waiting for him to respond. When he said nothing, she hung the jacket, shut the closet door, and added, "She says her husband's very supportive, and that for you to want to hospitalize me shows you're pawning me off. In fact, she wonders if you might be worse than Rick."

John knew she was trying to manipulate him, so he responded calmly. "Do you believe her?"

Her gaze remained strong. "Back then there was proof I needed help."

"What do you believe?"

"She's responding to the facts."

Another strong breeze swept through the trees outside. "Is she, Rebecca? Isn't there enough proof that you need help?"

"Kim believes there have been times in her life that people really have been following her. She thinks people could be following me, too. You just assumed they were in my head. But not her, she wants to know the truth. She asked if they're real, and do you know what I said?" In the darkness, John saw eyes of hatred staring at him. "I told her yes. And Kim said, 'Then they are.' So why don't you believe me? Instead of trying to lock me up—you should be protecting me."

Although the wind roared outside, a greater tempest raged inside. John could no longer fight against it. He stood up. His eyes burned and his heart raced, but it was time. This storm would break.

Inside the top drawer of his desk lay all the letters. He breathed rapidly as he entered the den, then he swiftly opened the drawer, picked up the letters, and marched back into the front room. "Here." His voice quivered. "Here's your proof."

Rebecca's eyes filled with fear. She took a few steps back. "John, I'm not crazy. Kim says I'm not crazy. I'm not." She scanned the room for an escape. "You're the one who thinks I am." She edged closer to the hallway. "So don't try to confuse me. Don't put ideas in my head."

He extended the three envelopes toward her and said softly, "Look at these."

"You can't deceive me." She picked up her book bag. "I won't let you. I'm going to bed."

"Rebecca, stop!"

"Be quiet," she said. "You'll wake Robert."

"Don't walk away."

She stopped. "What do you want to tell me?"

"Look at these." He repeated, extending the letters. "You'll see you need help."

She took the envelopes and glanced at them briefly. "I'm not crazy, John, so don't tell me I am." She started to open one, then paused. "You treat me like a child," she scolded him. "You try and tell me that I'm unable to live, that I'm not capable of finishing school, that I'm too fragile to do the things I want." Her voice crescendoed into an angry yell and she waved the letters at him. "You're manipulating me, wanting me to believe I'm crazy just to hold me back!"

He remained motionless. She stared at him, and he stared at her. Finally she glanced at the envelopes still in her hand. Then she crumpled them into a ball.

"Read the letters," John ordered.

"Don't create these fears in me. You're the one doing this. You're the one trying to control me."

"This is what you're doing to yourself. Read them."

Abhorrence filled her eyes. "Kim says that I'm prone to find abusive men." She stepped toward the fireplace. "Kim says you're another Rick."

"Don't, Rebecca." John watched her hand.

Her voice grew terrifyingly quiet. "But you're worse than Rick."

The words stung. Anger simmered inside him. It took all his self-control to keep still. Yet he did nothing as Rebecca opened the screen and tossed the letters inside. The envelopes crinkled yellow, then red, then disappeared into blackness.

With the letters gone, John felt an unfathomable void. He shut his eyes, yet he still saw her, distorted by hatred and spite. And her words—all the poison, the lies, the delusions she had somehow come to believe—kept raging inside his mind. When he opened his eyes again, he no longer faced the Rebecca that he knew and loved. Instead, he faced a stranger.

John's fingers wrapped up into a fist. His words were slow and stiff. "Do you really believe that?"

"I have to stop listening to you."

Every muscle inside him tensed. "I tried to give you everything." His voice was low. "I did my best. Never did I treat you badly."

She paused for a long moment, then said, "Don't lie to me."

Dark emotion erupted inside John. His fist tightened. "Am I?"

Her green eyes remained stable and strong. "Yes."

John reacted before he could think, swinging his fist hard against the fireplace. "You're lying to yourself!"

For a moment pain rushed over the anger. Rebecca stared at him, open-mouthed. "You're bleeding," she said softly. "On the rug." John looked down. Red droplets were falling from his knuckles to the Armenian carpet below, its crème fibers already absorbing the crimson blood.

Rebecca ran into the kitchen. Within seconds, she returned with a dishtowel and wrapped it around John's hand. The pain was strong but almost sweet, a release of the hot fury that had built up inside.

Then she stepped back. "Clean up the rug," she said, "hopefully you haven't already ruined it. I'm going to bed."

The bedroom door shut, and John glanced at the rug only to find that he didn't care. Instead of cleaning up the blood, he went to the closet. Favoring his left hand, he opened the door and slipped on his running shoes. Then he grabbed his jacket and headed outside.

Once outside, his feet worked as fast as his mind. If he was moving, the pain seemed to lessen, and since each movement led him away from his house and its problems, his steps became swift and vigorous. He wanted to stop thinking about her. He wanted to stop feeling. He was losing her, losing her after all their struggles and after all the years they'd spent loving each other. It was the irony of the human heart's quest for love: the more you loved another person, the more power that person had to hurt you.

John kept running. Raindrops fell but went unheeded.

When John reached the highway, he paused and struggled for a few breaths, only to conclude that he still had anger to vent. So he continued along the edge of the highway at a jog. The path was dark and quite close to oncoming traffic. Cars zoomed by him, some swerved wide around him, one honked at him. Then another honked and swerved onto the shoulder.

"Are you crazy?" He heard the yell, but only a second later did he recognize the voice. "Johnny Boy, what're you doing?"

John ran over to the passenger side of the Mazda as the window rolled down. "Randy?" John paused to gain control of his breathing. "What are you doing here?"

"Funny, I asked you the same thing." Randy tilted his head and shot John a quirky smile. "See, I'm in my car, on a place designated for cars, late in the evening on a rainy night. But then I see you, not in a car, running in a place not designated for runners, and also, mind you, in the rain. So the real question is, what are you doing here?"

"I have reflectors on my shoes."

"Get in."

John opened the door and slipped into the passenger seat. Amid short breaths, he tried to turn the focus away from himself. "Are you coming from Elle's?"

Randy's face broke into a huge grin. "Probably."

John nodded. "So things are good? With you and Elle?"

"Very." Randy adjusted the rearview mirror down, ruffled his hair, and then chuckled out loud. "Yep, it's very good."

"Rebecca wants credit for this."

"Oh, she can have the kudos—all she wants." Randy flipped the rearview mirror back into place and then flashed his blinker on. "So where am I taking you?" He flipped a U-turn back onto the highway.

"Cause in case you were lost, I'd like to inform you that your house happens to be in the other direction."

"You can take me home."

"Quite a vigorous exercise routine you got."

"Tonight was the first night."

"And quite the hour to finish too, especially on a school night." Randy shot John a concerned glance.

On the dash, the clock flashed a quarter till midnight. John shrugged and made a weak attempt to sound causal. "Sometimes you need fresh air."

Randy turned down Chimera Lane. "How is she?"

"Who, Rebecca?"

"Is there another 'she' we should discuss?"

John snorted a laugh. "Well, she's not who I agreed to marry."

"Yeah. Elle's still worried."

"Drop me off right here." John said. They were five yards from his drive.

"What?"

"Lately she's paranoid about everything. You drive me to the house, and she'll assume I got you involved in our problems."

"Leaving-the-seat-up problems, or shattering-nine-pointer-earthquake problems?"

John grabbed the door handle. "What do you think?"

"What happened to your hand?"

John glanced at his raw knuckles. They were stained with dried blood. Quickly, he dropped his hand out of sight and answered causally, "Robert's discovered the thrill of biting."

Randy shot him a skeptic look. "No two-year–old's teeth scrape up a hand like that." John shrugged his shoulders while Randy snorted a chuckle. "You're a terrible liar."

John could see his house through the trees. A single light shone from the front room. "The worst side of me is coming out."

Randy's voice was somber. "How can I help?"

John shook his head, knowing he was free to return to his home and change out of his damp clothes. Yet he did not move. He kept watching the single glowing light from his house. "What did you think when I decided to marry her?"

"You were happy."

"Was I stupid? Was I crazy to take on her problems?"

"You were happy," Randy restated.

"She's not the same person." John grasped the door handle with his bloody hand. "She's not who I thought she was. And I'm not the person I thought I was."

"John, we all have our good days and our bad days."

"And what if those days turn into years? Then what do I do?" He shook his head again and spoke quickly to cover his question. "I know what the right answer is. I know what I'm supposed to say."

"What's that?"

"I'm supposed to stand by her, support her through any of this. It's what I've said to her since the beginning. It's the right answer. I know that. But to be honest . . . I don't know if I can." John clenched his jaw shut, fighting off unwanted emotion. Once he'd regained his composure, he said, "She used to be the best mother—absolutely committed to Robbie. But lately, there are days where it's like she doesn't see him. It's scary."

The clouds released a downpour. Powerful raindrops hit the car.

"She's never seemed odd to me," Randy said.

"Get around her now, and she would." John watched the hefty drops splatter against the windshield and blur his view of the outside. "There's too much emotion, too many thoughts, and I can't separate myself. She does irrational things, and I fluctuate between anger and confusion. I don't understand her. I want to, but I don't." He took in a long breath, slowly exhaled, and said, "I should be able to step away from this and see her for who she is. I should be able to understand her fears and struggles. But to be honest, I can only be angry that she—or her illness—is destroying our family."

Randy shot him a concerned look. "Are you going to be okay?"

"I agreed to hard times, but this is humiliation. She's attacked my weaknesses, mocked my profession, and destroyed who we are. Or maybe her illness has. It's like her new world is centered on annihilating our family."

"John?" Randy's words startled him from his private thoughts. "Is that true?"

He ran his hand over his raw knuckles and felt the pain, yet he spoke without emotion. "I'm afraid of myself now. I'm afraid of how I'll respond."

"You're a good person." Randy's eyes were kind.

"Am I? I'm not sure I can last. Especially—" he swallowed, as an excruciating heartbreak ran through him, "especially if I can't remember why I wanted her in my life." He yanked the door open. "I need to go. Thanks for the ride."

"Wait, John." Randy glanced at the pouring rain. "You sure you don't want me to take you closer?"

"I'm fine."

"We're buds, Johnny Boy. I want to help, so let me know how I can."

John nodded and shut the door. By the time he descended down the drive, the sounds of Randy's car had faded far away. Each step toward his home brought back the rage, despair, anger, and mourning, but when he finally entered the home, he only felt numb.

He ignored the disgraced Armenian rug and turned off the overhead light. He relied on the night-lights to lead him past the kitchen and into their room. As he entered, she shot up in bed.

"John? Is that you?"

"Of course."

"I was worried." She lay back down.

He went into the bathroom sink and ran his hands under hot water. The excoriated flesh stung. As he scrubbed off the blood and cleaned the wound, he heard her low voice say, "Don't do that." He turned off the water to hear her mutter, "You shouldn't leave me alone again."

CHAPTER THIRTY-SEVEN

The next morning, John and Rebecca went through their morning routine like two roommates who tolerated each other's existence. Each politely moved out of the other's way, passing quickly around the other whenever possible. Words were sparse, monosyllabic, and exchanged only when necessary. Once John attempted peace, he offered Rebecca a compliment on a new shirt she wore. But his fury returned when she told him Kim had given it to her.

The only break from their rigid coldness came as John prepared to leave. He hugged and kissed Robert. Then he reached for Rebecca. Their hug was brief, their kiss tense, but when she said good-bye, John heard the slightest softness in her voice. He replicated the tone in his own good-bye.

Many hours later, after an encouraging therapy session with an advancing client, the receptionist's voice blared through his phone speaker. "Your wife called."

"Okay," John answered back.

But the new receptionist continued, "When she called the second time, she insisted that I get you, so I asked if it was an emergency." Her loud voice reverberated around John's office. "I told her I couldn't disturb you unless it was something like your house burning down. So she said your house was not burning down and hung up. Then she called again and again. I think it was, like, six times." The young girl gave a frustrated sigh. "Right now she's on line two. Do you want—"

"Thanks." He punched the connection over to line two. "Dr. Sanders here."

"John?" He could hear his wife choking through sobs.

His anger from the previous day was instantly replaced by concern. "What's wrong?"

"When will you be home?" Her voice wavered. "Please come now?"

"What's wrong?" He said calmly, trying to ground her frenzied emotions.

"I'm scared."

"Of what?"

"Of me."

John closed his eyes and held his breath.

"I saw that man again," she said.

"Where?"

"I was driving."

"Where?"

"On the corner where you turn onto Highway 18, underneath the stop sign."

"What was the message?"

"His sign said. . . 'I want a ride from you.' Then he pointed at me and started laughing." She was hyperventilating. "Calm down," John ordered.

"I am," she said through rapid breaths. "I drove away. But in my rearview mirror, he was still there. He was pointing at the sign, then at me, and he was laughing."

"Rebecca, listen to me. You are safe. You are going to be okay."

"Okay," she said, as if she were clinging to his words.

"Tell me what you did next."

"I drove a quarter of a mile," she said, slightly calmer. "Then I got mad at myself. I told myself I was wrong. I told myself that it was only in my head."

"Good for you."

"So I turned the car around and drove back."

"And what did you see?"

"Nothing. No one was there."

"See?" John revealed his smile through his tone. "You're doing better. You used logic to tell your mind what was real."

"But it feels real."

"Are you still on the Haldol?"

"It's not working."

"Are you still taking it?"

"Yes, but—"

"Remember, to make these hallucinations go away, you've got to give the medicine at least two months. Don't get discouraged." The words were as much for him as for her. "Give the treatment time to work."

"There's more." She choked on a sob.

"Okay."

"Less than ten minutes later, when I was driving toward Arrowbear, I knew he was there."

"How?"

"I just knew. He wasn't in my rearview mirror, but I knew he was hiding. He knew I knew, so he was hiding."

"Why? Why do you think he was still there?"

"I was going slow. Next time I looked up, he was there."

"Did you see him?"

"I saw a big truck. It was black and huge, and so close to me. He wanted to pass me, but wanted me to speed up. I can't do both—you know how I get. I can't speed up if I'm going to turn into a turnout. But if I slowed down, he would've run me off the road, and if I drove any faster I would've crashed." Her speech dissolved into quiet crying. John listened and waited. Finally, she continued. "When I pulled over, I thought I heard him laughing again."

"This will end," John reassured. "We just need to be patient."

"Come home."

"I will. Soon."

"Please."

"As soon as I can."

When the call ended, John paced the office. He sorted through his options. How could he show he cared, yet not feed into her fears? Amid his thoughts, he returned to his desk and flipped through his contact list until he found Elle's office number.

After a simple chat, John asked Elle to swing by the house and say hello to Rebecca. Of course Elle was pleased to help, but once she started prodding him with questions, John retreated. He told her he had an important therapy session starting but that they would talk more later.

As soon as he hung up, John questioned his action. Why had he voluntarily brought Elle back into the scene? She'd left the situation alone for over a week, and here he was asking her to reengage.

He rationalized that at least this way he knew Rebecca was fine and she would compose herself if someone else were there, at least until he arrived home. Then he turned his focus back to work, sorting papers back into their files and waiting for his next appointment. But as soon as he arrived at home, one look at Rebecca's face let John know he'd made a mistake. Rather than sending water to put out his wife's flames, it appeared he had sent over gasoline.

"She won't say anything to me," Elle said as John walked her to her van. "She's angry I came by."

"Is she?" He scrambled for words.

"She said she thought good friends called before they showed up." Elle stuck her key into the van's lock, but then paused and turned back to John. "I told her I just came to say hi, but her response was, 'Well, that's what a telephone's for.'"

"I'm sorry." No matter what he did, everything kept getting worse. He wanted to spare Elle's feelings by telling her the truth, but doing so would betray Rebecca's trust, and that was a step that John was not yet ready to take.

"Maybe she wasn't angry, just rude," Elle said.

"She's been under some stress lately."

"I could tell that when I got here. She was shaking and crying."

"I'm sorry," John said again. "When I phoned you, I must've misunderstood the situation."

"Robert was out near the drive." Elle pointed to the spot. "He was covered in mud, and she barely noticed that I brought him in. I don't think she's well."

"I know." He gave her as much truth as he could. "I don't think she's well, either."

Slowly Elle stepped closer. She looked up into his face and her eyes turned anxious. In a whisper, she said, "It's the letters, isn't it? She's been opening them."

"No." John offered Elle a consoling smile.

She took a step back and released a great sigh of relief. But then she looked him straight in the eyes. "The letters—are they still coming?"

"I think we have them under control."

She nodded her head in approval. "Randy made me promise not to worry. He told me to trust that you really did have everything under control."

John offered her a fake smile. At the moment, those words seemed too far from the truth. Yet, for her sake, he pressed forward. "Yes. It's all taken care of."

"Good." She opened her van door. "Randy insisted that I leave the situation alone. He said it was a personal issue, and that you had all the information you needed to handle things correctly."

"He's a good friend," John said sincerely, "and so are you."

She smiled at him until she appeared sheepish. "Sorry if I overreacted."

"I can understand where you were coming from."

She slid into the driver's seat, stuck the key into the ignition, and reached for the door. "I just know how awful that situation can be."

John nodded. "Thanks for coming by."

"Sure." She shut the door, then rolled the window down to lean her head out. "It wasn't a problem. I just finished showing a house, and Jade's with her dad." She glanced back at the house. "How long has she not been feeling well?"

"Life's been rough lately," John said nonchalantly, "but give her time, and she'll be herself again." Soon, he hoped.

Elle gave him a soft smile. "I hope so. I'm glad you called me. If I can help with whatever's going on, I want to."

He thought about the half-truths and outright lies he'd told Elle as he watched her drive away. The truth he'd shared was obvious: his wife was not okay. When he entered their home, Rebecca was staring out the front window. He reached out to hug her, but she pushed him away.

"What?" he asked in bewilderment. But the fight had already begun.

"I almost got sent off a cliff, and you don't even care."

"Of course I do."

"What were you and the crazy realtor woman talking about?"

John scowled at her. "About how she's your friend, and she's concerned about you."

She gave him a steaming glare. "She's not my friend."

"Of course she is."

"No she's not."

"Why would you say that?" John asked.

"She's got something against me."

"How do you know that?"

"First that tramp steals my mail, and now she's trying to steal you."

"Rebecca, listen to yourself."

"It's probably why she came over. She kept talking to me until you got here. I hinted that I wanted her to leave, but she wouldn't— not until you got here, and then she was ready, just so she could talk to you outside."

"Please." John took a deep breath. No matter the cost, he would remain calm. "What you're saying is not true. I asked her to come over here because I didn't want you to be by yourself."

She paused and studied John hatefully. "I don't want her help." She turned around abruptly and stormed off. Halfway down the hall, she yelled back at him, "I want a *husband* who will help me!"

A door slammed—and John knew he had nothing more to give.

CHAPTER THIRTY-EIGHT

Home had always been a sanctuary, a place of refuge that John had looked forward to after a day's work. Now his home was a battleground, a place of pain and heartbreak, ready to explode.

Something had to be done. A change had to be made. But on this particular evening, as John rolled into the drive, he was at a loss for what that change could be.

Two things he knew. First, that he dreaded facing the lies, the tension, and the excuses. Second, he didn't want another fight. Rather than fight against her, he wanted to fight with her to restore peace inside their home.

Yet as he turned the knob and stepped into his home, he squared his shoulders back, and braced himself for the night's events.

Instead of little feet running to meet him, there was stillness. No hugs, no kisses, just silence.

"Rebecca?"

Nothing.

"Robbie?"

Only the hum of the refrigerator answered him. Rebecca's car had been in the drive, but the silence suggested they weren't home. After yesterday's drama with Elle, John doubted Rebecca would be with her, but it was possible. Anything was possible.

But Robbie's diaper bag, as well as Rebecca's wallet, keys, and cell phone, were all near the front door.

Robbie's toys were scattered throughout the den, as though he were still in the act of play.

John moved quickly through the house, calling their names a second time only to be stopped by the letter on the kitchen table.

He felt weak. The letter rested on top of its envelope. He picked it up and read:

i wAnT a riDE from yOu

i

i

wAnT

wAnT

a

a

riDE

robert

fROm

fROm

yOu

yOu

i wAnT a robert from yOu

Very slowly, John set the letter back on the table.

Rebecca had read the letter.

This was what he had wanted, but now he feared the response.

He moved through the house, quickly looking in every room, searching for clues of where she went. But there was nothing.

Panic overtook logic. All his thoughts centered on his son. John grabbed his keys, ready to drive but unsure of where to go. Considering whether they'd left on foot, he looked out across their porch. Nothing. He ran back inside, through their bedroom, and out onto their deck. He scanned the forest below. Again nothing. He paced the hallway. He walked out onto the front drive. He felt anxious to leave, yet hesitated to abandon the home.

He returned to the kitchen, but glimpsing the letter sent him back to pacing the hall. Then he thought he heard the slightest muffled noise. Faint, yet definitely coming from Robert's room.

He stepped inside, scanning the walls, floor, ceiling, window. Then his eyes rested on the closet door. Adrenaline surging, John flung open the door.

His wife shrieked timidly. She was huddled down in a corner, wide-eyed. Robert was cradled in her arms, his eyes closed.

"Is he okay?" John said urgently.

Her face was a puffy, tear-stained disaster, but she swallowed back her cries and whispered, "He's asleep."

John reached for him. Rebecca cringed.

"No," she whimpered.

"Please."

Unwillingly, she let John take the child while sobs racked her body.

Relief rushed through John as soon as he had Robert in his arms. He kissed gently his son's head and pressed the little boy's warm body against his. He watched the sweet rise and fall of Robert's breathing.

Tenderly, John laid Robert down in his toddler bed, then turned back to his trembling wife. She was clinging to a stuffed bear, sobbing against the closet wall.

John lifted her up, and she fell into him. Sobs shook her body, her tears moistened his shirt.

At the slightest break in her cries, John led her out of the room. Rebecca looked back at their son, hesitating, but John placed his arm around her and reassured her with a steady nod.

Once they stepped into the kitchen, the letter grinned at them.

"It's horrible," she said, her face trembling.

"Yes." John looked at the cut and pasted letters. "It is."

"What does it mean?"

"No more choices." He reached over and touched her hand. "You have to get help."

"What?"

"It can't wait until you're ready." He spoke calmly, taking time to breathe. "We need to act now."

She stepped away, shocked. Her entire body shook. "What does that have to do with this?"

"It's your sickness."

"What?"

"Robert can't be a part of this."

"John," she whispered. "I'm scared for my baby."

"So am I. That's why we'll get you help—immediately."

"What does that letter," she said, clutching her head, "have to do with me?"

He released a heavy sigh. This was going to be difficult.

"Please, John. What are you saying?" Her eyes pleaded for an explanation.

He stepped toward her and placed his hand on her shoulder. "You sent this."

"This? This letter?"

"You sent four of them."

"Four?" Her hand covered her mouth. Soft whimpers shifted into louder cries.

"I tried to show you."

"Do they all mention my baby?"

"Not like this one."

"Why would I do that?" She looked like she might gag. "Why would I?"

"Schizophrenia causes people to act in unusual ways."

"No." Rebecca shook her head. "Something's happening here, and it's not me." Her hands were shaking. "It's not me." Her head was trembling. She clutched her face. "It's not me, John. It's not."

He wanted to protect her, yet he was terrified too. All he could do was pull her into his arms. "I know. It's not you, it's this illness."

She buried her head into his chest, and her entire body quivered. He stroked her hair, rubbed her back, and tried to soothe her as she clung to him.

He wanted to repeat his words that they had to act. They had to take control before something happened that they couldn't repair. But at that moment, he couldn't speak.

Suddenly a high-pitched ring filled the air. "It's your mom," Rebecca mumbled, holding tight to his shirt. "You should get it," she said, still clinging to him.

"The answering machine will."

The phone rang again.

"No." Rebecca looked at him with heavy eyes. "She's worried. She called right after I opened the letter. You need to answer." She reluctantly released him.

He picked up the receiver. "Hello?"

Rebecca had been right. His mother was restless. "John, what's going on? I spoke with Rebecca a couple of hours ago. She sounded awful."

John quickly put on a mask of calmness. "She hasn't been feeling well."

"She said something in the mail disturbed her, but she wouldn't say what—not until she'd spoken with you. I kept asking, but she wouldn't talk. I called again and asked if she'd talked to you, but she said she couldn't reach you. She sounded terrible."

John looked at his still-shocked wife. "I'm here with her now."

"What's going on? If she doesn't want to talk to me, that's fine, but I have to know—are you all okay?"

He had every intention to say words that would calm his mother, but when he looked at Rebecca, standing alone, with fear etched in her face, he knew he couldn't do this alone. "No, Mom. You're right. We're not okay."

"I didn't think so."

His wife watched him. "I don't know if I can explain it," he said.

"That's fine." His mother's voice was strong. "I've been talking with your father. We're coming to see you. We'll leave tomorrow morning, okay?"

"You want to see Robert?" John watched Rebecca for a response and was relieved to see her wipe tears from her check and nod in acceptance.

His mother's strained laughter echoed through the receiver. "I always want to see Robbie." Then she spoke gravely. "We'll be there early afternoon—unless you need us sooner."

John smiled at Rebecca. "No, Mom. It'll be good to see you."

CHAPTER THIRTY-NINE

When his parents arrived, they worked as a team. They had prepared a plan. After the hugs and hellos, Hal produced gifts for his grandson, gathering Robert's and Rebecca's attention while Cindy drew John aside.

"Should we ask her what's going on?" Cindy asked seriously.

John glanced at Rebecca, who was busy helping Robert set up his new train set.

"Not yet," John said.

His mother placed her arm around him. "Do you want to tell us?"

"Right now . . . just having you here helps."

She nodded. "That's what I needed to know." Then she stepped toward his father. "Hal, let the plan commence."

Without a word, John's father arose. He left the house only to return momentarily with two large grocery bags. Then, like two privates carrying out a drill, the parents gathered up John and Rebecca and herded them toward the door. They ran through the instructions: John was to take Rebeca away for the afternoon, and the two were not allowed to return until seven that evening, at which time dinner would be served. Then they lovingly forced the younger Sanders out onto their porch. As they did, John's mother tucked something into his hand. He looked down to see a rolled-up twenty-dollar bill and a note that read:

> ***Think Less.***
> ***Judge Less.***
> ***Love More.***
> *Please give her flowers & your love*

He chuckled as he headed to the car. The issue at hand was far more complicated than his mother's loving note.

As he slid into the driver's seat, he looked at his wife. Her hair was pulled up from her neck into a ponytail, her blue jeans accented her thighs, and her simple t-shirt matched her eyes. She looked stunning.

She also appeared much calmer since his parents had arrived. "You okay?"

"Is this a trick?" She looked at their house cautiously.

"Not that I'm aware of."

"Am I coming home tonight?

He reached for her hand. "Yes. They don't know what's happened. They just thought it'd be good for us to get away."

"They didn't even let me grab my purse."

"Do you need it?"

"No."

"Okay." John fired up the engine. "So where to?"

She offered a helpless shrug.

He turned toward the main road and thought of his mother's note, now tucked in his back pocket. The gesture was sweet, but they needed much more than flowers. They needed answers. They needed to explore what Rebecca's next step was, what arrangements needed to be made for Robert if she was hospitalized, and how his parents could help.

"Where are we going?" Rebecca asked.

"I have no idea."

At the turn onto Highway 18, he turned on the left-hand blinker. Then he turned it off. Then he turned on the right-hand blinker. Then he turned it off, too.

Suddenly she released a chuckle. "Are you feeling lost?"

John glanced at her and smiled. Her chuckle softened the day's strain. He nodded. "Yes. You could say that."

She smiled back at him. "We can just drive around."

"Good, because I have no idea where we're going," Those words rather aptly summarized their current life. What had once seemed to be a clear, well-paved avenue to peace and happiness was now a hazy, bumpy road full of potholes. John did feel lost.

But when he glanced over at his beautiful wife, he saw more than just her gorgeous features. He saw the beauty of their time together, and he remembered the hope she had represented in years past.

He wanted to turn back and find the path they had once been on. But the only way he could envision getting there was for Rebecca to heal.

He also needed a direction for that afternoon.

The route he was on would lead them to Lake Arrowhead and its lakeside path, but if another painful discussion ensued, the place would be too public.

There were other trails nearby, so he headed toward them. But as they drew closer, that too seemed wrong.

So he kept driving, hunting for the right spot.

In the meantime, they drove around the circumference of the lake.

Finally, John said, "I have an idea."

"Oh?" Rebeccca glanced at him.

He gave her a huge smile. "Let's hope it's still how I remember it."

For another ten minutes they drove in silence. Then, off to the side of the ice skating rink, he spied the small, hidden road. He drove down the lane until he found a turnout and parked. He glanced at Rebecca, feeling pleased with himself. "Let's go." He pushed open the door, but then turned back and touched her arm. "Wait just a second."

Her confused look fed his excitement. He strode over to the passenger door, opened it, and offered her his hand like an old-fashioned gentleman. She accepted it with grace.

"I think you'll like this." He escorted her down the road, past tucked-away houses, until they came to a bridge. "You ready?" he said softly.

"For what?" she said with an amused look.

His grin expanded. "If we're lucky, you'll see."

He led her forward, stepped onto the bridge, and watched her face light up in surprise. They stood in an oasis of ladybugs. Red and black oval insects danced around the bridge's dab gray, scuttled along the handrails and wheeled through the air. Others descended below, landing on wildflowers near the riverbank.

John had been right—the sight mesmerized Rebecca. "How did you know about this?" she asked as a daring ladybug climbed onto her finger.

"I heard about this place during my time at Clearcreek, and I came here once."

"It's amazing." Rebecca gently blew on her finger until the ladybug's wings lifted and it flew away.

Soon she was chanting ladybug rhymes and laughing. From deep within, John felt a smile emerge.

In time, as the ladybugs' magic lessened, John took Rebecca's hand to lead her across the bridge.

But Rebecca paused after a few steps. "Wait." She fished around in her pocket. "Good. They're still there." She held up two pennies and grinned. Then, laughing at John's bewildered look, she tucked one into his hand. "Robert found these the other day. I'm sure he'll forgive us if we use them." She touched his elbow and pointed down at the small stream below. John watched it flow and listened to it gurgle over the rocks. For a small moment, the world felt enchanted.

"We need to make a wish." She flashed a childlike smile, then stretched her hand back for the throw. "Come on," she prodded.

While feeling quite silly, John prepped his wrist for the toss.

"Okay." Again she laughed. "On three. Ready? One, two, three!" In unison, the two launched their coins.

She watched the river while John watched her. "I hope our wishes come true," she said.

After some time, her fingers slid into his hand and together they walked across the bridge while the ladybugs fluttered around them. He led her up an incline toward a tree with a sturdy trunk. They both sat and leaned back to look over the ladybug bridge and the water below. A gentle breeze rustled the tree's leaves. Wind chimes jingled in the distance.

He put his arm around her, and she leaned against his chest. "This is nice."

"It is."

For quite some time neither spoke, and John wished this serenity could heal them. Nevertheless, the issues pulled at him. Finally he said, "What should we tell my parents?"

She continued studying the ladybugs below. "What do you want them to know?"

"We can't face this alone."

"I know." Her body tightened.

John braced himself. He knew his words would separate them again. But before he could speak, she said, "I'm not delusional. I know it."

The strength in her voice surprised him. "We're looking for a cure, Rebecca. That's all I want—to find a way to make this right."

"John, I have my challenges, and there are warning signs I have to watch for, but this isn't one of them."

"Rebecca, it's okay if this is a small relapse. These things happen, we'll get through it."

"No." Her voice was firm. "I did *not* write those letters."

"I know." John gently rubbed her arm. "You didn't. But maybe the illness did."

"No, listen to me." She shifted so he could see her eyes. "I need you to believe me."

"I want to." John removed his arm from around her. "But how do we ignore the facts in front of us?"

They faced each other.

"I didn't write them," she said. "I couldn't have."

"Okay." John said cautiously. "Then who did?"

"I don't know." Her eyes were intense. "But I know it's not me."

He drew in a breath and spoke matter of factly, all emotion set aside. "There's a principle of logic called Occam's Razor that applies here."

"Okay." She drew her hands into a clasp and her body tensed. "What is it?"

"Well, you have a hypothesis that these disturbing letters are coming from someone else. My hypothesis is that due to your illness, you're sending the letters. Occam's Razor states that among competing hypotheses, the simplest explanation is most likely to be correct."

Her eyes became guarded. "How do you know that your explanation is simpler than mine?"

"Well," John said, trying to remain stoic, "I'm basing my hypothesis on three facts." He used his fingers to count off his reasons. "First, your behavior and diagnosis from Dr. Blythe suggest that your illness is out of remission. Second, the man you keep seeing has messages that are very specific to you—messages that only you would know about, and you yourself suggested that it's because he's in your mind. And third, the letters take the messages and shift them into threats addressed to you and Robert. So I'm led to believe that these letters are caused by your illness."

Rebeca turned away from him. She looked as if she had been hit by a splash of icy water. Her clasped fingers writhed and contorted as if they were trapped.

A callous question rested on John's lips. He wanted to get them back on the right path, but he dreaded what he had to say next. He had to remain strong. He couldn't let her cling to untrue notions. If he did, it would only injure her mind. "What facts are your assumptions based on?" he said softly.

Rebecca dropped her hands in her lap and stared at the bridge for a long time. Eventually she turned back and looked directly at him. "John, you've given me so much—so much of my life is tied to you. But right now, I need you to know that there are . . . forces that oppose me. I don't understand them, and I can't explain them. I only know that something is happening here."

"Something is." He reached for her hand. "And that's why we need to do our part to prevent it from getting out of control."

She let him stroke her hand. "I need you to believe that I am good."

"I do believe that. I know it."

Her body shifted toward him. "You never gave up on me before."

"No Rebecca," he said softly. "This isn't me giving up on you."

"Right now, you have to understand that hospitalization would mean I'm giving up on myself. I can't do that. And I'm asking you not to give up on me, either."

If they continued down their current course, they would eventually hit a dead end, a place where they could no longer travel together. John feared such an outcome, so he chose his words with care. "Can't you understand that by considering all our options, that's precisely what I'm doing? I'm not giving up on you."

"I have no recollection of ever creating those letters. When would I have done it?"

"What about your collages for school?"

"That doesn't make sense to me."

"Then tell me the alternative."

"The man seems *real* to me."

"Okay, but what about how personal the messages are? Your last name, the doll heads, the blanket, Robert's name. These are intimate messages—disturbing, but intimate. Not something anyone would know."

"I know, John."

"Not to mention that this man seems to always know wh you'll be."

"I'm terrified," she said gravely. "I need your support. R' I need you to believe in me."

"I believe you are fighting a very difficult battle." He squeezed her hand. "And I want to help however I can."

"Then I need something from you. It's possibly one of the most important things I've asked of you."

"What?"

"If I believed those letters came from me . . . it would destroy me. So have you ever . . ." her voice quivered, forcing herself to pause until she could speak calmly. "Have you ever once considered, that just maybe, somehow, those letters didn't come from me?"

"When I do, I always wonder how another person could know all these things." He released a heavy sigh. "Rebecca, help me out here. Who would know all this?"

She shook her head, and said softly, "Just you."

"Well, I'm not sending them," he tried to say lightly.

"If you were," she said, trying to mirror his light tone, "we'd have a different set of problems, wouldn't we?"

They exchanged a soft glance.

John wrapped his arm around her. "I'm sorry, Rebecca. All I have is logic. Rational thought. It's what I can clearly grasp. It's the only thing that will save us. If a thought or hypothesis, takes us away from rational thought, that thinking could cause us greater harm."

Almost as if ignoring his words, she said, "But would you consider it?"

The words from his mother's note haunted him. *Think Less.*

"Can you help me consider it?" he whispered.

As he sat with his wife under the tall oak, the word *irreplaceable* kept running through his head.

Judge Less.

Maybe it was the magic of the late afternoon, the warmth of a kind spring day, or the beautiful light that filtered through the trees and glistened on the stream. Maybe it was just sitting there close to her. But somehow, right then, he discovered he wanted to hear her hopeless plea.

"Will you listen to me?" she whispered back.

Love More.

Suddenly, he knew what he needed to do. He was not her counselor anymore—he was her husband. It was his responsibility, his duty, to offer her hope.

"You have a valid point," he finally said. "I need to listen to your side."

"Yes. You do." She sounded shocked—and pleased.

"So hear me out," he quickly added. "How about, for the next few days, we both strive to think from the other's point of view? I'll consider what you're saying if you consider what I'm saying. I'll explore your hypothesis if you explore mine."

Her lips broke into a small smile. "With an open mind?"

"Yes." John's face burned with a slight blush. "With an open mind."

On the way back home, John paused to give in to his mother's silly ways. He pulled into a parking lot, looked at his wife, and said, "I love you—and I'll be right back."

When he returned to the car, he handed Rebecca a bouquet of roses.

She gave him a rich smile and a tender kiss.

For the first time in weeks, John felt like he was on the right path.

CHAPTER FORTY

When they arrived home, John's dad had steaks sizzling on the grill. After a few minutes of helping, John turned to listen to his mom deep in play with Robert. Then John headed to the bedroom to find some recent photos of Robert to share with his mom. When he entered the room, he saw Rebecca sitting cross-legged on the bed, talking on the phone. "They're John's parents. They'll be here for a week," he heard her say as he located the album. "You'll meet Robert someday, I promise."

John sorted through a few photo envelopes while Rebecca listened to the person on the other end of the line.

"No," she answered. "They didn't know it was spring break until they got here." He looked over at her. She was watching him. "Yes." She smiled, then rolled her eyes. "He's got his whole family worried about me. Yes, I'm sure they'll watch me closely all week." Rebecca laughed, but her eyes were still on him as she shifted to a serious tone. "He really is a good husband. He's just trying to help me in the best way he knows how." Her eyes wouldn't leave him, so he kept watching her too. "I know," she said, "but I don't want you to get the wrong idea—he really is good to me." An embarrassed look crossed her face, followed by a change in tone. "Okay. Have a good break. I'll see you a week from Tuesday." Then she hung up.

"Was that Kim?" He pulled his eyes, hoping to appear indifferent, and sorted through the pictures.

"I'm sorry," she said.

"For what?" he asked casually.

"She wanted to get together over the break. She wants to meet Robert since I talk about him all the time. But with your family here, I said it'd have to wait."

John nodded his head, but inside he was counting down to the day when he would not have to hear Kim's name again. He turned toward the door. "It's about time to eat."

"John?" She tugged on his arm. "Are you okay?"

He drew in a breath, then slowly turned around. "You're asking me to believe in you, to trust you. Well, I'm asking for that same respect and trust from you."

He studied her. He needed to forgive, but the seed of doubt that Kim had planted in Rebecca by comparing him to Downley still embittered him. "Do you know what I'm talking about?"

Her green eyes were sad, but she nodded. "You're right, and I'm sorry."

"Please leave Kim out of our business," he said. "This is our personal life." The sadness in her eyes shifted to uncertainty. "I know she claims to understand," John added quickly, "and that she has experiences that give you two a bond. But your situations are different. She can't fully understand what you're experiencing, and she is not helping the situation. It would mean a great deal to me if you would separate her from our life."

There was a sudden knock on the bedroom door, followed by his mother's soft voice. "You two ready? Because the food is."

Rebecca slipped past John and approached the door, but before she opened it, she turned to face him. "You're right—it's not her business."

Once Robert was in bed, the adults sat around the table eating ice cream. The moment appeared calm, yet John sensed the tension. Everyone knew more was at stake than what was casually being shared.

But John remained committed to his promise. He tried to be open minded to her situation throughout the evening, even when he found himself leading the group through a cautious conversational tiptoe. As the topic shifted from the casual to the more substantial, the only clear thing shared was that Robert would be taken care of in whatever way was needed.

On his way to bed, John felt a mixture of regret and relief. He had originally intended to relate all the horrible events that had occurred. But all he had done was vaguely express concern around a difficult and unclear challenge that he and Rebecca currently faced. Judging by the worried look on his mother's face and the kind concern in his father's, John sensed they understood, and his relief began to outweigh his regret. They knew enough of Rebecca's history to piece together such little specifics and recognize the truth. He knew his parents would help, and he had not needed to go into detail, which meant he had shown Rebecca that he was still open to her request.

The following morning, there were dark circles under Cindy's eyes, but she nevertheless appeared cheerful and resolute. She announced she had a plan, undoubtedly concocted during her long, restless night.

She handed John the phone and, with a smile, said, "Call your work."

John accepted it dubiously. "Why?"

"You won't be coming in Monday, or Tuesday, or any other day this next week."

He was slightly entertained by her gusto, but needed to offer her an education into his life. "That would be great, Mom, but I have appointments, people who—"

"Who can wait."

"Actually, their situations are urgent, and they need me."

"Your life is urgent," She said, her voice steady and determined, "and it needs you more." Cindy pulled John into a half hug. "We are here to help your family, which means you need to take the same advice you give your patients' families."

"Mom, I need to be there in case of emergencies. Many of my clients are in—"

"I'm not here because of your clients. I'm here because of you. This is an issue of life and death," she stated. "You understand that—I know you do. So set all other disturbances aside, because right now your family comes first."

CHAPTER FORTY-ONE

For the following week, Cindy Sanders directed all the family's plans. First, John and Rebecca were sent on a mini-moon for some uninterrupted couple time. They ended up driving to a neighboring mountain town, checking in at a bed and breakfast, and settling into a lovely room that looked out over Big Bear Lake. For two days, John and Rebecca enjoyed their surroundings, the beauty, the view, and the priceless time to rediscover their endearing friendship.

When the two returned home, Cindy announced her next scheduled item: gender-bonding time. The following morning, John and his father set out early and found a quiet fishing spot on the banks of Lake Arrowhead. The sunbeams on the water looked like diamonds pushing their way to the surface. John and Hal kept quiet as they cast their lines and listened to the sounds of the spectacular spring morning. Ducks quacked at each other, motorboats roared in the distance, and a soft breeze rustled through the pines above.

The lake was fantastic. The fishing was less so.

After almost an hour without a bite, John finally looked at his dad.

"What do you think?" Hal asked. "Is it time to pack up?"

John shrugged. "Maybe." He looked out over the lake. During the stillness of the morning, John's thoughts had turned from his childhood to his youth and now to his current life. "Dad, I need some advice."

"On what?"

"You and Mom have been married for almost forty years, and I've always just expected that. But how?"

Hal offered him a perplexed look. "What do you mean how?"

"Did you have hard times?"

Hal shrugged. "I suppose we had our share."

"But you got through them."

Hal paused and looked out over the glimmering lake. The sun was making its way across the sky. "Well, we learned some things."

"Like what?"

"We learned what the word *us* meant. And that's how we built our marriage, trying to make choices not based on what's best for me, or what's best for her, but rather on what's best for both of us. That means we've made sacrifices—lots of them sometimes. But because of those sacrifices, we've grown closer as a unit, not just as two individuals."

A group of ducks swam past, leaving a long soft trail behind them. A helicopter passed by overhead, and another breeze rustled the branches above.

"Through the years we've learned about love, compassion, forgiveness . . . and maybe most importantly, to respect and believe in each other."

John swallowed a lump that had formed in his throat. "Thanks, Dad

"You have a good family, John."

"I do."

"Well, good." His father stood. "Because if all of this warm, mushy stuff doesn't help you see that, then a dog will." He winked at John.

"Dog?"

"Well, of course." Hal grinned. "Everybody knows a dog is a man's best friend, and I've been watching you since I've been here—I think you need that friend."

"You're joking, right?"

"Nope. I've already spoken to Robbie about it."

John rubbed his head. "Great. I'm sure he gave you full approval."

"So did Rebecca." Hal looked at John with serious eyes. "They told me that you'd resist the idea, so I volunteered to kidnap you and not return until we had a dog."

John thought back to the dog of his childhood. Kilee and their wire-fox terrier had been inseparable, and growing up John had been a little jealous that the dog had never bonded with him in the same way. "I don't know, Dad."

Hal picked up his pole and the tackle box.

"I need to give this more thought," John said. "Talk it over with Rebecca."

Hal chuckled. "I don't think you heard me. I already have. And Grandpa's not going to break his grandson's heart, so in case you didn't understand, I can't return to your home until I've got a dog with me."

"That's cruel," John warned. "You're abusing your grandparent rights. You can't use Robbie to persuade me."

"I don't need Robbie to persuade you. I need the dog to persuade you." Hal started his way up the hill. "Come on. We have an appointment down the mountain. They're already expecting us."

John shook his head and grabbed his pole.

Once they reached the car, his father reached in his pocket and retrieved a glossy brochure. He handed it to John. "I'll drive. You read."

The tri-fold brochure was entitled *Healing through Therapy Animals*.

On the drive down, John flipped through it. The first paragraph read: *We believe in pets helping people. Our mission is to enhance the quality of life through the human-animal bond, specifically through animal-assisted therapy services.*

Below was a picture of two Labrador retrievers, one cream and the other brown. The next paragraph read: *Therapy animals are there for crucial moments and delicate opportunities; they connect with people when their human loved ones and professional supporters often can't, when some special magic is needed to spark the healing process.*

Another picture showed a Yorkshire terrier sitting on an elderly woman's lap. Its caption read: *The presence of animals can provide comfort, humor, and joy; encourage appropriate behavior; and foster feelings of safety and self-esteem.*

During the hour drive, John found his reservations shifting toward amusement. By the time they finally reached their destination, he was actually excited. Perhaps a therapy dog did belong in his family.

After viewing the selection, the dog that won John over was Branko, an obedient, playful black lab that was not quite a year old and not truly a certified therapy dog. But the kennel's owner assured John that with proper training, Branko could eventually gain his Canine Good Citizen Certification.

Rebecca was timid around the bouncy animal at first, but Robert fell in love. By bedtime he had a new shadow that followed him straight to bed, which secured Branko's place in the Sanders' home.

On his parents' final night, while they packed up their things, John marveled at the week's strange events. So little of what he had expected to take place actually had; he now had an energetic puppy, a happy son, and a smiling wife. Somehow, in their odd way, his parents had indeed delivered help.

Right before bed, Cindy pulled John aside. "You were wrong," she said.

"What?"

She pulled him closer. "Do not hospitalize her," she whispered. Her voice was quiet yet forceful.

"We'll see," John said softly.

"Don't." Her touch turned to a grip, then a solid squeeze. "She's fine."

"She seems to be doing better."

"She doesn't need it."

It had been a wonderful week. "Let's hope she continues to do so well."

"I'm serious, John. Do not hospitalize her." She left him no room to disagree. "Motherhood can be very hard—much more difficult than some women suspect."

"I think it's more than that."

"Consider where she came from. She lived a very different life than she has now."

"And she has a good life now."

Cindy's eyes were firm yet full of love. "Things are better than before. She knows that. But even with all this good there are still challenges."

"We have a good life," John stated.

"I know. She and I have had some discussions about all of this—about being a mother, about our struggles. I know she's giving you a huge scare, but be patient."

"Did she give you all the details about her illness?"

"I didn't ask for details, and she didn't share. And I don't care. She really loves you and Robert—and that's what will get her through this."

The love in his mother's eyes prompted John to pull her into a hug. "Thank you, Mom. Thank you for everything."

Minutes later, he moved a mocha-colored pillow from the oversized chair in their bedroom and sat down. Rebecca, dressed in pajamas, folded her clothes from the day.

"My mom thinks the world of you," he said.

She stepped into the closet, tossed the shirt into the dirty clothes hamper, then turned back to face him. "It was nice to have her here."

"She said you had some good talks."

"We did." Rebecca smiled at him. "We connected in ways we haven't before." She continued tidying the room.

John leaned back in the chair and watched her. "I think Mom felt that too."

"She gave our house a deep clean while we were gone; did you know that?"

"That doesn't surprise you, does it?"

She grinned. "Of course not, but she found that stain."

"Oh." John rubbed his neck. "The rug."

"Yes."

"I'm sorry," he whispered.

"Me too. I'm sorry about a lot of things."

John gave her a sympathetic chuckle. "Maybe we should find a new rug."

"Actually, when it comes to her children, your mom's ready to rise to any challenge."

"Did she really . . . ?"

"She found a box of cleaning supplies." Rebecca sat on the edge of the bed.

"Did it work?"

"It was amazing. At first what she did made the color even more noticeable. But then, after some time, it was like magic. The stain lessened, and now you can't even see it was there." She reached for his hand.

He squeezed her hand softly. "I'm glad we're doing better."

"Me too."

"How are you feeling?" John asked cautiously.

"Good. Really good."

"Maybe the medicine's helping."

"I think it's been good to have your family here."

"I agree."

"Maybe you were right about school," she said. "Maybe it's been more stressful than I realized."

"I think . . ." He stood up and pulled her toward him. Then he touched the curve of her waist. "The break has been good for you."

She stepped into the hug. "It has."

John breathed in her soft lavender scent and let the seconds pass. The storm had ended.

"Do you think I should quit?" she suddenly asked.

"I never meant to imply that you should quit school altogether," he whispered in her ear, "and you shouldn't."

"I know. But do you think I should put it on hold? Just for right now, maybe until Robert's a little older?"

He considered, then pulled back to search her face. "Do you think you could finish the term?"

"There's three weeks left. Do you think I should?"

She appeared happy, healthy, and safe. "Do *you* think you should?" he asked.

"I would like to."

"It makes sense."

She stroked his face. "Thanks for believing in me."

"Rebecca," he whispered, "you'll do the best thing. I know that, and I trust you."

She pulled him into a passionate kiss.

CHAPTER FORTY-TWO

Once his parents left, John's regular routine returned. As soon as he arrived at work on Monday morning, he was thrown into meetings with Dr. Blythe and a prominent philanthropist. A detailed two-day show-and-tell followed with hopes that this potential donor would see Second Chance as a valuable community resource and choose to support it financially.

As he drove up the mountain after his second day back, John's mind was caught up in the philanthropist's departure. The man had made no promises, but he did offer a token of hope by saying he would contact John again in the weeks ahead. John didn't want to pre-plan on this financial relief, but the clinic would head into difficult times without it.

When John entered the house, he found that no toys decorated the living room, no aroma of dinner filled the air, and no noise greeted him. "Hello?" he called from the living room.

"Hi," Rebecca's voice immediately called back. "We're in the bathroom."

John discarded his briefcase and suit jacket, then headed down the hall to find Robert in the bath, surrounded by an assortment of water toys. Rebecca sat near him on a stool, frantically scanning her textbook. "Nothing's ready for dinner," she said while her finger skimmed the last page of a chapter.

John stood above her until she looked up, then he leaned down and gave her a kiss. "Hello."

She shut the book and gave him a smile.

"So do you remember anything that you just read?" he asked.

"No, but I have to go. There's a quiz, and Kim and I agreed to meet before class to review for it. But I just now finished the chapter, so if I don't run I'll miss getting her help."

"I could have bathed Robert," he said.

"I know, but it was something I needed to do tonight."

"Well, thank you."

"Can you believe they're giving us a quiz right after the break? Cruel, huh?"

"You'll do fine, and remember—this is only a class."

"That's your famous line." She pointed at the counter. "There are Robbie's pajamas, for when he's ready to get out."

John eyed the tub filled with water toys. "Which probably will be never."

Robert banged a plastic boat against the water and laughed. The movement sent a spray across the tub, hitting Rebecca's sleeve. "Robert!" She shot him a scolding look, then glanced at her watch. "I have to leave."

She grabbed her bag and hustled into the kitchen. From the bathroom, John could hear her slamming cupboard doors. Then she reappeared in the doorway with a granola box in her hand. "The trash compactor is still broken." She pulled out the last granola bar and handed John the empty box. "I talked to the repairman today and he said he'd come tomorrow. You'd hope, huh? How many times has he canceled?"

John's words were soft. "I think once, maybe twice."

She ripped open the foil wrapper and attacked the small bar, then looked at John. "Am I okay?" she said between bites.

"I think so."

"Tell me I'm okay. Tell me we're okay. That everything's fine."

"Do you feel okay?"

"Yes." Her voice revealed some slight agitation. "I know I'm fine, but if you want me to quit during this term, I will."

"Rebecca, I'm not going to worry about it. I trust you."

"Did you tell Dr. Blythe about the improvements?"

"Yes, and she agrees. If you want to stick it out, then you should. You have two weeks left and then finals. The end is almost here." He watched her shove the last granola bite into her mouth. "Do you feel okay?"

"Do I seem okay?" She searched his face.

"Definitely. Either the medicine's working or things have settled down." He offered her a huge reassuring smile.

"This last week helped, didn't it?"

"It did. You seem great. So get through this term, then during the summer we'll decide your next schedule."

"John, I don't know what was happening before. But I think I'm fine. Really I do."

"Then you are."

"Just don't worry about me."

"Do I seem worried?" He expected an answer, but she was too busy grabbing her bag. He waited, then pulled her into a quick hug. "All I want is for this family to be okay and for you to be healthy and happy."

"I'm working on it." She gave him a quick kiss. "I've got to go. I'll see you tonight." She grabbed the empty granola box from his hands, shoved the torn wrapper inside it, and headed for the kitchen. He heard her pull out the trash, open cupboards, and turn on the faucet for a drink. There was one last good-bye holler, and then the front door shut and the car rushed away.

John looked at his son, who was still hammering toys against the water. "Should I even try to get you out?"

"No."

"You get six minutes, then us men hunt for food."

Six minutes later, a father-son battle erupted over the steadily sinking water line. Not until the toys finally found land did Robert consent to leave his fleet and get dressed.

With a fresh diaper on and everything dry but his hair, Robert ran into the kitchen. "Uh-oh," he said.

John entered the kitchen. Branko had tipped over the garbage can and was busily rummaging through the trash. John rushed to grab the dog, which panicked the puppy into scattering more trash through the kitchen. On his second try, John scooped up the dog, marched into the laundry room, and, with a bit more force than necessary, flung Branko in and shut the door.

When he returned to the kitchen, John scanned the garbage. "This is Grandpa's fault." He crouched down and retrieved the scattered granola-bar box, wrappers, banana peels, assorted pieces of paper, and eggshells that still rocked back and forth.

"He ate garbage." Robert started to laugh. "Branko ate garbage."

"Robert, go look at a book."

"No."

"Now!"

Robert stood wide-eyed and frozen by the intensity of his father's tone.

In a softer voice, John added, "Please, go look at a book or play with your toys. I'll come get you when I have dinner."

Robert frowned but obeyed while John picked up the final pieces of trash, some sticky, damp junk mail. He picked up a grocery ad. A ripped envelope was stuck to its side. The contents were wet and discolored, but not defaced enough to hide:

E C C A

x 222

rest, CA

92385

The eerie type matched all the previous letters. John dug through the trash, frantically searching for the other half, only to find it further down, below a smashed milk jug. From the envelope, he pulled out the letter pieces, placed them together, and read:

Is knIGHt yOurS?
Is
I
knIGHt
kNOw
yOurS?
yOu!
I kNOw yOu!

John hurled the letter in the trash, then kicked the cupboard below him and slammed his fist against the counter.

"Daddy!" Robert ran in. "What's that sound?"

"Nothing."

"Can I eat?"

"What do you want?"

"Ketchup."

"And?"

"Hot dog."

"Fine."

John heated up Robert's food. Then he sat silently at the table and watched his son finger-paint in the ketchup. When Robert began applying it to his face and chest like war paint, John wanted to yell, but instead he simply cleaned it up.

"Why your mother had to give you a bath before dinner is beyond me," John fumed.

Then he tried to get Robert to bed, only to endure a bout of frustrated coaxing, followed by a dull and hasty book read. Eventually, John tucked the boy in, and leaned down to give him a kiss.

Once John left Robert's room, he re-entered the kitchen and looked in the direction of the trash. Too much was at stake. He couldn't stand idly back, waiting for the circumstance to resolve itself. This was dangerous, and John was afraid for his wife and his son.

He retreated to the den and picked up a book, but his mind raged. He stood and paced the hall, the bedroom, the living room, and then let Branko out. Finally he returned to the trash container and pulled out the pieces.

He pieced the letter and envelope together on the kitchen table. Then he read and re-read the message. After his fifth search for meaning, Branko began to bark. Headlights shone through the window, and her car crunched down the drive.

By the time the front door opened, John was in the doorway ready to greet her.

"Hi," she said.

"Hey."

"I did well on my quiz tonight."

"Good." He took a deep breath and reflected on the previous week. They had won back precious peace within their marriage. He would not lose that now.

He chose his words wisely.

But before he could speak, she continued. "It was hard, but I surprised myself. I remembered a lot, especially after barely reading some of it. What'd you have for dinner? I'm starved." She walked into the kitchen only to stop in her tracks.

She stared at the letter.

Then she stepped toward the table.

"I didn't want it to upset you," she finally said.

"Well, it has."

"What can I do?"

"You tell me."

"Everything seemed better." She sank into a chair, then picked up a piece of the letter. "We thought I was doing better; you and I were better. I felt like myself again. You and I . . ." She shook her head at the bits of paper. "Why do we have to acknowledge this?"

"There was just a letter this time?" John fought to hide the tension in his voice. "No dark-haired guy with a sign?"

"There was."

John's fist hit the table. "Why didn't you tell me?"

"It seemed better for us if I didn't."

"When?"

"Four days ago."

"Four days ago!" His mind raced through the shock and betrayal. "When? Where were you?"

"It was right after your parents left. Robert and I did some shopping down the hill. I was back up here by two."

"What was the message?" He had to remember he had options. Fear, distrust, anger—all these emotions had pulled them apart, and now they were returning.

Her voice weakened. "I can't believe it's me doing this, John. I just can't. If I think that, it destroys everything I'm trying to be. I want help, but your help is different than the help I want for me."

"Why didn't you tell me? Were you upset?"

"Of course I was upset."

"Where did you see him?"

"It happened before the turn off onto our street."

"On Chimera?" John thought back to the hospitals he had listed and made his decision. His parents would take Robert, just like they had tentatively discussed.

"About a quarter mile from here." She ran her fingers along the disturbing note.

The touch was unsettling. John thought of her cutting and gluing the pieces, preparing the message for its round trip through the mail. He glanced through the words again. "And the sign said something about a knight?"

"I know." Rebecca rolled her eyes. "It doesn't make sense. Is knight yours? I don't even know what that means."

"What's going on, Rebecca?" he said weakly.

She dropped her forehead into her hands and studied the letter. "If I have to believe this, then my mind is a strange thing . . ." She lifted her head, and her eyes reached out to him. "If you want me to, I can accept that my mind is playing tricks on me. If you really believe that's what happening here, then I'll acknowledge it. And I'll fight against my mind, I'll do whatever I have to, because I won't allow it to take over who I am. I have too much to lose." When he said nothing, she gave a small shrug. "Other than that, I don't know what else to do."

Once again John reread the letter.

"When your parents were here," her voice was calm. "I felt like me again. More than I had in weeks. I can't lose that now." She paused. "I should have told you. I know I should have, but I didn't." She reached out to touch his arm, but he did not respond. "Please, John. Understand me?"

Too much was running through his head. Yelling was pointless. Blaming was counterproductive. Discussion was fruitless. He had no options. But, he could not give up hope. He had to hold on to her somehow. Beneath his breath he muttered, "It was wrong, Rebecca."

She removed her hand. "I know. But I also know what the next step is, and I don't want it. But I'll get ready for it. If that's what you think I need, I'll do it." She watched him with clear, focused eyes. "I'm sorry I wasn't honest with you," she said, "but right now, I'm trying to be honest with myself."

He heard the calmness in her grand effort to accept hospitalization, but he was still angry. "You should have been open."

"I know."

His eyes scanned the words. Is knIGHt yOurS. She was right—the words were meaningless. He studied the letter's jagged pieces and obscure message. Then he scanned the envelope's eerie type, the food and grease stains from the garbage, the Santa Barbara postmark, Saturday's date, the American flag stamp, the . . . John gasped. How had he missed it? He jumped back, startling his wife.

"Please don't be angry," she said.

"I'm not." He grabbed the envelope pieces.

"What's wrong?"

"Nothing." He picked up the letter, avoiding her eyes. "I need to go somewhere. Just for a drive. I need to clear my head—please don't wait up."

"Why, John?" Her eyes were panicked. "Let's talk, please. I'm sorry. I'll listen to you. I'll get help. Whatever you ask—I'll do."

"Don't wait up." Then he cupped her face in his hands and looked her directly in the eyes. "I love you, and it's fine. *We're* fine."

CHAPTER FORTY-THREE

It was 9:20 when John pulled in front of Elle's house. Randy's car was parked in the drive. Lights were on and music echoed from the windows.

After a loud knock, Randy came to the door. "Johnny Boy. What's the occasion?"

"Hey." John walked past him. "Where's Elle?"

"In case you were wondering, yes, you happen to be disturbing a very nice moment between the two of us. Kind of intimate. Not really when you want your sidekick to be showing up, you know?"

"Hi, John." Elle appeared around a corner. "Don't listen to him. We were downstairs watching a movie with Jade, trying to get her to fall asleep. It's nice to see you."

"You were right," John said.

"About what?"

He drew in a quick breath and said, "We got another letter today."

"Really?" She sat on the large green couch. "Here have a seat."

John sat across from Elle. Randy sat next to her.

John glanced at Elle, then at Randy, and then pulled out the pieces of the letter. "It's someone who knows her," he said with eagerness.

"John," Elle said, alarmed, "Why are you smiling?"

"Because it's real."

"Really?" Randy watched John.

"Yes," John sighed. "It's real."

"I don't understand," Elle said.

"I didn't listen to you before," John said meekly. "I'm sorry. I was wrong—very, very wrong."

Randy released a large exhale. "That's good."

Elle continued to examine Randy. "What's good?"

"It's not her." Randy's eyes sparkled with joy and relief.

"Who?" Elle turned to study Randy.

"She's not sending them to herself," he said.

"What?" Elle's mouth dropped. "You jerk." She spewed out the words. "You think she impersonated a stalker?"

Randy threw up his hands. "No, of course not."

"You think this was made up?" Elle demanded.

"You don't know the whole story," Randy said defensively.

"You ruthless beast." She glared at Randy. "Do you know what a stalker *is*?"

"Yes." He looked to John for aid, but John was only partly listening to them. His wife had been right this whole time. He was the one who had been deceived. Furthermore, someone had wanted to deceive them, and he had fallen into their trap.

Anger at the stalker grew, but it couldn't overwhelm the joy in John's heart. Rebecca wasn't relapsing. She was sane. He had completely misjudged the enemy.

"They're real," Elle's eyes glared at Randy. "Real demented men that terrorize women."

"Hey, wait." Randy shook his head. "This wasn't me. John, back me up here."

"Or it could be a woman," John said.

"I can't believe you would say that." Elle scowled at Randy. "Are you saying she just wanted attention?"

"No." Randy stood up, his face earnest and resolute. "Enough of this game. John, she gets the truth. Now."

Still partially listening, John nodded. "We have to give Rebecca the truth."

"But Elle first! I don't care what you and Rebecca have agreed on." Randy glanced at John and then at Elle. "Babe, I'm not the bad guy." He flung up his hands again. "And I'm not in the middle of this—not anymore."

"What are you talking about?" Elle asked.

"John, either you tell her, or I'm going to. But no more secrets. Rebecca's not hiding; we're coming clean. We're going to be one big, happy, honest family."

John looked up at Randy. "This isn't a relapse."

Elle's eyes raced back and forth between them. "Who?"

"His wife," Randy said. "He thought she was crazy."

"You thought your wife was crazy?" Elle now stared at John in disbelief.

"She's not ill again." John's voice was low and soft. "I was wrong."

"What?" Elle looked like she was going to scream. "Because she received distorted mail—you both are—"

"She *was* crazy." Randy inserted.

"No she's not." Elle said.

"That's not what's happening here," John whispered.

"What?" Randy looked at John. "I'm not calling your wife names. I'm just stating facts. She's been unbalanced, Elle. She's been seeing some serious delusions. She saw a fake baby for years. That how's John and her met; he was her therapist at a psychiatric hospital. Not your typical place to find true love, I know, but it worked for John. Now he said her delusions are out of remission, and a dark guy with signs sends messages to her."

"It's . . ." John stumbled on his breathing. "It's all real. The man, the sign, the letters. It makes complete sense. They knew her maiden name, knew about her delusions, the baby blanket, its color, texture, the name she called the baby. They've been describing her all along. No random stalker would know those things." John pulled out the dirty envelope from his back pocket. "It's someone who knows her well, and they're telling her that. It's why I thought it was her all along."

Elle's eyes could go no wider. Her face appeared ready to pop. She shut her eyes, rubbed them, and opened them to glare at John. "What?"

Randy kept watching Elle. "John, you told me that Rebecca took the words from the signs, cut collages from the messages, and sent the letters."

"I was wrong," John said humbly. "Completely wrong. Elle, you were right. And now I've got to fix it."

"What?" Her eyes remained extremely large. "Why didn't anybody tell me this?"

"Rebecca didn't want you to know." Randy placed his arm around her. "She wanted you to be her friend. She didn't want you to view her differently. She's uncomfortable with people knowing her past."

Elle shook her head. "I don't care about that! Why didn't anyone tell me about all these other things connected to those letters?"

"I thought it made sense . . . at the time." John felt like a fool. In an effort to redeem himself, he extend the envelope toward them. "But I know now. Look." He pointed at the postmark. "All the letters were postmarked in San Bernardino. But not this one."

"Santa Barbara." Elle replied.

"And Rebecca wasn't in Santa Barbara?"

"Not anywhere close," John said. "She was with me all day on Saturday."

"The day it was mailed." Randy nodded, smiling. "That's how you knew."

"You were right, Elle," John wanted to give her a hug.

Elle looked close to tears. "I told you. I told you it was awful."

John nodded, his heart racing with happiness, adrenaline, and justice. "I understand now. Someone's trying to destroy her. I have to tell her, and then we'll get this taken care of and get it out of our lives."

"You can't tell her." Elle stated.

Now Randy stared at Elle. "But she needs to know."

"What do you hope to accomplish by telling her?" Elle asked John.

His eyes welled up with tears. "She needs to know she's not re-lapsing. I told her she was, and it's devastated her."

"And you think that knowing she has an actual stalker will be better?" Elle scowled at John.

John shook his head. "We take this to the police and they inves-tigate. They nab the person behind this, and we move on."

"It doesn't always work that way," Elle said cautiously. "We never found the person who stalked my sister. What happens if the police don't do enough? Or they can't find this person fast enough? Rebecca will live in fear for the rest of her life. What does that do for her?"

John turned back to the letter. Although ripped in half, it was powerful enough to make Rebecca hide it. She'd wanted to pretend it could all go away, and he wanted to pretend too.

"Elle," Randy said softly. "She's an adult. She needs the truth."

Elle shook her head. "You just told me she has a history of men-tal health issues, and the person behind this knows that. How is tell-ing Rebecca that she's being followed, threatened, and manipulated going to give her peace of mind? How can you be sure that it won't make her relapse for real?"

John bit down on his lower lip. He wanted to disagree with her. He wanted to rush home and grab Rebecca in his arms and tell her she was free from all the fears he had placed inside her mind.

He looked again at the letter. Is knIGHt yOurS? This stalker was preying on both of them. John had promised to protect her, to keep her safe and at peace. I kNOw yOu! Instead, John had been tricked into increasing her fears. In a way he had encouraged this; he had helped feed her the toxins that had eaten away at her health.

But this was not a time for blame. This was his opportunity to give her what she should have had before. He still could protect her.

"You're right," John said softly. "I'll take this to the police. Have them look into it. We'll get this taken care of, and it'll be over. Then I can tell her."

Randy's forehead creased. "John, would it really hurt her that much to have the truth?"

"The point is that it could," Elle stated.

"She has a right to the truth," Randy said.

"At some point she does." John looked back at the letter pieces. "All these events have placed her in a vulnerable place. If we share this with her now, with no definite resolutions, we'll increase her paranoia. She's grasping at healthy concepts, but there's nothing healthy about this. This is a critical time, and we need to be careful not to trigger more negative factors."

Randy rolled his eyes. "You're too protective."

"No." John slipped the envelope back into his pocket. "Why should I let her worry about something she has no control over?"

"These letters are designed to stimulate fear," Elle said, reaching for Randy's hand. "We can't allow the culprit to do that."

Randy accepted Elle's hand, but he looked away from them.

She stroked his arm. "I'm sorry, Randy."

He shook his head. "When I was younger, my cousin died in an accident that made the nightly news. It was my job to make sure my grandfather didn't watch it. He was still coming to grips with my grandmother's stoke, and we thought the news about my cousin would be too much for him. That was the worst night of my life. I had to lie to him to get him away from the TV. I felt like a traitor all evening. It was hard, and it was wrong."

"This time it's right," Elle said, leaning into him. "Just for right now."

John looked at Randy. It would be difficult to keep the truth from Rebecca. He felt his jaw tighten. "Only a very short time," John repeated. "Just until we know enough to tell her that it will all be ending."

Randy nodded, then looked at the carpet. "How can I help?"

Elle spoke up. "It's like John said. We need the police involved. They'll want to know if you can give them any leads." With my sister's sicko, since there was no direct threat on her life, the police weren't able to do much. But with her seeing a man . . ." Her voice suddenly caught. "Let's hope they can do more."

The room fell silent. John rubbed his cheeks, his face, his head. Then he stood and began roaming the room. "I know where the person's from."

Randy's mouth dropped. "You do?"

"It's someone who knows her past. They know who she once was, and they know how to make her react. It has to be someone from Clearcreek Mental Care Center."

"That's a start." Elle said.

"From Clearcreek," Randy restated.

"Yes," John said. "I just need to figure out who."

CHAPTER FORTY-FOUR

It was almost eleven when John arrived home. The bedroom light was still on. When he poked his head around the corner, he saw Rebecca curled up in the oversized chair reading a book.

"What are you reading?" he asked.

"*The Bell Jar.*"

"Is it good?"

"Sylvia Plath. She writes an award-winning novel all about insanity—inspiration taken from her own experience—then turns around and kills herself." Her fingers clawed into her arm. When she lifted them up, they left an imprint. "Now that's inspiring—she could capture craziness, could write about it, but couldn't cure it. She's considered brilliant and gifted, but what good is that?"

John pulled the book out of her hand and touched her arm. "Remember back at Clearcreek when you enjoyed reading fairy tales?" He looked into her sad eyes and offered her a guarded smile. "A book like that might be a better choice."

"None of Grimm's end happy. They were gruesome—meant to inspire childhood nightmares."

"Well, then not Grimm's."

"But they were true to life. They captured the darkness."

"Rebecca." His fingers brushed strands of hair away from her face. "Are you giving up?"

She pressed her lips together and shrugged.

Randy had been right—withholding the truth after these excruciating weeks was a second form of torture. She was hurting, and he was allowing her to internalize the lie that he had believed. But he replayed what Elle had said, about why he should protect her. Then John promised himself he would give her the truth as soon as he could.

He touched her thigh, and she slid over, giving him room to sit. Then he gently placed her legs over his lap. "Things will work themselves out. It'll be okay." He was a terrible liar, especially to her, so he turned away and dodged her eyes.

The culprit needed to be identified. As soon as they did that, Rebecca could have the truth. He tenderly caressed her feet and he causally asked, "Who do you remember at Clearcreek?"

Although he avoided her eyes, he felt them glaring at him. "Why?"

"Does anyone stand out to you? Anyone specific that you remember?"

"Is that where you went?" Her voice was tight. "You drove by that place?"

"No," he said softly. "I didn't go there."

"But you were thinking about it?" She touched his arm. "Why?"

"Who do you remember from there?" His eyes remained fixed on her feet, his hands still rubbing them.

"It's time to admit me, isn't it?" Her words held no emotion.

John felt trapped. If he looked into her eyes, he would open up. So he looked past her. "No. You're fine."

"Not if you're bringing up Clearcreek."

"I don't think we should worry about the letter right now, okay?" He glanced at her briefly. She gave him an unsure look. He spoke quickly and calmly. "I was only thinking about some of the people who both of us used to know. I was trying to remember certain things about them. It made me wonder what you remembered."

"About the people?"

"Sure. More specifically, some of the residents. Like Thomas, for example. What do you remember about Thomas?"

Her eyes grew wide. "Penciltop?"

"Yeah."

"He was gross."

"I know. Did you ever talk to him? Interact with him?"

"Once he grabbed me, shoved me against the wall, and pushed his tongue in my ear like he was trying to get it down my ear canal."

John gave her a disgusted look. "What did you do?"

"Screamed." She gave him a puzzled look. "What was I supposed to do?"

John chuckled and pulled her close. "I love you," he whispered.

"Thanks," she returned the whisper, however her voice was weak and empty.

Yet he had to push her a little further. "How well did Thomas know you?"

"I didn't talk to people there. You know that."

"Is there anything that sticks out to you?"

She pulled back slightly and studied his face. "Why are you like this?"

"I was just thinking . . . I don't know."

"John." She stroked his face with her fingers. "You know I love you. I'll do what we need to do."

His heart hurt. He took a deep breath and spoke in a low voice. "I was wrong."

"But Dr. Sanders," she teased, "fear and denial will not help me heal." Then she leaned against his chest. "Just don't leave me as I go through this, please."

"I couldn't." He tightened his arms around her. "Things aren't as bad as we thought. Not in that way. Really, Rebecca, let's not worry about this for now."

"Really?" She offered him a perplexed look. "What does that mean?"

"Let's be open to all the possibilities." He kissed her on the forehead. This was all he dared say. In a matter of days he would share the truth with her. Then they would rejoice in relief together. "Let's go to bed."

She looked at him, and smiled slightly. "Okay."

Hours later, John lay awake. He listened to Rebecca breathing next to him and thought about telling her the truth. How could he keep this from her while she was blaming herself?

He twisted onto his side and nudged her awake.

"Huh?" she mumbled.

"Does that man look like someone you know?"

"What?"

"The man with the signs. Does he look like someone?"

"Huh?" She was still asleep.

"Who does that man resemble?"

Her eyes slanted open to look at John. "A scary man."

Seconds later, she was back asleep. But John was still thinking, so he nudged her again.

"Huh?" She barely opened her eyes.

"What does Kim look like?"

"I don't know." She yawned.

"Does she resemble anyone from Clearcreek?"

Rebecca twisted her body deeper into the mattress. "I think so."

"Who?"

She pressed her head against the pillow. "I don't remember."

"Describe Kim to me."

"She's bigger than I am. Smarter, too. She likes chickens. She's Peruvian, I think. Or from   Alaska . . ." She went quiet, and her steady breathing resumed. Then she mumbled, "Good night."

The moonlight shone through the window and softly lit her face. *Is knight yours?* John had to protect her. This was his chance to redeem himself from his earlier mistakes, and, at this stage, there was nothing she could do with the truth.

He rolled onto his side and promised himself that he had to find the truth the following day.

CHAPTER FORTY-FIVE

At the slightest glimpse of daylight, John sprung into motion. He had a plan. The police would have *basic* facts. After that, with Elle and Randy's help, John would carry out his own plan. Then, after he had more proof, he would give the police *all* the facts.

Slyly, he reached into Rebecca's purse, retrieved her keys, and then stuffed them into his briefcase. Next he tucked her spare keys in a pocket of a blazer which then became lost in the far corner of the closet.

When she arose he gave her one tight hug. "I have something urgent today," he said. "Then I'll be home this afternoon, and it'd be good for us to talk."

She gave him a resigned look. "I assumed so."

"We're okay." He pulled her into a strong kiss. "We just need to talk and clear up some things."

Twenty minutes later, he called her on the cell phone and shared his recited speech. "Hey, I don't know how this happened, but I have your keys."

"Why?"

"I don't know; I must have grabbed them by mistake."

"Why?" She asked again.

He had to avoid any additional lies, so he plunged forward with his speech. "Do you need to go anywhere today?"

"I'll just use the spare set if I need to."

"Well, check and see if they're there. I used them last week, and I don't know if I put them back."

"John," she sighed in frustration, "what is going on?"

"If you need to go anywhere, call Elle. She'd be happy to help."

"I haven't talked to her in weeks."

"Well, this would give you a reason."

"No," she said. "I'm not going to call her for a ride."

"Okay. Well, where do you need to go? I can pick up anything. I'm leaving early today. I should be home around four, if not earlier. Is that okay?"

"John." She no longer tried to hide her annoyance. "This won't work. Not if I need to prepare for where you want . . . I mean, what we want me to do . . . I need today to prepare."

"Not today you don't."

"What about my appointment with Dr. Haden? You scheduled it for three-thirty."

"I canceled it."

"You did? When?"

"Don't worry about it."

"I'm confused."

"We'll figure it out tonight. So are you okay at the house until I get there this afternoon?"

She sighed into the phone again. "I guess that should be fine."

"Also, Rebecca, I've been listening to the news this morning. Lately there's just been a lot of scary stuff going on. Make sure you keep an eye on Robert. And keep the house doors locked."

"I usually do."

"Well, just make sure it's deadbolted, okay?"

"Funny," she said with a sarcastic chuckle. "I thought you said I'm the person suffering from paranoia."

"If there's anything strange, call the cops."

"Okay." Her voice shifted to a soft, accepting tone. "Are you okay?"

"I love you, Rebecca."

"I love you, too."

If he stayed on the phone for any longer, he would buckle; he would give her the truth. "See you tonight," he quickly added and hung up the phone.

CHAPTER FORTY-SIX

Dr. Landersen pulled out a file and scattered the contents over his wide, cluttered desk. "I'm surprised you think I know everyone's whereabouts. Most of the time I've got a terrible memory. Without an organized assistant, I'm lucky to not lose my own brain in here. It's been hard not having someone like Anita. She was amazing, wasn't she? Thomas Bass, is that who you want? No, no. Penciltop—that means Harlock. Thomas Harlock. All I have is what happened following Clearcreek's shutdown. At the time, the Board wanted me to be the surrogate father of every-one. It was up to me to place them in the right homes. He went to the County. Maybe you even touched his files during your short-lived stint there. Oh, no, wait, County couldn't keep the right treatments available. He needed something more permanent. He went over to . . . nope, my mistake again. County, you'd have to ask County."

"Would they tell me what happened to him?"

"Sanders, why don't you just take this to the police? Let them deal with it."

"I already have." It had been his first stop after picking up Elle. He had shown the police the remaining two letters, which showed the stalker knew Rebecca and wanted Robert from her. In return for the evidence, the police had only asked a few questions and prom-ised to have a patrol car observe the area. They were doing some-thing, but it was not nearly enough.

When he dropped Elle off at her home, she promised she would visit Rebecca for as long as she could before her afternoon appointments.

Now John faced the man who had access to the answers. Dr. Landersen knew Clearcreek's patients better than anyone. He knew each of their tragic circumstances, why they had been in psychiatric care, and what had become of them after Clearcreek's demise.

"We need names," John begged. "A suspect, some type of lead that can help the police."

"And you think Harlock is the one?"

"He just seems the type."

Landersen ran his fingers across his thick chin, and looked down at the document in front of him. Then he picked up the phone, and within seconds asked to speak to the facility's director.

Following some brief chit-chat, Landersen explained that a stalker might be pursuing a previous patient from Clearcreek. Could Thomas Harlock be their man?

But then John heard Landersen say, "I didn't know that. . . . Yes, that should prove helpful. . . . No problem, our mistake. Thank you." John's heart sank.

"It's not him," Landersen said as he hung up the phone.

"Why?" he pushed.

"He's in the state penitentiary as we speak. They're trying to get him out on an insanity plea, but the judge is being a stickler. He's been in for nine months, and he's not anywhere close to getting out."

"Do you know what he's accused of?"

"The director didn't say, but it doesn't matter. He's not standing on street corners or sending out random mail."

John had already visualized Penciltop as the phantom on the corner of Chimera. But now he'd been acquitted. "Any others?"

Landersen shrugged.

"Gravers wouldn't be behind this, would he?" John asked.

"No." Landersen's voice was adamant. "Besides, last I'd heard he's still got another three or four years behind bars."

"It couldn't be Gravers, then." John said.

"It's pretty inconceivable."

"Okay, well . . . what about Cameron Sears?"

"No." Landersen shook his head. "Not in his nature. Drugs and alcohol, yes, but not this. Besides, last I heard he'd really cleaned up his act. He's too healthy for that now."

"You never know," John said.

"No." Landersen was determined. "Besides, I wouldn't be able to track him down anyway."

"Why not?"

"He moved to Sacramento. I don't have any connections up there. The only place I could tell you to look is in the white pages—that's how helpful I am."

"Well, it's *someone* from Clearcreek. We just have to piece together who." Yet this was proving to be more difficult than John had first suspected. What he did know was that the person was crazy and knew Rebecca.

Landersen again shifted through the file that held Clearcreek's history.

"Somewhere," John pressed, "buried in those pages is the answer. Maybe it was someone before my time?"

Landersen rubbed his head and scrolled through the documents until he touched a small slip. Then a half-smile formed on his face. "Clarissa. Clarissa Spencer."

"Who?"

"She was there when you were there."

John cleared his mind of all other patients until he could see her face. "Oh, yes. I remember her. Why her?"

"It's exactly something she'd do. Remember the scare she caused the whole place? You were there, weren't you? That huge storm, the power outage, when she wrote threats to Jolene all over the bathroom mirrors?"

"In her lipstick?"

"No, in her blood."

"Oh, yeah." The memory came back stronger now. "I rescued her in the snow that night."

"That night's a classic example of how she works."

"Okay." John thought through the suggestion. "She was the type that liked to stimulate fear in others whenever she could. It gave her power."

"And she has a better memory than you'd think. She'll remember you, and she'll remember Rebecca."

"But why Rebecca?"

Landersen released a jovial laugh. "You think I can answer that? If I could tell you why these people do half of what they do, I'd be more than just an expert in the field; I'd be an exceptionally rich man."

"Would she know all the things the letters talk about?"

"She's too bright for her own good." Landersen set Clarissa's file on top of the stack. "It's like you said—building fear is her passion. Did Clarissa do this? I can't say. Is she capable of doing it? Absolutely."

CHAPTER FORTY-SEVEN

Once he left Landersen's office, John made three phone calls. The first was to Randy, who had called in a teaching sub and was at home, ready and waiting. Next was to Elle, who had just checked in with the police and had nothing to report but was on her way to see Rebecca for the next hour. Last, John called Rebecca. It was only a quick check-in, and under the circumstances she seemed to be doing fine.

When he hung up with her, he pulled into the familiar apartment complex, his home during his San Bernardino bachelor days.

Before he could honk, Randy approached. He opened the Jeep door, nodded a hello, and then buckled himself in. "I have a parent-teacher conference at four."

"We'll be back by then. Thanks again for your help."

"Sure. But say again why we're doing this?"

"If Clarissa and Kim are the same person, we'll have more to go on."

"But Harbor City?"

"That's where she lives."

"Let me get this straight." Randy heaved out a sigh, and then rolled his eyes. "She lives over an hour away, yet she sees Rebecca twice a week and mails all the letters from right here in San Bernardino?"

"It's likely."

Randy rubbed his chin, then said, "I guess so." But after several minutes of silence, he looked over at John and raised his eyes. "Hey, brilliant idea here. Why don't we turn our suspicion over to the police, instead of heading all the way over there ourselves?"

"They need more to go on."

Randy scanned John's face. "How much do they know?"

"Right now, they have sufficient information."

"So they don't know—"

"No," John cut him off. "They don't know her history, they don't know she resided at Clearcreek, and they don't know that one of those mental patients is responsible for this."

"Hey, I'm just asking."

"I know they're doing their job, and I'm sure it's the best they can do. But they were a real disappointment, very vague on how they would actually help us."

"Elle said they're keeping a watch on the area."

"Yeah," John grunted. "But once we know who to watch for, they'll want to do more." Then he spoke softer. "Thanks for taking off work."

"No problem."

They drove down Highway 91 in silence until Randy said, "You think we're making smart moves?"

"Of course."

"Okay." Randy leaned his head back and closed his eyes.

However, John kept the conversation going. "What other choices do I have?"

"None."

"Exactly."

"And you can't just do nothing about this. You have to do something. So that's why we're headed to Harbor City."

John was very quiet. "Something like that."

For the next forty minutes, Randy did not speak, and John assumed he was asleep until he muttered, "Is she dangerous?"

The exit was less than a mile away. "Not entirely." John changed lanes, ignoring Randy's stare.

"We're just talking to her, right?" Randy asked.

"We just want to confidently turn over our suspicions to the police."

"Remember I've got a parent-teacher conference at four."

"I remember."

At the bottom of the off-ramp, John glanced down at the directions clutched in his hand.

"Three-thirty would be even nicer," Randy said.

"You should be home in plenty of time." John turned right, staying on Huntington Avenue for about a mile.

"Unless she holds us hostage, right?"

"Exactly." Another left and he was proceeding down 27th Street. He saw a long row of apartments and parked on the opposite side of the street to face them.

"So here it is?" Randy asked.

"Here it is."

"Well." Randy clasped his hands together. "What're you going to do now, knock on the door and ask her to stop sending nasty letters to your wife?"

"We just need to talk to her."

Randy spoke like an actor in a British comedy. "A little tea time and chit-chat, eh?"

"We know it's not just her." John took in a moment to breathe. "Someone is following Rebecca and mailing those things from San Bernardino. So we just need to talk. Find out who, why, whatever we can."

"All of it's odd."

"I know." John feigned confidence. "That's why Landersen is right—this seems like the type of thing Clarissa would be involved in."

Randy shrugged and grabbed the door handle. "I don't understand it."

"I don't either."

"All right." Randy pushed the car door open. "Let's get this over with. And you should know I'm the mute private detective. I stand and I sit. I don't talk."

For the first time all day, John grinned. "Good. It's probably better that way."

The apartments were grim, dismal, and dilapidated. Apartment #35 was tucked down a short, darkened walkway. John drew in a breath and knocked on the stark gray door before him.

A woman answered. She had auburn hair that jerked around in bristled chaos. Her hazel eyes, sunken in and heavy with bags, paced back and forth like a trapped wild animal. "Yeah. What do you want?"

On the doorstep, an acrid chemical fume floated past them. The smell caught John off guard; his lungs wrestled for air. He released a quick choke, then spoke. "Clarissa. I'm John Sanders. This is Randy Case. We'd like to ask you a few questions."

"You cops?"

"No."

"They've already been here today. I don't need to answer any more questions."

"Wait." His voice sped up. "I need you to tell me some things about Rebecca Brownell."

Her rough eyes focused on John's face. "Do I know you?"

The intense stench burned his nostrils. He nodded his head, swallowed, and said, "From Clearcreek."

"Get out of here." The door slammed and toxic air smacked both men, forcing them to step back.

Upon recovery, Randy's face broke into a sympathetic grin. "Way to go, Sherlock."

"Yeah. Incredibly fine detective work, huh?"

"Well, we could knock again. Or," Randy continued, playfully punching John's shoulder, "give our lead to the real guys."

John studied the bare, solid door. It appeared to be a dead end, but leaving would make him feel foolish. They had come all this way, and John wanted some answers for their effort. "She's already seen the police today." John restated the only valuable words that had been shared.

"Great. Maybe they're one step ahead of you."

John kept studying the door. He couldn't leave, but he also could not confess to Randy that right now his only guidance came from a few detective dramas he had once seen.

He turned around in desperation. Nearby there was a courtyard with a picnic table in the center. "Give me a minute to think," he muttered. Then he strode the twenty paces, slid into the chipped bench, and angled himself for a clear view of Clarissa's door.

A few seconds later, Randy stood near him. "While you do the brain work, do you care if I walk around?" Then in a hushed voice and a twinkle in his eye, he added, "Perhaps I'll stumble on something important."

"I wouldn't be here if I thought we were wasting our—"

There was a creaking sound and then, just as John had hoped, Clarissa's door swung open. Out walked a girl. Her hair also was auburn, but her uncoiled curls were swept back into a ponytail. She wore short jean cut-offs and a pink T-shirt with a glittery star in the center. She walked straight toward Randy.

"Did you want Clarissa?" she asked.

"Yes." John stood.

"Well sit back down," the girl demanded. "She sent me to see what you want, not that I really care." Her thin legs slid over the bench. Then she crossed her arms and looked across the table at John. "I'm at least outside—it stinks in there."

"What's that smell?" John asked.

"Meth lab."

Randy's eyebrows shot up high. "Meth?"

"Sit down," the girl said. "You make me nervous."

"So that's a meth lab," Randy slid in next to John.

"Chill, Old Man. The Cops were just here; they're closing it down. It was her boyfriend's operation. He just used her for a place to work, but now that the cops are on to it, he split. And we're being evicted. The landlord comes down about every hour to cuss at us. I'm supposed to be leaving with some social worker soon. Mom's afraid the cops are coming back to arrest her. Anything else you want to know?"

"She's going to jail?" Randy asked.

"Not yet. But she's been forging checks for a while." The girl's finger played with a curl. "Right now the cops want Jake. He's got ongoing business around here, so they'll keep her for bait. I keep telling her that. But she doesn't listen. Mom's crazy—that's just how she is."

Finally, John spoke. "I worked at Clearcreek Mental Care Center when your mom was there."

She shrugged her shoulders. "She was at a million of those places. I don't keep track of their names."

"It was up in the mountains, about an hour and a half from here."

"Oh, yeah." Her mouth broke into a half-smile. "I think I remember when she was there. I think I was, like, six when she came back." "Six?" Randy's face turned sober. "How old were you when she left?"

"Five, I guess. They said she was only supposed to be in for a year, but she stayed like four months longer. Then I think the place shut down or something."

"It did." John studied the young girl; her shoulders were high, her chest stuck out, her head cocked. "What grade are you in?"

"Seventh."

John pointed at himself and Randy. "We both work with kids around your age."

Randy seemed preoccupied with surveying the dirty, run-down complex, but he shot John a puzzled glance. "I thought Clearcreek only took the rich."

"Ha." The girl snorted a laugh. "Don't you know? It's all about who you sleep with. Mom doesn't know who my dad is, which is too bad for me. But my sister, Cassie, she hit the jackpot because her dad is some big lawyer. Of course, Mom was sleeping with him back when she was pretty and not crazy. I don't remember it, but they'd already split up by the time Cassie was born. Typical; the better ones don't stick around very long.

"Oh." Randy's eyes were wide.

"But Cassie gets to see him all the time. And when Mom had the grand mother of all breakdowns and passed out from her pills, he stepped in. He said he didn't want his precious Cassie to have to live with Mom like that. But just between you and me, he didn't want Mom to die 'cause he didn't want full custody, you know? He has a nice family now—a real pretty wife and two perfect, spoiled kids. Cassie went there this morning while I got to deal with a banshee, disguised as a social worker. She plans to take me somewhere else, but I ran away." The girl sighed loudly. "But then I came back because I didn't have anywhere to go." She paused, folded her arms across her chest, and then looked at each of them for a solid moment. "Unless one of you wants to take me."

The pause was extremely awkward.

"I'm a good houseguest," the girl continued. "I don't drink or smoke. I don't bring boys around. I listen real well and I'll do your chores. I even stopped cussing yesterday. You won't even know I'm there unless you want me to be there, and then I'd be there. I'm really good."

At the moment, Randy seemed absorbed with peeling chipped paint away from the worn and weathered table. Out of shame and anxiety, John watched his friend's fingers work.

Finally, John looked over at her. "So you're going into foster care today?"

The girl's shoulders slouched. Then she too began picking at the table's ruts and crumpled paint. "I guess," she said. "I mean, once Mom goes to jail I can't exactly go with her. Not like I really want to.

And if neither of you will take me, then foster care's my only choice. I don't want to live on the streets. I tried that once while I was in a different foster home, and it sucked. Hard."

Randy cleared his throat and looked at the girl. His face looked troubled. "We need to know something about your mom."

Randy was back to business, so John followed his lead. "Has your mom ever mentioned Rebecca Brownell?"

"Does she hate her?"

"Maybe," Randy said.

"She only talks about women she hates."

"Well," Randy said, "then there is a good chance she talked about this one."

"Rebecca's my wife, and someone's been harassing her," John said. "We think whoever the person is, they're somehow connected to your mom."

The girl shrugged her shoulders. "Probably, if your wife's connected to meth. Jake was mad at a lot of people. I know he wanted to get even with some."

"She has nothing to do with that," John said.

"You sure?"

"Yes."

She shrugged her shoulders again. "Well, I don't know. I'd let you come in the house and ask her, but she won't talk to anyone—unless you have a way to keep her from going to jail."

Randy shifted his legs out from under the bench. "She needs a lawyer." His hand patted John on the shoulder. "That's not us, Sherlock." Randy stood up. "Let's go."

In a moment of desperation, John said, "She could still be our contact."

Randy frowned at the girl and shook his head. "I doubt it."

The girl followed Randy's lead and stood. "Well, I know the narc you should talk to." Her fingers slid down into her tight jean pockets. "Officer Howry is the cop on the case. I bet you they'll have this place cleaned out by the end of the day. Maybe they'll find some evidence about your wife."

"Thanks." John stood and watched the young girl, who had freed a hand and was nervously twisting another ponytail curl. "And good luck to you."

"Last chance," she said. "I'm the best houseguest you'd ever have."

"Jodi!"

The girl's shoulders dropped, and she cussed under her breath. A short, beefy woman with a husky face and a navy blazer stepped into the courtyard.

"Here's my banshee," the girl said.

"I was this close to reporting you to the Center of Missing Children. This is not a time to be running off—especially with strange men." The woman gave John and Randy a stern look. Both of them stepped away from the table.

"Is your mother in the house?" The woman began pounding on the door.

"Wait," the girl, Jodi, called out to the woman. "You don't need to talk to her." Taking strong steps toward the door, she added, "I'm ready to go. I just need my suitcase." However, before falling into the building's shade, she stopped and turned back to John and Randy. "Good luck." Then she disappeared back into the toxic household.

Twenty minutes into their drive home, John finally dared speak. "So do you want to rub it in?"

However, Randy feigned innocence. "Rub what in?"

"That you were right, this trip was probably a waste of our time. Not to mention awkward."

"Hey." Randy threw his hands up. "I wasn't thinking any of that." He released a grunted sigh followed by a steady head shake. "Actually, I got that kid stuck in my brain. I mean, what kind of environment is that?"

"I know."

"She's got it rough, doesn't she?"

"Yes."

Randy leaned his head back. "So, what do you think? Is her mom our woman?"

"I don't know." At the moment, John saw how foolish his eager hope had been. "It doesn't look promising."

Randy's tone was kind. "We don't know that for sure. She still could be. And if she is, the letters will stop as soon as she ends up in jail."

John released a sarcastic chuckle. "I really believed we could outsmart this predator with logic, but you were right. All we did today was uncover someone else's distorted world."

"Why don't you call the Harbor City Police?" Randy suggested. "Have them look into it. Like the girl said, they're already going through her stuff."

John smiled weakly and tossed Randy his cell phone. "Maybe so."

"What?" Randy looked at the phone.

"Thanks for calling."

Randy rolled his eyes. "I didn't exactly offer." Nevertheless, for the rest of the drive, John listened to Randy make a series of phone calls, none of which seemed promising, though Officer Howry agreed to let them know if he found anything useful.

At 3:20, John again drove into his old apartment complex. Randy jumped out of the Jeep but lingered with the car door open. He gave John a serious look. "Hey, Johnny Boy. I know you thought you could deal with this yourself, but it's time to give the police all the details."

John nodded. "I know." Their time was up. The truth had to be shared.

CHAPTER FORTY-EIGHT

John still yearned for a legitimate lead, so on the way to the police station, he called Landersen again. After sharing the events at Clarissa's, John finally said, "Why couldn't it be Gravers?"

Landersen hummed into the phone. "Can you see Gravers behind this?"

The pines that surrounded the town were getting closer, and John hated that he had no solid hopes to share with Rebecca. He didn't even have any to comfort himself. "I don't know what I think anymore The person is mimicking her illness deliberately. Could Gravers do that?"

"Maybe." Landersen said thoughtfully. "He knew her symptoms quite well."

John's hands tightened against the steering wheel. "Exactly." A chill went down John's spine. "Could he be out on good behavior?"

"I don't know," Landersen said grimly. "But he has motivation, knowledge, and probably the craftiness to do this. It's quite the elaborate plan, but he would have time to think it up in prison."

"Wouldn't you have heard if he was out?"

"I would think so."

"Well, he certainly didn't make Rebecca's life easy before. Mine either. And after all these years in prison, I'm sure he's even more bitter towards us. This would be his way to get revenge."

"Okay, "Landersen said firmly. "Let me check into this. I'll keep you posted."

The call ended, and John felt some comfort—he had a real lead.

At the police station, John shared his hunch about Gravers. Lieutenant Campbell, a middle-aged, barrel-chested officer preformed a quick search only to confirm Landersen's initial assumption—Gravers still dwelt in medium-security prison.

Instead of replacing this disappointing news with any other hope, Campbell became hung up on Rebecca's history. John tried to keep him focused on the urgency of finding the stalker, but the term *schizophrenia* made every other fact seem to fade. In the end, without anything other than two letters and his wife's account of a man with signs, Lieutenant Campbell could only promise the same thing as before— that a patrol car would routinely check the area for anything suspicious.

It was the final blow. John headed toward home knowing he had failed. He had to tell Rebecca the truth without any solid understanding of why she was in this awful situation.

Grasping at one final straw, he stopped at the post office. The key slid into Box 222 and the knob turned. Then John sorted through the Stater Brothers ad, the power bill, a credit card statement, and an internet price plan postcard. Finally, there on the bottom, lay the business envelope with the plain type:

R E B E C C A

His heart raced. He took the mail into the comfort of his Jeep and stared at the envelope. This time there was no postmark, just a simple stamp. For a short second, he closed his eyes, then he ripped through the envelope and pulled out the thin typing paper. Across the top, and down at the bottom, were the words *I see you, I see you, I see you, and you see me too.*

Then in the center of the paper, the cut and glued letters read:

ARe yOu reaLLy CRAZY?
ARe
ANd
reaLLy
remeBEr

CRAZY?
COMPANY?
ANd yOu remember COMPANY?
R.D.

Twice he skimmed it, running his fingers over R.D. Then reality hit.

CHAPTER FORTY-NINE

Instantly John fired up the ignition and threw the gearshift into reverse. An oncoming car honked and swerved around him. He yanked the stick into drive and floored the gas pedal.

The Jeep lurched around corners as he sped toward Chimera Lane. At the first straight away, he reached for his cell phone and called home.

After two rings, Rebecca answered.

John struggled to hide the terror in his voice. "What's going on?"

"I'm just reading to Robert."

"Are you okay?"

"Yes, I'm fine. Why? Did you just try to call me?"

"No." Pine trees were whizzing past him. Home was at least five miles away.

"I was on the phone with Kim. She's making plans to come see Robert this evening."

"No!"

"I know you don't like her, but there are some good things about—"

"No," John cut her off. He wanted to blurt out right then how dangerous all this was, but the news would completely terrify her. "Please, I'm almost home." Once he had her in his arms, once she knew he would protect her, then he would tell her the awful truth, and together they would get through this. "Right now, stay away from Kim."

Rebecca laughed off his concern. "That's right, you said you were coming home early. Elle was here most of the day, then Kim called a couple times, and I've just lost track of time."

"Rebecca, this is urgent."

"John?" Her voice finally sounded troubled. "What's going on?"

"I know what's happening, I know the truth. You were right, and you won't believe what I have to tell you."

She paused. "Okay. I'll need to call Kim to reschedule, but she might already be—" Rebecca stopped. "Oh, there's the door now."

"No, Rebecca—"

"I'll tell her you're on your way home. Here, Robbie wants to say hi."

"Wait!" he pleaded, but it was too late. Instead he heard, "Hi, Daddy," followed by an awful, high-pitched scream.

In that same second, John heard the phone thud against the floor.

Another yell carried through the phone line, followed by pounding feet and muffled voices.

A horn blared. The Jeep had strayed toward oncoming traffic. John yanked the vehicle back into his lane. A man's low, deep voice resonated through the phone, followed by Rebecca's screams and Robert's cries.

John had stopped breathing. His foot thrust down against the gas pedal. The Jeep's tires squealed around the mountainous curves, but all he heard was Rebecca's voice speaking fast and tensely. A loud crash followed, and suddenly the man's voice turned clear, thundering loud against her escalating shriek, "Don't fight me, Becca."

"You don't want him!" Her voice drew closer to the receiver.

"Shut him up."

The Jeep's tires squealed as John turned off the highway. He was on the final stretch—only another two miles to go. But the car in front of him was going the blasted speed limit. John leaned on the horn and let it blare, knowing full well there was no turnout between the switchbacks.

"Leave him alone," Rebecca's voice held a strange calmness.

The man growled, and she screamed in pain. Another loud crash followed.

Finally the car ahead of John pulled onto a small embankment near the side of the road. John swerved around and ground the gas pedal to the floor. He took the next two turns at a suicidal rate, only to fall behind another slow car. He slammed on the brakes. Dark laughter echoed through the phone. John felt paralyzed. He slammed on the horn, only to watch the car ahead press on the brakes and crawl at a mere 27 mph.

Amid the panic and frustration, John felt the smallest relief to hear Rebecca's voice again, this time tremendously strong. "Run, Robbie! Go where I told you!"

Then a sound of banging, over and over again. "You ruined me, Becca!"

"And you . . ." Her voice was again close to the phone, whimpering and submissive. "You almost destroyed me."

"You know," the man said, his harsh voice deepening, "how much I hate unfinished business."

A high shriek transformed into a faint whimper.

Terror had kept John listening, but now he to act against his wishes. He ended the call and dialed 911.

CHAPTER FIFTY

At Chimera Lane, John broke free of the trundling vehicle in front of him. He slammed on the acceleration, and the Jeep immediately swerved around the drawn-out corner. Just as John pulled out of the strong curve, something caught his eye. There, at the stop sign on Chimera, a black Land Rover idled. John locked eyes with a dark-haired man seated inside. He looked exactly as Rebecca had described him.

But John's foot remained firm on the gas. He had to reach Rebecca and Robert—they were all that mattered.

Sirens were ahead of him. A police car was in his drive; two more skidded in ahead of him. John threw the Jeep into park and sprinted toward his home. The door was wide open. Rebecca was on the floor, blood seeping through her hair.

"Rebecca!" John cried. He knelt down next to her. Her hands felt cold.

More police officers rushed through the house, searching the rooms. A female officer held Robert in her arms.

"Daddy!" he screamed.

"Robbie." John stood. His lips trembled. He reached for the crying boy.

"Take him out," the officer whispered, nodding at the scene on the floor. John turned back to look at Rebecca while the officer pushed him toward the door. "You don't want him to see her like this."

John nodded. His throat was dry. He surveyed the room of dark uniforms then numbly moved onto the porch.

Branko met them, whimpering and dancing. Robert clung to his father's neck, his grip far too powerful for a two-year-old boy.

"I need you to do something," John said, focusing on his son. "It's very important. I need you to be very brave."

Robert nodded his head, afraid to speak.

"I need you," John said as his mind raced, "to take Branko and stay right here with him. Can you do that for me?"

"A man hurt Mommy," Robert whispered.

"I know."

"She was crying."

"Are you hurt?"

The boy shook his head, but tears continued to flow.

Carefully, John set the boy down. His mind strained for clarity. "Okay. Sit here with Branko. Make sure he doesn't leave you."

"No." Robert started to whimper. "Stay with you."

"No." John's voice quivered. "Be strong for Daddy, okay? Right now I need you to be strong."

He walked away from his son just as the ambulance arrived. As soon as he was back at Rebecca's side, John was pulled away again. More people crowded into the room. A stretcher rolled past.

Lieutenant Campbell, the uninvested officer John had met less than an hour ago, stormed down the drive.

"The Rover!" John yelled at him. "The man in the black Land Rover. He knows. He's responsible for all this."

"Where is he?" the lieutenant asked.

Robert was crying.

"Corner of Chimera and Pine. At the stop sign."

The stretcher was rolling past with Rebecca's limp body. John was being pushed back. Robert was running inside. The world was out of control.

Thankfully, the lieutenant understood enough. He reached for his radio.

"Dispatch. We need an alert. Be on the lookout for a black Land Rover last seen at the corner of Chimera and Pine."

Campbell nodded at John. The search had begun.

CHAPTER FIFTY-ONE

The next hours passed in a daze. The ambulance headed to Mountains Community Hospital, only to be re-directed to Loma Linda Medical Center at the base of the mountain.

Elle came and took Robert. Not long after, Randy came to support John who stared lifelessly at the pale blue walls of the ICU waiting room.

"How is she?" Randy asked tentatively.

John swallowed a heavy lump in his throat and wiped his eyes before turning to face Randy. "She's still unstable." His voice cracked. He paused to control himself. "There's blood clots. And swelling." His lip trembled. "She's in surgery right now."

Randy pulled John into a hug.

For over an hour, the two sat in the waiting room. Then FBI Agent Glen Newton arrived.

He wore beige slacks and a pressed black shirt with the top button open to accommodate his thick neck. The mustache seemed to have been stolen from a walrus, and his baritone voice, according to Randy, had to be the envy of some barbershop quartet. All John saw was the FBI badge, and all he heard was that this man had been on Downley's case for years.

John and Randy were escorted to a small, quiet room, where the walls were a pale beige and the chairs were orange plastic scoops. Then a string of questions began—questions that all surrounded Richard Downley.

With each answer John gave, he tried to not re-live the screams heard over the phone hours before. Downley had been in their home, that monster had assaulted his wife and son.

When Detective Newton asked about the man who assisted Downley, John felt like he would vomit. He glanced over at the trash can. In addition to the horrid man who'd haunted Rebecca with signs, John had been an aide. He had hurt Rebecca with his own misjudgments and fed her words that had endangered her. He bit his lip and let the nausea pass.

Finally he spoke. "All I know is that I saw the man waiting on the corner while Downley was in my home."

The detective nodded. "What did he look like?"

John gave a basic physical description, then stared at the ground.

"Okay. Is there anything else you can tell me?"

John shook his head.

The detective stood. "Thank you for your time and cooperation, Mr. Sanders. We'll keep you posted."

"Wait," John looked up to meet Detective Newton's eyes. "Now it's your turn. What can you tell us about Richard Downley?"

Detective Newton's large shoulders rolled back and his knuckles glided over his chin. "I can tell you this was a well-meditated plan."

"Apparently," Randy said. "The man's been dead for nearly five years. So explain to us how he assaulted my friend's wife."

The detective appeared unfazed. "He deceived us."

"He deceived all of us." John mumbled.

Newton sat back down. "What do you remember about his death?"

"It was in the news." John thought back. It seemed so long ago. "Suicide on his boat. They didn't find his body right away, but eventually they did."

"About a year later, actually." Newton said. "Found off Catalina Island, right?"

"Yes." John felt dizzy.

"And you heard the body had partially decomposed, but the dental records verified it was Downley's?"

"Something like that."

Randy looked at John but spoke to Detective Newton. "So what really happened?"

"Downley's crafty. Clever," Newton said. "He used that body as a decoy to stop our investigation."

"But you knew he was alive?" A vein protruded from Randy's forehead.

"Not at first," Newton said calmly. "We assumed he was dead until we discovered that Downley's dental records had been modified to match the stolen corpse—"

"You're joking. A stolen corpse?" Randy said tersely.

Newton released a stiff laugh. "You'd be amazed at what people steal and sell. This one was a cadaver from a small nursing school in Kansas. The odd thing was that it appeared right as we were digging into the financial records of Downley's investment in an overseas company that had suddenly ceased to exist."

John tried to steady his mind. "So why did the public hear it was Downley's body?"

"Red tape," Newton said. "A little tiff between our FBI unit and the San Pedro Police." Newton looked to the ceiling, heaved in a breath, and released the air. "How much do you want to know?"

"All of it," Randy said.

Newton nodded. "It was an ordeal. The police packed the body away before the FBI could run any tests on it. A slight power struggle followed." He looked at John sympathetically, cleared his throat, and softly added, "Had those events happened differently, it could possibly have prevented your current situation." His words came slower. "Anyway, media got wind of it from the police. By the time we got the body back, completed the proper testing, and learned the truth about it, we decided to leave things as they were. We figured that if Downley thought we'd taken the bait, we had a better shot of nailing him."

Randy appeared disgusted. "So you left him dead?"

Newton refused to react. "We did what we needed to do. We never had a good hold on him, and we made some mistakes. I'm sorry the price has been so high for you, Mr. Sanders. It's unfortunate that Downley accomplished so much."

"Yes," John said. "It is."

CHAPTER FIFTY-TWO

Two hours later, John and Randy were whisked into a room with an illuminated wall displaying brain images at various angles. Dr. Weici Chang, a short woman with cropped dark hair, kind eyes, and petite voice, introduced herself. John searched her face. All he wanted to know was that Rebecca would be okay, but this young doctor's smile offered only compassion, not answers.

"Your wife has experienced an epidural hematoma." Dr. Chang reached for a red marker and began marking the black-and-white exposures on the wall. "Between the skull and the brain is a tough, leathery covering called the *dura*." She made an indentifying mark. "The dura attaches to the brain just beneath the skull. Normally, the dura protects the brain and keeps it nourished with blood and cerebrospinal fluid. When a person receives a severe blow to the head, like your wife has, the brain bounces within the cavity." Her red pen waved back and forth, playing out the trauma. "This movement may tear the blood vessels surrounding the brain and dura."

The replay of events from Rebecca's attack sickened John. Hatred and fear swirled within him.

"When the vessels tear," she continued, "blood accumulates in the space between the dura and the skull. This is known as an epidural hematoma—a blood clot at the covering of the brain."

Randy looked at John. "Did you get all that?"

John nodded. "How bad is she?" But John had spent years studying the brain, and he already knew enough. The situation was not good.

"When the blood accumulates between the dura and skull," Dr. Chang continued, turning back to the photo and circling an area, "Swelling of the brain occurs. There's not enough extra room inside the skull for the brain to swell and for blood to accumulate. The only way the brain can compensate is to shift out of the way. This puts pressure on delicate structures and can impair vital functions, such as eye opening, speech, awareness, or even breathing."

John understood what she was saying, at the moment there were no clear answers. He tried to sound composed. "When do you think we'll know?"

"We just removed the blood clot, which will prevent any further swelling."

"So that's good news, right?" Randy asked.

Dr. Chang offered a soft, compassionate smile. "Right now, we don't know anything. We can only wait."

Dr. Chang tried to prepare John for what he would see, but when he finally arrived at Rebecca's ICU unit, his knees almost buckled.

Machines beeped, a ventilator hummed, IV lines dripped, and monitors recorded her neural activity. Other machines tracked her blood pressure and the pressure inside her head. Amid all the machines, a deformed woman lay in a hospital bed. Bandages wound around her shaved head and her broken nose. The parts of her face that lay exposed were swollen and bruised. Close at hand, a nurse watched and waited.

Rebecca was barely alive.

During the hours that followed, John saw his parents and Elle and confirmed that Robert was okay. His loved ones came and went, but they always left someone at his side.

John saw Rebecca again during a blood transfusion before she was whisked away for more testing. Linda Blythe came for a while. She gave John a hug and offered encouraging words. Someone placed food in front of him, but he couldn't eat. A counselor came and talked about the necessity of taking care of himself and gave John a handout about the hospital's support group.

John stayed close by Rebecca. He listened and watched.

And waited.

CHAPTER FIFTY-THREE

Time passed. John listened, paced, waited, and hoped fervently. Eventually good news came—she was stable.

The group moved to the east waiting room, a slightly larger area with nice, green couches and oak end tables, one of which had been moved to the center of the room to support Robert's coloring book. On the wall was a wood clock, a painting of a young girl in a bonnet walking through weeds, and a glowing TV arched in the corner. The walls were a very pale yellow, so pale that John wished that basic white had been selected instead. It seemed wrong, as if the color wasn't healthy enough to be its normal, vibrant self.

In time, Elle brought Robert. John moved a table to the center of the room to support the coloring books. Then John's father appeared with two large In-N-Out® bags in his hand. "Any updates?" he asked.

Cindy shook her head. "Nothing new since they stabilized the bleeding."

Hal approached Robert's table and ruffled his grandson's hair. Then he started scooting toys and crayons away to make room for lunch.

Cindy looked troubled. "Hal, can we eat in here?"

"It's fine." Hal nudged his head toward a list of rules stuck to the pale yellow wall. "We just need to keep the room clean."

"But what about him?" Cindy gestured at Robert, who had already abandoned his coloring to fish through the bags.

John watched his son reach in and pull out some french fries. "Robbie's fine. Let him stay."

"Okay." Cindy, now with new purpose, began busily preparing Robert's food.

Hal offered John a cheeseburger "Will you eat?"

According to the ticking clock, it was 1 p.m. John couldn't remember when he'd last eaten. Certainly hours before he'd driven to Clarissa's. How long had it been? It felt like a lifetime ago.

His backward thoughts mingled with the aroma of grease and meat hit John with a wave of nausea. Yet his father kept his hand outstretched, and his mother's eyes pleaded with John. He accepted the offering, but the initial bite was tasteless.

Fortunately, Randy entered the room and all eyes shifted toward him. John quietly abandoned his meal on a neighboring chair.

"Hey." Randy touched John's shoulder as he walked by. "How is she?"

"Stable," Cindy answered, lifting Robert onto the couch next to her. Then she handed him a perfectly semi-wrapped burger.

Hal pulled out more burgers. "Here, have some lunch."

"Thanks." Randy took a burger and sat next to Elle. "I just got through speaking with Detective Newton." He eyed John. "Are you ready for another update?"

Perhaps it was Randy's solemn voice, or the way he touched Elle, or how Cindy doted like a mother over Robert. Maybe it was everything. But at that moment, John felt emotion well up from deep within. He had been suppressing so many thoughts, feelings, and emotions, but now all of it was gathering like an enormous tidal wave. If he spoke, the wave would break. All he could offer was a simple nod.

Hal moved next to John on the couch. "More on Downley?"

"Actually his lackey." Randy kept watching John. "They have him in custody."

Cheers broke out through the room. John offered Randy a weak smile.

"He's name is Ethan Hovan," Randy said. "He's an ex-private eye, and he's furious about being caught, so he's willing help the authorities locate Downley."

The group cheered again, and John's smile grew larger.

But then Randy's voice turned somber. "Unfortunately, Hovan doesn't actually know very much. He was only hired a year ago. He got all his instructions over a pre-paid cell phone, and he was paid from an offshore account. The only time Hovan and Downley ever met face-to-face was yesterday. Hovan was on lookout, and when he saw you, he drove off. He thought for certain Downley would be caught and he would be a free man. He's furious that it didn't work out that way."

"Wait." Hal waved his hand and pointed at the television set in the corner that flashed Downley's picture. "They're talking about him on the news. Where's the remote?"

Elle grabbed the remote and unmuted the TV.

"No," John said. "Not with . . ." he nodded at Robert, who was fortunately still busy picking at his sandwich." Cindy nodded and picked up her grandson.

"Let's go find a treat," she whispered and stepped out of the room.

Then the rest of the group listened to the report. First, Downley's familiar mayoral portrait from six years ago appeared next to a computerized estimation of his current, rougher look. The anger boiled inside John. A picture of Hovan appeared next to Downley's, and the anchor's voice blared through the room. "Former Mayor Richard Downley was most recently suspected to be in the company of Ethan Hovan, an ex-private eye, who is now in FBI custody. All tips about Richard Downley are to be directed to the FBI." The FBI's tip line number flashed across the bottom of the screen.

The tidal wave inside of John was cresting.

When the anchor shifted to world news, John looked away from the TV. Then he saw Elle. Her eyes were wide and trembling. One hand covered her mouth, and the other held the remote in a white-knuckled grip. She looked back at John with panic in her eyes. "John, please forgive me."

"For what?" he asked.

She muted the TV and set down the remote. "I've seen him before. He came into the agency months ago and asked some generic questions. Nothing that stood out, but now . . . he must have found you through me." Her face was pale.

"The soft serve," Randy whispered.

"He was the one who broke into your office," John said dryly.

Tears brimmed in Elle's eyes.

"It all makes sense," Randy said. "He scoped out the place, and when he returned he knew exactly where to find what he needed."

John grunted. "And the police found nothing wrong."

"Everything seemed fine." Elle looked close to tears. Randy stroked her hand.

"Downley is sly," John said, carefully controlling his emotions.

"And Hovan's skilled," Randy added. "Even if it hadn't been through you, Elle, he would have found a way."

John nodded. "He had sufficient information to track Rebecca—to watch her, follow her, and memorize her routine. Randy's right. He would have found a way."

"I still don't understand," Hal said. "Even with Hovan's help, Downley still knew too much—more than is logical."

"Yeah. It's almost like he had someone watching Rebeca's life," Randy said.

"Kim," John whispered. He stood up and clutched his head. His entire body was tense.

Hal looked at John, concerned. "John, you don't look well."

"Through school," John said. His body was shaking. "Kim kept tabs on Rebecca's life. And she brainwashed Rebecca into believing what Downley wanted her to believe. Downley hired Hovan to terrorize Rebecca, and he hired Kim to make Rebecca doubt her own sanity. He needed Rebecca to question who she was. Because if he could do that, she would mistrust everything."

"See if you can get him to eat." Hal pointed at the cheeseburger next to John's chair.

"I'm fine." John yelled.

The room went silent.

John pulled out his cell phone. "The FBI needs to find Kim, too."

CHAPTER FIFTY-FOUR

For a small moment, John felt empowered. He phoned Newton and paced the halls, sharing everything he knew about Kim. But since she had been planted by Downley, much of what Rebecca knew of her was probably a lie. Still, the tip gave John something to share, and that was a relief in itself.

But as soon as the call ended, John felt empty again.

He checked the nurse's station, and confirmed that there were no updates. Then he paced more of the hospital floor.

Once he retreated back to the waiting room, the pale yellow walls stirred a feeling of helplessness in him, especially as he watched Robert.

"Here, Grandma." Robert stood and handed Cindy a drawing. "I'm all done."

"Is this for me?" she asked.

"No. For Mommy."

Grandma took it, exchanged a brief, painful look with John, and turned back to Robert. "Very nice," she said. "Now, will you draw one for me?"

He shook his head and pointed at the picture. "Mommy."

Cindy drew in a breath. "She's still asleep, Robbie."

He began to fuss. "No."

John swallowed a tight lump in his throat. Then he stood and pulled Robert into his arms. The boy looked at his father in frustration. "Mommy should stop sleeping!"

"The doctors are helping her," he said.

Cindy was back, coaxing Robert from John's arms. "I'll color with you."

Robert shook his head.

"Please?" she added.

He didn't smile, but he did return to the coloring table.

A minute later, he stood up and extended the paper with his distinct scribbles to Cindy. "Here, Grandma."

"Very nice, Robbie." She took the paper. "What did you draw?"

"Robbie and Branko," he said. "Branko took care of me."

She stretched out her arms and pulled her grandson up on her lap, cuddling him into her arms. "Tell me what you did when Mommy got hurt. How did you know to squeeze behind the dryer?"

"Mommy told me to," he said.

"And Branko helped you?" she asked softly.

"He barked."

Elle moved closer and touched Cindy's knee. "We're lucky he's here," she said softly. "After it had happened, when I picked him up, he told me the man called for him, and tried to reach him, but Branko barked until the sirens came."

The entire room was silent.

"Is that right?" Cindy finally said, her voice cracking.

Robert nodded. All eyes were on him.

Cindy's hug tightened. She rocked him while she brushed tears from her eyes. "You did well," she whispered. "You did very well."

In time, Elle took Robert home. Cindy, Hal, and Randy rotated in and out of the room.

Time crawled by.

Eventually the hospital lights dimmed. The walls now appeared to be a dark tawny. Randy had gone, and John's parents were leaving, but John refused to return home.

From the hall, only a faint glow filled the room. The clock above read 2:20 a.m.

Occasionally John heard the hum of monitors, the striding of feet, or low conversations at the nurses' station.

In the dark, empty waiting room, he tried to bend his large body into one of the small green couches. But after a few tight turns, he determined that his effort were pointless. So he sat and allowed his mind to flow in and out of consciousness.

Finally, the clock lost its focus. Sleep approached, and John felt the smallest sense of relief as he drifted into a world of dreams. The soft subconscious atmosphere calmed him, and he began to hope he'd never wake.

He stood on the bank of a lake. The sun was setting in the distance. Pink and orange hues covered the sky. Birds whistled nearby.

Several yards away, he saw Rebecca. She wore a white dress that flowed in the wind. Her curls fell against her shoulders. She looked astounding—invigorated, healthy, and at peace. She was perfect.

Right then, John felt intense joy; it was stronger than anything he had ever felt before.

He stepped toward her. Then everything shook.

John looked around. He was back, on the granite tower, but this time he wore no armor. His shield was gone, and his helmet was missing.

Rebecca stood near him. She was fully dressed in battle gear, her shield raised, another shield in her hand. She looked sad.

"Are you going to leave me?" he called to her.

"It's you," she said. "You won't fight. You're leaving us." She extended the extra shield toward him.

He shook his head. Something was clutched in his hand. He opened his fingers and looked down to find an orientate key. He glanced back at Rebecca.

"Don't, John."

He knew where the key belonged. He scanned the granite tower and spotted the large wooden door. It appeared to beckon to him, almost audibly calling his name, and he felt a hunger to be there.

The key would unlock the door.

He glanced through an opening in the battlements. The enemy soldiers below were filtering in, coming up the tower steps, waiting for him.

And he would open the door.

He turned back to face her. She was now Rebecca from the ICU, battered, bruised, and bandaged. Yet she still offered him the shield. He stepped away from her. "No. I'm too weak," he said. "I did this to you."

Blood began seeping down her forehead.

He grimaced and turned away from her to glance again at the door.

Then he ran for it.

"Wait, John!" Her shouted plea stopped his feet, but he still faced the inviting door. "Don't hurt us."

He spun around to see her standing there, fully armed again. The injuries were gone. "Please," she said.

He kept his gaze fixed on her, but his hands desperately sought out the knob. His fingers fumbled with the key. He knew his place in this excruciating war. He was the traitor.

She spoke with power. "They want you to hurt us. They want you to destroy what we've built. Don't let them, John."

His fingers closed around the cold knob.

"Please don't," she said. "Stay. Fight. Defend your post."

"Will you be here too?" Tears streamed down his face.

"I don't know," she whispered as if next to his ear.

"If you are, what will be left of you?" he cried out. "How much of you will be here?" Would her body remain? If so, would her mind be gone forever? He turned back to the door.

Yet her voice, clear and strong, rang in his ears. "No matter what, you need to be here."

"I can't." He yanked the door open.

"No!" Rebecca let out a terrified scream.

He whirled back toward her. But she was gone. There was only darkness and a ticking clock, and the scream that still echoed in his mind.

CHAPTER FIFTY-FIVE

At ten in the morning, John was allowed to see Rebecca again. There were no updates or changes. She still relied on the ventilator, the IV, the monitors and machines. She looked so broken, so marred, so lifeless.

He wanted to speak to her, wanted her to hear his fears, his confessions, his apologies. But he couldn't bring himself to speak.

He just touched her hand and squeezed it lightly. "Please just stay with us," he managed to say.

Then he walked down the hall, trying to keep at bay the blame, the worries, and the uncertainties ahead. But once he saw his father and Randy in the waiting room, John knew he had to be alone. He quickly excused himself, retreating to a private walk around the hospital grounds. His steps led him to a large fountain. Water shot up and cascaded down. Time slipped by as he watched the mesmerizing motion, the constant, ordered sequence of rises and falls.

Suddenly the calm frustrated him. He didn't want to feel soothed or serene; he wanted the bitterness to flow.

The shock was cracking. The wall of grief that had built up around him was breaking. The numbness that had held him together over the past days shattered against the crash of the tsunami. Anger, bitterness, and guilt flowed through John's heart. He no longer could escape. He was forced to feel.

His family had been attacked. His wife might never wake up. He marched toward the parking structure, then to the chain linked fences, then to a rose garden, and then back to the fountain. Nothing helped. Everything reminded him of his wife.

All of it made him angry.

Then a sharp image of Rebecca's father shot through his mind. Yet of all the thoughts he could have, why would he think of this disturbed man?

Again he walked, but he couldn't clear his mind. Snippets of Robert Brownell's journal echoed through his thoughts.

Mia is gone.
Never will I smile again.
There is no life to live for.
I am empty.
Alone.
Destroyed.
Becca is too much for me now.
Reminds me of Mia.
I cannot be more.

John clutched his head, but the ghost still chanted inside his mind.

Robert Brownell was a man John had no respect for—a person who crumbled under the weight of life. That man had exhibited his weaknesses to Rick Downley, and Downley had used those weaknesses to ruin Brownell. And because of Robert Brownell, Downley had slithered into Rebecca's life, inflicting years of horrific pain and suffering. The anger swelled in John. If her father had been stronger, Rebecca would have never suffered like this. What a waste of a man Robert Brownell had been.

But what of his namesake? What about the young Robert, John's son?

Thinking of him was just as hard. His innocence had been shattered at the age of two. Only two, and witnessing an attack that could very well take the life of his mother. And if she survived, in what state might she be? Robert may never know the woman who had cherished him.

The sharpness cut through John's guarded heartstrings, and pain took over. He sat on a curb and finally let the tears roll down.

Robert was too important.

No matter the outcome, his son deserved a good life, and it was John's responsibility to ensure that Robert had one. John would have to find the strength.

Amid the tears, his thoughts turned to Rebecca. She had undergone so much pain, faced so much confusion—an isolated childhood, an abused adolescence, and an institutionalized life, until he had offered her so much more. He had believed in her. He had seen who she could become. Then she exceeded those dreams in a thousand ways, and he had fallen in love with her. They had created a beautiful home, a wonderful child, and an almost perfect life.

And then it had all gone wrong.

Downley had manipulated John into becoming the person who had questioned and doubted her.

Now John ached.

Despite all of Downley's crafty work to poison their home, Rebecca had not given up. Over the last few months, there had been hard times, dark times, and evil times—anger, confusion, and deceit. But in the end, she had kept trying—steadily striving to do what was required.

And now she deserved a husband who would do the same for the sake of their child.

When he went back to her room, he brushed his fingers across her face, her forehead, and her hand. Finally he leaned down and whispered, "I'm sorry, Rebecca. I am so very, very sorry." He wiped away his tears that continued to flow. "I need you to know that. And I need you to know that we'll be okay. We will be okay."

CHAPTER FIFTY-SIX

That afternoon, for the first time in two days, John finally returned home to grab a few hours of much-needed sleep. His parents remained at the hospital, promising they would call with the slightest news. Kilee had arrived and now had Robert in her care. So when he stepped inside his home, the overwhelming stillness jarred him. Someone—probably his mother—had pieced the shattered living room back together. He paused there long enough to register this fact, then headed to the bedroom.

As soon as his head hit the pillow, he slid into desperately needed sleep.

But after two days of minute napping, dreams dangled around him. His subconscious mind wandered, leading him up the winding path of an ocean-side manor. He moved through the estate with familiarity, as if he owned the place. He saw a maid in the hall, then a nanny and a cook. He rushed past, anxious to be away from them all. Once the French doors of his office locked, he retrieved a book, slid into his leather chair, and looked out over the vast ocean. Then he retrieved a heavy pen from his suit coat pocket and uncapped it. The book fell open and he let the pen flow across the pages.

I feel trapped in this home
Must get out

The pen stopped. From an open window he could hear the distant sound of the ocean waves crashing against the shore. Seagulls flew past. Then the pen flowed quickly again.

Becca looks like Mia every passing day
Must get out
Rick came by today
Talked for hours
Finally someone who I can talk with
Keep close at hand

Another pause and a glance outside, but this time he caught his reflection in the glass.

It was Robert Brownell.

John's own rapid breathing awoke him. He had seen Robert Brownell, the man he despised, eye to eye. No, he had *been* him.

"I'm not you," John muttered out loud. "I'm different." But the words of Robert Brownell's journal still echoed in John's mind.

The beast. He comes

John arose. He needed that journal. The man's words would prove they were different.

It used to be seldom
In the dark corners of my life

The phrases kept coming. John tore through Rebecca's nightstand, yanked open drawers and searched her books, her jewelry—her whole present life.

Seeping into my mind

These were articles that Rebecca might never touch again. John attacked her dresser, throwing underwear and clothes to the floor.

Turning me into a man I do not know
Yet this is who I've become

John yelled, with all his fury. He screamed at Robert Brownell, and he screamed at the fragility of life.

The beast visits frequently now
Calling me away from my home
I miss my dear Becca
If I stay I could hold her again

John ran to her closet, tossing shoes and purses aside.

Everyone sees the beast
I cannot hide him
So I hide

Up in the corner, there was a floral box with a gold latch. John reached for it, holding his breath.

Rick has seen the beast
He says he understands

His fingers brushed against soft leather, and his hand closed around it.

He says he will care for Becca
I can leave

John pulled the dark green journal out of the box. Relief filled him; this was the key to his sanity.

He stepped over his wife's belongings, now strewn across the floor, and clutched the book to his chest. He climbed back into bed and turned on the bedside lamp. Light burst across the pages of the tome.

He flipped to the very back, where Robert Brownell's obituary was precisely pasted against the inside cover. The man died in his home on January 10, 1984.

John was choked with fear that Rebecca may join her father soon.

Or perhaps she would return here, to their home, where she belonged. John envisioned her scolding him for tearing through her things. He smiled meekly, and it eased the pain. Before she returned, he would restore each item back to its rightful place.

The thought of her back, moving through the house in her regular routine, caused tears to well up in John's eyes. He swiped at them then quickly looked down at the heavy journal.

He flipped through the entries, which spanned from December 29, 1961 to January 9, 1984. Twenty-three years. Rebecca had been born in the middle of it.

With the journal in his hands, John confronted the reality of Robert Brownell. For John, it felt as if Robert's soul was there, sitting in the room.

He let the pages fall open.

Mia convinced me to buy the place
It is private
A resort for us to retreat to
A home near the exquisite bay
I'm in love with our La Vida Que Cubra
I am a fortunate man
Mia is my everything

La Vida Que Cubra. Rarely had Rebecca spoken of their beach house. But when she had, John always sensed a deep sorrow in her voice.

He flipped through more pages, and once again the name caught his eye.

For her birthday
Becca and I went to La Vida Que Cubra
Her face reminds me so much of Mia
So many memories of Mia
Yet her memories all live here
Happy times
Where she smiled so much
I love Zihuatenjo Bay
Our La Vida Que Cubra
This is my place
The place where Becca loves me too

What had Rebecca said about their Mexican Riviera retreat? Her father had taken her there often when she was a young girl, but less frequently as she grew older.

But it had been a good place, a home where Brownell was a father, a private beach where the whole world stopped for them to be alone.

John continued to skim pages, searching for more about La Vida Que Cubra.

Rick is here
He loves La Vida Que Cubra
He tells me it is a den
Hidden from everything else
He is good for me
He sees things
And he knows me

In ways no one else understands
It is good to have him here
He says he belongs here

John kept turning pages.

Tomorrow
Rick takes me again to La Vida Que Cubra
We will talk business
And relax on the sands
And he will tell me what to feel
And how I will heal

More pages, and John found another reference.

Rick asked today
If I would ever
Leave this world
And live forever at La Vida Que Cubra
I told him I might
He asked if we could bring Becca next time
This is a good idea

A few entries later, it was there again.

Becca is becoming a woman
I don't know how to take care of this
Rick has offered to talk to her
He has such a way with her
She looks at him
Like he understands her too
Perhaps he can help her see what a precious girl she is
And what a beautiful young woman she will become

John continued scanning for entries about the place.

Becca wants to visit La Vida Que Cubra again
I don't know why
This is not a good idea
Rick has offered to take her
Especially since he senses my reluctance
She seems to truly want to go
And is fine to go with just him
Rick assures me
He will care for her

That entry was enough. John shut the journal. He could read no more about Downley. The man had been like a snake that slithered in, sunk his fangs in deep, and poisoned their lives.

Rebecca had been so young when he had bitten her.

John stared at the closed journal. He reviewed Rebecca's life as if it were ending, then reshaped it as if it were just beginning. When John brushed at his eyes, he found they were flowing with tears.

Finally, he laid the journal on the nightstand and flipped off the lamp. Then he helplessly curled up against the bed and begged sleep to rescue him.

But Robert Brownell's words still echoed through his mind.

He will care for her . . . Rick has offered to take her . . . She looks at Rick . . . Like he understands her too . . . Hidden from everything else . . . Rick tells me . . . Leave this world . . . And live at La Vida Que Cubra forever . . .

He loves La Vida Que Cubra. . . He says . . . He belongs here.

John threw his body upright, knocking his head against the headrest while grabbing the phone.

"Randy," he said, before he had finished punching in the numbers. "Randy," he said again, once his groggy friend answered. "I know where Richard Downley is."

CHAPTER FIFTY-SEVEN

Newton's team responded quickly. Alongside the Mexican govern-ment, the FBI located La Vida Que Cubra. Twenty minutes away from the buzz of tourism at Zihuatenjo Bay, the home was a quiet, solitary place, an ideal hideout for the faux ghost of Richard Downley. The FBI researched and hunted with great care, and when they raided La Vida Que Cubra, they captured both Downley and Kim.

The news thrilled John. Someday he would share it with Rebecca. Someday.

Then two and half days later, as John sat near Rebecca holding her hand, her eyes fluttered. The nurse saw it too. It wasn't much, but it was enough. The nurse ushered John out, and more testing began.

John anxiously paced the hallway for the next hour. This little movement implied that Rebecca was still there. She had passed the greatest hurdle. Anything was possible now.

He met with Dr. Chang. "You understand, don't you?" She said as John grinned at her.

"Yes." It was their starting line for her road to recovery.

"Every once in a while, you get a special case," Dr. Chang said.

"She's a fighter." John's cheeks hurt from smiling.

"We've run all the tests." Dr. Chang's own smile remained cau-tious. "Right now, they all look good. Plus, she scored a twelve on the Glasgow Coma Scale, which indicates a less severe brain injury and a better prognosis for recovery. It's very encouraging news."

"Yes. It is." John wanted to hug the woman.

"She'll still need to stay in ICU for a while," Dr. Chang continued. "She'll be in and out of consciousness for the next few days. From there, we'll need to move her to inpatient care."

John nodded.

"Here's a brochure that talks about postconcussion syndromes and what she might experience in the next year."

Even though Dr. Chang was reinforcing the unknowns, John couldn't restrain his grin. He took the brochure, but he already knew what it said. There would be warnings about dizziness, headaches, mental confusion, behavioral changes, and memory loss—a long and ugly list. But it was still okay. They would deal with those things.

"It will be a full year before you'll know the exact extent of the damage."

"But it looks good," John restated, the grin still plastered to his face.

"As of right now, it looks exceptionally good." Dr. Chang gave him a tender smile. "It seems your wife has a very strong and resilient brain."

"Yes. She does."

The rest of the day was spent rejoicing. It had been nearly a week since the attack. Now the family shared cheerful hugs and relieved tears over the good news. Exuberant phone calls were followed by eager visits, exultant laughter, and radiant smiles.

But when John again sat by her, alone, with monitors still humming, the reality of their life settled in. Here lay his beautiful wife, who he had almost lost, and he could have prevented this tragedy. The reality hurt.

John hunched over and dropped his head into his hands. He tried to reign in the emotion and swatted at tears. Then he reached for her arm. She was warm. He thought of the blood flowing through her veins, sustaining her life. It humbled him. More tears plummeted down.

He did not deserve her. She should be gone. But now he had a second chance; a merciful opportunity to redeem himself.

Since the attack, John had struggled to find the right words to share with to her. Suddenly now, the words tumbled out.

"I don't know how to say how badly I messed up, Rebecca." John shook his head. "I did things, I said things, I assumed things, and I can't change any of them . . . even though I desperately want to. I wish I could fix the past. I wish I could have been what you needed me to be. I stopped believing in you, and I was a fool, and you—you believed in yourself even when I didn't. I'm sorry you were alone. I'm sorry you didn't have my support when you needed it most.

"I messed up, Rebecca. But please give me a second chance. Please let me show you that I can be the husband you deserve."

Her eyes fluttered open. She blinked and looked at him.

"I love you," he said quickly. She offered him a modest smile.

He found an unbruised spot on her face and carefully stroked her skin. "You're the greatest thing in my life."

He kissed her gently, and then she was asleep again.

But the smile remained on her face.

CHAPTER FIFTY-EIGHT

A week later, Newton phoned John. Downley's interrogation had yielded more news. Although John had already pieced together most of the information, the facts were still disheartening.

When Downley entered their house, his target had been to hurt Robert, not Rebecca. He had studied Rebecca's new life and plotted his method to make her suffer as much as possible. He's goal was to destroy Robert physically, to cripple Rebecca mentally, and to break John emotionally.

But Rebecca had interfered.

After the call, John surveyed his home. It was late at night and he was all alone, but for the first time in a long time, he felt peace. His family had been forced to enter an awful war. All of them had been injured, yet somehow all of them would survive. They had been victorious.

A month after that, John walked out of Second Chance for the day. His administrative duties had been reassigned, and his clinical duties had been reduced to a minimum during Rebecca's rehabilitation. Now he eagerly left to visit his wife.

"Sanders!" Dr. Blythe's called from across the parking lot. John turned and walked back, meeting her halfway. "How are you holding up?"

"I'm good."

Dr. Blythe nodded. "You seem like it, especially this last week. How's Rebecca?"

"Good."

Dr. Blythe gave him a huge grin. "I want a better update than that."

John smiled. "They say it's still too early to be confident about her status."

"But where is she on the Cognitive Functioning Scale?"

"Her current level is extremely high."

"Then that's excellent." Dr. Blythe pulled him into an eager hug. After she had released him, John added, "It's still sounding like there's plenty of room to hope for daily functioning and independence."

Dr. Blythe released a long sigh and smiled. "That's great to hear."

"Her therapists always have positive remarks. They say she's right on track, recovering with exceptional mental strength."

"I'm not surprised."

"They only think her coordination's slow because she's still in a great deal of pain."

"Yes." Dr. Blythe studied John's eyes. "Time will cure many things, won't it?"

"That's exactly what they're telling me."

"How does she seem emotionally?

"She doesn't want to talk about what happened."

"Does she remember it?"

"I didn't think so at first. I've said minor things about it once or twice, but she's shrugged it off. If she does remember, she's not ready to talk about it."

Dr. Blythe pressed her hands against her slacks and studied the ground. When she glanced back at John, a frown covered her lips. "We made some mistakes, didn't we?" For the first time, John saw tears in Linda Blythe's eyes.

He could only nod.

She reached out and clutched his hand. "Are you okay?"

"She doesn't seem angry," he managed to say.

"That's because she's a good person. A very good person."

"Robert has helped."

A huge grin replaced Linda's frown. "Children are blessings, aren't they?"

John reflected on the mother-son reunion. When dark spikes of hair appeared on her head, and the severe bruises began to fade, Rebecca finally welcomed Robbie back into her arms. Robert had been completely ecstatic, full of giggles and hugs. "You slept for a long time," he had said over and over, laughing and smiling.

"Is he with you now?" Linda asked.

"He comes this weekend. He's been up with my parents, and they've been amazing. They bring him down often, and Rebecca improves each time he comes. She works harder after seeing him, especially since he's growing up so fast. She doesn't want to miss it. In many ways, he's her best motivator."

"You have an amazing family."

"I do," John said. "I'm very fortunate."

Without any warning, Linda pulled John into another hug. "I'm so glad you're all okay."

A beautiful summer afternoon greeted John as he arrived at the rehabilitation center. The physical therapist was challenging Rebecca with a strength exercise. Since the injury, she now favored her left side, so today's exercise focused on Rebecca placing weight on her right leg. The therapist helped her stand, then moved the right leg back. Rebecca shifted her weight, grimacing as the sensory feedback hit her brain. Yet she listened to every instruction from her therapist and pushed herself forward. With each shift to the right, Rebecca bit down on her lip. But she worked hard, repeating the movement over and over again until the pain seemed to lessen. When the therapist finally lowered her back into her wheelchair, Rebecca looked exhausted but pleased. The therapist praised her, and John joined in. Rebecca beamed at them both.

But when John wheeled her toward her room and offered her a side trip out into the garden patio, she declined. Instead she leaned back in the sturdy wheelchair. Her body looked fragile and small.

"Do you want to rest?" he asked, as he rolled her into her room.

"No," she said firmly.

Over the last month this room had become her home. It was decorated with plants, get well cards, and an abundance of paintings and drawings from Robert. One cupboard held her stash of snacks and another cupboard held her personal items—hair clips that she couldn't use yet and makeup that she wasn't coordinated enough to apply. But those abilities would come in time.

As he quietly shut the door, she said, "Push me over to the window, please." On their way past the bed, Rebecca stretched out her hand and picked up the most recent drawing from Robert.

He pushed her wheelchair up close, then opened the window to allow the breeze to blow through. Rebecca studied the scribbled drawing in her hand.

He pulled up a chair next to her and reached for her hand. Birds chirped from the tree outside, and the air felt soft and warm.

"You sure you don't want to go out?" he asked again.

"Not today." She kept her eyes on the paper.

John listened to the birds' continuous song. Finally, he asked, "Are you okay?"

"I need to tell you something."

From her demeanor, John sensed that the conversation he'd both hoped for and feared had finally arrived. If the memories of that fateful day had returned, it more than explained her tired eyes and dismal attitude. To help the moment, John stroked her hand. "Okay."

She gave him a modest smile, one that looked almost exactly like the one she'd given him in the ICU after he'd begged her forgiveness. It brought back all the shame that had consumed him that day. They had never spoken of it, and John wondered how cognizant she had been during his verbal remorse.

He dropped his head and whispered, "I'm sorry, Rebecca. I am so very sorry."

"John Sanders." Her sweet voice spoke a solid command. "It's in the past. Rick knew the challenges I face, and so did you. He used your knowledge against us. I don't blame you. Okay?" He glanced at her stern eyes and nodded. "We have many more days together," she said. "A new life together, and I look forward to it."

"Me, too," he whispered.

She leaned back, still clutching his hand, still in pain, and watched a bird bounce across the limbs of a tree outside. "I need to tell you something. And I need you to believe me."

"I'll believe you," he said humbly.

"There are still some things I don't understand."

"I know." He wondered how much she knew. "Do you want answers? I'll give you whatever I can."

Her hand gave him a light squeeze. "Later." Then her body shifted and resolution covered her face. "Rick will no longer be allowed to terrorize me."

He gave her a soft smile and nodded. "I know."

"He won't be allowed to have influence, or power, or control over my life. Never again. I won't allow it." Though tears ran down her face, she spoke of Downley with a control and strength that John had never seen before. "He will not enter our home or our lives. He will not be the means of destroying us." Triumph filled her eyes. "I won't allow him to have that kind of power over my mind ever again." John leaned closer and brushed a tear from her face. The movement made her smile, and she laughed her words with overwhelming relief. "Never again, John!"

"I know."

"Rick was my greatest nightmare, a demon from my past. And then he was *there*, a living ghost. I had buried that fear, fought it for so long, and then I was face to face with it in my own home. I was paralyzed. The fear completely crippled me. Until he made it clear that he wanted Robert." She paused to gain control of her voice.

"I was holding Robert, and I knew that if I was going to save him, I needed to let him go. So I whispered in his ear what he needed to do, and I released him. And then I tore into Rick with everything I had. I fought like a bear; I fought like I'd never dared fight him before.

"Of course he was stronger. He had me pinned in less than a minute. And then he stared at me with his hateful eyes and breathed into my face, and said, 'I could kill you right now. But what fun would that be? I'd much rather watch you suffer.' He wanted Robert, and he told me exactly what he intended to do. In detail. It was the most awful thing . . . so I fought back with everything I could. I knew he was going to kill me. Whether he meant to or not. He used such force . . . it was only a matter of time. I always knew he'd be the one to destroy me, and it was coming true."

John cringed.

"I was ready to surrender," she continued. "But he had twisted my head at an angle where I could see all the pictures on our mantel. I saw you, and I felt strength. I saw Robert, and I knew I had to survive. The thought of the two of you made me able to shut out Rick's words. And then I saw Kilee with her family, and I remembered how much she makes me smile. I saw your amazing mom and how much she believes in me, your incredible dad and how much he loves us. And I felt . . . this bond, a connection that made me different than what Rick wanted me to believe." She paused. When she continued again, her voice was soft and reverent.

"I saw all of you, and I no longer saw Rick. I no longer felt him. His influence—the pain—wasn't as strong. Instead I saw pictures of my own father, and as complicated as his life was, I felt his love. Then I saw my mother, and for the first time ever, I knew I would be okay, that I was not alone. That I'd survive." She turned back to the scene outside. More birds flew, carefree, through the sky. "From there I don't remember anything else."

There was no right thing to say, so John just stared at her radiant face.

Eventually, Rebecca filled the silence. "The only reason I survived was because I was not alone. The love I felt from all of you validated me. It gave me what I needed to know."

John swallowed a stagnant lump of emotion and whispered, "What was that?"

"That I was *good*. I was valuable. I was important. I had a right to exist, a genuine purpose, and I needed to survive." Tears streamed down her face, but her eyes remained peaceful and clear. "And the good I had wasn't just equal to his hate—it was far, far more powerful."

"That's one of the truest things I've ever heard you say."

She smiled at him and released a soft sigh. "Yes. It might be." She squeezed his hand and said, "Do you remember that night after Gravers's trial, sitting on that bench outside of Champion's?"

"Of course."

"And what I said to you? That I needed to find something more powerful than Rick?"

"Yes."

"I found it."

ACKNOWLEDGEMENTS

To see this book in print means many people helped get it here. For all those who believed in this project and supported my efforts – thank you.

Daniel Friend and Savannah Wood, thank you for your exceptional skills and editorial talents. Your dedicated work strengthened this novel. Also thank you Nyssa Silvester for your assistance with the early chapters. Brett Peterson – special thanks for your vision and goals.

Thank you Provo K12 team. Joseph, Rodney, Lael, Mike B, Mike H, Michael, Rachael, Todd, Cory, Mel, Robert and Karin, I've learned a great deal from rubbing shoulders with such a talented group of individuals.

Dearest Austads – my year as the resident author of Temple Hill changed me forever. Wayde, Tana, Tylor, Aaron, Kyle, Morgan, and Robbie—thank you for your example, love, support, and for your unwavering faith in me.

I appreciate all the psychiatric and clinical professionals who assisted in the research for this novel. Special thanks to Dr. Dennis Staker for the insight and the kind reminder to do my best but in the end this is a work of fiction.

Special thanks to SannDee Stowell, Amber Bignell, Mike Hansen, Christie Austad, Karen Thomas Hansen, and Megan von Niederhausern for your assistance on this project at its various stages.

Dori Nottingham and Ryan Mendenhall, thank you for coaching me through new territory, for encouraging me, and for sharing your amazing talents.

Libby Lloyd, Staci Mitzman, Marni Law, and Linda Miller – thank you for the special friendships and for cheering me along through the highs and lows of this journey.

My dear family, I love you. You gave me the core, the foundation, the love, and the passion to write this book. Amber, I loved sharing with you the early story threads. Thank you for reading the novel at its various stages of development and for all your encouragement through the years.

Chuck—you have brought hope, love, and joy back into our lives. I love you so much for that and many other things.

Mom, I would not be where I am without you. You are amazing. I'm humbled to be your daughter. Thank you for your continual support through every phase of my journey—in writing and in life.

Niekamps – I'm forever blessed to be part of your family. Your love and support has blessed me in countless ways. Thank you!

To all my incredible friends and extended family that have helped me through this project – thank you. Your support means more than I can adequately express. I feel extremely fortunate for all the love that surrounds me.

Especially, thank you Jeff for all your support. I am a better person because of you. You make life fun, exciting, and beautiful. How incredibly blessed I am. Thank you for being right about so many things!

25163597R10223

Made in the USA
Charleston, SC
21 December 2013